Book Three: Bitter Arrow

And so those who'd abhorred suc
cast upon that flèche
That by such
they'd

- Metrick Ru
of the Childre

“Here it is,” announced Coma Veronice proudly, “one illegal and experimental overdrive device.”

The bridge crew of the independent vessel Almagest stopped what they were doing and turned to look at her as she entered. The large control room seemed to contract upon her entry. The thin and attractive humanoid female was grasping a metal case and wearing a wide, closed smile. Captain Farril Calico, the strong and well-liked commander of the ship, was leaning against a bulkhead as she entered and nodded his bald head approvingly.

“It's only illegal in this star system, and we're not sticking around,” Calico said with a smile.

“It's heavier than it looks,” said Coma, striding up to him.

“I want you to start working on the installation immediately, Gueyr,” Calico said to his Kau’Rii engineer.

“Yes, sir,” replied the sage-furred youngster.

Unlike most of his kin, Gueyr preferred to sit in his chair on his haunches with his tail curled around his feet, making the challenge of recognizing the panther-like humanoid for an intelligent being that much greater for Coma.

"Excellent," Calico said, taking the case. "If we can get this overdrive device working properly, we'll have a huge advantage in a pinch."

"It went off without a hitch," replied Coma. "Their captain was six inches from my face and he was convinced I was a male Residerian."

Knoal's cybernetic enhancements whirred as he spun his chair around. The devices replaced some of his body parts, and Coma found the external structures unsettling. She had to remind herself that there was little difference between them other than outward appearance.

"I'm sure Bugani will be very happy," said the large Residerian.

"I'm sure he will, Knoal. Perhaps you can be the next volunteer for imaging."

"Heh, no thanks."

"There was some variation in the electrostatic field when their ship engaged the sublight drive," Coma said to Calico. "Fortunately no one was looking at me when it happened."

Calico nodded. "All right. Make your report to Bugani, then. Gueyr, set a course for Misrere Prime, then get to work on integrating the device into our systems."

"Aye, sir."

Coma entered the main corridor. Captain Calico followed her and closed the door. The two shared a brief embrace.

"You're getting better at controlling your arms," Calico said.

"I'm so sorry about that," Coma replied.

Calico smiled. "Don't be."

"I feel almost normal."

"I'm worried about you, Coma. You've only had the cybernetics for three weeks, best we can tell. Your adaptation and recovery is unusual."

"That worries you?" asked Coma, smiling.

"Yes. I can't help but feel like we're waiting for the egg to break."

"Huh?"

"It's an expression. It means everything is fine now, but disaster is inevitable."

"Are you superstitious?"

"Not usually. I've got to take care of some things on my end, Veronice. Hopefully Bugani can figure out what happened. After that, I thought we might take a meal, if you're up to it."

"I should be. Thanks."

Calico returned to the bridge. Coma walked down the length of the corridor and descended the stairs to her right. She continued down until she reached the third deck and walked the length of the ship, which was about one hundred and fifty meters. She stopped in front of a hatch that was labeled "workshop" in Z'Sorth, or so she had been told. It was one of a few languages her former masters had deemed unnecessary for her to learn.

Inside the shop, Coma had to let her eyes adjust to the lower light. Typical of a Z'Sorth chamber, it was cluttered without being messy, organized with pieces of equipment creating a L-shaped foyer next the entrance, and smelled like mud. She emerged into the central area, where several projects were underway on various tabletops.

"Bugani," she said loudly.

There was a clatter as a pile of something was knocked over, and a purplish-green Z'Sorth emerged from the back.

"Was it a success?" Bugani hissed.

As much as she didn't like Z'Sorth, Coma had a hard time transferring this bias to Bugani, since he was really a very nice person and the slow cadence of his speech belied a considerable intelligence. His lack of greeting was typical, however. The fact that she was communicating at all with a giant humanoid lizard had long since become irrelevant.

"Yes, it went almost perfectly. There was some visual distortion in the field when their ship engaged their subluminal drive. It probably had something to do with the electromagnetic coils on those old ResZor-Con transport vessels."

Bugani shot Coma a look of disdain that was so universal even his reptilian face couldn't hide it, and said, "Give me the control unit."

Coma reached into her pocket and withdrew a small device constructed of aluminum and plastic. Bugani activated it and a small display lit up.

"What are you doing?"

"Accessing the log. Yes, there was a disruption. I can program the system to anticipate variations in EM fields and compensate for them. Such a feature should require no more than seventy-six parhet."

"Seventy-six? That's what, four hundred and fifty calories? Using this thing is already exhausting enough."

"Better than being discovered, no?"

Coma leaned on a table, her fatigue rapidly catching up with her. She sighed.

"No, of course not. If you marketed this thing as a weight loss device on my home planet you could make a fortune. How long will the modifications take?"

"Come back tomorrow."

"Fine by me. I'll be passed out in my quarters if you need me."

He was the only human on Misrere Prime. For most of the species, this would have been the cause of a great deal of anxiety. For Commander John Scherer, it was just another alien planet where almost everyone ignored him. It was the fourth such planet that he had visited. John couldn't count Macer Alpha; all the aliens there had tried to kill him.

Even though he didn't feel particularly threatened on Misrere Prime, he was still quite glad to have a much more traveled companion with him. Fernwyn Rylie had been here before, although not to this particular city. Fernwyn had a sharp eye, a quick draw, and was loyal to John. That added confidence, however, did not diminish the thrill of seeing a new alien world. Their current environs seemed safe enough, but as they both well knew, the lack of any obvious danger was never a good indication of reality.

John and Fernwyn sat in an outdoor cafe in a massive commercial center known as Requiem Ziggurat. The base of the central building measured a full kilometer across; the central cone itself was fifty stories tall. Encircling the complex every ten stories were circular structures which jutted out fifty meters from the side, creating additional square footage inside and flat surfaces without. These flat areas were either covered in domes or left open, and the latter were used for either landing platforms or as outdoor shops or restaurants. According to Fernwyn, the weather was agreeable 95% of the year at this particular latitude, and indeed it was a beautiful, warm day.

"Chrysanthemum," said John.

"I'm sorry, my translator missed that, John," replied Fernwyn.

"It's a kind of Earth flower. I couldn't remember the name. That's what this place looks like from above. A chrysanthemum."

"I'll have to take your word for it. I thought it looked like a layer cake."

A Kau'Rii waitress approached the pair. She looked different than others of the species that John had encountered, and he struggled to identify the discrepancy. As she turned to speak to Fernwyn he realized that she was slightly taller than usual and she was dressed much less modestly than those in the Residere system. The waitress, whose nametag was written in an unknown language, began to speak. John recognized the words as Residerian, and did not notice the split-second delay as his translator earpiece kicked in.

"I'm sorry, Fernwyn," she was saying, "but we are definitely out of yutha beans. The kitchen manager says the shipment from Residere Beta has been delayed."

"No big deal, Lyra, thanks for checking," Fernwyn replied. "What's the closest thing you've got?"

"Genaro. It's a brescaré fruit. It's sweeter than yutha, more like tea, really, but definitely dark and smoky."

"Sound good to you?" Fernwyn asked John.

"Sure," said John.

The waitress moved away. Fernwyn shrugged and smiled.

"Was the girl's name Lyra?" asked John.

Fernwyn nodded, and said, "Yes, that's right."

"What's brescaré?"

"It's, uh... a plant that grows close to the ground. The fruit is harvested by allowing the vines to grow on trellises."

"Ah, you mean vineyard. Got it."

"I'm sorry the software on that thing isn't better."

"On the contrary, I'm surprised it isn't worse. Since we stole them, I can't complain."

"I wish I had more time to teach you Residerian."

"As long as I have this device, I'll be fine, but knowing my luck it will quit working in about an hour."

Fernwyn smiled, and resumed scanning the cafe patrons. They had given good descriptions of themselves to the man they were supposed to meet, and considering the dress of the other customers present, John was confident there was little chance of confusion. He was wearing a green Gore-Tex jacket (his favorite Army jacket long since destroyed), blue jeans, and hiking shoes. It was a little too warm for the jacket, but removing it would reveal the Beretta 92FS pistol he was carrying. Most visitors to the Ziggurat did not conceal their firearms, but the practice was not forbidden. John was happy to keep his weapon hidden; he was already too distinctive as a species for his liking and carrying a weapon no alien could identify would only add to the problem.

Fernwyn's own vestments, a flight jacket, cargo pants, and a baseball-style cap were fairly generic compared to the local populace, but her physical features made her stand out. She could easily be mistaken for a human, as her Residerian heritage and borrowed Kau'Rii blood were well blended. Together, John and Fernwyn were hard to miss, if one happened to be looking for them. So far they hadn't been treated any differently than any other visitor with money to burn.

"Interested Rakhar on my three," Fernwyn said without looking.

John glanced up. A lithe, fawn-colored Rakhar had entered the terrace from the interior of the cafe. He was dressed in a long coat and sported long hair tied back into a ponytail. He was also wearing sunglasses, which were almost certainly augmented with various useful devices. He finished scanning the patrons, settled his gaze on Fernwyn, and began to walk over.

"Officer Rylie, I presume," he said upon arrival.

"Please, have a seat," Fernwyn replied.

The waitress appeared and placed two mugs of a dark liquid on the table.

"Something for you, sir?" she asked.

"Is that genaro?" he queried, pointing at the mugs.

"Yes, sir."

"That will be fine."

The waitress nodded and turned away. When she'd returned inside, the Rakhar spoke again.

"My name is Hzolter. I'm with the Galactic Free Warriors Guild."

"You already know my name, although you can dispense with the title. This is my associate, John. We represent only ourselves."

"Yes, as your message indicated. So you're trying to get in touch with one of our members?"

"The captain of the Almagest, specifically. That's one of yours, right?"

"He's a member in good standing, yes. What is this regarding?"

Fernwyn leaned back. "That's between us."

John sipped his genaro. It was reminiscent of bergamot tea with a drop of barbeque sauce.

"I'm not going to arrange a meeting without more information," said Hzolter.

"Fine. We believe the captain has something that belongs to us. If so, we are willing to offer a price for its return."

"Credits or material?"

"Whichever strikes his fancy, Hzolter."

"You're going to have to give me some idea of what you're offering... excuse me, I have a call coming in." The Rakhar reached inside his coat and activated an unseen communication device. "Hzolter. Yes. I'm there now. Already? I... understood, I will comply."

"Everything okay?"

"Yes. The Almagest is already here. Once the captain gives me his landing platform number we can go see him."

"You weren't expecting him so soon, were you?"

Hzolter shifted in his seat. "I am authorized to negotiate for members of my guild. Captain Calico simply decided to do this deal in person."

"I don't like this, Fen," said John.

"Relax," said Fernwyn, and looked at Hzolter. "Most mercenary guilds play by the rules."

John rolled his eyes, and said, "Like the Universal Mercenary Guild?"

"I understand you were involved with some sort of altercation with the Black Crest," said Hzolter. "I'm sure you know that they were fined millions of credits for their actions on Residere Beta."

"What about the way station?"

Fernwyn shrugged. "There was nothing illegal about the Black Crest's actions there. The GFWG has a better reputation than the UMG anyway, regardless of the actions of a few overenthusiastic members."

"I never thought I would hear a shuffler compliment a merc guild," said Hzolter.

"Former shuffler."

"Obviously. I also never thought I would hear a plank compliment a merc guild."

"Former plank. Is your file really that incomplete?"

"A Z'Sorth doesn't change its scales, Rylie."

John peered into Hzolter's sunglasses. For a moment he saw reflections of light on the Rahkar's face.

"Do you really think I'm going to investigate crimes now that I'm not wearing a badge, Hzolter?"

"Only those of a personal nature."

"What does your file say about me?" asked John.

Hzolter looked at John and smiled. "You are much more interesting. Tell me your full name and I'll add it to the file. There are a lot of people out there who would like to know the names of the crew of the ship that destroyed Aldebaran, liberated Umber, and almost crippled the Zendreen fleet."

John leaned back, sipped his drink, and said nothing.

"He doesn't think it's wise to reveal anything more," said Fernwyn.

"I don't blame him. Everyone in the Tarantula Nebula is still trying to sort out what happened over the last few weeks."

Hzolter was distracted for a few moments as he answered an incoming call.

"If it's best for Umber we might want to reveal more about us," began John, "but I'd just as soon remain a mystery."

Fernwyn nodded. "You never struck me as the type to enjoy fame."

"Okay," said Hzolter. "Captain Calico is waiting for you down at the yard."

Five minutes later, John, Fernwyn, and Hzolter emerged from an elevator onto first floor. The Almagest was too large for any of the landing platforms, so it was parked in an area adjacent to the building known as the yard. An above-ground shuttle was available as the far end of the yard was over four kilometers away. Hzolter lead the way to the shuttle station and the three waited for the next car to arrive. John watched people go about their business. The first level was either travel-related services or facility administration and maintenance, so there wasn't anything particularly interesting to see. John had been watching for signs that they were being tailed but so far he hadn't picked up on anyone. Fernwyn was certainly doing the same while still managing to make small talk with Hzolter.

A car showed up and the three boarded. They were joined by half a dozen other travelers. The Almagest was only four stops out so it was a short ride. The heat of the desert hit them as they exited the car and crossed the tarmac. The ship was the only one parked nearby and looked huge from the ground. Three men waited for them at the bottom of a personnel ramp. The man on the left was a sage-colored Kau'Rii. The one on the right was a Residerian with obvious cybernetic enhancements.

The man in the middle was of an alien species that John had never seen. He looked human but was completely bald - not even eyebrows - and his ears lacked any upper lobes. They resembled inverted teardrops and hung a good four or five inches down his neck. The neck itself was a bit shorter than that of a human (or Umberian for that matter), and his shoulders were broad. His torso was shorter as well, but his legs were longer, so as a result he stood the same height as John. His arms were the same length. He took a step forward and spoke. John's translator didn't hesitate as the man was speaking Residerian.

"I am Farril Calico, captain of the Almagest," he said, then gestured toward the others. "This is Knoal, my bosun, and this is Gueyr, my senior technician."

"Fernwyn Rylie," said Hzolter, "and her mostly unidentified companion."

"Some might think it rude not to introduce yourself, sir."

"Call me Temerity," said John.

"Nice to meet you. Please join me in my galley and we can discuss business."

Everyone but John moved toward the ramp. Fernwyn turned around.

"Come on, T," she said.

John shook his head. "I don't like this one bit."

"I really don't think we have anything to worry about."

"Forgive me, Fen, but my experience out here hasn't exactly warmed me to trusting new aliens."

Fernwyn moved closer to John. "They don't stand to gain anything from being hostile toward us. Mercenaries are like shufflers. They don't care about anything but getting paid, and they don't dabble in revenge if a deal doesn't go their way, well, certain Rakhar groups notwithstanding. It's bad for future business."

"I suppose."

"Tell you what. If they kill us, I'll buy you a cup of yutha."

John smiled, then gestured ahead. "Lead the way, then."

The group made their way up the ramp and into the ship. They walked down a central corridor for fifty meters and entered the galley. The room was much larger than the galley on John's own ship and was set up like a cafeteria. Only one crewmember was present when the group entered, and he was too far away to be a concern. Captain Calico took a seat and offered the chairs across from him to Fernwyn and John. The others sat at the adjoining table.

"Now then, what are you looking for?"

Fernwyn cleared her throat and leaned back. "Rumor on the net is that your ship raided a Zendreen ship, the crew of which was stricken by the Vengeance virus. They must not have put up much a fight."

"You should know better than to believe every rumor you hear."

"This rumor also indicated that the ship was headed to the Zendreen's now-defunct research facility on Gamma Misrere VI. Among the things reportedly taken from this ship was a sentient female of unknown genetic heritage."

"And you think that this female is a friend of yours?"

"It's possible, yes. Our friend was captured by the Zendreen some time back."

Calico raised an eyebrow. "Captured how?"

"That's really not relevant, is it?"

"I suppose not. Even if your friend was an Umberian, there's no profit in it now."

"The Zendreen aren't in the habit of experimenting on sentients, are they?" asked Gueyr.

Calico shot the Kau'Rii a look of annoyance. "It was long rumored during the occupation that Umberians would disappear in the night, never to be seen again. Not nearly all of them were dissidents either. Exactly what they were doing with the balance was never determined, but many suspected that the Zendreen were engaging in cybernetic and genetic experimentation."

Gueyr shrugged. "Why?"

"To make them more efficient slaves," said John.

"Sorry, what?" asked Calico.

"We know of Umberians that were fitted with cybernetic devices meant to directly control their behavior," said Fernwyn.

"No kidding. That's awful. However, it is the inevitable result of power bereft of ethics."

John stood up and crossed to an empty salad bar. He folded his arms across his chest and stared at the bulkhead.

"What's the matter with your friend?" Calico asked, genuinely surprised.

"He knows first hand how effective the mind control devices were. He had to fight Umberians that were ordered to kill him. He never told me the details but I gather it was a very nasty experience."

A look of shock crossed Calico's face. He looked at Hzolter.

"You had the same information I did," said Hzolter, "and you still doubted my conclusion?"

"They're eight light years out of their way in a two-seater fighter craft!" Calico said, then turned to John. "Is it true? Are you a member of the Perditian ship that created the Vengeance virus?"

"What do you care if I am?" John said lowly.

"It doesn't make any difference, does it?" asked Fernwyn. "The bounty is defunct."

Calico stood up. "In terms of sheer curiosity, it does. Everybody wants to know the truth about what happened. The Zendreen aren't exactly well-liked around the Cloud. If you are responsible for liberating Umber and virtually destroying the Zendreen's war-making capabilities, then there are a lot of people out there who would like to shake your hand. Myself included."

The door to the cafeteria opened and Coma entered. John inhaled sharply and Fernwyn leaped to her feet.

"Ari!" John yelled, and rushed across the room.

Embracing Ari roughly, John began to cry. She pushed him away and grasped his shoulders.

"Hello, John," she said calmly.

"I can't believe it," said Fernwyn. "You did survive."

"My God, Ari," began John, "tell me what happened to you. You look fine. We heard you were badly injured when the way station was destroyed. Did Captain Calico give you medical treatment?"

Ari smiled half-heartedly. "Not exactly."

"Are you all right, then? Aren't you glad to see us, Ari?"

"Arianna Ferro might as well have been killed on the station, John. I don't want that life back. I'm happy living as Coma Veronice. The Almagest is my home now. Frankly, I'm surprised you came all this way looking for me, after what I did to you."

"You know I would never give up on you if I thought you were still alive!"

"You're too forgiving, John. It's a significant weakness."

"We've had this conversation before. I still believe that Aldebaran was chiefly responsible for your actions. Even still, you sacrificed yourself to save us at the way station. And despite the trouble the two of you caused for us, you still made significant contributions toward the liberation of Umber. We never would have gotten off the ground without you, let alone made it to the nebula. The others understand all of this. You have a second chance with us, Ari."

"What happened to Aldebaran?"

"Aldebaran is dead," said Fernwyn. "He died shortly after the station was destroyed."

"Too bad. He's the one who deserved a second chance. I am responsible for my actions, despite what you say. Aldebaran only made it easier to live with what I did."

John stepped back. "Please, Ari, come back with us. There is still a lot that needs to be done. We need you."

"Stop calling me Ari, God damn it! I didn't ask you to come out here! If I wanted to go back to the Faith then Calico would have brought me. I have made my choice. Ari Ferro is dead. I am Coma Veronice."

2.

The Almagest was an older Res-ZorCon cargo ship, refitted for a general purpose role and for use by a non-Z'Sorth crew. While not many spacecraft were manufactured by the conglomerate, the ones they did produce were of legendary quality and durability. For Captain Farril Calico, the Almagest was a source of immense pride.

A ship was only as good as the crew, however, and Calico knew it. He worked hard to hire only the best and most determined mercs, and this practice had proved fruitful. He made an exception with Coma Veronice, a woman with an unknown past and no willingly offered credentials, but so far she had proven to be quite useful. The success of the last mission had increased her reputation a hundred-fold among the crew of the 'Gest.

The fourth cargo hold of the Almagest was empty save for an ancient armchair. The walls and ceiling bore the evidence of a fire, but whatever had been consumed by the flames had long since been removed. The chair itself was made of the hide of an unknown animal. The material was well-processed and comfortable. Ari sat in the chair, adding an unappreciable amount of carbon to the soot-streaked bulkheads with her cigarette. The filler of the brown-wrapped cylinder was similar to tobacco and contained a chemical almost identical to nicotine. The net result was an acceptable substitute to the variety with which she was familiar. The hold was completely dark save for the glow of the cigarette.

The hatch opened, spilling soft light from the hallway into the large chamber. Captain Calico entered and shut the door. He stood in silence for a few moments, then took a single step forward.

"So your real name is Arianna Ferro," he said.

"That's from a life I'd like to leave behind, Farril," replied Ari.

"You know I'm not going to pass judgment on you. You can tell me as much or as little about yourself as you please. However, you should know that your friend John wants to speak to you again."

"Just off-load their ship and let's be on our way."

"We're not in a hurry to go to Residere. There are several recent job postings. I think you should give your friends another chance. They went through a great deal of trouble to find you. They seem willing to remain on good terms. Why aren't you?"

"That's none of your business."

"Fair enough. I want you to look at it this way, Coma. I would love to find out more about how the Zendreen were kicked off of Umber. If you were once a member of the ship that did it, I hope you can work through whatever's troubling you and tell me about it."

"Maybe. That doesn't mean we need to entertain Scherer and Rylie."

"I'm going to invite them to dinner."

"What? I didn't mean it literally! And why are you going to do that?"

"Scherer and Rylie are understandably reluctant to talk about themselves and the Reckless Faith. I'm hoping that a friendly dinner will loosen their reservations."

"You don't seriously expect me to attend, do you?"

"I'd prefer that you didn't. Honestly, Scherer doesn't need the distraction."

Back in the galley, John kicked a chair across the room. Fernwyn leaned back in her chair and crossed her arms behind her head.

"Give her some time, John," she said. "She's obviously gone through a lot."

"I can't believe she still hasn't forgiven herself," replied John, pacing in a small path.

"Right now, all we represent to her is a reminder of the part of herself she hates. I don't think that she told Captain Calico about her past, or at least not the truthful version of it. Calico didn't recognize our names and he didn't know Ari was a member of the Faith."

John scowled at the bulkhead. "Go on."

"So, I think she saw a perfect opportunity to start a new life aboard this ship. A life without a past. I think that in time she will be ready to confront her past, but for now she needs a safe environment where she doesn't have to worry about whether or not anyone secretly resents her or lacks any trust in her."

"I don't. She must know that."

"Yes, but there are five other people on our ship she can't be sure about. And for the love of the core, how do you think she's going to react when she finds out that... well, you know."

"About us?"

"No, the other thing."

"Oh, right."

The hatch opened and Captain Calico entered.

"Any luck?" asked Fernwyn.

Calico frowned, and said, "Coma, excuse me, Arianna, has been severely traumatized. I consider myself lucky that she is capable of serving as a member of my crew after what happened to her. I don't know what kind of past she has with you and your ship, but your presence here seems to contradict her reaction to you."

Fernwyn furrowed her brow. "To explain it as briefly as possible, she was kidnapped and held under the control of Seth Aldebaran. She did things of which she is not proud. John and I are willing to understand that such acts were made under duress, for lack of a more accurate term, but she holds herself more than fairly responsible."

"What happened to her?" asked John. "What did the Zendreen do to her?"

"He wants to know what..."

"Yes, I got that," said Calico. "I splurged the whole one hundred credits to download your friend's language from the net. Mister Scherer, she was very badly injured when the Zendreen got their appendages on her. In order to sustain her life, they installed cybernetic enhancements. I strongly suspect that they attempted to probe her mind as well. I don't know if they gleaned anything from it."

"I should hope not," said Fernwyn.

"Cybernetic enhancements?" asked John. "What sort?"

"Both arms needed to be replaced due to extensive burns. Her left leg was severed at the knee. Her left kidney was destroyed and most of her small intestine was shredded. Her lungs were damaged by moderate decompression..."

"Stop!" said John, sinking into a nearby chair. "Dear God."

"If it makes you feel any better, the replacements were top-notch. Nobody would have suspected that the Zendreen were capable of working on a life form as different from themselves as a Perditian."

"What function does she serve on your crew, Captain?" asked Fernwyn.

"She asked for a chance to show her capabilities as a gunner. She did well, so that's what she does now. We haven't needed her yet, though."

"Did you do a full medical scan on her when she first came aboard?"

"Of course."

"Did you find any suspicious Zendreen technology? I mean, cybernetics you couldn't identify."

"No, but I think I know where you're going with this. When we rescued her, the Zendreen were about to install some sort of mind control device into her brain."

"It's fortunate that you intervened. We had a bad experience with those damned devices back on Umber."

"I see. I just wonder what those scientists had in store for her."

"I wish we had more time to talk to her," said John.

"How long are you going to be on Misrere, Captain?" asked Fernwyn.

"I don't have any reason to stay. We're heading to the Residere system once we've concluded our business with you. I wanted to invite you to dinner, though. I would like to learn more about both of you, at least as much as you're willing to share."

"You're heading to Residere?"

"That's very interesting," said John, perking up.

"We only came out this way to find our friend. We need to get back to Umber."

"I take it you're hoping I'll give you a berthing," said Calico.

"You ever spend 36 hours straight in a cockpit?" asked John.

"Not quite that long, but I get the point."

"What's it going to take?" asked Fernwyn.

"It costs me practically nothing to take you. Don't eat more than your fair share, or cause trouble, and I don't see why you can't ride with me. Just be aware that Coma will probably avoid you the whole time."

John nodded. "A shame, but it's her decision."

"Come on," said Calico, gesturing, "let me show you to your quarters. Dinner is in one hour."

Fifty-five minutes later, John was stepping out of a tiny shower stall in a small but inviting room on the second deck. He finished toweling himself off and had pulled on his underwear when there was a knock at the door.

"Just a minute," he said.

Donning his jeans, John crossed the short distance to the hatch and opened it. Fernwyn stood in the corridor.

"You're just getting dressed now?" she asked.

"Come in. Yes, I fell asleep, if you can believe it."

Fernwyn entered the room and John closed the door. He grabbed his shirt and put it on.

"Sure I can. I fell asleep, too. Once my backside hit a clean, comfortable mattress it was all over."

"I still shudder at the thought of that dive of an asteroid we stayed on."

John armed himself and drew on his jacket. Fernwyn sat down in a sofa chair.

"So what do you think of Captain Calico?" she asked.

"He seems like a professional. I don't entirely trust him because he doesn't know of any way to profit from us right now, and that could quickly change. I can't help but feel a little jealous of him, since Ari likes him more than me at the moment."

"Maybe. I agree that we can trust the captain for now. I disagree, however, that he would..."

There was a tone that was obviously a doorbell. Fernwyn stood up and opened the hatch. Captain Calico stood there, smiling.

"Ready?" he asked.

John and Fernwyn nodded, and followed Calico into the corridor. They began walking aft.

"I could down a wolrasi," said Fernwyn.

"My cook didn't know of any Perditian meals," began Calico, "and I have no idea what you are, Miss Rylie, so I hope you like Hayakuvian cuisine."

"I'm Residerian, and that sounds great."

"Hayaku?" asked John.

"The captain's home planet," replied Fernwyn. "You will like it, there's nothing weird like grilled Zendra or anything still moving."

"You've never heard of Hayaku?" Calico asked with a raised eyebrow.

"It may go by another name on my planet. My translator may have simply missed it. How far is it?"

"A hundred and fifty-nine thousand light years, in the left spiral of the core galaxy."

"I take it you don't get home much."

"No."

The captain stopped at a hatch and opened it. He gestured to the others and they stepped inside. A large, simple room met them, with a single window at the end that displayed the seemingly motionless glow of the nebula. A metal table at the center of the room had been set with four places. Several dishes of food were already in place and were responsible for a wonderful aroma.

"Please, have a seat," said Calico. "Megumi, my first mate, will be here shortly."

John and Fernwyn did so. John attempted to identify the food in front of him. There were meat and vegetables, things that looked odd but very much edible, a pitcher of water, and two bottles of wine, one red and the other white. Captain Calico sat at the head of the table and held out his hand.

"I'm sorry about the room," he began. "I don't entertain guests very often. Feel free to try the wine. It's Hayakuvian, nothing special I'm afraid, other than being so hard to come by in the cloud. You may want to try just a splash of the red first, it's got a bit of an acquired taste to it."

As John and Fernwyn reached for their glasses, the door opened. A female Kau'Rii entered and crossed to the table. She had ruddy brown fur and a scar down her right cheek. Fernwyn stood up and bowed slighty, and John followed her lead.

"Megumi Rukitara," the Kau'Rii said, returning the bow. John's translator told him the last name meant "fisher cat."

"I'm Fernwyn Rylie, this is my associate John Scherer."

"Nice to meet you. Shall we?"

All four present took their seats. Fernwyn resumed pouring herself a small amount of red wine, and offered the same amount to John. She then passed the bottle to Calico, who poured himself a quarter of a glass. Megumi filled her glass to the brim.

"I'm surprised we're just meeting you now," Fernwyn said to Megumi.

"I had other matters to attend to," she replied. "Calico has filled me in on the results of his meeting with you."

"Please, eat," said Calico. "No need to stand on ceremony here."

"So Captain," began Fernwyn, procuring a hunk of animal flesh, "how long have you been in the mercenary business?"

"Ten years. I started out in the Hayaku system as a merchant trader. One day I was offered a job moving valuable wares to the cloud, and I took it. I didn't really have anyone back home that would care if I was gone for twelve years. The contract paid so well that I was able to purchase this ship, and I saw an opportunity to join the guild. I haven't looked back."

John took a small portion of nearly everything, then decided to try the wine first. It tasted like grape juice mixed with scotch. John grimaced as he finished the small amount and refilled his glass with water.

"And you, Megumi?" asked Fernwyn. "How long have you been on board?"

Megumi finished draining her glass, and said, "Since the beginning."

"Megumi and I have known each other for twenty years," said Calico. "We met at an orphanage on Hayaku when we were still kids."

John found everything on his plate to be delicious, especially whatever creatures had died to provide their protein. He quickly finished and loaded up his plate again.

"You were both orphans?" asked Fernwyn.

"Yes. My parents died in an accident, and Meg... well, she can tell you if she wants."

Megumi refilled her glass and chewed on some bread.

"So you said that you're going back to the Residere system." John said to Calico.

"Yes. There has been a spike in mercenary and freelance job postings in that area recently, which shouldn't surprise you. I have a lot to offer a potential employer and I believe there's a great deal of money to be made."

"I'm sure I'm being quite premature by saying this, but it's possible that Umber might hire you as supplemental security. I have no idea what kind of compensation they could offer, however."

"I'll consider any reasonable offer. Mister Scherer, I have to say that I'm quite curious about your home planet. What can you tell us about it?"

"Perditia? You already know the first part of the story. We decided to withdraw from the galactic community all those years ago because we were concerned about the rapid advancement of alien technology. The idea was to spy on other races rather than interact with them, and supplement any knowledge gained with our own research efforts. We hoped to remain strong enough to repel any invasion while remaining hidden to further discourage any unwanted attention. Eventually the espionage part of the plan fell by the wayside, and the isolationist movement continues to the very day. As you probably already figured out, my crew and I do not represent the Perditian government."

"Aren't you concerned that your actions here in the cloud could revive the galactic community's interest in Perditia?"

"No. My ship was built with Umberian technology and my allegiance lies with them. I don't expect anyone will make the long journey to Perditia based on any curiosity my actions have fostered. If someone did, they would find a fleet of very capable battleships guarding Perditian space and a rather terse transmission telling them to turn around or be atomized."

"I see. So Perditian technology has kept up after all."

"Based on what I've seen, yes."

"This only makes me all the more fascinated with your involvement in Umberian affairs."

"Let's just say I was in the right place at the right time."

"And you, Miss Rylie? A former shuffler, a former plank, and now a freelancer? That's quite a resume."

Fernwyn sipped from her glass. "Resume or rap sheet, depending on to whom you speak."

Megumi refilled her glass again, finishing the bottle of red wine and earning a glare from Calico.

"You don't refer to yourselves as mercenaries," said Megumi, "but I don't see any difference between your line of work and ours."

"Oh, you could definitely call us mercs," replied John, "except that since Umber is our first and only employer, I think a better term would be private soldiers."

"So what will you do when Umber no longer requires your services?"

"I doubt that will happen for a long time."

Calico swallowed a bite. "If you're officially a member of the Umberian military, then I've been very rude to you by calling you 'Mister,' haven't I?"

"I see what's going on here," said John, smiling. "You're going to try to get us drunk so that we'll reveal more about ourselves."

"I, uh..." said Calico uncomfortably.

"I'm kidding, although you did manage to coax that detail from me. Yes, my official rank is

Commander, and no, I'm not offended that you're not calling me that."

"Commander of what?" asked Megumi, amused.

"Commander of the Royal Umberian Space Fleet," said John sarcastically.

Megumi laughed heartily, and said, "A fleet of one ship right now!"

"I'm an optimist. If the Umberian government hires you, then there will be two."

In a dark, freezing cold room in an unknown place in deep space, a young woman was screaming. She had just awoken after an indeterminable time unconscious and was not where she expected herself to be. Her eyes darted around the small room even before her mind resumed rational thought. There was little visual information to improve the situation for her. The room was bare except for a metal desk in one corner. The only light was supplied by a single bluish neon fixture on the far wall, a light that flickered and threatened to extinguish itself at any moment.

The girl gulped down the frigid, stale air around her and brought herself to a tight, almost feral crouch. She held her bathrobe tight around herself, a garment that was rapidly becoming useless against the cold. Her eyes met the figures of two other people in the room, lying motionless on the floor. She gasped as she recognized them as her parents, and rushed to their side. Afraid to speak, she shook them both for a few moments and received no reply. Indeed, they were as cold as the metal deck on which they lay. Her eyes welled up with tears, but before grief gripped her completely, the moisture on her face reminded her that the room was far too cold for wasting any time. Her hands were already becoming numb, and her bare feet and knees were in considerable pain. The girl fumbled with the bodies of her parents, searching once more for any sign of life. It was a futile effort.

Pushing back the awful temptation to give in to her sadness and join them, the girl instead stripped off her father's heavy Air Force N3B parka and put it on. The voluminous jacket came down all the way to her knees, but it would not be enough. She stripped her mother of her wool sweater, jeans, wool socks, and galoshes, and painstakingly added them to her own body. The girl discarded her bathrobe after this effort, and buried herself in the parka. She drew the fur-rimmed hood tight over her face and plunged her hands deep within the pockets. There were some objects in the pockets, but identifying them would have to wait until feeling returned to her fingers. She jumped up and down in place for a minute, and found her warmth returning to her at last.

The girl stood in silence for several minutes. The parka was doing an excellent job. She opened up the hood and let it rest lightly on the top of her head. The air was no longer such a threat to her. She withdrew the objects in her pockets. In her left hand was her father's metal-bodied torch, and in her right was his Colt .45-caliber pistol.

Her last moments of consciousness returned to her in a flash. She remembered the freezing Romanby night, the terrifying light in the sky, and her father's warning to stay inside the house. She remembered her mother running after him, pleading with him to come back inside himself. There was nothing further after that.

The girl hiked up the hem of the parka and checked the pockets of the jeans. She found a disposable lighter and her mother's cigarettes, maybe half a pack remained. She transferred these items to an exterior pocket on the parka. Withdrawing the torch, she turned it on and pointed it around the room. As bright as it was, it wasn't enough to reassure her. Neither of her parents had been wearing gloves, so she withdrew her hand into her sleeve and grasped the torch with her palm. It was awkward, but warm.

The room was in fact empty save for the desk, which was a simple table with one open drawer, also empty. There was one door, and the girl considered whether or not to open it. If she had been kidnapped, her abductors might not appreciate her emergence. On the other hand, proving that she was alive and well could work to her benefit. She took a deep breath and moved forward. The door had a long lever set into a recess, with markings in an unknown language around it. She moved the lever down with some difficulty, and the door unlatched. She slid it to the side, which created quite a racket, and peered past the threshold.

She was standing at the top of a dual curved staircase, each path leading down into darkness and forming an open oval in the center. To her left was another such staircase, about ten yards down, and to her right was a metal wall. The room itself was immense; her torchlight had no hope of reaching the opposite end. The ceiling was vaulted, and alternated panels of glass with some sort of gleaming black material. Through the glass she could see thousands of stars and the swath of the Milky Way, which looked more brilliant than anything she remembered from Romanby.

"I'm not so much worried about where we are, Miriam," she said to herself, her breath condensing before her, "but who the bloody hell took us here."

3.

It was a warm spring evening in the temperate zone of the northern continent of Umber. The clear sky revealed the pink and green swirls of the Tarantula Nebula, distant stars, and the steady trace of hundreds of satellites. For the human named Chance Richter, it was a welcome opportunity to spend some time with his feet on solid ground. His attention was not skyward, however. He was leading a team of eight men on a combat patrol.

Richter had been granted the rank of Major for this operation, and though he thought that was a bit of a stretch for himself personally, considering the current size of the Umberian military it wasn't so ridiculous. The Umberian word for the rank was of course different, but as it was the fourth grade of officer Chance had instructed his translator unit to change it into Major. He wasn't in uniform, and only one of his men came close. There was little uniformity to the weapons they carried either. Richter was one of the lucky ones, with his Res-ZorCon Mark IV Phalanx select-fire rifle.

The next man in line was Sergeant Jack Smith, an Umberian. Richter knew him by a different name, but for the present situation an alias was required. He wore a green field jacket of the old Umberian military, as well as the proper buzzed haircut, and lacked any facial hair. Even though he was second in command of the squad, the other men took him more seriously than Richter. Not one of them was sharp-eyed enough to notice that several patches had been removed from Smith's jacket, although none of them doubted that he had once been a soldier. He carried a rifle previously unknown to the men, which had been identified by Richter as a

Springfield Armory M1A, and he seemed completely confident with it.

The other men were a indistinct conglomerate of various clothing choices and weapons. Such variety, which would make even the most forgiving Sergeant Major kill himself in protest, was only acceptable since as of five days ago none of the men had even held a rifle before. Richter and Smith had only agreed to take control of this mission out of a sense of charity, both leaders sure that the squad would be wiped out without their guidance. After two days of training with the men, they were somewhat certain that the new soldiers would at least refrain from accidentally shooting each other.

So far, the seven privates were doing well enough. The squad was moving single file on a mountain trail, flanked by deciduous trees and glacial rocks. Somewhere overhead their support ship circled. It was hidden by an invisibility shield and stood ready to provide additional firepower. Unfortunately, due to compromised systems, it could not detect any enemy troops that might be present; but the ballistic response, if needed, would be more than adequate.

Richter held up his fist, signaling the squad to stop. He had found the entrance to a cave. He carefully removed some of the brush that had been placed in front of the entrance and glanced inside. Despite the darkness he could see a metal hatch a few feet down. The door was divided into two halves and did not look like it had been used recently. Richter again held up his hand, this time extending his fingers outward and then bringing his arm down horizontally. The other members of the squad passed along the message, and slowly formed a semi-circle around the cave entrance facing away from it. The two men closest to the cave were careful to place themselves below the line of sight of the hatch. Smith nodded at Richter and the two of them moved inside. A brief inspection revealed the control panel for the door. Smith slung his rifle on his shoulder and retrieved a multi-tool from his pocket. Richter searched the jamb for booby traps as Smith popped the faceplate from the panel and scrutinized the wiring inside. He grabbed a small flashlight with a red lens to aid in the process. Richter gave him the thumbs-up signal. Smith cut two wires and wrapped them together. The hatch groaned and opened by three inches.

Richter and Smith grabbed the two halves of the hatch and wrenched it open. The squad rushed inside, attempting to cover all possible angles. Since the interior was adequately lit this was a simple task. After a few moments Richter called out the obvious.

"Clear!"

Smith and the other soldiers called out the same word. The frigid cavern was large and full of the distinctly-curved architecture of Zendreen equipment and computer terminals. Personal equipment and some trash lay scattered around. There were no other chambers. Once Richter was sure they'd checked every corner, he ordered the squad, save Smith, outside to pull security.

"It looks like they left in a hurry," said Smith.

"I agree," replied Richter, zipping up his black fleece jacket. "I'm surprised they bothered to lock the door."

"I don't see anything of immediate value here. We should suggest that central send a team out here to hack these computers for intelligence."

"Definitely."

Richter and Smith headed outside. The seven squad-mates were in a tight semi-circle a few feet from the cave entrance.

"Do you want to make the call?" asked Smith.

Richter yelled at the soldiers. "Spread out, men! What the hell? I told you that you need at least fifteen meters between each other. Move it!"

"Major?"

"Yeah, Smith, I'll have Andrews contact central." Richter obtained his radio and spoke into it. "Andrews, this is Richter, over."

Dana's voice came through the speaker. "Dana here."

"The facility has been abandoned. Contact the central government and request a data recovery team."

"Will do."

"Meet us at the extraction point."

"Roger, I'll see you there. Dana out."

"Alpha squad, fall in," said Smith.

The extraction point was a small clearing half a mile further up the hill. Richter chose to take rear security this time, and Smith led the squad. The uncloaked Reckless Faith was waiting for them at the clearing. Ray Bailey, Christie Tolliver, and the Umberian Professor Fugit Talvan were at the bottom of the ramp to the cargo bay. Smith motioned for the squad to enter the cargo bay, then waved hello at his companions. Richter seemed satisfied that they hadn't been followed and joined the others.

"Well, that was a waste of time," said Christie.

"Not if they can get something off of the Zendreen computers," replied Smith.

"Good job out there," Richter said to the soldiers. "Hang out here, drink some water, and we'll be back at the base in a few minutes."

Richter headed to the bridge so the others followed him.

"Are you satisfied with Sergeant Smith's performance on his first mission?" asked Smith.

"You should have chosen a different pseudonym, Aldebaran," replied Richter. "I keep almost calling you Seth."

"Sorry, but it's too late now, at least if we continue to work with the locals. Talvan, any luck with the computer systems?"

"Yes indeed," Talvan replied, grinning. "I got the matter replication system back online."

"That's incredible," said Richter.

"Thank you. I've made good progress on the other compromised systems as well. Unfortunately, I haven't been able to determine why the virus causes such a serious reaction in some Umberians."

"What's this about the virus?"

"You haven't heard? A small percentage of the population has experienced severe anaphylaxis after exposure to the virus. There have been two fatalities due to asphyxiation."

"Oh, shit."

"Excrement indeed. If we should ever again have to deploy the virus in the presence of humanoids, we should determine the cause of the reaction. I'm working with Umberian scientists on the problem, and I'm confident I can further modify the virus to mitigate that behavior."

"That's probably of little reassurance to the families of the dead," said Aldebaran.

"They're casualties of war," replied Richter. "I hate to sound callous, but the loss is minor compared to conventional warfare."

The group entered the bridge. Dana rose from the pilot's chair and smiled.

"Have fun?" she asked.

"Oh, tons of fun," Richter said.

Dana smiled. "Central reports that they don't have any data retrieval teams available, so they want us to secure the facility."

"No problem," said Aldebaran, "I can fix the hatch controls and input a new code."

"Thanks, Seth," said Talvan.

"That will have to be done after tonight's ceremony," said Dana.

Richter raised his eyebrows. "Shit, when is that again?"

"Two hours from now."

"I almost forgot about that. I really wish we could skip it."

"The central government is just trying to express their gratitude," replied Talvan.

"Somebody is going to have to stay behind to watch the ship," said Dana, smiling.

"Hey, yeah," said Richter. "I volunteer."

"We'll have to flip a coin, then."

"Or draw straws," said Christie. "I don't want to go either."

"Are you humans that loathing of ceremonies?" asked Talvan.

"It's just that we're very busy and it seems like an unnecessary distraction."

Talvan smirked. "They're planning on granting each of you a gift, you know."

"What sort of gifts?" asked Ray.

"You'll just have to show up to find out."

"Great," began Richter, sitting at the communications station, "I'm sure a planet that's been under occupation for ten years has some really valuable gifts to give."

"You don't find Umberian females attractive?"

"Whoa. Good point, professor!"

"Sounds like a just reward to me," said Ray.

"Don't even think about it," growled Christie.

"It's a moot point, my friends," said Aldebaran. "I'm obviously not going, so I'll mind the ship."

"Seth is right," said Talvan. "He can't risk being recognized. Young soldiers are one thing, but there are some Umberian officials that stand a good chance of remembering him by sight."

"Then it's settled," said Richter. "Andrews, please set a course for the base. Let's drop these guys off and get ready for the party."

"Roger," said Dana, resuming her spot at the controls.

"I've been awake for over a day," began Aldebaran. "If you don't mind I'd like to get some rest while I can."

"Of course," said Richter.

Aldebaran exited the bridge. Dana lifted off and began the five minute flight to the Umberian base.

"Let's get together a list of things we want to replicate," began Richter. "I'm sure the central government can get us the raw materials we need. I would like to replicate as much five-five-six as possible, and a couple more Phalanxes wouldn't be a bad idea. Additionally, we might as well replenish our supply of thirty-mil and fifty-cal, even if the plasma cannons are our primary weapons."

"I though you were all out of five-five-six," said Christie.

"I am."

"Without Seth the AI, we need a representative sample in order to replicate something."

"Shit! If I had just saved one damn round... well, it's not like we're hard up for small arms. The Phalanx can cover short ranges and the Springfields can cover long."

"Do you really think that we're going to see that much more action?" asked Ray.

"That depends on how aggressively you want to pursue the Zendreen," replied Talvan. "We've decimated their space fleet and they can never land on Umber again. It will take them decades to become a threat to anyone again."

"And who knows where we'll be at that time."

"Are you opposed to rearming?" asked Richter.

"Of course not. I'm sure the Umberians can supply enough iron to replicate whatever we want."

"Fine, then. So, get your needs together and I'll compile a list. Other than that, what's going on?"

"Christie and I have finished studying the fifty-cal systems. We're confident that we can repair them if necessary."

"Good, now there are three of us qualified to do so. Assuming you haven't forgotten anything, Dana."

"I'm still up on the fifties," Dana replied.

"Good."

"I'm continually amazed that John was able to design something as complicated as a fully-articulated gun turret," said Christie.

Ray said, "They're modified turrets from the Boeing B-29. With Seth augmenting John's analytical abilities it wasn't much of a stretch for him to integrate the originals into the ship."

"Scherer is a good man," said Richter. "I just hope he and Fernwyn make it back okay."

"Amen to that."

"I'm going to make sure the soldiers are ready to depart. Professor, any dress code for this shindig? Not that any of us have any formal wear aboard."

"John mentioned that you have uniforms," replied Talvan. "Perhaps you could wear those."

"We have black BDUs, but they're hardly formal. They don't have nametapes or patches or anything."

"I think they'll be better than the casual clothes you've all been wearing so far."

"Good enough. Ray, do you think you could make sure everybody gets a set?"

"No problem."

"Thanks. Let's hope none of us fall asleep during the ceremony."

Two hours later, the crew of the Reckless Faith minus Aldebaran had gathered at the bottom of the cargo ramp. Before them was a large building recently reoccupied by the Umberian central government. It was five stories tall and resembled an early 20th-century hospital back on Earth. The bricks were greenish in color, and it was topped with gleaming copper roofing. A delegation of Umberian officials were crossing the lawn towards the ship. They wore deep olive-drab hoodless robes tied at the waist with blue sashes. They appeared to be unarmed, in contrast to the crew, who with the exception of Talvan wore sidearms. The professor had assured the crew that weapons would not be seen as rude, which was fortunate since most of them, especially Richter, were rue to go anywhere unarmed.

Each of the seven Umberian dignitaries, four men and three women, had some sort of elaborate hairstyle. While the form of each varied, they all centered around how the hair from the top of their ears was integrated into that from their heads. The hair that grew from the earlobes was lighter than the rest, and was patterned into either braids, swirls, or both. The men shared the style of a single ponytail from the nape of the neck down to their waistlines, while all but one of the females had a ponytail growing from one side of the head and wrapped around the neck.

The two groups converged and halted. Two of the men stepped forward and bowed slightly.

"Good evening," the first man said. "I am First Minister Amian Braese. This is Acting Second Minister Pall Lalande. On behalf of the central government of Umber, we offer you our sincere and limitless gratitude for the service you have provided."

Talvan stepped forward and returned the gesture. "Thank you, First Minister. I am Professor Fugit Talvan, also Lieutenant Colonel of the Royal Umberian Space Fleet Center for Research and Development. I am proud to present to you the crew of the Reckless Faith. This is Ray Bailey, and his fiancée, Christie Tolliver; Dana Andrews, and Major Chance Richter."

The crew nodded and smiled as their names were called.

"We can never truly repay you for your actions," said Braese. "We feel the least we can do is hold a ceremony in your honor and offer you some meager gifts as tokens of our appreciation. Since most of you are unfamiliar with our customs, we have streamlined tonight's ceremony. But come, let us walk."

Braese led the crew into the building and the other dignitaries followed them. The front hall was obviously a museum, and was in perfect condition. There were several displays and glass cases, and the theme was military technology and warfare. The hall arched two stories up, and was clad primarily in pink marble.

"Each of the surviving Prefects had submitted speeches that they wished to deliver tonight," continued Braese, "but in the interest of not boring our guests to death, we will instead log those texts into the official register. Anyhow, as you can see, the Zendreen had no interest in this museum. All we had to do was get rid of ten years of dust and restart the infrastructure. This is a great blessing."

"Isn't the Royal Zymurgist's office here, too?" asked Talvan.

"As I said, a great blessing."

"Aren't there any members of the military who wanted to greet us?" asked Ray.

"Some members will be in the audience during the ceremony, but the officers you've met couldn't make it tonight. General Zeeman sent his personal apology..."

The entire procession stopped. Richter had left the group and was looking into a display case.

"See something that interests you, Major?" asked Talvan.

"What's the deal with this sword?" asked Richter detachedly.

The others approached the object of query. Inside the case was a single-edged sword approximately three feet in length, with a slight curve to the blade and a snub point.

"That is the sword of Vesper Tarsus," replied Braese, "One of Umber's most famous heroes."

"The story of the Seven Shepherds," added Talvan.

"Correct."

"It looks just like a Japanese long sword," said Richter.

"This sword was forged using a technique that was a secret for two hundred years. Only modern metallurgists were able to determine how it was done. There is a naturally occurring ore on Umber that emits radio energy when exposed to heat energy. It's properties were first discovered by Professor Talvan."

"We're quite familiar with Talvanium," said Ray.

"Oh? Good. Well, once we knew that, we were able to discover how Vesper Tarsus' blacksmiths forged this sword. They must have discovered that heating a lump of Talvanium and keeping it near the forge resulted in stronger steel. This was due to the ability of those radio waves to help the molecules line up. This, in addition to the normal techniques of folding the metal, resulted in this blade. It is virtually indestructible and never needs to be sharpened."

"First Minister Braese used to be the curator here," said Talvan, smiling.

"What gift did you have planned for me?" asked Richter bluntly.

"I beg your pardon?" said Braese.

"We're each supposed to receive a gift, right? What's mine?"

"You'll just have to wait until the ceremony to find out," replied Braese, a little confounded.

"I'm only curious because I'd rather have this instead."

"Corporal Richter!" objected Talvan.

"Richter, shut up," said Ray.

"My dear distinguished guest," began Braese, "this sword is a planetary and historical treasure. It is simply not available."

"You said you could never truly repay us," replied Richter. "Don't you think that sort of thing is better defined by the creditor? If you want to consider the debt settled, I'll be mollified by this."

"Seriously, Richter, what are you going to do with it?" asked Dana, smirking.

"Carry it. I studied Kendo while I was in the Marines. I was on my way to Japan to study Kendo when I was recruited by the CIA. I can think of at least two times since we got out here where a blade like that would have been useful."

"Are you going to grow dreadlocks and start spending all of your time in the Metaverse, too?" asked Ray.

"This is not a decision I can make by myself," said Braese. "I will consult with the council after the ceremony and you will have our decision then."

"Fair enough," said Richter.

The group resumed walking. Christie approached Richter and spoke quietly.

"You are now officially the world's biggest asshole," she said.

"I was just being honest," he replied. "Besides, the worst thing that can be done to a perfectly serviceable weapon is put it in a museum."

Christie rolled her eyes and returned to Ray's side. The group entered a packed meeting hall. About fifty tables had been set up with ten chairs each, all full of Umberians. At the front of the room was a long table, yet unoccupied. Braese directed the crew to take up one side of the table while the dignitaries took the other. Once everyone was lined up with a table setting, Braese gestured for them to sit. He remained standing and clipped what was obviously a microphone to his collar. All eyes were on the crew.

"My dear friends and honored guests..."

Braese was almost immediately cut off as each of the crew's radios beeped.

"If you would silence your devices, please," said Braese, covering up his microphone.

"I'll take care of it," said Richter. "If you'll excuse me, I need to answer this call."

"Now?"

"Yes, now. My ship wouldn't be calling me now if it wasn't important."

Richter stood up and returned to the display hall. He keyed his radio.

"This is Richter, over."

"Major, this is Sergeant Smith. Are you able to speak freely?"

"Yes, go ahead."

"Scherer and Rylie have returned. They want to link up with us."

"Damn, that's good news! Any word on Ferro?"

"They said they'd explain it when we picked them up."

"Uh... okay. Where are they?"

"They're still in orbit. Scherer wants to meet at the Tarsus bakery."

"We're kind of in the middle of the ceremony right now, Smith. Is this urgent?"

"He said they're okay, but they want to be picked up immediately."

"Okay, fine. No need to bring along the rest of the crew. I'll excuse myself and return to the ship."

"Roger, out."

Richter returned to the meeting hall. Second Minister Lalande had taken the podium and was making a speech. Richter leaned in next to Ray and spoke quietly.

"John and Fernwyn are back," he said.

"Thank God," replied Ray. "Any news?"

"None yet. Smith and I are going to go pick them up. We should be back in half an hour. Make my apologies to the bigwigs."

"No problem."

Ray immediately began to share the news with the rest of the crew. Lalande realized he was being upstaged but continued to drone on. Richter made his way out to the ship, staring forlornly at the blade of Vesper Tarsus on his way out. He boarded the ship and climbed the stairs to the bridge. Aldebaran turned to meet him.

"I can't say I'm upset to miss the rest of that ceremony," said Richter.

"I'm familiar with Umberian ceremonies," Aldebaran replied. "Try standing at attention for the duration of one."

"I've been there myself. Like a change of command ceremony?"

"For starters! Anyway, we're ready to launch."

"Good, let's get going. I'm eager to see Scherer and Rylie safe and sound."

Aldebaran put the ship into the air, then said, "When I asked him if they'd found Ari, John said 'yes, but... just get over here.' It's not like him to be enigmatic."

"It sounds like they found her but she wouldn't or couldn't come with them."

"I agree. Maybe a rescue mission is in order."

Richter grinned. "Dear God, I hope so."

4.

A solitary man stood outside the entrance to a handsome stone building, apparently staring at the spectacular night sky. The Tarsus bakery, as the building was known, was set on a bare hill, surrounded on three sides by forest. The man, named Stackpole, was in fact reluctantly waiting for the landing of the Reckless Faith.

With a rush of wind, a spacecraft approached and touched down about fifty meters away from the ancient stone structure. He stared in anticipation at the ship until the ramp opened and a figure in black approached. Stackpole recognized him as one of the men who had rescued Professor Talvan a few weeks ago. While he would have preferred an apology for the manner in which the rescue was conducted, he had little reason to expect one. On the contrary, he was far more concerned that this visit had something to do with his fiancee, a woman with a famous name and an inherited responsibility.

"What in the name of the core galaxy are you doing here?" Stackpole asked the visitor as he approached.

"Hello, Stackpole. I'm Major Richter. I'm looking for Commander Scherer, isn't he here?"

"The other ship hasn't arrived yet. What's this all about? Why are you meeting here?"

"This location was chosen by Scherer. Is that a problem?"

"I suppose not," Stackpole said angrily.

"I was told that the Zendreen never retaliated against you after we showed up. You're not still upset over the way things went down, are you?"

"Just because the Zendreen were too distracted to punish us doesn't mean you didn't put us in terrible jeopardy by leaving us here."

"Stay mad, then, I don't care. Scherer just wanted a convenient place to meet that would also afford some privacy. You don't have to be involved, I only called ahead as a courtesy."

The large wooden door behind Stackpole opened and an Umberian woman emerged. Richter raised his eyebrows at what he saw. Striking a stunning figure, the woman shared the typically svelte form of the species, and was wearing cargo shorts and a loose t-shirt, the most casual clothing Richter had yet seen on an Umberian. She had a Res-ZorCon Gladius pistol in a medium-slung belted holster and a small knife with a fixed blade stuck in what for all the world looked to Richter like jungle boots.

"I told you to stay inside," Stackpole said to her.

"Relax, Giclas," said the woman. "I was eavesdropping and I can't believe the way you're treating this man. We owe him and his crew so much."

"Yeah, I know," muttered Stackpole.

"I'm Viere Tarsus," the woman said to Richter.

"Major Richter. Nice to meet you."

"Do you have a first name, Major?"

"Chance. Are you any relation to Vesper Tarsus?"

"I'm a direct descendent."

"No shit. Does that get you anything around here?"

"I'm a rightful member of the Umberian Royal Family."

"That's gotta be nice. Weren't you invited to the party tonight?"

"I don't really care for such formal gatherings. I was only a child when the planet was invaded so I never developed a taste for proper royal customs. I'm happy to stay here with my fiancée until the reconstruction gets fully underway."

"Say, there's this sword I've got my eye on, the one that belonged to your great-great-whatever grandfather?"

Viere blinked, then said, "You mean the one in our museum?"

"That's the one. I was hoping, seeing as how my crew and I liberated your planet and everything, that I might be allowed to carry it."

"You've got huge gonads if you think the central government is going to give you that sword."

"Doesn't it technically belong to you?"

"Yes, and if it was up to me I'd let you have it. However, I'm not really in a position to bargain for you right now."

"Oh? That's too bad."

The whine of a descending spacecraft filled their ears.

"This must be the other ship," said Richter.

Those present watched as a much larger ship touched down nearby. The only available spot was right next to the Reckless Faith, giving Richter an idea of just how small his ship really was. A hatch on the larger craft's lower level opened, and four people emerged. He immediately recognized John and Fernwyn, who walked behind another humanoid and a female Kau'Rii with brown fur. The aliens waited outside the hatch, and Richter met his friends halfway.

"Good to see you again, Scherer," he said, shaking his hand.

"Still so formal after all we've been through," John replied, smiling.

"Rylie, you're looking well."

"Thanks," said Fernwyn. "It's good to be back. Where is everyone else?"

"Remember that ceremony the central government kept threatening to hold for us? It's going on right now. Smith is waiting for us on the Faith and everyone else is at the ceremony. So what's the situation with you?"

"Here's the short and dirty version of the story," began John. "Ari is on board that ship as a member of the crew. However, she feels too guilty about what happened to come back to the Faith."

"How did she survive the destruction of the way station?"

"She was picked up by the Zendreen and held prisoner for a short time. Captain Calico," John pointed at the man, "and the crew of the Almagest rescued her during a raid on the Zendreen ship. She's been through absolute hell, Richter. She doesn't even want to talk to the rest of the crew."

Richter took a few moments to absorb the new information. He sighed.

"I suppose I can understand where she's coming from. I'm glad she survived. Maybe in time she'll be able to face us again."

"I hope so too." John's gaze rested on the Reckless Faith. "What in the world?"

Richter smiled. "Oh, the artwork? Cool stuff, huh? It was a gift from the Umberian people."

A picture had been painted near the nose of the ship. About five feet in diameter, it depicted a woman dressed in classic Greek garb, blindfolded, and about to fire an arrow. Above the woman in a military-style scroll were the words Temeraria Fides, inexact Latin for Reckless Faith.

"Nice. Anyway, let me introduce you to the captain of the Almagest."

John led Richter back toward the Almagest, followed by Fernwyn. Calico smiled and Megumi nodded curtly at Richter.

"Corporal Richter, this is Captain Calico and his first mate, Megumi Rukitara," said John.

"Corporal or Major, depending on which military you choose," said Richter, shaking Calico's hand, "nice to meet you. Rukitara, the same."

"I guess I'll use major, then," began Calico, "from what I hear, you earned it."

"We did okay. So, Ferro's aboard your ship?"

"She is. Commander Scherer tells me you were all good friends at one time."

"I still consider her a friend."

"That's good. By the way, Officer Rylie, some of my men are unloading your ship now."

"Excellent, thank you," said Fernwyn.

"Who do we need to talk to about a job?" asked Megumi.

"General Zeeman is in charge of the provisional space fleet," replied Richter. "You can reach him directly on local channel 57. I have no idea what Umber may have to offer you as payment, but we could certainly use some help out here."

"What's the status of the Zendreen in this area?" asked Calico.

"What's left of the fleet has withdrawn to parts unknown. Here on Umber there are limited pockets of resistance but the virus has doomed them anyway. Our greatest concern is that they're consolidating and reorganizing for a counter-attack."

"Is that likely?"

"We really have no way of knowing. Once the fleet withdrew past normal shipping lanes it… we…"

Richter trailed off as he became distracted by something in the sky. The others naturally followed his gaze. Amid the faded swirls of the nebula and starfield, a bright point of light distinguished itself. Even the newcomers could tell it hadn't been there before.

"Another ship?" asked Megumi.

"Looks like another Zendreen satellite decided to blow itself up," said Richter.

"I don't think so," John said, confused.

Aldebaran's voice crackled across the radio. "Richter, Scherer, you'd better get back here. I just got some extraordinary readings from the direction of the Zendreen's former homeworld, Sanduleak."

Calico's communicator beeped and he answered it. Gueyr's voice could be heard.

"Hey Cap," he began, "I just got a new reading from nearby space. You're going to want to take a look at this."

The leaders acknowledged their respective transmissions as the point of light faded and disappeared.

"Speak of the devil, perhaps?" asked Richter.

"It looks like we have to go," said Calico. "I will contact General Zeeman as soon as we sort out this event."

"Indeed," replied John. "Let us know if you and the general can come to an arrangement. Until then, good luck."

"Same to you."

"Oh, and Captain?"

"Yes?"

"Take care of her for me."

"I promise I will."

"Goodness, is it getting loud in there!"

Dana all but stumbled from the chaotic meeting room into the display hall, followed closely by Second Minister Lalande. They were both holding half-full wine glasses, and Dana also had a bottle with her. Under his arm, Lalande was cradling a long box tied with a ribbon.

"So many want to talk to so few," replied Lalande. "I'm glad we could get away from them. So you were trying to tell me about your ship's computer?"

"Oh, yes." Dana smiled at Lalande. The dignitary was quite handsome in her estimation, and the wine was the first drink she'd had in weeks. "First the artificial intelligence was damaged, and we had to struggle to figure things out. Then Professor Talvan fixed the AI, but it was so damn specific that getting finer details out of it was a struggle. Then Aldebaran..."

"The space pirate."

Dana laughed, almost spilling her drink. "Yes, the fearsome space pirate Aldebaran. He stole the sentient personality of our AI and turned it into a simple computer system, no longer capable of lingual interaction. Deciphering the computer on our own has been a long and difficult process."

"I can only imagine."

"A good example is the work we've done trying to determine the capabilities of our stardrive. Our maximum sublight speed is ninety percent the speed of light, and our maximum superluminal speed is 1.56 million times the speed of light. Most of our actual cruising around has been with the superluminal drive engaged at nine hundred times the speed of light. I had to ask Seth just the right questions to find out why."

"Seth?"

"Our AI."

"Wasn't the infamous pirate Aldebaran's first name Seth?"

Dana's expression suddenly fell. "Quite a coincidence, don't you think?"

"Especially if Aldebaran wanted to steal it. You'll have to tell me the whole story sometime."

"Yeah, sure," said Dana, smiling sheepishly. "So anyway, it turns out that the optimal efficiency range for our stardrive is below nine hundred times the speed of light. Operating in that range allows the drive to recharge at the same rate it burns fuel, so the net result is neutral."

"I seem to remember that figure holding true for most of the stardrive types used in the galaxy."

"Yes, and actually, eight hundred times the speed of light is the maximum speed for the best hot fusion nuclear stardrives. You have to use a cold fusion drive like Umberian technology to break that limit. Once you do, however, you're really hauling ass."

"Yes, uh, I believe Umber is only a handful of races that can offer that level of technology. Unfortunately the Zendreen is one other."

"Refill your glass?"

"No, thank you."

"You know, Richter is going to shit himself when you give him that."

"He's going to what?"

"Shit myself," said Richter, appearing from the direction of the main entrance, "lose bowel control, you know, since I'm such a lightweight."

Dana and Lalande turned to see John and Fernwyn approaching.

"You made it!" exclaimed Dana, and hugged Fernwyn and John at the same time.

"Good to see you, too," said John.

"What did you find out about Ari?"

"It's a long story."

"Richter, check this out," said Dana, tapping the box and smiling broadly.

Accepting the box, Richter said, "I'll be damned, the Umberians really do know how to thank a guy."

Richter took a few steps away and unwrapped his new sword. He began to test its balance. It was obvious that he had a significant amount of experience handling a similar weapon. Impressed, John turned back toward Dana.

"We need you back aboard the Faith," he said. "There's been some type of stellar anomaly in the nebula."

"What kind of anomaly?" asked Dana.

"That's what we need you to find out. We haven't been able to interpret the data."

"Okay, then. Do you want me to grab the rest of the crew?"

"They can stay at the party, I suppose."

"They're not enjoying it as much as I am. I think they'd appreciate an excuse to get out of there."

"Let's not appear rude to the dignitaries," said Richter, flicking his blade downward. "At least, any more rude than we have been tonight."

"I'll ask you what you mean by that later," said John, eyeing Richer with curiosity. "Right now we only need Dana.

"Second Minister Lalande," began Dana, "duty calls. Stick around, though, I may be back to the party tonight."

Lalande bowed slightly, and said, "As you wish, my lady. Commander Scherer, Officer

Rylie, you would honor us with your presence, if you can."

John shrugged. "Second Minister Lalande, we need to investigate this anomaly. Please offer your compatriots my apologies. If it turns out to be nothing then we will join the party."

"I understand. Good luck, then."

Lalande bowed again and headed back into the conference room. John looked at Dana.

"Are you in any condition to work right now?" he asked her.

"There's only one way to find out," Dana replied.

Ten minutes later, John, Richter, Fernwyn, Aldebaran and Dana were on the bridge of the Faith. Dana was at the sensor station and a cat named Friday sat on the console next to her. The others were gathered near the door to the conference room.

"Honestly, I'm not surprised she doesn't want to say hello to us," Aldebaran was saying.

"Hopefully General Zeeman will hire the Almagest to augment our fleet," said John. "I'm not ready to say goodbye to her again just yet."

"The future is a long time, John," said Fernwyn. "You shouldn't be so fatalistic."

"I've finished analyzing the data from the stellar anomaly," said Dana.

The others moved over to Dana's station. Friday meowed at John.

"What do you have?" asked John.

"Well, the results are very confusing. It seems that two stars appeared in an otherwise empty area of space, then disappeared a moment later. The data is absolutely clear on the fact that they were stars, and the Reckless Faith got a good look at both of them. The brighter of the two stars is a G1 II spectral type, at four solar masses and twenty times the size of Sol. The other star is a G8 II spectral type, a cooler bright giant. Both stars have a luminosity over three hundred times that of Sol." Dana brought up a diagram of what she'd described. "Now, either of these stars appearing alone could be related to any number of astronomical phenomenon, such as gravitational lensing or a change in a star's magnitude. However, when I ran those stars through the database I got two exact matches, Alpha Sagittae and Beta Sagittae. Their positions relative to each other confirm it."

"And those stars don't lie in that direction?" asked Fernwyn.

"No, they belong to the constellation Sagitta, and not only are they in a different direction from the anomaly but they're also back in the core galaxy!"

"Were you able to get a distance on the anomaly?" asked John.

"Two hundred AU, current right ascension twenty hours, four minutes..."

"So about twenty-seven light-hours," interrupted Aldebaran.

Richter nodded. "Right smack at the last reported position of the Zendreen fleet."

"Hell, that can't be a coincidence!" said John.

"Maybe not, but I think it's worth checking out," said Dana. "Our invisibility shield will keep us hidden from the Zendreen if we run into them, as long as we keep our distance."

"It won't take us long to check it out. I don't see anything going on in this neck of the woods that could be more important than confirming the source of this anomaly. If the Zendreen are responsible then it could represent a new threat to Umber and the SUF."

"What about the Almagest?" asked Richter.

John nodded. "I'll contact them and find out if they reached an arrangement with General Zeeman. If so, they will probably be ordered to accompany us."

Richter's radio beeped at him and Ray's voice came through.

"Hey, anybody home?"

"How's it going, Bailey?" replied Richter.

"We're at the bottom of the ramp! Let us in."

"Roger. I'll go."

"Bring some help, we've got a lot of alcohol and some other stuff to load up."

Richter grinned at the others. "This may be a wild goose chase, but at least we won't be bored!"

On the Almagest, Calico and Megumi entered the bridge. Gueyr, Knoal, and Ari were waiting for them. Calico approached Ari and kissed her on the cheek.

"General Zeeman is holding on channel 57," began Gueyr, "and Knoal and I have analyzed the anomaly that occurred a few minutes ago."

"The General can wait a couple more minutes," replied Calico.

Knoal nodded. "Cap, the anomaly is right in the middle of the last reported location of the Zendreen fleet. Two stars seemed to appear out of nowhere, and disappeared a moment later. Our computer database was able to make a match to UAS 1006 and 1026, which are approximately 160,000 light years away in the core galaxy."

"That's back in your neck of the woods, isn't it sir?" asked Gueyr.

Calico nodded, then asked, "Explanation?"

"I have none. The phenomenon may be something else, but the match to those distant stars was exact. Either something moved them here temporarily, or more likely, something briefly opened a window to them."

Calico shrugged. "A wormhole?"

"Maybe," replied Knoal, shrugging back.

"If the Zendreen are fooling around out there, you can be sure the Umberians and the SUF are going to want to know about it. The Zendreen were out at the edge of the solar system, right?"

"Correct," said Gueyr.

"Okay. Thank you, gentlemen. I'll take General Zeeman in my room."

"Roger," said Knoal.

Calico entered his personal chamber. He grabbed a mug and poured himself some yutha from a pot brewed not too long ago. He sat down, sighed, and pressed a button on his console. General Zeeman's severe visage appeared on the screen. He was an austere Umberian, dressed in the usual olive drab military utility jacket, with close-cropped hair and shaved ears. He also sported a goatee, which was more typical of non-commissioned officers than the brass. He looked like he was frowning, but Calico recognized his expression as one of calm.

"General Zeeman, I'm Captain Farril Calico of the Almagest and a member of the Galactic Free Warrior's Guild. I'm looking for work, and Commander John Scherer of the Reckless Faith suggested I contact you."

"I see, Captain," replied Zeeman. "How do you know Commander Scherer?"

"We met on Misrere Prime a few days ago on an unrelated matter. We established a professional relationship based on that mission."

"Excuse me for a moment while I access your public file. All right, I see that the Almagest is a Res-ZorCon Class Five freighter. I assume you have upgraded it to better suit your purposes?"

"That's correct, sir."

"How many aboard your ship?"

"Nine crew, including myself."

"Your public file says you have a plus six reputation, that's very impressive."

"Thank you. I take pride in a job well done."

"Captain, what I'm looking for are ships to be part of an orbital patrol and a quick reaction force. Your contract would be for as few as one investigation or interception to as many as you would care to take. You would remain a private entity but under the command of the Umberian Space Fleet for that contract. That would effectively make Commander Scherer your superior officer."

"I understand. And compensation?"

"Uranium and gold, equivalent to the rates listed on the GFWG home page."

"Those are always easy to move. I agree to those basic terms, General. Send me a contract for a two week term, unlimited engagements. I'll review it and if I like it, I'll sign it electronically and return it to you."

"Sooner would be better than later, Captain. There seems to be an incident occurring as we speak."

"If you're referring to the stellar anomaly, sir, we've been following it. Do you intend to launch an investigative team?"

"Yes indeed. Would you be interested in going out there?"

"Absolutely, sir. Are you sending the Reckless Faith as well?"

"Most likely, yes. I will contact you shortly with the contract. If you sign it, I will brief you on the specifics of the mission."

"Sounds good, General. Thank you.

"Zeeman out."

The General's face disappeared from Calico's monitor. Almost immediately, Knoal's voice came in over the intercom.

"Sir, Commander Scherer is holding on the radio, audio only."

"Pipe him through, please. Commander?"

"Hello again, Captain," said John's voice. "Knoal told me you were on the phone with Zeeman."

"Yes, I've agreed to sign on for two weeks. He said we're most likely going to be sent together to check out that anomaly."

"Good. How long before you're ready to leave?"

"I just have to review the General's contract and sign it."

"If you could expedite that, I would appreciate it. Word just came across the 'net that the SUF has dispatched a nearby squadron of fighters to investigate the anomaly. If at all possible I would like to arrive there well in advance of them."

"I agree. I'm receiving the contract now, and I can't imagine it will take me more than fifteen minutes to review it. Establish orbit, if you want, and I'll join you soon."

"Roger, thank you. Scherer out."

Calico worked on his computer console briefly, then stood up and returned to the bridge. The others looked at him expectantly.

"Everybody grab a console and check the shared folder. There's a contract in there for employment with the Umberian Space Fleet. Review it immediately and let me know if any of you have a problem with any part of it. Gueyr, pass this along to the rest of the crew. If anybody thinks they're too busy right now, correct them vigorously. We need to get this document approved as soon as possible. I'll be in my room going over it myself and I expect everyone to be finished in twenty minutes. Understood?"

Megumi, Gueyr, and Knoal all agreed and sat down at a console. Ari approached Calico.

"We're going to work for the Umberians?" she asked softly.

"For at least two weeks, yes. Do you have a problem with that?"

"No, it's just..."

"You were hoping to distance yourself from your old crew."

"Yes."

"Come with me."

Calico opened the door to his room for Ari and followed her inside. He offered her a chair then sat down himself. He topped off his cup of yutha and opened the employment contract on his console.

"I'm okay with this, Farril, I really am."

"Honestly, Coma, it wouldn't matter to me if you weren't. I have to do what's best for this crew and right now General Zeeman just offered us flat rate with no negotiation. We won't get a better contract this side of the Tarantula Nebula. I sincerely hope that this contract doesn't have any surprises in it or that one of us doesn't decide to nit-pick some minor detail. Now, you don't have to communicate with the crew of the Faith if you don't want to, but if simply working with them is a problem then you are more than welcome to vacation planetside instead."

"All right, forget I said anything."

"Coma, nobody understands what you went through better than I, but you are a member of this crew first and my daught… my friend next."

Ari raised her eyebrows. "Did you almost call me your daughter?"

Calico looked slightly embarrassed. "Well, I suppose I almost did."

Miriam sprinted down a semi-darkened tunnel, a group of very angry creatures fast on her heels. While they bore little resemblance to humans, they did react in a similar fashion upon having some of their food stolen. In her seventeen years of life, Miriam had never had to fight for anything, but in this bizarre, seemingly endless structure of rooms and hallways, meeting every basic need was a struggle.

This was not the first time she'd stolen food from the natives, and she was confident she could outrun them. They were slow of foot, but not of intelligence. If she was careless in where she made her raids, they would almost certainly have her surrounded in a short time. In this case she had numerous escape routes; her pursuers would most likely lose track of her in a few moments and return to the comfort of their encampment. They were not short on provisions, as far as she could tell, and gave chase after her thievery only out of anger and a desire to capture her. Miriam preferred not to think about what might happen if they ever got hold of her. She still had five rounds left in her pistol that she was saving for just such an occurrence.

Miriam ran with little effort. She had adjusted to the cold air after several days, and she believed her constant physical activity had turned her into an ad hoc marathoner. The only thing holding her back was her near-starvation diet. She ran in a straight line down the tunnel, ignoring several opportunities to turn off, enjoying the thought that she was gaining on her antagonists. She was completely surprised when one of them took a shot at her, both because they'd never used deadly force against her and because the shot was a bright ball of light moving impossibly fast. She peeled off into an adjoining tunnel, her adrenaline surged. These blokes were getting serious.

Miriam took a few more random turns and ducked into an alcove. She listened intently for what seemed to her like an hour, then looked at her take. She had a half a loaf of something that was probably bread, or at least baked in the same fashion, and a tin of something completely unidentifiable. She ate the former immediately. As for the latter, it was unlikely to be poisonous (several days of trial and error had proved that) and would be consumed later in the comfort of her hideaway. It was there that she headed next, still reeling from the homicide attempt.

Her path back to her hideaway led her across a bridge. The bridge spanned a large open area, still contained within the structure but partially covered with a glass roof. The area, like much of the structure, was a combination of tunneled rock and metal construction, serving some sort of industrial process that was long since discontinued. A steady breeze passed through this section, so Miriam put up the hood on her parka. She had found random discarded clothing here and there during her wanderings, but so far nothing exceeded her parents' vestments in terms of quality and utility. She had picked up a pair of fingerless gloves, made out of an unknown material but still toasty warm.

The only other item of use that she'd found that she kept on her person was a wickedly sharp knife from a long-abandoned mess hall. She'd also found a tin opener, several tabs of solid fuel, and a relatively clean saucepan, all of which she kept in her hideaway for heating meals.

Miriam's stomach was already growling at her again by the time she reached her room. It was originally someone's private quarters, and indeed there were many such chambers, but what set this one apart was that the door had been welded shut, and one could only gain entrance through a ventilation grate in the next room. Miriam had dragged some debris in front of the door to disguise it, although thanks to her daily scattering of dust over the deck of the hallway, she knew nobody had ever ventured though this section of the structure.

The girl wriggled her way through the vent and leaped dexterously to the floor. She turned around and closed the vent grate, shoving a metal rod through two of the slats and fixing the grate in place. Sound carried very well in this place, so she was confident she'd have plenty of time to escape if the room was discovered. Her alternate route out of there was through a long passage under the floor, in a conduit for cables, and while uncomfortable to navigate did get her far away from the hideout.

Inside the room she'd gathered many items to make her life more tolerable. In addition to some emergency rations that she'd found (edible but foul-tasting), she had several blankets, a synthetic mattress, books and magazines (she couldn't read them but the pictures were interesting), an electric lantern that never seemed to run out of power, and a huge box of pre-soaked cleansing wipes. She used the last item every few days, or as needed, even though the process required her to strip naked and her room was no warmer than any other part of the station.

Kira'To.

The word crept into Miriam's mind again. It happened every time she felt happy about something, which wasn't often, and it bothered her because the mere thought of the word was enough to ruin her good mood. She was smart enough to recognize that the conjuring of the word may have simply been latent guilt over the death of her parents, even though she had nothing to do with it, but she couldn't shake the feeling that the word itself led to an explanation of how she'd gotten to this strange place. Her parents would have believed it straight away, naturally, and even considering her current environment she reserved final judgment on the matter. They tried to hide their activities from her; of course, a curious teenager has ways of finding things out nonetheless.

Kira'To.

They believed in this thing, or person, or animal-vegetable-mineral. Exactly what it was supposed to be was never clear to Miriam. She only knew that it had consumed her parents' lives, almost to the exclusion of all else. Including her.

The tin contained a fleshy fruit and heavy syrup, and Miriam was momentarily in heaven.

5.

Bright orange flames licked at the windows of the bridge of the Reckless Faith as the ship flung itself out of the atmosphere of Umber. John, sitting at the controls, rolled back the throttle and locked down the autopilot, activating the orbital path that Christie had just calculated. He sighed in satisfaction; he found that breaking atmo was one of the most enjoyable aspects of space travel. Not all of his companions felt the same way, however, and even after several iterations of the event a few of his friends still felt rather nauseous afterward. Ray, one of the most unfortunate in this aspect, found that breaking atmosphere in a room without windows was far worse, so he did not avoid the bridge during such. Adding to the peril at the moment was the fact that he was still drunk from the party earlier that night.

"I'll get the mop," he said, exiting the bridge.

"Ray has the worst luck," said John.

"You know, John," began Christie, "you don't always have to scream out of the atmosphere like that. Next time can you at least try a calmer ascent?"

"I'm sorry, Christie, I tend to let my enthusiasm get the better of me when it comes to piloting the ship. Besides, I had to play second fiddle to Fernwyn during our trip out to Misrere."

"You wouldn't let him fly your ship?" Christie asked Fernwyn, who was sitting across from her.

"You have to be able to read Residerian to properly pilot my Neutrino," replied Fernwyn.

John stood up and smiled. "I did all right back at the power station."

A beeping sound drew Christie's attention back to her console, and she said, "The Almagest is approaching."

"Captain Calico is signaling us," added Dana.

"Put him on the HUD display," said John.

Calico's visage appeared in the center of the forward windows.

"Commander Scherer, I stand ready to take your orders," he said.

"Okay, Captain, here's the deal. We're going to head to the anomaly at 13c, which will get us there in about two hours. The SUF squadron has an ETA of three hours. That will give us some time for my crew to get a bit of badly-needed rest and to see what's going on before the squadron arrives. Dana Andrews," John gestured at her, "will work with her counterpart on your ship to sync up our Superluminal Relativistic Compensator and neutrino sensor arrays. We should be able to accomplish the latter in transit, so once the former is complete we will depart."

"Everything sounds good to me," replied Calico. "Lieutenant Andrews, it's nice to meet you. You will be working with Knoal Maiers on those systems."

"Hello," said Knoal from off-camera.

"Good, Dana, please get started. Once you're done, go ahead and lock in the coordinates and get us going."

"No problem," replied Dana.

"Thank you, Commander," said Calico. "I'll talk to you later, then."

John nodded. "Roger."

Calico's face was replaced with Knoal, who introduced himself to Dana. She switched the video image to her normal station and began working with the Residerian on the task at hand.

John pulled out his pipe, which was ready to smoke, and turned to Christie and Fernwyn.

"I'm going to do my tour, you are both welcome to come with me," he said.

John's tour was a quick walk through each part of the ship, a habit he'd gotten into a few days after leaving Earth.

"I think I'll stay here," said Fernwyn.

"I'll go with you," said Christie.

John and Christie exited the bridge. When the door had closed behind them, John lit his pipe and puffed vigorously. The ventilation system on board the Faith quickly distributed the bluish haze around the upper bulkheads and thinned it out. Christie waited until John pocketed his lighter then hugged him.

"I missed you while you were gone, John," she said, and released him.

"Me, too. How's it going with you and Ray?"

John walked a few steps down the corridor, took a left turn, and entered the lounge area. Christie followed at his right.

"We're well. We have some philosophical differences about certain details regarding marriage, but that won't stop us."

"Oh, really?" asked John, entering the conference room.

"Well, you know Ray, he wants a traditional wedding, at least so far as having an official proclaim us as married. Since we're in short supply of priests out here, I don't see the point. A small ceremony with the whole crew in attendance would make me happy."

John returned to the lounge and made his way down the corridor towards the aft of the first deck.

"Technically, I could perform the ceremony," he said. "It's naval tradition."

"Oh, could you?" asked Christie, grabbing John's arm. "That would be so perfect! I think we can talk Ray into that fairly easily."

Passing the crew quarters, John arrived at the Zero-G room, opened the hatch, and looked inside. As usual, this room was completely empty save for the controls to the airlock.

"Just name a time and place," said John.

"Right here, with the walls transparent would be great. Residere Delta would be awesome, but who knows when we'll be able to get back there."

John closed the hatch and headed to the mid-deck stairwell. Ray was coming up from the galley with a mop and bucket.

"Feeling better?" asked Christie.

"For the most part," replied Ray. "It is far past time for me to rack out."

"Let me clean up the mess, then. You go get ready for bed."

Ray nodded and gratefully handed the gear off to Christie. He walked a few feet to the door to his quarters and entered.

"There's something else, before you go," said Christie to John. "Other than our own research, Dana and I haven't been able to access any more information on Talvanium from the database. But more annoying to us than that, we haven't been able to get any information about it out of Professor Talvan, either. He says that information is classified and he's not at liberty to disclose it."

"That's drastically out of character for him," replied John.

"We've only known him a few weeks, John. Still, it's strange. He seems totally committed to this ship, but he refuses to explain how Talvanium really works."

"Talvanium is the basis for Umber's best military technology. It makes sense that he would be under orders to keep the details secret, even from us. I'll ask him about it."

"I'd appreciate that. In the meantime, Dana and I have prepared a brief on what little we do know about Talvanium. It's in the shared folder on the network."

"Thanks, I'll look at it."

"Enjoy your tour, then," said Christie, heading back toward the bridge.

"Thank you," said John.

He descended the stairs and emerged in the galley. Aldebaran and Richter were arranging large wooden kegs against a wall, opposite from the kitchenette. Dappled light from the H2O storage tanks mixed with the smoke from Aldebaran's pipe.

"You know what you forgot to design into the ship?" Richter said to John. "A wine cellar."

"Is that all beer?" asked John.

"This isn't the half of it," said Aldebaran. "We've already stashed twelve cases of wine in the hold."

"This could have a serious effect on our war-fighting capability," said John, grinning.

"Definitely," said Richter.

"Unfortunately we'll be at the anomaly in two hours, so you'll have to go easy on it right now."

"No problem."

"What kind of beer is it?"

"I don't know. When I asked, the reply included a bunch of words my translator didn't know."

"This one is ale," began Aldebaran, "this one is lager, and this one is stout. It's the universe's largest sampler pack."

"Fantastic. Come to think of it, we should have enough time for a few rounds of poker and a pint or two, are you up for a game?"

"Definitely," said Richter.

"I have to talk to Professor Talvan for a few minutes, but after that I'll join you."

"Okay then."

"Do you know where he is?"

"I let him crash in my quarters," said Aldebaran.

John nodded. "Thanks."

John turned around and headed into the orb room, a title that was no longer accurate. The room still contained all of their Earth computers, however, and as such it was kept at a slightly lower temperature than the rest of the ship. For a moment John thought he could feel Seth again, but he brushed it off and continued forward.

He emerged in the arms room, a chamber that smelled every bit as wonderful as it looked. He immediately noticed that there were two extra Res-ZorCon Phalanx rifles, and remembered that Professor Talvan had repaired the ship's matter replication system. He also noticed that Richter's M4 carbine was gathering dust, and began wondering if he possessed enough engineering skill to replicate a 5.56mm cartridge without a representative example. It would be a project for a quiet time, although reversing the distinct lack of any energy-powered small arms was a more pressing need than getting another slug-thrower back online. John picked up his M1 rifle, smiled, and returned it to the rack.

Stepping out into the cargo bay, John found himself at the top of a flight of stairs. He descended to the floor, taking note of the large block of lead that had been donated by the Umberian government as fodder for the replication systems, and Fernwyn's Neutrino, a two-seat fighter craft. He crossed to the ramp, and ascended the grade next to it to the forward gun room. The entrance to this room was a three meter hatch while the room itself was barely five feet tall. The gigantic helical magazine at the rear of the GAU 8/A 30mm cannon took up almost the entire room. Cleaning the weapon was a major pain in the ass, and a decent job could only be done on the surface of a hospitable planet.

Everything seemed to be in order, so he backed out and returned to the floor of the bay. At the rear of the lower level was the door to a short corridor, which led to the ventral gun room. This room contained a computer that controlled the fully articulated .50 caliber GAU 19/A machine gun directly below it, and mirrored the room on the upper deck that John just realized he'd forgotten to inspect. The computer included a joystick for elevation and rudder pedals for traversing. Six monitors provided a panoramic view. The rest of the room was filled with ammo cans and a large wooden crate, which was open, and a belt of cartridges led through the hatch in the floor to the feeding mechanism on the receiver. One thousand rounds were linked together for the gun; once the gunner ran through that he or she would have to open an ammo can and add 200 rounds - more if time permitted. It was strongly advisable to the gunner not to run the gun dry, at which point a reload would require opening the hatch in the floor to access the weapon. This computer was left on at all times, so it didn't take John long to check the weapon system.

Proceeding aft, John passed through another short corridor and entered the first hallway. Directly in front of him was the entrance to the cargo hold. John stuck his head inside briefly, noting the cases of wine, and continued down the hallway. That led him to the engine room, where the stardrive lived. This took up most of the two-deck chamber and resembled a section of a 1950s-style rail car with two smaller cylinders on either side. Various conduits connected these features and ran into the rear bulkhead. A computer console displayed information relevant to the drive. The crew rarely entered this room as the stardrive required no maintenance and was visible from a window to the galley.

John reversed course and headed for the dorsal gun room, this time taking the stairwell that connected the cargo bay with the upper deck. The only difference from the other gun room was that the weapon was above the computer station, and the ammo belt stretched from the ceiling to the wooden crate on the floor. Here, it was a good idea to reload as soon as the belt hung free from the ground.

Satisfied, John went back upstairs and stopped in front of Aldebaran's quarters. He removed his folding knife from his pocket and tapped the handle loudly on the steel door. A few seconds later, Talvan opened the door, blinking in the light.

"Commander Scherer? What's going on?"

"You and I need to talk, Professor Talvan. Christie tells me you're withholding information about Talvanium from us. Why?"

"Information on Talvanium is classified to the highest level. It's nothing personal, Commander, you just don't need to know."

"The highest level? Only General Zeeman outranks me. Nobody else is left!"

"Not even General Zeeman had clearance for that information. It is simply too valuable for more than a select handful of people to know. I am, in fact, the only one left who knows everything. Not even the quantum grid database has it."

John crossed his arms. "I think we've earned the right to know. It has always bothered me that we're totally reliant on the stuff for our stardrive and weapons, but we don't know how it can generate so much power. What do you have to lose by telling us? We've proven ourselves as trustworthy a dozen times over."

"And I would hope you trust me enough to make that decision, Scherer. Besides, you already know everything you need to know to utilize the material. How it works is purely academic."

"Then why keep it a secret?"

"Experimentation on the material is extremely dangerous. If you were to start researching new applications for Talvanium, you might blow yourselves up."

"Did I say we wanted to do that? Professor, I'm starting to get the feeling that you're messing with me."

"You are not in any danger, John. You will simply have to accept that the information you desire is unavailable, and trust me to it. If you ever need to know, I will tell you. That's all."

John turned around in frustration. "I don't like secrets on board this ship, Talvan. I'm not sure I'm going to be able to take your advice at face value as long as you keep them."

"I'm sorry, but I made a promise to my superiors, and I will not betray that promise."

"Fair enough. Get some rest, Professor Talvan, we'll be near the Zendreen fleet soon."

John descended the nearby stairs without waiting for a reply. In the galley, Richter and Aldebaran had just installed a spigot in each of the kegs' bungholes and had tested them for function.

"What's the matter with you?" asked Richter, noticing John's expression.

John looked at Richter. "Nothing, forget it. How's the beer?"

"Which one do you want to try first?" asked Richter, pointing at one of three mugs on the table.

"I'll try the stout," said John. He sipped from the mug, which only contained a few ounces. The stout was sharp in flavor with a mellow finish and reminded him of an extra special bitter on top of a typical oatmeal stout. "Very, very agreeable."

The ship shuddered and made a subtle flanging noise that marked the activation of the superluminal drive. A moment later Dana's voice came over the intercom.

"Dana to John, we're underway. Travel time is two hours, fifteen minutes, barring any interruptions."

"Excellent, thank you Dana. We're getting ready to start a poker game down in the galley, if you want to join us when you're finished with Knoal."

"I don't think I'll have time for that, but thanks."

"How about you, Fernwyn?"

"Fernwyn went to her quarters, John," said Christie's voice.

"Oh. How'bout you, Christie?"

"I'm going to take a power nap, I'm bushed."

"Roger. We'll try not to have too much fun without you."

"Yeah, right."

A click signaled the termination of the connection, so John turned to the others.

"Looks like it's just we three for now," he said.

"Scherer, before we get started, Aldebaran and I have something we've been meaning to show you."

"Oh?"

"Yes, a demonstration. Shall we go to the Zero-G room?"

"Okay."

John followed the other two men upstairs to the Zero-G room. Upon arrival, Aldebaran removed his jacket.

"You are aware that I have all of the skills and memories of everyone who was ever connected to the orb," said Aldebaran.

"Of course," replied John.

"I have all of Richter and Ari's martial arts training, in addition to some skills I learned in the Umberian military."

"Dear God, you don't want to spar, do you?"

"Not if you don't want to, not right now anyway. Richter and I have been, however, and the results are impressive enough to show off to you."

John said to Richter, "If you die, can I have all your stuff?"

"We won't hurt each other, Scherer," said Richter, smiling.

Aldebaran and Richter began to spar. Richter's training was primarily in Aikido, and his tactics reflected the style of side-stepping and redirection of force. Aldebaran fought with a broader style, incorporating full-power kicks and blocks in response to Richter's blows. The fight went on for what seemed like an hour, but when Aldebaran finally ceded the battle John realized only five minutes had passed.

"You two could give Jet Li a serious run for his money," said John, visibly impressed.

"Aldebaran can beat me in a real fight," said Richter.

"But Richter is in much better cardiovascular shape than I," panted Aldebaran. "In an intentional stalemate I can't go on as long as him."

"I want to get as many members of the crew to start training on a regular basis," said Richter. "We're all competent with firearms but some of us could stand to improve in unarmed combat."

John nodded, and said, "I'm on board. You may have trouble convincing some of the others, though. Even when we had the orb…"

John trailed off and the others looked at him expectantly.

"John?" asked Aldebaran.

"Sorry, it's nothing, it's just for the second time today I almost felt like Seth was trying to access my mind. Seth the AI, I mean."

"You and I always had a particular kind of relationship. The kind of technology we were dealing with was never tested with any species other than Umberians. I don't mean to scare you, but we don't know how being possessed by the AI might have effected your mind."

"I don't know. Maybe I'm stressed out over reuniting with Ari. Maybe I'm still tired from our last combat mission. I intend to get as much rest and relaxation as possible on our way to the anomaly, but I'll let you know if I have anymore problems. It was just a passing feeling, nothing substantial."

"Why don't we run an active scan on the ship, just to be safe?" asked Richter.

"I suppose that couldn't hurt. I'll get started on it, you two go have fun."

"Fine by me. Come on, Aldebaran, let's get some beer in us, for God's sake."

Megumi stood in the small bathroom adjacent to her quarters, brushing her teeth. For a Kau-Rii living among furless humanoids, personal hygiene was extremely important. Certain grooming deficiencies that would be completely overlooked by other Kau'Rii or Rakhar were more noticeable among those without so much hair. Of particular issue aboard spacecraft was the frequency of bathing; only the Umberians had ever created a water reclamation system that afforded the luxury of frequent showers. Initially this problem was compounded aboard the Almagest as the ship had originally been constructed for Z'Sorth. Captain Calico had installed showers in all of the crew quarters but they were small and using them was not unlike trying to bathe in a wall locker. Knoal couldn't fit in his at all and had to use one of the frigid empty cargo holds. The typical frequency of showers, thanks to water rationing, was once a week.

Fortunately for Megumi and Gueyr, a piece of readily available technology made life easier. It was just like a typical hairbrush, but was augmented with a harmless electrical field that lifted dirt away from hair and sterilized the body. Combined with normal deodorant sprays, one could get by without offending all but the toughest critic.

It was this device that Megumi grabbed upon completion of cleaning her teeth. She removed her clothes and sat on her bed. A proper job of brushing usually took five minutes, although she also liked to do a one-minute pass upon waking. She let her mind wander as she started working. Being under the employ of the

Umberians was something she couldn't have predicted, and she hoped that the captain knew what he was doing. The contract was fairly standard mercenary boilerplate, but representing an entity that so recently had such a significant falling-out with its neighbors troubled her.

Coma's presence (Meg was tempted to call her Arianna just to be difficult) was also a concern for her. At first, Coma was simply a prisoner in need of rescue, but in light of recent events Meg began to wonder if there wasn't something more to the woman. Her particular skills would make her an excellent spy, and indeed that's how Calico was presently using her. Meg had come to suspect that Coma might be spying for someone else, too, and if it was the Solar United Faction then they were all in serious trouble. Her suspicions were premature, however, and expressing her concerns to the captain would simply seem like sour brescaré.

A beep alerted Megumi to someone at her door. If it was Gueyr, she was tempted to open the hatch naked. The younger Kau'Rii had few redeeming qualities other than his looks and technical ability, but space is a lonely enough place to change anyone's mind about just about anything. As his superior officer, however, there was no way she could make the first move. Captain's rules. Meg suspected Gueyr was interested, as he had given her a rare copy of a book of historical poetry written by her great-great-grandfather. It was a nice gift, but Meg found the content impenetrable.

Megumi donned sweatpants and a t-shirt and answered the door. Coma stood in the corridor.

"Veronice," Meg said.

"Hello, I'm not bothering you, am I?"

"Not really. What's up?"

"I want to talk to you about Farril."

"By all means, come in," replied Meg unenthusiastically.

Coma entered, crossed to Meg's desk, and took a seat. Meg closed the hatch and sat on her bed.

"Thank you."

Megumi folded her arms across her chest, and said, "You must realize that I'm going to take the captain's side, no matter what you have to say."

"That's fine, I'm not stupid enough to play you two against each other. It's that Farril just revealed his true feelings about me. Unintentionally, and unexpectedly."

"So screw him. You don't need my permission."

Coma blushed. "He sees me as his daughter, Rukitara."

Meg put her hand over her mouth. "Oh! I'm sorry!"

"Don't worry about it. I wasn't entirely sure myself. If he'd acted in a romantic manner toward me, I would have returned it in kind. And I won't insult you by saying that it would be for purely romantic reasons, either."

"I think true love is a myth. Still, I appreciate your honesty. I also think I can predict your next question. Yes, the captain did have a daughter. She died at age sixteen."

"That's terrible. What happened?"

"She was a very bright girl and had an aptitude towards flying. She and her dad restored an old single-seat fighter craft and launched it on her birthday. After a few flights in the atmosphere, she felt ready to break atmo. She calculated her own re-entry path, and got it wrong. The ship burned up."

"That is just awful. I can't even begin to imagine how you can recover from a loss like that."

"You never really do. People cope with tragedy in different ways. Calico became a mercenary. Drink?"

"Yeah, sure."

Meg reached behind her bed and pulled out a growler.

"Knoal may be an annoying brute but he is one hell of a brewer."

"Knoal brews beer on board? It's not in the same hold where he…"

"Fortunately, no. Glasses are behind you. His setup is sanitary, best I can tell."

Coma grabbed two mugs. "That's good."

Meg poured the ale. "In case you're wondering, by the way, Calico and I never had a relationship beyond friendship."

"I guess it's irrelevant now, isn't it?"

Coma sampled the ale. It tasted like India pale ale with hints of black currant. Meg drained most of her glass and topped it off.

"You weren't kidding, this is good stuff," Coma said.

"Some people are only attracted to humanoids of similar appearance, how about you?"

"I would like to beat the hell out of a Rakhar and force him to mate with me; that's normal, right?"

"I do hope you're joking," replied Meg, her expression deadpan.

"Almost entirely. I once knew a Rakhar with impeccable grooming, and the thought crossed my mind. Unfortunately I was distracted by someone else at the time and the Rakhar got killed soon thereafter."

Meg took a swig from her glass, and asked, "Were you involved in the liberation of Umber?"

"No."

"No? That's it, just 'no?' "

"We can talk about our sexual predilections all you want, but talking about my past is far too intimate at this stage of our relationship."

"Suit yourself," said Meg, and drained her glass. "Let me ask you this, though. Is what happened between you and your crew really bad enough to warrant your reaction to Scherer and Rylie? They were ready to reconcile with you."

"Scherer is a sentimental fool and Rylie is a mystery to me. Suffice it to say that I almost cost the entire crew of the Faith their lives. I'm not certain the rest of the crew is as forgiving."

6.

It was a simple enough dream, but for John it was a nightmare. In a fantasy concocted by his confused mind, he saw himself packing up Ari's old apartment in Boston. The premise was not stated but John knew it inherently: Ari was dead, and for some reason the burden of disposing of her personal effects had fallen on him. It was a recurring dream, to John's dismay, and found him during sleep at least twice a week since Ari had disappeared into a distant, silent explosion in the cold darkness of space.

John awoke in his quarters. At first he was relieved, as usual, to realize the nightmare was over, then annoyed that his reunion with Ari hadn't allowed his subconscious to dispense with the imagery.

One hour had passed since a single glass of beer had overcome John's wakefulness and sent him to snooze in his quarters. A scan of the ship had revealed nothing, and by the time he joined the poker game he was almost completely spent. Despite the ineffectiveness of his subsequent nap, he freshened himself up in the bathroom and got dressed. He armed himself, and headed for the bridge. He was met there by Christie and Ray, who were sharing in the luxury of fresh Umberian artisan bread and hot yutha.

"Good morning," he said, "at least I think it's morning."

"It is morning," replied Ray, "by the ship's clock, anyway."

"Feeling better?"

"A little. A catnap is better than nothing, I suppose."

"Good. How are you, Christie?"

Christie nodded. "Fine, thanks."

"I hate to interrupt your breakfast, but how about a status report?"

"No problem. We're cruising at 13 c on course, no deviations. The Almagest is holding a thousand meters behind us, according to the SRC. Obviously we can't maintain visual contact right now. Dana finished working with Knoal on our sensor arrays; she's napping in the lounge. Unfortunately we weren't able to increase our range or sensitivity , but at least the redundancies will increase our chances of catching something interesting. That's about it... oh, Professor Talvan has a theory about the anomaly he wanted to share."

"What is it?"

"One of the many projects..." Talvan began to say.

"What the hell?" barked John, startled.

"What the hell yourself, Scherer!" replied Talvan angrily.

"I'm sorry, Professor, I didn't notice you come in."

"I've been here the whole time."

John turned to Christie and Ray. "Really?"

"Yes, really," said Christie earnestly. "You walked right by him and started talking to us."

"I've had a lot on my mind the past few days. Please continue."

Talvan grimaced slightly, then spoke. "I was saying, one of the many projects that my colleagues and I were working on before the war was a new form of superluminal travel. This involved a device that could create and sustain a stable wormhole for a short time, through which a ship could pass. We got far enough with the theory to design a device on paper, but the war began before a prototype could be built and tested.

Still, the idea was grounded quite solidly in superluminal theory."

"Do you think the Zendreen have discovered your research?"

"Maybe. It may be coincidental that the anomaly has manifested similarly to a wormhole. What makes me suspect that the research from Project Wishing Well is being used here is the size and spectral type of UAS 1006. What was your name for it?"

"Alpha Sagittae," Christie answered.

"Right. Stars of a specific size and spectral type are essential to the device functioning properly, in theory. The idea was that a certain density of high energy protons in the solar wind could be used as a carrier wave for a cascade flux implosion."

"Ah, technobabble," said Ray.

"Excuse me? My translator didn't catch that."

"The specifics are a little beyond our level of education," said John.

"Oh, I see. Well, to simplify, a star like that can be used as a stable exit point for a ship."

"How, in simple terms, is the entry point generated?"

"A really big invisible lightning bolt."

John smirked. "Naturally. Okay, so let's assume for the sake of argument that the anomaly was caused by a working model of this device, and that the Zendreen are the ones responsible. Why would they want to go to Alpha Sagittae?"

"I don't know, but if they ever want to return to the Cloud they'll have to settle for the area of the Nursery of the Gods. There isn't a star of the correct type within one thousand light years of Umber. Come to think of it, Sanduleak was a star of that type. Perhaps they're looking to settle a new colony near a familiar-looking sun."

"Maybe. What else is near there?"

"That's within striking distance to the Hayakuvian system. The Zendreen have never strayed outside of the Cloud. They have little or no reputation in the core galaxy. If they were planning on giving up their bellicose tendencies, at least temporarily, Hayaku and the surrounding settlements would be a good place to do it."

"I might believe that, if the fleet is indeed that bad off."

"Also, keep in mind that the Zendreen's plan for their future isn't a ten year plan, or even a fifty year plan. The Zendreen think in terms of millennia. They have no problem with the idea of a thousand years of reconstruction. If the vicinity of Hayaku is the safest place to do it, then they will go there. It would certainly ensure that they'd be safe from retaliation from us or the SUF."

"Do you realize the implications of what you're saying?" asked Christie.

"What do you mean?"

"If the Zendreen are using information from Project Wishing Well, then where did they get it?"

Talvan thought about this for a moment, then said, "Christie is right, it's impossible. If it is a wormhole, then either the Zendreen aren't responsible for it or they've created their own form of technology."

"Are you absolutely sure that the orb was the last repository of Umber's technological archive?" asked John.

"Positive, John. I was not only responsible for programming Seth, but also for purging the planetary computer systems of all data. There were twelve central servers where the data was stored. Any scientist who had authorization to access the servers could do so from any terminal, but the data was not downloaded to that terminal and remained in flash memory. When the user was finished, any changes were saved to the central server and the terminal was cleared. When the war was obviously not going our way, I transferred everything to the orb and wiped the servers."

"All right, Talvan, we..."

"I'm not finished, Scherer! I personally traveled to each server station throughout the globe to ensure compliance. I deleted the files, bombarded the quantum matrices with gamma radiation to scatter the code, and just to be sure, dropped incendiary grenades inside the server rooms. There was no record of an illegal download prior to that. It's simply impossible that any other archive could exist."

"The Zendreen occupied Umber for ten years," said Ray, "if there was an unauthorized archive, they had plenty of time to find it."

"If they did find such an archive, why didn't they begin production on Talvanium 115-based forms of technology? The whole point of the invasion was to gain that ability."

Christie said, "The discovery could have been concurrent with our arrival. Once the Vengeance virus was deployed, it was all over for them on Umber. They might have taken as much Talvanium as they had on hand and made off with it during their evacuation. Then they began development in on-board laboratories."

"I simply hope you are wrong, my friends. Missing an unauthorized archive would be the greatest failure of my entire professional career."

"There is another possibility," said John grimly. "Ari was a prisoner of the Zendreen for at least a week. Ari, like most of our crew, was in direct contact with the orb. If what happened to Aldebaran holds true for the rest of us, even to some degree, then the Zendreen could have obtained the technical data from her mind."

Christie leaped to her feet, knocking her cup of yutha to the deck. "Oh my God, I can't believe I didn't think of this before!"

Moving swiftly to her console, Christie accessed her astronomical program.

"What is it?" asked Ray.

"Alpha Sagittae is only 475 light-years from Earth."

John joined Christie at her console. "Christie's right. We have to assume that the Zendreen were able to gain one critical but easily discovered fact from Ari: there's Talvanium on Earth."

"Hell," said Ray, "if Earth is the Zendreen's ultimate destination, then we've got to stop them!"

"I don't think anyone on this ship is going to disagree with you, Ray, but I doubt two light cruisers and one fighter escort are going to intimidate the Zendreen fleet very much. We are going to have to convince the SUF that this is their fight, too, and I don't see how. Once the Zendreen go through that wormhole then they are no longer the SUF's problem."

"Maybe we can convince them that the wormhole device is actually a weapon," said Christie.

"You mean lie to them?" asked Talvan. "Even if we were able to draw the SUF into the fight on our side, once the truth came out it would destroy Umber's reputation even as we're trying to repair it."

"At this point this is a discussion that needs to be held with the entire crew," said John, and activated the intercom. "Attention please, this is Commander Scherer. There is a mandatory meeting in the conference room in ten minutes. I apologize if you were asleep, but this has to happen now. Thank you, out."

"Richter and Aldebaran are not going to be happy," said Christie. "They played poker and drank beer for another half-hour after you went to bed."

"Tough shit. If this turns out to be nothing then they can catch up on sleep all they want. Open a channel to Captain Calico, I need to talk to him."

Eleven minutes later, the crew of the Faith was gathered in the conference room. John had just given a quick summary of the conversation on the bridge. Richter looked miserable; Aldebaran was comatose. The others took a moment to let the information sink in.

"I contacted Captain Calico," continued John. "I asked him about Ari's experience aboard the Zendreen ship. He said she's understandably tight-lipped about what happened to her, given the trauma of the event. He said she remembers being interrogated and can't honestly say whether or not she revealed anything compromising. If so, and the Zendreen are on their way to Earth, then we have to come up with a plan to stop them that doesn't involve direct action. We simply don't have the force necessary to take on the fleet."

"Professor Talvan," began Dana, "if the Zendreen are trying to generate a wormhole, is there any way we can stop it short of destroying the emitting ships?"

Talvan thought about this for a moment. "Theoretically, if the emitters were too close to a large source of stellar radiation there would be too much interference to create a cascade wave. Unfortunately the only way we can generate that kind of energy is to overload the Faith's stardrive, burning all of our fuel within a few seconds. If we don't control the reaction properly, we'll destroy ourselves. Then, if the Zendreen have enough energy remaining, they can just restart the process."

"And we'll be stuck five years away from the nearest source of fuel," said Christie.

"If Captain Calico can spare ten gallons of deuterium," said Aldebaran, rubbing his eyes, "that's all we need to make it back to Umber."

John nodded. "Is there any way to determine how much energy the Zendreen are using to generate this wormhole, and if so, how many times they can attempt it?"

"Once we know how many ships have been modified to emit the energy pulses," said Talvan, "then we can estimate their energy expenditures based on known variables. If the stardrives have been modified, however, there would be no way of knowing."

"Ballpark it."

"Excuse me?"

Aldebaran said, "Our last intelligence report put the Zendreen fleet at twenty ships. They have one battleship, five heavy cruisers, and fourteen various other smaller craft. The first six are the only ones normally equipped to generate the kind of energy that Talvan's theoretical device called for, although if all fourteen were linked up somehow they could account for a seventh emitter. What was the energy level we're talking about here, Professor?"

"Four point five trillion parhet."

"That's about one terawatt for you Earthlings."

"Six ships could generate a packet burst of that magnitude twice without refueling. A seventh ship, or the equivalent, wouldn't make any difference. So they may indeed have only one attempt remaining."

"What would the process of generating our, I guess you could call it a dampening field, entail?" asked John.

"First you would have to override the appropriate safety protocols. Then you would set the engines to create a resonance cascade at the rate of five point seven Kruelar. Each tier of the cascade would have to be stabilized at the appropriate time with a electromagnetic carrier wave generated by our radio transmission system, which will have to be tied into the stardrive. If the carrier waves are not implemented at precisely the right times, the reaction will either cease or overload. An overload would effectively destroy the Faith."

"Who here is qualified to perform that sort of operation?"

"Myself."

"I can do it," added Aldebaran.

"I'm sure Christie or I could learn how to do it with some practice," said Dana.

"Good," said John. "You four work together in the time we have remaining to make it possible. Obviously I hope not to use that measure. If the time comes, anyone who doesn't wish to be fatally irradiated or vaporized can evacuate to the Almagest, time permitting. Only the best candidate for the procedure need stay aboard with me."

"Sounds like a plan," began Ray, "but how long will generating the interference take?"

"Five or ten minutes," replied Talvan.

"How long will it take before the Zendreen will be able to detect the radiation?"

"Oh, they'll be able to detect it almost right away."

"Then I'll stay behind, too. Somebody's going to have to help John man the weapons if we're attacked."

"Count me in," said Richter.

"Me, too," said Fernwyn.

"Your best place in that event will be in your Neutrino," said John. "Anyone else who wants to stay behind is welcome to do so, of course. Our best hit percentages come from each gun station having a live person there. I will not fault anyone for evacuating to the Almagest. There is no need for all of us to die. That reminds me, what kind of a fight can the fleet put up? I mean, I know we don't stand a chance, but can we hold them off for ten minutes?"

Aldebaran nodded. "If the large ships are busy generating the energy pulses, then we can expect the response to be mainly Zendreen single-seat fighters and any of the other fourteen ships that are significantly armed. The normal compliment for a battleship is one hundred, and each of the cruisers usually carries twenty. Hopefully the Vengeance virus will have depleted the pool of qualified pilots, since we'll be limited to sublight speed during the generation process."

"But the worst-case scenario is two hundred fighters?"

"Yup. They'd be limited in how many could attack at once, but there will be plenty to fill in the casualties once we started picking them off. The only other good news is that Zendreen fighters normally carry plasma cannons that are only capable of destroying us with dozens of direct hits. Otherwise we can simply shunt the energy into our own plasma cannons and laser banks."

"What about our other option of shunting the hits into the stardrive?" asked Christie. "Would that speed up the process?"

Talvan shook his head, and said, "Theoretically, yes, but for mere mortals it will introduce too many variables to compensate for that rapidly. Maybe if Seth were still in orb form, otherwise an overload would be inevitable."

Christie shrugged. "Okay, never mind."

"Are we just assuming that Captain Calico will back up this plan?" asked Richter. "What will that kind of radiation burst do to his ship?"

"Unless he's significantly modified his stardrive," replied Talvan, "it will only disable his superluminal ability for a few hours. He'll still be able to…"

"Oh, just a few hours, no big deal," said Richter, interrupting. "We need to make sure Calico is on board with this plan, Professor."

"I plan of briefing Calico, don't worry about it," said John. "His help was always a bonus and we can proceed without him if necessary."

"Will the radiation burst have the same effect on the engines of the Zendreen ships?" asked Dana.

"I don't know, maybe," replied Talvan.

Dana continued. "If we fail to stop them this time, won't our next option be to follow them through the wormhole? How long will the wormhole stay open? If the Zendreen fleet can still go light, will we have enough time to follow them?"

"We will have to pursue them at all costs," said John. "Earth forces cannot repel the Zendreen without help. We can only hope to find allies on the other side of the wormhole if we cannot stop them on this one."

"That's why we can't afford to lose Calico," said Aldebaran. "He's Hayakuvian, he may have valuable contacts in that region."

"I will talk to Calico as soon as we're done here. His contacts may not help if he's unwilling to follow us through the wormhole. Other than that, between now and when we arrive,

Richter, I want you to run some weapons drills. Make sure that we're still sharp on the weapons systems and reloading procedures for the slug-throwers. Those of you testing the cascade procedure, you can participate as soon as you're available, but that takes priority for you. Add the stardrive restart process to your agenda. I want to be able to go light as soon as possible after the radiation burst. Does anyone else have anything to add right now?"

Those present indicated they did not, and John stood up.

"Ready to rock and roll," said Richter.

"Good luck, then," John said, and exited to the bridge.

Richter stood up, and the last evidence of his fatigue disappeared instantly. "Okay, people, first drill is in one minute. Pick your favorite station and that's the one you won't be manning. I want everybody to work on the weapon system they have the least time on. Fernwyn, after that I want to go over launch procedures for your ship, since we've never done a vacuum deployment before. Let's get this done as soon as possible, so that we're refreshed by the time we get there. Move it!"

"I'll be right with you, Richter," said Fernwyn, and followed John onto the bridge.

"Was there something else?" asked John, sitting at the commo station.

Fernwyn sat at the station next to John. "There is, John. My thoughts have been dwelling of late on the state of local politics. If the Zendreen are responsible for a wormhole, then I will help you try to stop them from going through. However, if we can't stop them, I'm afraid I have no desire to follow you through to the Hayakuvian system."

John sighed and looked at Fernwyn. "You've been a great ally and a good friend, especially to me. I'm sorry to let you go, but I think I understand your feelings. You should know that I never meant to lead you on. This whole situation with Ari…"

"That's got nothing to do with it, John. You and I had fun together but I never considered it a serious relationship. If the Zendreen depart this region of space, then the process of repairing the relationship between Residere and Umber can proceed unimpeded. I can contribute a lot to that effort, and that's where I feel like I belong. I'm also reluctant to end up back in the core galaxy, considering the effect of time dilation on the return trip."

"You've already given more to this crew than anyone could have asked of you. I don't know where we might end up in the future, but you will always have a place on this ship."

Fernwyn picked up John's hand and squeezed it. "Thank you."

In Calico's chamber aboard the Almagest, John had just brought the captain up to speed on his plan. Calico nodded and thought about his reply.

"You don't have to answer now," said John, his image flickering on the monitor.

"No, I can tell you what I think," said Calico. "Honestly I think you're getting awfully far ahead of yourselves. There could still be another explanation."

"My crew and I like to think ahead as much as possible."

"Fair enough, nobody ever died from too much planning. If it is the Zendreen wormhole, and we can't stop them here, then I will follow you through. The Zendreen may be going after Hayaku, after all. However, if they are headed to your home planet, then I don't expect anyone from my neck of the galaxy will care to help. The best you could hope for would be to hire more mercs, and I'm not sure a promise of payment from Umber will be sufficient enticement. Hell, if I follow you through the wormhole it will take me a long time to collect that compensation myself. Barring another handy wormhole to return through, of course."

"Then I hope the threat to your homeworld is enough."

"It is. Of course, Commander Scherer, I couldn't help but notice that Perditia is a lot further away from Hayaku than five hundred light years."

"Perditia was a cover story to protect my home planet. I'm sorry I lied to you, but I hope you understand why I did."

"Don't worry about it. The other thing, though, is that Perditia would have nothing to fear from the Zendreen fleet. Is the status of your homeworld really that weak?"

"Calico, next time we are together in person I will tell you all about Earth. Until then, please be content to know that Earth cannot repel a Zendreen invasion without help."

"Fine. Now then, as far as the possibility of using a radiation pulse. I can either withdraw to a safe distance just before you activate it, or I can shut down my superluminal drive. The latter choice will give me fewer tactical options if we're engaged, so I'm inclined to the former. It could even act as a diversion and take some of the heat off of your ship."

"Sounds good to me."

"Another aspect we haven't discussed is the arrival of the SUF squadron."

"I forgot about them. They're ultimately irrelevant to our goals, aren't they?"

"Not entirely. Commander Scherer, between our two ships, we have just enough firepower to take down one of the Zendreen heavy cruisers. If I understand your tactical analysis, if we can take out one of them then they can't generate the wormhole. If the SUF fighters cover our way in, we might be able to succeed."

"That sounds even more dangerous than overloading my stardrive."

"Perhaps, but the Zendreen won't be expecting it. Surprise can count for quite a bit. If the SUF agrees to this idea you should seriously consider it. If we can't destroy a cruiser then you can always back off and activate the radiation pulse."

"I'd have to be alive to do that. I will keep it in mind, Captain. Thank you for your support. When we get to the anomaly, let's keep an open channel between our ships."

"Agreed. Commander, enjoy the time we have left until then. This could be one hell of a fight."

"Roger. Scherer out."

Calico deactivated his console, stood up, and exited to the bridge. Gueyr, Megumi, and Coma were present. The SRC-generated image of the surrounding nebula graced the viewports.

"I have good news and bad news," Calico said. "The good news is that we may get some action on this mission. The bad news is that we may never get paid for our services."

"Are you trying to be glib about our odds of survival?" asked Megumi.

"No, I mean we may be heading for Hayaku via wormhole."

"Oh," said Gueyr, crestfallen. "Oh, wow."

"That's a little too far from home for your liking, Gueyr?" asked Calico.

"Excuse me, sir. My commitment to this ship takes priority. I'll get used to it."

"There's a higher population density of Kau'Rii out that way. The right girl in the right port can make you feel right at home."

Gueyr turned away, embarrassed. "Come on, sir, you know I'm not like that."

Calico grinned. "You don't have to be, that's the beauty of it!"

"How will the rest of the crew react?" asked Coma.

"They can react all they want. Everyone except you has signed a contract that forbids withdrawing from the contract during an active mission. If they do, they are subject to administrative review by the guild, and may be jettisoned."

"Jettisoned?"

"I mean kicked out."

"Ah. Why didn't you have me sign the same contract?"

"You didn't come to me by way of the guild, and the standing policy is to allow independent agents to work for guild members without a contract. They are subject to fewer restrictions but entitled to no benefits. If you were to be accused of a crime, for example, the guild would not represent you in court. You should have a contract between you and I, as an agent of mine, and I have one ready to run off should the situation require it."

"Can I read it?"

"Of course. Megumi, have the crew prepare the ship for combat. We're going to have to adjust the static charge on our armor to resist Zendreen plasma, Knoal should be able to help you with that."

"Understood, Cap," said Megumi.

"Veronice, now would be a good time to learn the armor system. You should get a good sense of things during the adjustment."

"What about that contract?"

"I'll give you copy now. Gueyr, Megumi, get going, I'll send Coma down shortly."

The others nodded and Calico entered his chamber. Coma followed him.

"Sir," she began.

"This contract is standard GFWG material," said Calico, accessing his terminal. "Any part of it can be modified as long as we both agree on the change. The guild maintains a significant presence in the Hayakuvian system, so it's not a bad idea for us to hammer something out after all."

"Farril, we need to talk."

Calico stopped what he was doing and turned around. "This can only help you in the long run. It's nothing personal."

"This isn't about whether or not I trust you, you know I do. I want to talk about our relationship, because frankly I was working off of some assumptions that apparently aren't true."

"Okay," said Calico, sitting down. "Go ahead."

"Megumi told me about your daughter."

Calico became visibly upset, and after a moment he pointed sternly at the door. "Megumi, that… she should know better. That part of me belongs to me alone."

Coma gestured apologetically. "You don't have to tell me anything. And Megumi was just making sure I knew why you were treating me the way you were. You completely shut me down yesterday after you inadvertently called me your daughter. There is nothing wrong with our relationship, Farril. I'm flattered that you think of me like that. You and your daughter must have had a good relationship too, because not once did I feel like you were treating me as a child."

"If I had treated her like a child," said Calico sadly, "at least for a few more years, she might not have been killed."

"Look, I'm curious as to why you feel that way about me. Is it just a physical resemblance to her, or are our personalities similar?"

Calico turned away. "Neither. It was how you looked when we found you on that science ship. You were in a featureless metal cell, naked except for a tattered jacket, face streaked with tears, shivering, and half out of your mind with fear."

"I don't remember that," Coma said flatly.

"That doesn't surprise me. I think the Zendreen were starving you on purpose to let your damaged digestive system heal. We didn't test the substance in the intravenous line attached to your arm, but it could have been nutrients, just enough to keep you alive. You didn't snap out of that stupor for a couple of days."

"Is that why you suggested the name 'Coma' to me?"

"No, the name means 'lucky' in Hayakuvian. What does it mean in your tongue?"

"A prolonged state of unconsciousness."

"That's an interesting irony."

"So your feelings for me were simply born of a paternal instinct to protect me?"

"I suppose so."

"I can take care of myself now, obviously. Does the feeling still hold?"

"You must not have had a close relationship with your father if the sentiment perplexes you."

Coma would have been insulted if Calico hadn't been right. She nodded thoughtfully.

"I never knew my father," she said.

"Well, I'm not here to replace him. We can simply be friendly without being familiar, as we have been. The rest of the crew already know we have a bond that goes beyond the professional, but the attention I've given you is not beyond what I'm willing to offer to any member of this crew. Wait a second…"

"What?"

"Coma, what assumptions had you made that were wrong?"

"I thought you might be open to a romantic relationship." Calico turned the color of a chilled Cabernet, so Coma added, "See what I mean?"

"I am not in the habit of keeping a lover on board. It interferes with my ability to effectively implement my crew."

"I'm not sure whether to feel comforted or slighted."

"If we were to become romantically involved, then I would be compelled to dismiss you. Since my line of work is not conducive to keeping a lover planetside, the thought never crossed my mind. Also, you are far too valuable to me to waste on indulgences."

Coma smiled. "You are a complicated man, Captain Calico, but I think I understand your logic. Would you ever give up your command for the right woman?"

"Not a chance in hell."

The eyes of Miriam's mother were locked open in shock. Miriam tried to cry, but this time nothing came. In the constant cold of the structure, her parents' bodies had remained almost the same since they'd arrived. Miriam had lost track of time. How long had they been there? A week? Ten days? Longer? It didn't seem to matter anymore. She only wished that she'd closed her mother's eyes before they'd frozen that way.

"Why did you die and not me?"

It was a question that she asked herself every time she visited this small room where her parents lay. After four visits, Miriam had lost any hope that this was all a bad dream. The bodies lying on the deck were the only things that seemed real. Yet, she knew this was the last time she would enter this room. She was weighing two possible strategies to take with the natives. One was to attempt to open up a dialog with them. Other than the most obvious problem of the language barrier, there was also the open hostility between them. The second idea she had was to take them out, one by one, until she'd captured enough territory and supplies to be self-sufficient. That strategy suffered from the fact that Miriam had almost negligible combat skills and the thought of killing one of these creatures, however much it might be in self-defense, sickened her. She was compelled to do something, anything, as she couldn't bear the thought of this lifestyle indefinitely.

Miriam whispered goodbye to her parents, and turned around. There was a woman standing in the doorway. She appeared human at first glance, although the details of her features were difficult to discern underneath her cold-weather gear. Her beige fur-rimmed jacket was cropped at the waist, her black pants were form-fitting, and her head was covered with a fur hat and clear goggles. She held a pistol of some sort down by her side, and gave the girl a half smile. Miriam tensed up, her fingers closing around the pistol in her pocket, and prepared to fire.

"*Malchem, prase, fealva baruchin kai metsu*," the woman said, holding out a small device with her other hand.

Miriam looked at the woman, and at the device. It was obviously an earpiece. The woman slowly placed the device on the floor, and calmly motioned for Miriam to put it in her ear. Miriam craned her neck to see past the woman. It was impossible to tell if she was alone from this angle. Still, there was nowhere to run, so she leaned over carefully, keeping her eyes on the woman, and retrieved the device.

"Well, I suppose if you wanted to hurt me you'd just shoot me," she said, and placed the device in her ear.

"Now then, can you understand me?" the woman asked, the words in English following the unknown spoken language by a split-second.

"Yes. And you me?"

"Yes. Identify language."

"It's called English."

"Excuse me, I was talking to my translator. English it is. Aren't you curious as to how we came to know your language?"

"It's not near the top of all of my questions," replied Miriam, still scared but grateful for the conversation.

The woman nodded. "Why don't we try one-for-one. I'll go first. What's your name and where are you from?"

"That's two questions, but I don't mind. My name is Miriam Fenchurch Colchester, and

I'm from Romanby, Yorkshire. How about yourself?"

"Call me Cassie."

"Where are we?"

"This is the Vulture, last of the three great Stymphalian raptors. Eagle, the noble explorer, went toward the galactic core. Swan, the beautiful diplomat, disappeared near the eye of the demon, Gorgon. Only we remain, free to fulfill the original intent of the Vulture: to profit from the suffering of others."

"So you've lost your marbles, is that it?"

"Uh-uh, my sister, it is my turn for a question. If you please, on what planet is Yorkshire, I believe you called it."

"Are you daft? The same planet as the rest of Britain. Earth."

"Have you seen the sun since you arrived here?" asked Cassie in a condescending tone. "Surely it will be the least of surprises for you to learn that we are not on Earth."

"Ridiculous. We are clearly near one of the poles, which easily explains the long period of darkness and cold temperatures. What is this, some kind of Arctic or Antarctic research station?"

"Even if it were, what about the dog-like creatures you've been stealing from this whole time?"

"It's the 21st century, ma'am. I've heard about cloning, and DNA manipulation. All of this is within believability, but not your queer assertion that we are on another planet."

"Miriam, you are not the first human the Kira'To have brought here."

Her adrenaline hit her chest like a fast pitch, and Miriam's mind stopped working for a moment. When she regained her ability to vocalize her thoughts, she was stymied as to what to say. Cassie's words had an undeniable ring of truth to them, even if Miriam couldn't explain why. Her only option was to deflect the entire subject.

"What do you want from me?" she asked.

"Your uncooperative presence is proving to be a problem among our ranks," replied Cassie. "The troops are frustrated, in more ways then one, and as far as the more complex reason, they will not believe that they cannot mate with you until all of the empirical evidence has been exhausted."

"You are hardly making a good case for my surrender!" exclaimed Miriam.

"On the contrary. I intend to prove to you that bringing you under my protection is your best choice. The only reason why we haven't systematically cordoned off and searched this entire place is because I wished to reason with you. If you choose to withdraw back into the darkness, I will be forced to find you and take you in an undiplomatic manner. If that happens, I cannot be held responsible for the conduct of my troops."

"Are you telling me that I'm free to go?"

"For now," said Cassie, moving aside, "but I urge you to consider my words. This place was once a grand palace, full of delights both mental and physical. Time and distance have reduced us to a pale shadow of our former glory. Your arrival is the portent of a resurgence of that greatness, and although you alone are not enough to regain it, your help could be instrumental in the process. In the immediate future, I can promise you a warm room, a hot bath, and enough food to fill your belly for a week."

"You strike me as a lunatic," said Miriam, moving onto the landing, "so I think I'll take my chances on my own."

Cassie grabbed Miriam by the shoulders. The younger woman resisted the urge to stick her pistol in the strange female's ribs, and stared into the flashing green eyes behind the rubber-rimmed goggles.

"We will find you," Cassie said ominously.

Miriam pushed her away and flew down the stairs, three steps at a time. Her tears finally returned, and she felt the wetness soak the fur rim of her hood. The word 'purgatory' crossed her mind as she fled into a nondescript corridor. Perhaps that was the true nature of this place. If so, what would that make the Kira'To?

As she ran into the gray bleakness, Miriam thought that she heard echoing laughter follow her.

Tho they have no voice or form
they're heard and seen by the mad
This so claimed also by the wise
and rulers who wished they had
- Metrick Rukitara, Specter of the Kira'To

7.

The Besser Expanse was a relatively open area of the Tarantula Nebula, just beyond the comet-forming region at the extreme limit of the Umberian solar system. The next closest planetary systems were Residere and Misrere, in almost a straight line to the galactic axis (which was somewhat artificially defined in a diffuse sub-galaxy). In any other direction the nearest star system was over 100 light years distant. The luminescent colors of the nebula were dimmer in the expanse, and a large patch of open space sat above the area like the eye of a massive hurricane. It allowed a glimpse into a darkness that the crew of the Reckless Faith hadn't seen since they first arrived at Umber weeks ago.

When the Faith and the Almagest dropped down to sublight speed, they had only a few minutes to admire the scenery before the Zendreen fleet was spotted. On the bridge of the former ship, Dana activated the invisibility shield and began to scan the area. The crew of the 'Gest listened in via an audio link.

"The intelligence reports were correct," she said. "There's one battleship, five heavy cruisers, and fourteen smaller support vessels. According to our database, two of the smaller ships are medical frigates, two are supply ships, and the rest cannot be immediately identified. Incidentally, one of the cruisers is a Res-ZorCon starliner heavily retrofitted and broadcasting a Zendreen power signature."

Aldebaran stood next to Dana, and viewed the data over her shoulder.

"The fleet is maintaining a standard escort echelon," he said, "with the smaller ships clustered together inside the perimeter of the larger ships. The ships in the interior area are maintaining a relative distance of one thousand meters. The ships on the perimeter are five thousand meters apart in a hexagonal formation. There is little variation along the Z-axis."

"Our scans agree with yours, Major Richter. I'm also reading very small unmanned vessels above and below the fleet," said Calico's voice. "I'll forward you the coordinates."

"Roger," replied Dana. "Receiving telemetry now."

John said, "Captain Calico, stand by for a couple of minutes."

John gestured to Christie to mute the transmission channel, which she did. Aldebaran turned to John.

"Calico thinks I'm Major Richter," he said, "which reminds me…"

"That they don't know about your true identity," said John. "I completely forgot about that. Ari is most likely on the bridge of the 'Gest, or listening to our conversation. Aldebaran, I'm sorry, but I'm going to have to ask you to stay quiet. Either that or you can swap for the dorsal gun with Ray."

"Nobody has as much space combat experience as I do, Commander. It will be inefficient to ask me to send you a text message every time I have something important to add. Listen, why not reveal my identity to Calico and his crew? Offer me as a bounty once they fulfill their obligations to Umber."

"They already know that 'Sergeant Smith' is a valuable member of this crew. I doubt they'd believe that handing you over is a genuine offer, and they'd be right. I'm not giving you up to anybody."

"I am still master of my own fate, John, but I see your point."

"Nevermind the fact that you could emotionally cripple Ari at a time that the crew of the 'Gest really needs her."

"Why don't I send Talvan up to the dorsal gun with you? He can speak for you, and the microphone gain won't carry from you to him to Calico."

"Uh, excuse me?"

"I mean Calico and his crew won't be able to hear your voice."

"Reloading the dorsal gun is much easier with two people anyway," added Talvan.

Aldebaran nodded. "All right, Commander, I'll go. Ray, did you copy that?

"Roger, I'm on my way up," said Ray's voice.

"Thank you, Seth," said John.

Aldebaran smiled, and he and Talvan exited the bridge to the corridor. John gave the thumbs-up to Christie, and she reactivated the audio connection.

"We're back with you, Captain," said John.

"Everything okay?" asked Calico.

"We're fine."

"Good, listen up. Those drones we detected are limpet mines. When armed, they will automatically seek out an enemy ship, get as close as possible, and detonate. One of those devices will seriously damage either of our ships, and completely destroy Rylie's Neutrino. If we engage, your gunners should make them a priority."

"Understood. How many are you detecting?"

"Six hundred," said Calico and Dana simultaneously.

"Oh shit. Richter, did you copy that?"

"You bet your ass I did, Scherer," replied Richter from the ventral gun room.

"Christie, tie the laser banks into the fifties. Ray, I would rather have you as Richter's assistant gunner than as a dedicated laser operator."

"Copy that," said Ray.

Christie crossed to the station that Aldebaran had just vacated and made the necessary changes.

"Sergeant Smith, Major Richter," began John, "you will now have the laser banks at your disposal. Remember that even if you run out of ammo on the fifties you can continue to fire the lasers, but don't forget that they have different fields of fire."

"We know, Commander," said Richter.

"What about the rear cannon?" asked Christie.

John shrugged. "Tie it into your station if you want, but I'm not too concerned about it."

"Are you short on personnel?" asked Calico.

"One more wouldn't hurt, but the rear cannon is fixed so there are few opportunities to effectively use it."

"Understood. Still, if you really want an extra hand, I can spare one of mine. Now would be the time to dock 'cause we sure won't get a chance once the particles start flying."

"I'll do it," said Ari's voice.

"Are you sure?" asked Calico.

"It makes the most sense. I'm already familiar with the Faith's systems. Assuming I'm still welcome, Commander."

"Of course," replied John, standing. "Christie, begin docking procedures. Dana, you have the controls. Ari, I'll meet you at the airlock."

"Roger, see you soon," replied Ari.

John exited the bridge to the corridor and was slightly surprised when Christie followed him.

"John, are you sure this is a good idea right now?" she asked.

"Ari is always welcome on this ship, I thought you were on board with that."

"I'm only worried about the timing. Ari might be trusted to keep Aldebaran's existence a secret, regardless of how she might feel about the fact that he's still alive, but think about it. Ari knows manning the rear cannon isn't a priority. Do you think she just wants to help us out in a general sense or that she's got something else in mind?"

John opened the hatch to the Zero-G room. "I think she's homesick and she wants to be here again, even if only for a little while. If she still wants to stay after she finds out about Aldebaran, then that is her right."

John and Christie stopped at the inner airlock door. A light on the wall turned from red to green, and John entered a code into the keypad. The hatch slid open, admitting a rush of cold air and Arianna/Coma. She was wearing a sage green flight suit, boots, and, conspicuously, nothing else.

"Welcome back," said John.

"It's good to see you again, Ari," said Christie.

"Where is he?" Ari countered. "I want to see him now."

"You know about him already?" asked John.

"Do you think I could ever forget that voice?" Ari replied with urgency. "Why didn't you tell me, John?"

"Aldebaran still has a huge bounty on his head, and Calico was standing right there. If you'd agreed to talk to me in private…"

"Forget it," Ari interrupted. "Does he want to see me?"

"We haven't asked him yet. I imagine he will. Ari, Aldebaran's reconstitution with Seth was a complete success. He is not the man who seduced you; in fact, he's an incredibly valuable addition to this crew and a genuinely good man to boot. If you plan on any sort of revenge, whether it be physical or verbal, please reconsider."

"I haven't thought about it past the first few seconds. Don't worry, John, I don't plan to kill him."

"I'd like you to wait in the conference room. I'll talk to Aldebaran and find out how he feels and send him up if he's amenable to a meeting."

"John," said Christie. "The fleet?"

"Christie is right, we don't have time for this right now. I know Aldebaran is enough of a professional to wait until after this engagement to talk to you. Can you do the same?"

"I'll deal with it," said Ari.

"Good. Let's get back to the bridge."

The trio entered the corridor and headed forward.

"I take it my room didn't go vacant," Ari said as they passed it.

"Fernwyn took it over," replied John. "Don't worry, she didn't throw out any of your stuff."

"How's Richter been?"

"Great. He and Ray are manning the top turret right now. Poke your head in for a moment if you want, but keep it short."

"Nah, I'll leave them be."

The group entered the bridge. Dana turned to greet them.

"Welcome back to the ship, Ari," she said. "We've been keeping your station warm for you."

Ari nodded. "Thanks, Dana. I'm glad you're doing well."

Dana vacated the pilot chair and John sat down. Dana returned to her station and Ari and Christie took theirs.

"Just like old times, eh?" asked Dana.

"Yeah," replied Ari, "right before reality came along and fucked us right in the…"

"Are you still online, Captain Calico?" asked John.

"Yes, Commander," said Calico. "Now that we're out of superlume, would you like to establish a visual link?"

"Sure," said John, then to Christie, "put him on monitor one."

"Okay, I can see you."

John looked over his shoulder at the rear left station, and confirmed that he could see the bridge of the Almagest. He allowed his gaze to rest on Ari for a few more seconds before Dana got his attention.

"I'm reading power fluctuations from the fleet," Dana said.

"They may be preparing to reactivate the wormhole," said Christie.

"Look sharp," said Gueyr over the radio. "The SPF squadron has just arrived. They're half an AU to our 90, declination plus 47. It looks like thirteen single-seat fighters."

"They're early," said John.

"Contact them on the freq I gave you," said Fernwyn, entering the bridge.

"Too late, they've already hailed the fleet."

"Can we listen in?" asked John.

"Of course. I'll patch in the call."

A new voice speaking Residerian came in over the radio. The Faith's translator program immediately changed it to English.

"This is Lieutenant Colonel Masel of the Solar Police Force. We are investigating a stellar anomaly. Please state your intentions in this region."

Another voice was heard, this time initially the bizarre chirping of the Zendreen tongue.

"This is Commander Lithilkin. You are outside of your jurisdiction and our presence here is none of your business."

"The Provisional Enforcement Act of 3521 authorizes us to enforce SUF laws within ten light years of faction interests. You are compelled to comply with our demands."

"Feel free to enforce your act at any time, Colonel."

"If you do not communicate your intentions in this region, we will observe your movements for as long as necessary until you comply. In the meantime, a task force will be dispatched to back us up."

"He must be out of his mind threatening them like that," said John.

"Maybe he was hoping the fleet was in worse shape than estimated," replied Calico.

"You can observe all you want," said Lithilkin. "Otherwise you'd better be more than an opportunity for gunnery practice. Lithilkin out."

"That's it," said Gueyr, "he terminated the transmission."

"Then I guess we wait and see what happens next," said John.

"Do you want to contact the squadron like we initially planned?" asked Calico.

"I'm not so sure anymore. Are they aware of your presence yet?"

"Didn't Dana explain our measures yet?"

"I forgot about that," said Dana, then to John, "The channel that we're using with the 'Gest is a VLF signal using the minimum amount of power possible for this distance. From where they are, the squadron won't be able to distinguish it from background radiation."

"VLF?" Ari whispered to Fernwyn.

"Very low frequency, I would assume," replied Fernwyn quietly.

John nodded, then said, "Captain, let's hold off on contacting the squadron. I was hoping they would send more than a baker's dozen to investigate. I doubt those guys will be too eager to get in the middle of things with us."

"We may not have to wait long," said Dana. "Those power readings from the fleet are increasing in intensity."

"Can you lock down the emission points?"

"They are definitely coming from the six largest ships, John."

"If we're going to go through with attacking one of the cruisers, now would be the time," said Calico.

"Screw it, let's do it. Care to pick which one?"

"Our best bet would be the converted Res-ZorCon starliner. The power systems are more susceptible to overload so we stand the best chance of knocking it out."

"Roger. I suggest the Faith go in first, and hit it as hard as we can once we reveal ourselves. Then you can join us."

"Agreed. Good luck, Commander, we'll be right behind you."

Calico closed the channel. John pushed the throttle up.

"Look sharp, people, here we go. Ari, we'll probably get a couple of clean passes on that cruiser before we have to get fancy, so get ready with that rear cannon."

"You got it," replied Ari.

At maximum sublight speed it didn't take long for the Faith to cross the distance to the former pleasure ship. The almond-shaped craft was at least four hundred meters long, with about ten decks. There was no visible weaponry or propulsion systems. John cut his relative speed to five hundred miles per hour and approached the ship from the low six o'clock position. When the Faith had closed two thousand meters John commenced firing with the forward plasma cannon. The impressive weapon had a sound reminiscent of a large truck engine-braking, and drowned out almost everything else. Five salvos of superheated matter crossed the distance at nearly the speed of light and struck the cruiser. John pulled back on the stick, passing within a hundred meters of the other vessel, and evened out to give Ari a shot. The same distinct sound was heard more quietly, muffled by the superstructure.

"Three hits," reported Ari.

"Effect?"

"Indeterminate," replied Christie. "The plasma definitely impacted the hull, but we'll have to come back around to spot any damage."

Bright light filled the expanse as laser turrets on the cruiser began firing in all directions. The focused energy beams were pale red in color and seemed to pass into infinity as they streaked by the Faith.

"Relax, they're firing blind," said John. "I'm coming about."

"The energy output of this ship just increased exponentially," said Dana. "I'm also reading a similar buildup from the other large vessels."

"They're getting ready to generate the wormhole, then. We may only get one more shot at disabling this one. I'm going to cut my speed and add some thirty-mil to my attack. Then I'll turn with the ship and we can broadside it with the lasers and the fifties. Then I'll give you another chance with the rear cannon, Ari."

Ari nodded and John began his second run. He pressed a key on his joystick until both main weapons were selected, and aimed the Faith at the cruiser. The plasma cannon barked as he fired nine salvos, the GAU 8/A adding several decibels of noise to the din, then John pulled along the starboard side of the larger ship. The laser banks silently streaked their purple-tinged energy as the fifty caliber guns added their own subtle vibration into the ship's superstructure. As John turned away, a compartment on the cruiser rather clearly experienced explosive decompression. Ari fired three more times with her weapon, and again space was filled with return fire. This time, several shots hit the Faith, flickering the lighting and the computer monitors.

"It looks like we blew out a compartment," said Dana, "but there wasn't any other visible damage. John, the energy radiating from that ship is starting to compromise our invisibility shield."

John grimaced, and said, "Keep it up as long as you can. Break radio silence and contact Calico."

"Roger," said Dana, and did so.

"You're creating quite a spectacle out there, Commander," said Calico over the horn.

"Heads up, the battleship is launching fighters!"

"Captain Calico," began John, "we need more time to attack this cruiser. Do you think you can hold off the fighters for a little while?"

"That depends entirely on how many there are," replied Calico, "but I'm on my way."

There was a bright flash of light off of the Faith's port bow, and those on the bridge involuntarily turned away. A moment later the light faded.

"Was that a limpet mine?" asked John.

"That was Alpha Sagittae," Christie said. "I read it as one astronomical unit to our two o'clock. It's gone now, but the power emissions are still coming from the cruisers."

"I'm counting twenty-one fighters, Commander," said Calico. "It looks like two squadrons are headed your way and one is intercepting me."

"That's all, huh?" said John. "Maybe we stand a chance after all."

"It also looks like the limpet mines are moving into a wider pattern," said Dana. "So far, none of them are close enough to be a concern. There's also too much electromagnetic interference from the emissions to maintain the shield. I just can't make corrections fast enough."

"Take it offline before it gets knocked out, then."

"Understood. I would also like to mention that it is probably too late to implement the radiation pulse. It would make us a sitting duck for those fighters."

"I agree."

"I think it's time for me to get out there and do some damage," said Fernwyn.

"I appreciate the sentiment but I think it's too dangerous out there," John replied, pushing the throttle up. The volume of fire from the cruiser had increased at the same moment that Dana lowered the invisibility shield.

"Each laser blast that hits us takes a fraction of a second to dissipate," began Christie, "so don't let them pile up on us."

"I'm increasing throttle to compensate," replied John.

"It's my decision, John," said Fernwyn, "and I want to go."

"Fine, just take it easy out there. Ari, go with her and help her mount up. Make sure all the cargo is still secure, too."

"You got it," said Ari, standing.

Fernwyn and Ari left the bridge.

"Commander," said Calico, "the other four cruisers have launched seven fighters each. All of them are headed your way."

Aldebaran's voice came in from the dorsal gun room. "Commander, I was wrong! Those fighters are armed with magnetically-enhanced rail cannons with high explosive plasma projectiles. Only one in five is luminescent. We need to take these guys very seriously, Commander."

"We've got enough time for one more pass before we're swamped," said Dana.

"Understood," replied John. "Captain Calico, I'm taking one last pass on this cruiser, then I'm going to head for the largest concentration of limpet mines and deal with these fighters. Then you should be clear for a pass on the cruiser."

"I will comply," said Calico.

As John took the Faith about and closed within three kilometers of the cruiser, the larger ship resumed firing. This time, the laser blasts were much more accurate, and as John began his attack run the nose of the Faith was barraged with hits.

"Channel the excess energy into the forward cannon," he said.

"The capacitors can only handle about half of this volume," replied Christie. "I'm channeling the rest into the thrusters."

It was a smart move that John had overlooked. The thrusters were almost irrelevant at this speed, and directing the energy through the aft assemblies would have no discernible effect. John allowed himself three combined salvos before breaking off and heading away.

"Power levels from the cruiser have dropped ten percent," began Dana. "The other ships are increasing power to compensate."

"The wormhole is beginning to stabilize," said Christie.

An odd yellow streak passed by the bow of the Faith, and a fraction of a second later the entire ship shuddered.

"The fighters are on us," said Aldebaran. "Four from the six and four from the three."

"Most of them are setting up for repeated lateral passes," said Richter from the ventral gun room.

The expanse was abruptly filled with the light from Alpha Sagittae. This time, the star remained in view. Each of the Faith's gun stations rattled with intensity as the fighters jockeyed for a shot. John headed directly toward a nearby limpet mine and veered off less than a thousand meters from it. A moment later a silent explosion enveloped two Zendreen fighters. Three more ventured too close to the Faith and were vaporized by a deadly combination of copper-jacketed lead and energized particles.

"I just lost the energy signature for most of the mines," said Dana.

"They're not stupid enough to let that happen again…" said John, cutting himself off with a squeeze of the trigger as a fighter happened into his field of fire. As he destroyed it, a nearby Zendreen cruiser seemed to break in two and explode into a brief but brilliant blue fireball.

"Did you see that?" asked Calico.

"We sure did," said Dana.

"What did I miss?" asked Aldebaran.

"One of the Zendreen cruisers just destroyed itself. There was a huge increase in power output, and the entire thing exploded."

"What's the state of the wormhole?" asked John.

"It appears to be stable," replied Christie. "It is a circular, two-dimensional window from our region of space to Alpha Sagittae. It's currently five AU from the fleet… wait, standby. The wormhole is collapsing at a rate of sixteen meters per second. At this rate it will be gone in ten minutes, twenty-five seconds."

"That cruiser probably sacrificed itself to stabilize the wormhole," said Talvan over the intercom.

Several HE plasma rounds impacted the Faith, and John again turned his attention to the fighters.

"The fleet is moving toward the wormhole," said Calico. "They're moving as fast as their slowest craft, which appears to be the starliner. They'll be clear of the wormhole in approximately nine minutes."

"Fernwyn is ready to launch," said Ari from the corridor.

"Roger, I'm opening the ramp," replied Dana.

There was an eerie roar that culminated in a thump as the vacuum of space displaced the air in the cargo bay.

"Everyone stand ready to cease fire," said John.

"Ramp is deployed."

"Cease fire, cease fire, cease fire."

At the conclusion of John's command, the bridge became deathly quiet. A couple of seconds later, Fernwyn's voice came in over the radio.

"I'm clear," she said.

Before John could pull on the stick there was a loud bang and the ship shook violently. John rolled the Faith hard to port as Dana closed the ramp. Ari stumbled into the bridge and took her station.

"Status report!" John barked.

Christie shook her head, and said, "Starboard laser bank is out. Rear cannon is down. The air exchangers for the cargo bay are offline."

"Do you still want to target the starliner?" asked Calico.

John swore to himself, then replied, "No, there's no point. Meet up with me. We need to hold off these fighters and get through that wormhole."

"Why don't we just accelerate and go through first?" asked Christie.

"What if they don't follow us? Then we're stuck on the other side of the galaxy."

The ship shuddered as a few more shots struck the hull.

"I hate to interrupt," said Richter over the intercom, "our weapons are effective against these fighters but we need you to fly more evasively."

"Roger," replied John. "Everybody hold on, these maneuvers may be too much for the inertial compensators to handle."

"The ventral fifty is critical on ammo," said Aldebaran's voice.

"Christie, get down to the cargo bay and replicate some more ammo."

"We can't repressurize the bay right now!" responded Christie.

"Okay, do it from here, then."

"Fixing the replication system required a specific Umberian circuit that we were only able to integrate into the cargo bay's terminal. We haven't gotten around to splicing the system into the main computers."

"Are you fucking kidding me?"

"It wasn't a fucking priority, all right?"

"What about the heating elements?" interjected Ari. "Are they still working?"

"Yes, but there's no atmosphere in there."

"I can handle that as long as it's not too cold. What are we using for source material?"

"What did the Zendreen do to you?" asked Dana, looking over her shoulder.

"They gave me the Lindsey Wagner treatment."

"If you think you can handle it," said Christie, "there's a giant block of lead in the cargo bay for you to use."

"So that's what that is. I'll get right on it."

"Go through the arms room," said John while maneuvering. "Leave the hatch open and we'll repressurize the bay through there. "

"Understood."

Ari stood up and stumbled into the corridor. The fifty caliber weapons systems imparted an almost constant vibration to the deck. She descended the mid-deck stairway into the galley, pausing briefly to look at a dedication plaque on the wall, and reversed direction into the orb room. Passing through this room gave Ari cold chills and the hair on the back of her neck stood up. She entered the arms room and glanced at the new additions to the collection, and began to hyperventilate. The Zendreen had tested this ability before, and Ari braced herself in anticipation of the experience. She accessed the manual override for the hatch and carefully opened it, gulping down one more lungful of oxygen and holding her breath. Air whistled vigorously from the arms room into the cargo bay as Ari pulled against the suction with every fiber of her strength. Eventually the pressure dropped enough and the door gave way. Ari felt the familiar pain begin to build up as cybernetic micro-vacuoles all over her body clenched shut at the change in pressure. She knew that the air exchanger for the arms room wasn't capable of enough volume to pressurize the cargo bay in any reasonable length of time, so she had to work fast.

Ari entered the silent cargo bay, descended the stairs to the deck, and crossed to the terminal. Accessing the replication program, she noticed that Christie or Dana had vastly simplified the interface, even adding pictures of everything that had been scanned or previously replicated. She became dizzy as she chose the picture of an ammo can with the right description and ordered ten such items, or two thousand rounds, and instructed the computer to deposit the new ammunition outside of the hatch to the ventral gun room. She then sent a text message to Aldebaran asking for confirmation of the delivery. The reply came ten agonizing seconds later. Ari headed back up the stairs to the arms room and closed the hatch.

Sitting on the floor, Ari picked up a M14 barrel wrench and began banging it against the wall. She didn't have control over the micro-vacuoles, so the only way she could know that it was safe to breathe was when she could hear again. Her vision narrowed and she struggled against the temptation to exhale. She was no longer afraid of dying, but simply wanted to avoid the inconvenience of passing out for an unknown amount of time. Her arms began to tingle and she accidentally threw the wrench across the room. It clattered like hell as it knocked over a cleaning kit and Ari exhaled thankfully. She stood up, gulping greedily at the thin but sweet air, and remembered John's directive to leave the hatch open. The short corridor connecting the arms room to the orb room didn't have a dedicated air exchanger, unless one was added during her absence, but it wouldn't matter in the long run. She opened the door to the corridor, bracing herself against the rush of air, hyperventilated again, and held her breath. The hatch to the cargo bay was a little bit easier to open this time but still required a tremendous effort. When the pressure equalized, Ari moved into the corridor and closed the door. She entered the orb room to another rush of air, and resumed breathing normally. She headed to the bridge, and by the time she arrived the functional air exchangers had returned the pressure to normal.

Nothing had changed on the bridge except the amount of sweat on John's brow. He was concentrating on flying the ship to the exclusion of all else, and didn't seem to hear Ari's announcement of success.

"Are you okay?" asked Dana.

"I'm fine," Ari replied, returning to her station. "How goes the battle?"

"One of the cruisers just launched another wave of fighters, this time thirty. Between us, the Almagest, and Fernwyn, we're keeping them busy. The fleet will enter the wormhole in another two minutes, and we'll be right on their heels."

"What about the SPF squadron, are they still watching?"

"Yup, they still don't want to get involved. Calico just spoke with their commander and was unable to convince him to help."

"We'll be entering the first loop of the wormhole's magnetic field in a few seconds," said Christie. "Don't be surprised if this causes turbulence or effects our power system."

"Roger," said John tersely.

As Christie predicted, the ship began to vibrate. John felt the stick wobble for a moment, then return to normal.

"Power systems are stable," said Christie.

"Rylie, do you copy?" asked John.

"I read you fine, Commander," replied Fernwyn over the radio.

"I think it's time for you to break off. See if you can get some of the fighters to follow you."

"Oh, several of these little bastards are already trying to nail me. No problem there."

To punctuate her situation, Fernwyn flew her ship across the Faith's bow. She was followed by at least six fighters, two of which John blasted into vapor with his cannons.

"Goodbye, Fernwyn. We will always be in your debt."

"Goodbye, John. I hope you happen by the Tarantula Nebula again someday."

"Me, too."

"The first of the Zendreen ships is crossing into the wormhole…" began Christie. "It looks like it made it through just fine."

Several shots impacted the Faith, and Richter's voice came in over the intercom.

"Those fighters are becoming suicidal, Scherer," he said. "I recommend you increase speed and make a run for the worm..."

There was a very loud bang from midship, and Richter's transmission was terminated.

"The dorsal gun just went down," said Christie urgently.

"Shit!" yelled John. "Somebody get over there and check on them!"

"I'll go," said Christie, standing.

"Be careful."

Christie exited the bridge to the conference room, then entered the lounge area. Ray was coming up the midship stairs with an ammo can in each hand.

"What happened?" he asked, panting.

"The top gun has been hit."

"Jesus, Richter."

Ray dropped the ammo and joined Christie at the door to the gun room. A green light on the panel indicated that the room was still pressurized and unlocked. Ray and Christie pulled the door open and were met with smoke and darkness.

"Richter!" shouted Christie.

There was no reply. The smoke began to dissipate and Ray pulled a small flashlight from his pocket. The dorsal gun room was a mess. The GAU 19/A machine gun had partially collapsed into the chamber, and a pale blue emergency force field kept the vacuum of space at bay. The receiver of the large weapon had crushed the computer station. Ray spotted a boot sticking out from underneath a pile of empty ammo cans. Ray and Christie began throwing the cans out into the lounge area. They soon uncovered Richter, who was unconscious and bleeding from a head wound.

"I think his left arm is broken," said Christie.

"I can't find any other injuries right now," Ray added. "Let's get him out of here."

"No, we need to wait until we have the backboard. I'll go get it."

"Okay. I'll get the first aid kit from the bridge."

Christie nodded in agreement and descended the stairs to the galley. Ray entered the bridge via the conference room. He hesitated for a moment and stared at Ari, as he'd almost forgotten she was aboard, and all but whispered an apology to her as he accessed the first aid kit in the compartment underneath her station.

"Richter's wounded," he said, opening the kit. "I can't tell how seriously. The gun room is a mess, and the only thing between him and space is the emergency force field…"

"Hold onto something!" said Dana. "We're about to cross the threshold of the wormhole and I don't know what will…"

There was a brief sound like a locomotive impacting a cement truck, the power went dead, and the bridge was plunged into bright light and silence.

8.

"Are we dead?" whispered Dana.

Still in shock from the sudden loss of power, the crew of the Faith on the bridge looked at each other as a hope to refute their fears. The main view screen had been set to automatically shade the crew from light sources, and without this feature the chamber was radiant with the glow of Alpha Sagittae almost directly ahead. John had turned around in his chair and was facing the others, who had to shield their eyes to see him.

"What the hell just happened?" said John.

"It looks like a system-wide power failure," said Dana. "Does anyone else's station have power?"

"Negative," said Ari.

"Oh my God, Richter," said Ray, and moved quickly to the door to the conference room. He opened it manually and was about to exit.

"Ray, wait!" said John. "Did you leave the door to the dorsal gun room open?"

"Yes. Oh, no... If that force field went down, then we just depressurized half of this deck." Ray's expression turned to terror. "John, Christie may have been in the corridor."

Ray moved to enter the conference room and John grabbed his arm.

"Ray, stop," he said.

"Let go of me!" Ray looked like he was about to strike John.

"God damn it, stop! If you open that door to the vacuum of space you'll only kill yourself. We need to get the computers back up before we can be sure."

"I can't just stand here!"

"You don't have a fucking choice! Scherer to all stations, sound off, over!"

John's order was met with more silence. Ray hit the wall with his fist and swore. John stood up and opened a drawer beneath his console, removing a small but powerful flashlight and a hand-held radio. He switched on the radio just in time to catch Talvan's voice.

"... come in, over."

"Professor, this is Scherer," John replied. "What's your status?"

"We're okay, what's going on?"

"It looks like a power failure right now. Does your station have power?"

"Negative. Aldebaran's rummaging around in a box looking for a hand-light. Oh, he found one."

"I need you to check the console in the engine room. If that one isn't active then we're all in big trouble."

"Why that one?"

"In the event of a catastrophic loss of power, the reserve batteries are connected directly to two stations. One is on the bridge and the other is in the engine room."

"Roger, we're heading there now."

"I can see the Almagest and at least one of the Zendreen cruisers," said Ari, looking out of the starboard side window. "The Almagest is about two hundred meters off our three, and the Zendreen cruiser is maybe two clicks to our two. Neither ship looks powered up right now, although I can't be sure about the cruiser. I can also see one of the fighters about one hundred meters out there, tumbling out of control."

Another voice came through over the radio. "This is Tolliver to any listening station, come in, over."

"Thank God!" said Ray.

"This is Scherer," replied John. "What's your status, over?"

“I’m in the galley. Can you tell me if the force field in the gun room is still up?”

“Do not, I say again, do not attempt to open the hatch to the corridor. We cannot confirm that the force field is still up.”

“Understood, over.”

“Christie, are the storage tanks luminescent?”

“Yes, as usual.”

“Roger. Stand by for further instructions.”

“Roger, out.”

“That’s a good sign,” said John. “It means the engines have maintained a latent charge.”

The radio crackled to life. “Scherer, this is Aldebaran, over.”

“Scherer is on.”

“John, I’m in the engine room. The terminal is active.”

“Roger, please give me a status report.”

“Main engines are down. Thrusters are inoperative. All weapons systems are down. Environmental systems are active except for the cargo bay air exchangers... they‘re showing a low voltage error. Passive sensor systems are operative, active systems are down. The starboard laser banks have been destroyed. The rear cannon and dorsal fifty are both showing a critical error. There are emergency force fields in place above the dorsal gun room.”

Ray immediately exited the bridge to the conference room.

“Anything else?” asked John.

“That’s about it.”

“Roger. Aldebaran, get up to the dorsal gun room and assist Ray and Christie with Richter. You will have to use the emergency hatch from the cargo hold to the galley as we can’t confirm that the cargo bay is back to safe pressure yet. You should find another hand-held in the port storage compartment, please give it to Talvan."

"I will comply. I'll hand you off to the professor, how about that?"

"Okay. Professor Talvan, can you hear me?"

"Yes, John," replied Talvan.

"Good. I need you to find out why the bridge terminal isn't receiving power."

"That's an easy one. The emergency force field system on a Mark Seventeen draws fifty-five thousand parhet. I bet your batteries are devoting almost all of their power to keeping those fields active. There may only be enough to spare to run one terminal."

"All right, we'll get Richter out of there and seal it up. When I give you the signal, I need you to override the force field. Then hopefully the rest of our computer system will come online."

"Understood."

John sighed, and turned to Ari. "Do you remember how to access the air exchangers?"

"Of course," Ari replied.

"When we restore power, I'd like you to see if you can repair the ones for the cargo bay." John handed his radio to Dana and headed for the conference room. "I'm going to check on Richter. Call me if anything changes."

"No problem," said Dana.

John passed through the conference room and into the lounge area, securing the doors behind him. Christie and Ray were bent over the unconscious form of Richter. A bandage had been applied to his head, which had already soaked through, and Ray was finishing strapping him to the backboard. There was a heady smell of smoke and ionized air. John looked into the dorsal gun room, which was illuminated by two green high-intensity disposable glow sticks. The computer station was a total loss, and the Nineteen looked heavily damaged. The dorsal turret, which along with the ventral turret were the most time-consuming parts of the Faith's construction, was completely trashed. Shielded from the direct light of Alpha Sagittae at this angle, the blackness of space loomed overhead through the barely visible force field. John swore to himself and turned toward the others.

"How is he?" he asked.

Christie said, "He's got a substantial laceration to the scalp, and probably a concussion. His left arm is severely bruised, but I don't think its broken. I also don't think there's any internal bleeding. If we can keep his cranial pressure down he should be okay, I think. Ray, get the ice packs."

"Is there anything salvageable in there?"

"I doubt it," replied Ray, pulling an instant cold compress out of his bag. "I already grabbed the remaining ammo out of there; Richter and I were down to our last two hundred rounds. If I hadn't run downstairs for two more cans I would have been in there with him."

"Okay. Help me get this door sealed up, the force field is drawing too much power from the dry cells."

"We might want to try to pull the Nineteen out of there first, or at least strip out the receiver parts."

"I agree but we don't have time for that."

Ray activated the ice pack and handed it to Christie, then stood up to help John. Together they closed the door and turned the handle. To their relief, the indicator light on the panel turned green, meaning the hatch was sound. John picked up the radio that was on the deck next to Christie and activated it.

"Talvan, this is Scherer, over."

Aldebaran arrived in the lounge area and inquired about Richter's status. A moment later John's radio squawked at him.

"This is Talvan, go ahead."

"Professor, the gun room has been sealed. Deactivate the force field."

"All right, here goes."

Nothing happened.

"Nothing happened," said John.

"Power has been restored to the first two decks," replied Talvan, "but the lines to deck one have been compromised somehow."

"Compromised? All four of them?"

"It's probably just the circuit breakers," said Christie.

"If it was the circuit breakers then it would show up on the… forget it, I'll check on them. Talvan, what's the status of the cargo bay air exchangers?"

"They're still offline," replied Talvan. "One of them is showing a blown fuse, and I have a general fault error on the other one. The exchanger in the arms room will restore safe pressure to both chambers in approximately thirty minutes."

"What about the engines?"

"The screen says, 'initiate cold start sequence'."

"Okay. Hold off on that. When I'm done with the breakers I'll meet you at the galley station and we'll do a complete system-wide diagnostic."

"I understand."

"Scherer out, break, Scherer to Andrews."

"Go ahead, John," replied Dana.

"Please tell Ferro she can go ahead and start working on the air exchangers."

"Roger."

"Thank you. Scherer out."

Christie, Ray, and Aldebaran moved Richter onto the coffee table and the first two resumed working on him. Aldebaran walked up to John.

"I'll help Ari with that," said Aldebaran.

John looked at him, and said, "I'm not sure that would be the best venue for a reunion, Aldebaran."

"Can you think of a better time?"

"Sure, when you're not alone with her?"

"If you thought Ari was a threat, why did you let her on board? Or is it just that you wanted first crack at debriefing her?"

"Double meanings aside, Seth, I'm simply concerned that you will distract each other from the task at hand."

"Just knowing that she's on board is enough of a distraction for me, John. I imagine she feels the same way, but we're both willing to put the mission first."

"I believe you, but I have another task for you anyway. I need you to go down to the galley and see if you can contact the Almagest and find out their status. Just be sure the transmission is audio only and maintain your Sergeant Smith alias."

"Fine, then."

Aldebaran rather tersely exited the lounge area and descended the midship stairs.

"Scherer, this is Andrews," said John's radio.

"Go ahead."

"I think you'd better get up here, John. It looks like the Zendreen fleet is back under power and moving away."

"Damn it! Wait, you said they're moving away?"

"Yes."

"Their weapons must still be down. That's good news for us, we need all the time we can get. Let's get our sails back up as soon as possible and hope Calico isn't any worse off."

"Gotcha!"

Fernwyn grinned as the last Zendreen fighter exploded into a brief fireball. Two of them had stayed behind, apparently to try to prevent her from proceeding through the wormhole. If so, they might have died thinking they succeeded. Fernwyn double-checked her sensors and her heart leaped into her throat as thirteen new bogies appeared. She swore to herself, remembering a second later that they were most likely the SPF squadron.

"Unidentified craft, this is Lieutenant Colonel Masel of the Solar Police Force, Solar United Faction. State your intentions."

Fernwyn answered, "This is Officer Fernwyn Rylie, SPF, Beta Station assignment."

There was a pause over the radio. Fernwyn remembered that she had switched off her IFF transponder and reactivated it.

"You are currently listed as suspended, Officer Rylie. If you want any chance of restoring your career in the SPF, you are strongly advised to immediately report to your duty station."

"That's it?" asked Fernwyn, surprised. "There's nothing about criminal charges there, Colonel?"

"Unauthorized absence from duty is a rather serious offense, Officer Rylie."

"I mean something that can get me locked up, not just fired."

"Is there something you want to admit to me?"

"Just do me a favor, sir, and tell me who the SUF held responsible for the destruction of the Umberian System Way Station."

"The Zendreen, obviously."

"My, my, how things can change so rapidly. To perpetuate the stalemate, the SUF hangs innocents out to dry. Once we kick the crap out of the Zendreen, the truth is allowed to come out."

"I don't know anything about your involvement in the destruction of the station. If any charges were dropped, then maybe the powers that be simply realized they were wrong."

"Does that sound like business as usual for the SUF?"

"I'm a law enforcement officer, I'm not allowed to have an opinion on political matters."

"What about your opinion of the battle you just observed?"

"You were clearly allied with that Umberian ship, although I'm mystified as to why they intentionally followed the Zendreen fleet to the core galaxy. Why prosecute the Zendreen when they're no longer a threat to the planet?"

"The Reckless Faith is an independent ship, allied with Umber only to assist them in driving off the Zendreen. They came all the way from out in the eastern spiral arm to help liberate Umber. As long as the Zendreen still pose a threat to any world, they will oppose them. That's their fight. I became friends with them and assisted them in liberating Umber, which in my mind was far better option than continuing my beat on Beta Station. However, my home is still Residere, so I decided not to go with them."

"Fair enough, Rylie, but if you ever want your job back you'll have to face the consequences of your actions; real, or perceived. If the evidence is on your side, then you should report to Beta Station now."

"Do I have a choice?"

"My only duty is to log a report of this encounter. You are free to go if you want."

Fernwyn mulled over her choices. As an official heroine of Umber, she had solid evidence of her recent activities. Even if her career as a plank was finished, she could either retire on Residere Beta, or even go back to shuffling. She might even try her hand at the quarries in the neighborhood of Earth someday.

"I think your advice is sound, Colonel Masel," she said.

"Good, you can follow us back there now. For what it's worth, Rylie, I hope you get your job back. You're one hell of a fighter pilot."

"Thanks," she replied, "Rylie out."

Fernwyn set a course for home and looked out at the Besser Expanse one last time. "Good luck, John Scherer. The galaxy is no place to go it alone."

9.

Gueyr Ryoujin walked down the rear corridor on the lowest deck of the Almagest. He stopped at an access panel and removed it. Underneath was a charred and smoking power transfer coil. Gueyr put down his toolkit, which included a replacement coil, and removed a voltmeter. He plugged the meter into a socket above the blown coil, confirmed that power had been cut to the station, and began removing the damaged part.

Upon crossing the threshold of the wormhole, the Almagest had experienced primary engine failure. Several power transfer coils had been blown out by some sort of overload, and the crew was currently attempting to replace them. Gueyr examined the station. The coil was fried but the connectors were still good. This replacement would be easy; based on the reports from his compatriots he knew his case was an exception.

Gueyr had been on the bridge during the fight to the wormhole, principally concerned with operating the 'Gest's rear articulated twin plasma emitters. The weapon system did not have as high of a yield as the fixed cannons that graced the bow of the ship, but did have a higher rate of fire, making them perfect for a close engagement. Gueyr had lost count of his kills at six due to the frenzy of other activities, but he fully intended to check the recordings later to confirm the total. The younger Kau'Rii had won the honor of operating the tail guns from Megumi in a coin toss. The losing position was the less desirable dorsal turret, which due to Captain Calico's budgetary constraints consisted of a single laser emitter. While the inclination to use the more powerful weapon simply to try to get more kills may have been juvenile, they still had to flip on it. For his part, Calico did not encourage or discourage that sort of behavior as long as time permitted the discussion.

Gueyr was still riding an adrenaline high from the battle, which was far longer and more intense than anything else to which he'd been exposed since he joined the crew. He was also excited that the fight created a higher level of simpatico with Megumi, which naturally served to increase his affection for her. Unlike a lot of other mercs and long distance shufflers, Gueyr was only attracted sexually to his own race; however, he worried that pursuing Meg would seem like nothing more than an attempt to mate with the only other Kau'Rii on board, and not the hope for a meaningful relationship that he had fooled himself into thinking he wanted.

Having finished replacing the coil, Gueyr activated his radio, a small device on his shoulder which was tied into the ship's intercom system.

"Bridge, this is Gueyr, restore power to coil number seventeen."

"Standby," replied Knoal's voice.

The coil began to hum appropriately, and Gueyr said, "Looks good, Knoal. Shall I assist Bugani or Railyn with the other coils?"

"Negative, Cap wants you back up here."

"Okay, see you soon."

Gueyr packed up his gear and headed to the bridge. Because of the ovoid shape of the 'Gest he had to ascend one deck before he could access a lift, which then only took him as far as deck two. The lift stopped at deck three and opened to admit Megumi. Gueyr smiled at her as she entered.

"The number nine coil was a bitch to replace," she said as the doors slid shut.

"That sucks."

A moment later the doors opened again, and the two felines walked down the corridor to the nearest set of stairs.

"Hey," began Gueyr, "how many fighters did you tag?"

"I don't know," replied Meg, ascending the stairs. "My hit percentage was good, but those fighters can take quite a pounding from lasers before they go up."

"Next time, the rear guns are yours."

Meg entered the top deck corridor. "Next time I hope to be piloting the ship. Calico was supposed to let me do it this time. He changed his mind at the last minute."

"Captain's prerogative. I guess he saw the size of the opposition and figured he'd better do it himself."

"I am every bit as good of a pilot as he is."

Gueyr raised his eyebrows, and replied, "Oh, really?"

"Yes really," said Meg, turning to face him. "Before you joined us I spent a lot of time at the helm."

"Yeah? What changed?"

Meg resumed walking, and said, "Things."

"Things named Coma Veronice?"

"Didn't I just say this was before you joined up? For the love of the core, you are starting to annoy me."

The pair entered the bridge. Knoal sat at his station, and Captain Calico stood near the helm. He was having a conversation with a member of the Faith's crew, someone whose voice Gueyr couldn't recognize. Whoever he was, he was speaking Umberian, which was evident not by a delay in the translator's efforts but by his intonations, which did not extrapolate well into Residerian.

"…be back up within two hours," the man was saying.

"Understood, Sergeant," replied Calico. "This presents a problem as the Zendreen fleet has just resumed course. They're only going one-quarter c but if we don't follow them soon, one or two course changes and we'll have lost them."

"Where are they headed?"

"Well, currently they're headed directly toward UAS 1026, but we can't assume that's their ultimate destination."

"For the sake of argument, is there anything valuable out there that they might be after?"

"There's a Hayakuvian colony called Freedmen located at 1026. Last I knew they were an independent entity. Unless they've attracted a large influx of well-armed colonists in the last ten years, there is no way they can defend against the Zendreen fleet. The Zendreen may be interested in requisitioning supplies and resources there."

"What about Hayaku itself?"

"They have more than enough ships to counter the fleet. Open warfare would be suicide for the Zendreen."

"Captain, Commander Scherer is now available. I'm going to turn this conversation over to him."

"All right, Sergeant Smith, thank you."

John's visage appeared on the nearest monitor as he joined the transmission. Calico could see the bridge of the Faith behind him. A panel was open in the deck and Coma was up to her elbows in a piece of equipment.

"Captain Calico, this is Commander Scherer."

"Hello, Commander. Did you hear the last part of our conversation?"

"Yes, I did. We restored power to the Faith but we're having trouble with the engine restart sequence. I would ask you to follow the fleet now except that our main transmitter is still offline. Once you leave we will no longer be able to contact you via the VLF channel."

"I would still suggest that we depart now. Being out of contact for a while is something we will just have to deal with. Freedmen is 8.3 light years from here, and Hayaku is 13, so if you can't restore your main transmitter before you get your engines up, look for us at the colony first."

"If we get the engines back up to full capacity, we can be at Freedmen in less than three minutes. If that happens, we'll look for you on the way."

"Sounds good."

"Excuse me, Captain," said Knoal, "but there's something that requires your immediate attention."

"Hold on for a minute, Commander. What is it, Knoal?"

"One of those Zendreen fighters is drifting toward us. All of its systems are down except for life support. If we act now we can harpoon it and bring it into the cargo bay."

"I'm not sure we have the resources to deal with a prisoner right now," said Megumi.

"I disagree," said Calico. "Megumi, Gueyr, make it happen. Commander Scherer, once we load that fighter I'll begin tailing the fleet. Hopefully the pilot will be in a talkative mood and we'll get something useful out of him."

"Roger," said John. "Be careful with him, the Zendra's carapace is coated with a powerful neurotoxin…"

"We know about that."

"Good. I will talk to you at Beta Sagittae, if not sooner."

"Understood. Good luck, Commander. Calico out." Calico terminated the transmission and turned toward Meg and Gueyr. "I meant now, people."

"Yes, sir!" said Megumi, and exited the bridge.

Gueyr followed her, closed the door, and said, "I agree with you, Rukitara. We don't have time to deal with a prisoner."

"Maybe the rest of the crew doesn't, but you do," she replied, heading down the corridor.

"Me? Why me?"

"Seriously, Ryoujin, because it's something I know you can handle and I trust you."

"Thanks, I think."

Megumi descended the stairs to deck two, and asked, "What do we have in cargo hold one right now?"

"Just that old jalopy that Railyn has been trying to repair. Rukitara, how do you want me to deal with this fighter pilot if I can't touch him?"

"Listen to me and I'll tell you. When we bring the fighter into the cargo bay, keep it decompressed. Then move the ship into cargo hold one and keep that decompressed. Activate the force field between the two, then repressurize the cargo bay. You can communicate with the pilot via a laser amplifier from the deck of the bay. If he tries to exit his cockpit, he dies."

The pair stopped at the lift. Meg hit the call button.

"Good idea. What if he's injured or his life support system fails?"

"Ask him the same thing and use it against him. We're trying to interrogate him, after all."

The doors opened and Megumi all but pushed Gueyr inside.

"What if that doesn't work?"

"Repressurize the hold and allow him to exit his ship. He'll be confined to the hold and you can think of something else to threaten him with."

"I'll do my best."

The doors closed. Gueyr sighed and hit the button for deck seven. He leaned against the back of the car and fumed. Megumi was angry with either him, the captain, or both of them. He hoped it was just Calico. Even after a year he couldn't figure out the nature of their relationship, and neither one of them was particularly chatty about their mutual past.

The lift arrived on deck seven. Gueyr began the short walk to the cargo bay. He entered the control room and was greeted by Railyn, a jovial if slightly bookish Misrerian. He was thin for his race of humanoids, completely hairless, and wore a baseball-style cap in addition to his overalls. The door to the cargo bay was already open and the Zendreen fighter dangled at the end of a pair of magnetic harpoons. The harpoon spools were slowly retracting, pulling their quarry into the bay. The boxy, trapezoidal ship was only slightly aerodynamic, and Gueyr guessed that it wasn't meant for atmospheric flight.

"Hello, Gueyr," said Railyn.

"Nice catch," replied Gueyr.

"I assume you want him in cargo hold two."

"Number one, actually. Keep it depressurized once you get the force field up."

"What if he trashes my Impulser?"

"I don't think he cares about that pile of junk, Railyn."

Gueyr watched Railyn work. Once the spools had retracted, the Misrerian closed the outer hatch. A wheeled sled had been placed in the center of the bay, and when the ship was above it, Railyn slowly restored gravity to the bay, gently setting the ship upon it. The pilot was very much alive, and stared at the two men with what appeared to be ire. Railyn opened the connecting doors to cargo hold one, and air rushed into the bay until the pressure equalized. He grabbed the controls to the sled and moved the ship into the hold, activated the pale blue force field, and pumped the remaining air back into the bay.

"I knew they were giant insects..." began Railyn.

"I know, they're rather creepy in the flesh, aren't they?"

"One atmosphere achieved." he said.

"Good work, Railyn. I'll take it from here."

Gueyr opened a storage locker on the rear wall and obtained a small device attached to a tripod. He entered a separate stairwell that led directly to the cargo bay and entered. His breath condensed in the cold air and he shivered. Crossing to the force field, he set up the device and activated it. A constant, narrow crimson laser beam shot out and he adjusted it until it was aimed directly at the cockpit. He set the filter to triple redundancy to compensate for any interference the force field might create.

"Can you hear me?" he asked.

A bizarre clicking sound filled his ears, and a split-second later the translator changed it for him.

"Yes," said the Zendra.

"I am Gueyr Ryoujin of the Galactic Free Warrior's Guild. Welcome to the Almagest."

In a dark access conduit between decks on the Reckless Faith, Seth Aldebaran slowly crawled forward. His shirt had soaked through with sweat, and grime covered his arms and face. He had just finished evaluating the level of damage to the rear plasma cannon, and the results were not positive. A Zendreen projectile had impacted the emitter head, sending a shock wave down the collimator coils and into the Talvanium 115-lined reaction chamber. This resulted in a hairline crack in the chamber wall, which would require an additional five micrograms of Talvanium to repair. If the Talvanium from the destroyed starboard laser bank couldn't be salvaged, the rear cannon was toast.

Aldebaran reached the access panel to the galley, which he'd left open. He executed the difficult maneuver of dropping down from the conduit without falling on his head, and brushed himself off.

"I finally get to see you again."

Turning around, Aldebaran found Ari sitting at the kitchen table. Her face and hands were also streaked with grease. She had a mug of ale which was almost full, and she looked terrified.

"Hello, Arianna," he said flatly.

"I thought I was ready to talk to you," she said, her voice trembling, "but now I'm not so sure. I don't know whether to slap you, kiss you, or break your neck."

"You're welcome to the first two if you want."

"I've been told that you possess my memories."

Aldebaran grabbed an empty mug. "That is more or less correct."

"How far back?"

"I'm not sure." Aldebaran filled his mug with stout. "Since I have your memories, my own as Seth Aldebaran, both sets of memories during my schism, John's, Ray's, and the rest of the original crew, I often have to be thinking of a specific thing in order to call up a memory. However, my dreams are interesting, to say the least."

"What do you think of Silas Blodgett?"

Aldebaran finished a swig from his mug, and said spitefully, "That asshole?"

"So it's true, then. What about your… ability?"

"That seemed to dissipate when I reconstituted myself with the orb. Why, do you feel something?"

"Honestly, I'm not sure. I thought I felt something when I first came aboard, and then again in the old orb room. It may have just been my imagination."

"I am not consciously aware of any extrasensory ability, and nobody else has sensed anything from me. You and I have a special bond, however. You're the only surviving person to be manipulated by Aldebaran the pirate, and the most recent. You know, that ability has never been quantified or explained by science. Maybe there is still something between us that is more than just emotion."

Ari shed a tear, and said, "Maybe. I'm still confused. The more I want to love you, the more I resent you for manufacturing those feelings inside me."

"I'm not a philosopher by any stretch of the imagination, but I do know that emotions, whether original or manufactured, are real to the person feeling them. If you are as strong of an individual as your memories seem to imply, then I believe you still have a choice you can make. You can embrace or reject your feelings, even if the latter takes a long time."

"What's your opinion?"

"My feelings are irrelevant. Making a suggestion to you would be just as inappropriate as implanting your affections in the first place."

"Unless you don't love me."

Aldebaran began to reply, then faltered. He looked at Ari in silence for a moment.

"Can you tell me you don't love me?" Ari insisted.

Speaking deliberately, Aldebaran replied, "I do not love you romantically. You are like a sister to me, or, like a daughter."

Ari laughed bitterly, and shook her head. "Why do I keep coming off like that? Do I need to be more direct?"

"Are you talking about Richter?"

"No, I'm not. Forget it. Actually, maybe it would make me feel better if I threw myself at him. I hear guys with serious head injuries are maniacs in the sack."

"Ari, I..."

"Frankly, you're not the worst crush I've ever had to get over. I'll be fine."

Aldebaran sighed, and said, "Maybe we should keep some distance from each other."

"We're in the middle of a combat mission, how do you propose we do that?"

"I mean emotionally. Beneath all of my shared memories I am still a professional soldier. If you can treat me like that, I will return the favor."

"I think I can do that."

"Good. How did the air exchangers go?"

"Well, one is fried and will need to be reinstalled. The other just needed a new power cord. We can pressurize the cargo bay, it will just take twice as long until the first one is fixed. How 'bout the rear cannon?"

"We need a little bit of Talvanium to fix it. I need to check the starboard laser banks to see if there's any available. How is it going with the engines?"

"John and Dana are working on the cold restart now," said Ari, her voice wavering. "I should go help them."

"No, you stay here and take a break. I'll go. You're a little distracted right now."

"No shit. Thank you. Listen, who was Nathalier?"

"Nathalier? Oh, you must have seen the plaque on the stairs. He was a Rakhar who rescued the crew after we abandoned them on Residere Beta. He was a friend of Fernwyn Rylie and he was kind enough to extend that friendship to the crew. He was killed by a Tenchiik during the mission to Macer Alpha."

"I don't know anything about that mission. Actually, I have no idea how you succeeded in liberating Umber."

"I'm sure John will be happy to tell you all about it. In fact, Ari, and I'll leave you with this: I think you should seriously consider what John did to find you. If there's anyone you should be discussing your emotions with, it's him."

Ari simply looked at him and drank her ale, so Aldebaran ascended the stairs to the lounge area. He walked up to Christie and Ray, who were still attending to Richter. The wounded man was awake and oriented, so Aldebaran waved at him.

"Hey, there," Richter groaned.

"Hey yourself," he replied. "No worse for wear?"

"My arm hurts worse than my head. It was better than letting my noggin absorb the full weight of the falling receiver, though."

“You’re like the Charlie Brown of space, you know that?”

Ray looked at Aldebaran in surprise, and Richter said, “Ray already made that joke five minutes ago.”

“I feel particularly connected to Ray right now. John and Ari, too. I think it’s because Ari just reminded me of your experience with Silas Blodgett.”

Ray laughed. “You must have an interesting take on that whole situation.”

“Let me give you my summary. You were put in an impossible position and it was completely unfair, John should have knocked that guy’s teeth out of his head, and Ari should have dumped him two months earlier than she did.”

“I concur.”

“However, if either of the latter situations occurred, I’m certain the friendship wouldn‘t have survived, which means you never would have had a reunion at the cabin, and you would have never met me.”

“Are you saying that Silas Blodgett is responsible for the creation of the Reckless Faith?” Ray asked incredulously.

“Indirectly, yes.”

“Don’t tell Ari, she’ll put her fist right through the bulkhead.”

“Excuse me, I need to get to the bridge.”

Aldebaran entered the conference room as the three resumed the conversation without him. He sat down at the large table and stared out into space. Despite his willingness to joke about it, the invocation of this Silas fellow brought about so many memories from so many different perspectives that he was having trouble processing it all. He sympathized most strongly with John’s version of events, solely for the reason that John had a crush on Ari at the time. Aldebaran’s lies to

Ari in the galley seemed to be taken for fact, but he feared that if there was indeed some sort of bond between them, then she would see through him. How ironic, it seemed, that the very thing he warned her about may have been the cause of the same dissonance in his own mind. Was it his own infatuation for Ari that made him feel the way he did, or were the emotions simply borrowed from John? Even more confusing was the lust he had toward her. John seemed to deny that desire on all but the deepest level, and Richter's memories expressed frustration at never having become intimate with her (although little else). Aldebaran tried hard to remember his own feelings on the matter, but since this involved a time when he was apart from his conscience, it was akin to trying to remember the taste of a particular bottle of beer while already dead drunk. Seth the AI, on the other hand, could no more lust after a woman than a blind eunuch.

Aldebaran tried to push these thoughts out of his head. He found himself wishing that Ari had never come aboard, and he wondered if her presence on the ship would ultimately prove a problem for himself, John, or both. He resisted the temptation, as a coping mechanism, to conjure up memories of Ari's many character flaws, not the least of which involved a cold-blooded murder for which she was more culpable than she herself dared to admit. He also pushed aside the thoughts of suicide which had dominated his waking hours in the weeks since he restored his psyche. Condemning Ari's single murderous act would have been the height of hypocrisy after ten years as the Terror of the Tarantula Nebula.

He cursed under his breath. If only Richter's reflexes hadn't been so fast on the way station.

10.

Rafe Pyramis was pissed. He strode down the octagonal corridor to his commander's office, stomping his feet as he went. He paused in front of the desired door, took a deep breath, and knocked.

"Enter," came the reply.

Pyramis entered the office, and saluted Commander Ballard. The older man returned the salute, and gestured at the chair across from his desk. Pyramis instead presented the piece of paper in his right hand, and remained standing.

"Sir, with all due respect, what the hell is this?" he asked.

"Major Pyramis, when you say, 'with all due respect,' you're supposed to mean it."

"Excuse me, sir, but…"

"I can only assume those are your transfer orders. Congratulations, you got your own command."

"Out at Freedmen? That's as much an exile as it is a promotion."

"You want to wear the rank, you get the responsibility. Go ahead and contest the orders; see what happens to your career."

"Sir, when I joined the Hayakuvian Space Fleet, I joined to protect Hayaku. Freedmen is one step away from becoming fully independent, and then they will be none of our business."

"Then your command will end and you can return to Hayaku with honor, Major. By the way, here are your O4 pips. Has it escaped your mind that this would make you the youngest major in the history of the fleet?"

Ballard opened a drawer and removed a rank pin, which was four small circles in a diamond pattern. Pyramis looked at them with obvious desire, then returned his gaze to the commander.

"Can I at least have some time to think about it?"

"Take five days."

"Really?"

"Then divide it by ten. You're leaving tomorrow morning."

"Shit."

"I beg your pardon?"

"I mean, yes, Commander, sir."

Pyramis took the pips, and he and Ballard shared another salute. He took a step to the rear, executed a crisp about-face, and exited. Once alone in the hallway, he removed his communicator from his pocket and pressed four keys.

"Yo, Rafe," said a voice on the other end of the line.

"Mert, what are you up to right now?"

"I just got off duty, didn't you?"

"Do you want to go to the officer's club?"

"No, not really."

"Can you do me a big favor and come anyway?"

"Sure, if you want. Don't expect me to engage in another asinine contest, though."

"Don't worry about that. I'll see you there shortly."

"Roger. Garufi out."

Returning the device to his pocket, Pyramis headed down the corridor. Hayaku station was large, but was well-connected with a series of high-speed people-movers without and within. It was one on the circumference of the station that he chose, and ordered the lift to take him three-eights around to the evening side.

The spherical station was on an accidental day/night cycle of twenty hours, which despite being unintentional on the part of the designers still fell in nicely with the military duty day of ten hours. The Hayaku day was 29.8 hours, so duty on the station was actually a time increase of 50% versus working at a planet-based facility. Pyramis always found it curious that there was no pay differential to make up for this, but there was no shortage of spacers who preferred the station to a terrestrial assignment. Even so, it was much less desirable than a shipboard assignment, even if Hayaku's ten powerful battleships rarely left the orbit of one of the two moons. The length of the day on those ships was equal to the planet.

It was one of those battleships that Pyramis had hoped to join as a flight chief. Such an assignment had all the glory of a command position without the tedium of a long-range patrol cruiser or, regretfully, the squadron based at Freedmen. Pyramis, like most Hayakans, was a homebody, and enjoyed the ability to frequently take leave on the surface of the planet. Here on the station he could be at his parent's place (or at the largest gambling city) in a matter of hours, making it feasible for a weekend run. Out at Freedmen he would have to wait for his twice-a-year vacation, and he would burn two full days just in transit.

The lift stopped and Pyramis resumed walking. The officer's club was fifty meters down the corridor on the right. He entered the large, triangular chamber and immediately spotted his friend at the bar. Typical for a mid-week night, the club was sparsely populated, guaranteeing an easy atmosphere for the kind of conversation Pyramis had in mind.

"Hello, Mert," he said, taking a stool next to his fellow.

"Hello, Rafe."

The bartender, a second lieutenant named Koller, approached and said, "Hello, Captain. I haven't seen you since the trivia contest last month."

"That kind of sapped my enthusiasm for this place, LT, no offense of course."

"None taken. What can I get you?"

"Ale, please, thirty halets."

"You got it, Cap."

Koller poured Pyramis a huge glass of ale and placed it in front of him.

"Got some issues to work out, Rafe?" asked Mert.

"Mertag, I'm being transferred."

"Wow! That's good news. Right?"

Pyramis took a long swig from his glass. "They're sending me to Freedmen."

"Oh. Well, it makes sense. You're young, motivated, ambitious, and you don't have a family. But don't you have to be at least a major to command a squadron?"

Pyramis deposited his pips on the bar. "Yes."

"Hey, congratulations, Rafe! I mean, sir! Hey, LT, the major here drinks on me tonight."

"Thank you, Mert."

"I can't help but wonder, though, I mean, I don't think the current commander out there is retiring or ill or anything. Why change command now, when the colony is so close to full independence?"

"I bet you it's only because the current commander doesn't want to deal with the shit storm that is coming. The colony has been hostile to the squadron's presence for a few years now."

"You mean philosophically hostile, right?"

"For now."

"God, Rafe, you don't think there will be a civil war, do you?"

"Of course not. However, I don't think it would be wise to maintain a squadron there one day longer than necessary."

Mert leaned in close to Pyramis, and whispered, "Would you fire on the colonists?"

"You bet your ass I would. I'm a loyalist, you know that."

"So you don't think Freedmen should be independent."

"I didn't say that. They're fourteen light years away, they can do whatever they want. I will simply follow orders as they are given."

"Then let's hope our bosses have the wisdom to keep the peace."

"I'm just happy I get to keep my Stylus. Which reminds me, I need to alert the hangar crew to prep it for long range."

Pyramis took another swig of ale and stood up.

"You don't have to do that this instant, do you?"

"I don't know the night crew very well. It would be polite to go down there in person."

"That's a diplomatic way of saying you don't trust them to do a good job."

"Something like that, Mert. I've got an early morning, too, so I'm reconsidering tying one on."

"I'm sure that's the best idea. Listen, Rafe, I'll be there in the morning to give you a proper send-off, okay? You probably want that holovid back, too, I'll have it for you then."

"Okay, Mert, I'll see you then."

Pyramis retrieved his pips and exited the club. He hated to leave his friend on their last night together, but prepping a single-seat fighter for two days of continuous superlume was complicated enough to make him paranoid about a screw-up. This time he needed to take an internal lift, as the hangar was at the end of a long shaft running parallel to the station's southern axis. Pyramis found the closest one and entered. He pressed the button for the appropriate level and waited.

The lift stopped one floor prior to the hangar, at the hangar control room. The doors slid open and admitted Flight Chief Casimar, who was the night shift supervisor. He was wearing the dark blue flight suit typical of officers, but also allowed to non-commissioned flight crew members.

"Ah, Chief Casimar, just the man I wanted to see," said Pyramis.

"Hello, Captain," the older man replied. "I don't see you down here much these days."

Casimar correctly assumed that Pyramis was going down, and resumed the lift's descent. A moment later they arrived on the floor of the hangar.

"I must inform you that I'm being transferred," said Pyramis as the pair entered the busy hangar. "I need my ship prepped for sustained superlume."

"I'll get my crew on it right away," said Casimar. "Where are you headed?"

"Freedmen."

"I see. I'll triple-check your weapons systems, then."

"If that was a joke, I don't think it's funny."

"Forget I said it, then."

"I'll begin the flight systems check myself, chief."

"Yes, sir."

Pyramis stopped at his assigned Stylus, and Casimar proceeded to the duty desk at the other end of the hangar. The single-seat fighter craft was shaped like a pub dart, with retractable wings for atmospheric flight. It was the best ship Hayaku had to offer the combat pilot, and included powerful plasma cannons and fifty layers of nanometer-thin ablative armor. Each square decimeter of a layer could absorb a solid hit from any of the known weapons systems currently being employed in the galaxy up to the power level of a cruiser, with the exception of c-torpedoes.

Entering his personal code into a small console on the craft's fuselage, Pyramis activated a ladder and climbed to the cockpit. The canopy retracted as he arrived, and he jumped inside. He turned the power selector dial to batteries only, and turned on the flight computer. It would not take him long to do a systems check.

The Stylus' top speed was 3600 c. At that rate it would take Pyramis almost exactly 34 hours to reach Freedmen. It was a long time to be confined to a cockpit, and three times longer than he was used to being awake. Fortunately the station's surgeon was aware of the rigors that awaited Pyramis, and would almost certainly dispense a few milligrams of amphetamine for him. There were no way stations between here and there. Disposing of urine was easy; anything more complicated would require uncomfortable gymnastics to accomplish properly. Pyramis wished that his trip could coincide with a supply run, but a quick check of the schedule proved this to be impossible.

Pyramis completed the computer diagnostic. Everything was in order. He would have to rely on Casimar and his crew to check everything else.

Casimar approached, and said, "Your departure time is on the plan, sir. I hope you're planning on catching some sleep before then."

"Oh, definitely. Hey, chief, I know we didn't work together often, but thanks for everything."

"You're welcome, Captain. In a way I'm jealous of your new assignment."

"Yeah, but not so jealous that you'd take my place."

"Freedmen is no place to be… well, let me just say I hope your assignment is a brief one."

Pyramis smirked, and said, "Me, too, chief. Me, too."

On the bridge of the Almagest, Captain Calico and Railyn were watching the Zendreen fleet from a distance of 15 AU, the limit of their active sensors. The fleet was proceeding at a lethargic 100 c, which was apparently the fastest speed most of the support ships could manage. At that rate it would take over a month for them to reach Freedmen, and Calico was already bored.

"If they can see us, they don't seem to care," said Railyn, in response to an earlier question.

"I would like nothing more than to beat them to Freedmen," said Calico. "I doubt anybody there has ever heard of the Zendreen, and they might be willing to aid them."

"Are they the sort prone to charity?"

"No, but last I knew the colony could use all the allies it could get. If that's still true, and the Zendreen approach in the spirit of friendship, they'll most likely consider it. If my contacts are still there, we might be able to convince them to aid us instead."

"Who did you know on the colony, sir?"

"You get to find that out when we get there, Railyn."

Knoal entered the bridge and approached the captain.

"Excuse me, Cap," he said. "I have good news and potentially bad news."

"What's the good news?"

"All of our systems are back up. The other news is that our passive sensors have finished scanning star positions for this region of space."

"Are we not where we thought we were?"

"No, we're definitely just outside the Hayaku system. It's that we detected a minor variance in the relative position of the galaxy."

"Uh, what?"

"Sir, that wormhole didn't just move us in space. It moved us in time, too. Twenty years into the future, to be precise."

Calico and Railyn leaned back in their chairs and let the new information sink in. After half a minute, Calico nodded.

"That means it's been a total of thirty years since I was last on Freedmen," he said pensively.

"Making it much less likely that your contacts will still be there," added Railyn.

"Exactly."

"Captain," began Knoal, "I would be remiss not to point out that this means our guild membership has expired and we're now technically freelancers."

"Indeed, Knoal, but it doesn't change anything. I am still committed to assisting Scherer for as long as he needs."

"I guess we can really forget about ever getting paid by Umber now," said Railyn. "Who knows if the reformed government even survived this long?"

Knoal nodded. "No kidding."

"I know you two are okay with this news, but Rukitara may take it hard. She knew it would be at least ten years before she could return to Hayaku, but twenty-five? I'd better go tell her."

Railyn and Knoal continued to discuss the possible ramifications of the time shift as Calico stood up and exited the bridge. He thought about his contact on Freedmen on his way down to Megumi's quarters. She would be sixty years old by now. Calico countered the melancholy that this fact caused by reminding himself that she had most likely lost her figure. What he couldn't chase away with mirth was the thought of his daughter at age 41. She would have most likely been married, with children, and even grandchildren. The thought sickened him. Then, to his surprise, he found himself missing Coma with an intensity that didn't match the time of her absence. He hoped she was fitting in back on her old vessel.

Calico stopped at the appropriate hatch and rang the bell. Megumi's groggy voice demanded an answer.

"It's Farril," Calico replied.

"Come in."

Calico did so. Megumi was in bed, buried under her blankets. A video played on her bedside monitor. It was a serial that Calico had loaned her the night before, and Meg had obviously fallen asleep watching it. He also noticed a keg of ale (in fact a converted fuel drum) with the bung removed.

"You're supposed to be on duty in twenty minutes," he said.

"Is this a wake-up call?" groaned Megumi.

"I guess so. You were planning on showing up, right?"

"Do you really need me right now, Cap? I could use a couple more hours of sleep."

"Don't tell me you've been up all night watching these vids, Rukitara."

"No, of course not. I think I passed out during episode three."

"That's four and a half hours into it! For the love of the core, we're in the middle of a mission. Go see Doc Trewler and get yourself a stimulant. I can't have you snoozing the day away."

"All right, I'm getting up already." Megumi threw off her covers. "Why did you come down here, anyway?"

"I was going to tell you something important, but now you'll have to wait until you get your ass up to the bridge to hear it. I want you up there in twenty minutes."

"Fine, I will see you then."

Calico exited and made his way back to the bridge. Just before he entered he felt the ship drop out of superlume. He opened the door and was met by Gueyr.

"Oh, hello, Captain," he said, "I was just about to call you."

"The Zendreen fleet has come to a stop," said Knoal from the pilot seat.

Calico said, "Take us within visual range."

"Yes, sir."

The fleet came into view, framed by a universe much darker than the beautiful swirls of the Tarantula Nebula allowed for, and even though they were moving along the galactic plane, light-absorbing dust normal to the region kept the environment muted.

"How did Rukitara take the news?" asked Railyn.

Calico sat down at a station, and replied, "Later, my friend. Let's see what the Zendreen are up to."

"The fleet is still in a defensive formation," said Gueyr. "Some of the smaller vessels are moving around inside the perimeter."

"I've got six ships headed to the center of the formation," said Railyn. "It looks like they're getting ready to dock with each other. Estimated time is eighty seconds."

"Curious," said Calico. "Keep an eye on them. Gueyr, how did it go with our new guest?"

"He's not afraid to die, Captain," began Gueyr, "so he's not too chatty. He did bring up the fact that it is unlikely that Umber will ever compensate us for our allegiance, and strongly implied that his people would pay us if we left them alone."

"Interesting. I may be able to get some more information out of him if I pretend we're willing to deal. Let's see what the fleet is trying to accomplish here first."

"They could be getting ready to launch a counter-attack," said Railyn.

"Without the Faith we'll have no choice but to withdraw," added Knoal.

Calico frowned. "I don't think that's it. The cruisers and the battleship aren't doing anything."

"We could always hail them," Gueyr said, shrugging.

"If they wanted to talk they would have done so already."

"The ships are now docked with each other," reported Railyn. "Sir, one of the other support vessels is moving away from the rest of the formation. It's resumed a course toward Freedmen… speed, one-quarter c."

"That's the same ship we took a pot-shot at during the fight," said Knoal. "I was sure we damaged it. Maybe it can no longer maintain superluminal travel."

"They must not be aware of our presence after all. That ship is a sitting duck without an escort."

"Either that or it's not worth protecting."

"Maybe they're trying to draw us away."

"Let's just wait and see what happens," said Calico, slightly annoyed.

After three minutes of uncomfortable silence, Railyn said, "Cap, the ships have decoupled. The fleet is commencing superlume flight."

Almost instantly the fleet disappeared from sight.

"They're still headed to Freedmen," began Gueyr. "Three of the ships that docked are still going one hundred c. The rest of the fleet has achieved 800 c."

"They dumped their dead weight," murmured Calico.

"Apparently, sir."

"Bring us within scanning range of the slowest ship."

"It could be a trap."

"I'm aware of that, Gueyr. Don't worry, even if they self-destruct, a ship of that size can't hurt us at scanning range."

"We're in range," said Knoal.

"It's a medical vessel," Railyn began, "with eighty-seven life signs on board. The propulsion system is indeed damaged. I'm not reading any weapons systems or anomalous power sources. There are markings on the side that the computer informs me is likely the name of the ship, which is pronounced 'Rikilish,' I think."

"Open a channel," ordered Calico.

"Done."

"This is Captain Farril Calico of the mercenary ship Almagest. We will avoid the obvious temptation to destroy you in exchange for information. Please respond."

There was no reply, so after a few seconds Calico signaled to Railyn to terminate the call.

"I have a bad feeling about this," said Knoal.

"I think I might know what's going on," said Calico. "I'm going to have a talk with our prisoner. Gueyr, come with me. Knoal, Railyn, let me know if anything changes."

"Cap," replied Knoal, "This delay will eliminate the possibility of us arriving at Freedmen before the rest of the fleet."

"Let Freedmen deal with them; when we're done here we're going to Hayaku."

Calico exited the bridge before the others could express any surprise. Gueyr followed him into the corridor. By the time they entered the lift one deck below, the Kau'Rii could no longer hold his tongue.

"What about the Reckless Faith?" he asked.

"Scherer isn't stupid enough to attack the fleet on his own, so if he gets to Freedmen before us he can wait. Hopefully they'll have restored their long-range transceiver by then. We would be scurrying up the wrong vine at Freedmen anyway, Gueyr. If we really want to enlist help against the Zendreen, we should be asking the Hayakuvian central government. Going through the military outpost, if it's still there, would just be an unnecessary delay."

The lift arrived and the two men headed for the cargo hold. Bugani happened by and nodded at them as they passed. The temperature in the cargo bay still hadn't returned to normal, and Gueyr again wished for a heavier jacket as they entered. Calico seemed unaffected. He stared at the Zendreen pilot for a moment, then activated the laser communicator.

"I am Captain Calico, this is my ship."

"I would be willing to forgive your lack of knowledge of the Zendreen customs involving interrogation," the Zendra said, "if you would assure me that no one else but you will question me from this point forward."

"I will have the last word, one way or the other. And you are?"

"A loyal warrior in the service of my people."

"Okay, fine. Listen, I wanted to tell you that I am seriously considering opening up a dialogue with your superiors regarding our relationship. This mission is no longer profitable for my crew and I, and we're far too distant from our normal business lanes to simply forget about the whole thing."

"If you repair my fighter's propulsion systems I would be happy to relay your message, Captain."

"That is not feasible, warrior. Fortunately for you, we damaged the engines of one of your support vessels during our engagement, and they are now limited to sub-light speed. As such, it would be easy for us to overtake them and release you into their custody."

The Zendra blinked. "Which ship is it?"

"What does that matter?"

"I am friends with the commanders of some of our ships, but not others. If this vessel belongs to one of my friends, I will have a much better chance of convincing him of your veracity."

"It's the medical frigate Rikilish."

The color seemed to drain out of the Zendra's face and he looked terrified, although it was hard for Calico and Gueyr to be sure.

"I'm sorry, Captain, that ship is not commanded by someone I know. Perhaps if we rendezvous with the rest of the fleet, you will have better luck."

"That is not an option. In fact, you will be transferred to the Rikilish no matter what. We don't have the resources to keep a prisoner on board this ship. If you don't have enough air to survive until then, I will have some loaded into your tanks."

"That's… that's not necessary. I think I can repair my ship from here after all. I'd like to save face if at all possible and return under my own power."

"I hate to ruin the chance of a budding friendship here, warrior, but we haven't yet developed the level of trust required to let you out of your cockpit. You will be transferred to the Rikilish in fifteen minutes."

Calico switched off the laser device and turned to Gueyr. He put his arm around his shoulder and turned away from the hold.

"Cap?" asked Gueyr.

"Now we let him sweat for a few minutes, then put fixing his ship back on the table."

"I don't get it, sir, what are you playing at?"

"Watch and learn."

Calico and Gueyr turned back around. The Zendra had opened his cockpit and was flopped over the side of his ship, quite dead.

"Oops," gulped Calico.

"Gee, Captain, awesome."

“Well, Gueyr, at least we were able to determine one thing. Everyone on board that medical frigate is infected with the Vengeance virus, and we’re going to get a sample.”

11.

His mind struggled to rectify reality with memory as conflicting emotions surged through his chest. The warm, wind-swept rooftop of a San Diego hotel seemed real, but his logical side assured him that it was in the past and very far away. He felt the pain of combat, the sting of gunshot wounds, and the joy of victory and the countenance of his first lover. All of these things had been real, and almost simultaneous, a scant four years into his past. He focused on the beauty of the young woman instead of the ache of the injuries, only slowly realizing that a different pain was real and not just a memory. Her face, smiling and accepting in his mind, faded away, and was replaced by another. The latter face was just as beautiful but had never offered the same kind of carefree affection as the former. Both kinds of love were all too brief, and he knew he had blown his chance in each case. Still, the face that was real was an incredibly welcome sight to him in the dim light of his quarters.

"Hello, Wildcat," Richter said groggily.

"Hello yourself," said Ari.

"You look exactly the same as the last time I saw you."

"Right before you knocked me out cold, if I remember correctly."

Richter smiled. "It seemed like a good idea at the time."

"You knocked some sense into me," Ari said, blushing slightly.

"I saw the look in your eyes just before I landed that blow. It had to be the same time that Aldebaran reintegrated himself with the orb. The link between you was severed. If not for that shock, Ari, you would have beat me."

Ari gazed sadly at the floor, and replied with complete humility. "I know."

"Are you embarrassed by that?"

"Of course I am. I was on the wrong side of that argument; I didn't deserve to win."

"I agree. Still, the fact that you went on to free the Faith from the docking clamps made up for it. Everyone on board the ship that day feels the same way."

"Tell that to your friend Nathalier."

"No apology is ever perfect, Ferro. And your presence here at this moment confirms that John, who should be your biggest critic, has accepted you back."

"What about Aldebaran?"

"I don't know; I haven't discussed it with him. However, knowing he has an integrated set of memories from you, me, and the other original crewmembers, he probably accepts you too."

"You have always been so kind to me, Richter. I wish I could make it up to you."

"You can. Tell me you brought some contraceptives and that you're free for the evening."

Ari smirked. "You're not in any shape for that!"

"Try me. I guess you'll have to do most of the work, though."

John's voice came in over the intercom. "All crewmembers report to the conference room in two minutes."

"I'll tell you what," said Ari. "When your forehead isn't seeping plasma and you can use both arms, get back to me. Until then, you should probably know that I can't get pregnant. There was too much damage to my reproductive system and the Zendreen weren't interested in repairing it."

"Oh, my God. I'm sorry. It's very brave of you to even entertain the idea of sex."

"That's the oddest compliment I've ever received."

"I've got more where that came from."

"Richter," said Ari, leaning in close, "so much of me is cybernetic now, I'm eager to embrace what's left of my humanity."

With sudden swiftness, Richter gently grabbed Ari with his good arm and kissed her on the lips. She didn't resist, but her response lacked a certain enthusiasm. She broke away, and shot Richter a curious expression of both frustration and amusement.

"Either lock the door," he said, "or help me get to the conference room."

"Are you sure you're able to walk around? Aren't you drugged up?"

"Professor Talvan knew the chemical formula for a painkiller similar in composition to morphine, so he replicated some for me. I'm mellow and ambulatory."

Ari assisted Richter in standing, and the two traveled the short distance to the conference room. The rest of the crew was already present, and it was standing room only. A fresh pot of coffee had been brewed, and Aldebaran and Talvan were eating a meal at the table. Friday was obediently waiting for a scrap of food on the other side of the table, and she meowed and purred at Ari when she drew near. John stood next to the wall-mounted plasma monitor, which displayed a diagram of the ship's systems. Dana immediately rose and insisted that Richter take her seat, which he did. Despite his hazy state, he noticed Ari and Aldebaran share an extended glance.

"Are you sure you're up for this, Richter?" John inquired.

"It will take more than a weapon system falling on my head to keep me from one of your briefings, Scherer."

"Good. All right, everyone, here's the state of affairs. Our propulsion systems are back up and fully operational; however, we had to do a patch job on the power relays so we should go easy on them. The air exchangers have been repaired, thanks to Ari, so we've pressurized the cargo bay. The rear plasma cannon is inoperable as there was not enough spare Talvanium to fix it. The jury is still out on the starboard laser bank but there is some hope for it yet. The dorsal gun has been heavily damaged, and may not be reparable until we make planet-fall somewhere. The invisibility field is down, naturally. All other systems are in the green, except for the Superluminal Relativistic Compensator component of our navigation array. Dana?"

Dana moved forward, and called up a diagram of said array.

"As you know," she began, "the SRC provides us with a real-time picture of the galaxy, as well as the ability to detect and/or communicate with other ships in superluminal travel. It has not been functional since we got the computers back online. This has left us in the unenviable position of having to guess where we really are. Based on Calico's assertion that this star is in fact Alpha Sagittae, I can extrapolate which stars are Beta and Epsilon."

"What's wrong with the SRC component?" asked Ray.

"We don't know. Professor Talvan and Christie and I have been trying to figure out what's going on. In simple terms, we can't get the device to load its drivers properly. Obviously we'll continue to work on it, but without it, operating in superlume is going to be a lot more dicey. Christie and I will be earning our degrees all over again just trying to properly calculate a precise course."

"It also means that we will continue to be out of contact with the Almagest," added John.

"There's something else," continued Christie. "When we compare the relative positions of the three nearest stars to our Earth program data, there's a slight discrepancy. When Dana and I attempted to rectify it, we discovered the simple solution." Christie stood up and crossed to the monitor. She activated the program and called up a multi-layer image of the surrounding stars. "Watch this. The blue stars are the positions of Alpha, Beta, and Epsilon Sagittae on the date that we left Earth. The green stars are the expected positions, and the red stars are the observed positions. If I speed up time…" Christie did so. "You can see that the blue and green positions overlap after about five years, which is the amount of time dilation I estimated that six weeks at our top speed would result in. However, in order to reach the observed positions, we have to keep going. You can see that they match in another twenty years."

"So you're saying that twenty-five years have passed on Earth since we left?" asked Ray.

"Until we get the SRC device back online," began Dana, "we can't be sure, but the observable evidence is pretty solid."

"You're also saying that twenty of those years were a result of the wormhole," said John.

"Apparently," replied Christie. "The only other possibility is that I screwed up the Lorentz transformations by a factor of five, which I doubt very much."

"This is the first time in recorded history that anyone has ever passed through a wormhole," said Talvan.

"Really?" asked John, surprised. "You seemed rather unimpressed by the entire affair."

"I never thought the Zendreen would actually succeed. My point is that anything is possible. We're lucky we didn't end up a thousand years in the future. No one has ever attempted to predict wormhole characteristics."

"Why not?" asked Ari.

"There was never a confirmed, stable example to study."

"Look, it's kind of a shock," began John, "but it's ultimately irrelevant to our mission. The Zendreen fleet, the Almagest, all of us, are in the exact same situation we were before. If we're twenty years in the future now, then so be it."

"Maybe Earth is better equipped to deal with an alien invasion by now," said Ray.

"I seriously doubt it," said Richter.

"I would still prefer to stop the fleet well before then," said John, "if they are headed that way. For now, we need to rendezvous with Calico at the colony at Beta Sagittae. Christie, I'll need your help to determine the correct speed to get us there simultaneously."

"Are we sure that we want to arrive simultaneously with the fleet?" asked Dana. "Wouldn't it be better to beat them there and establish contact with the colony?"

"I want Calico to handle that, remember? He's got a better chance of accomplishing an alliance with them, even if it is twenty years later than we thought. If neither the 'Gest nor the fleet are at the colony, then we have to assume that the Zendreen changed course and went elsewhere. Hopefully we'll get the SRC component back up and we can resume real-time contact with Calico. Otherwise, our next logical choice would be Hayaku-slash-Epsilon Sagittae."

"What if Calico loses track of the fleet entirely?" asked Ray.

"I don't know how that would happen, but if he does then we have no choice but to return to Earth and warn them. If we have to face this threat alone, then maybe our scientists can reverse engineer enough Umberian technology in time."

"Why can't we send them the plans for Umberian ships like we were supposed to the first time?" asked Ari.

"There are several specific aspects of starship construction that we haven't been able to access since the orb was destroyed," replied Talvan. "Aldebaran and I can only remember so much between the two of us. Building another Mark Seventeen without more detail is not feasible. However, I should be able to assist your Earth scientists in building a hybrid vessel, using the Faith as a template. Unfortunately I expect such a task would take longer than the Zendreen's minimum travel time to your planet."

"What's your best case scenario?" asked John.

"Five years, at least. And that's assuming full cooperation from your government."

"Governments," added Richter. "Plural."

"Let's not worry about that nightmare quite yet," said John. "Christie, Dana, Aldebaran, and Talvan, once you get the SRC component back up, I want you to make restoring the Umberian technological database your top priority. At this point, any scrap of new information will be invaluable. Let Richter, Ray and I worry about the mission. Obviously I still welcome any insight you may have, and we'll continue with our normal, twice-daily briefings."

"What would you like me to do?" asked Ari.

"You are welcome to assist whomever you please. You were the resident computer expert at one time, but I'm afraid that Christie and Dana have surpassed you in that arena. I could make better use of you on the bridge."

"Fine with me."

"Assuming they can still do 800 c," said Christie, looking up from a piece of scrap paper, "the Zendreen fleet will arrive at Beta Sagittae in three and a half days."

John nodded. "Good, that will give us some breathing room. I'm sick of doing everything with razor-thin margins of error."

"Come on, John," said Ray, smiling, "you wouldn't want our missions to get boring, would you?"

"That would be a welcome change of pace, Ray. Okay, if there's nothing else, we'll get underway. Christie, Dana, please take care of it."

"You got it," said Dana, heading for the bridge.

"Once we get going," said Christie, standing, "we'll continue working on repairs to the SRC."

Dana entered the bridge, and immediately turned around and addressed the others.

"Everyone, you've got to see this!"

The crew rapidly gathered themselves on the bridge and in the port hallway, and in a moment each available port-side window in both locations were taken up by one or more crewmembers. They were gawking at a massive, potato-shaped asteroid, its mottled gray surface pockmarked with craters both large and small. The asteroid was of unknown diameter and mass, and although it appeared huge, relative sizes were unreliable without scanning equipment. The only thing the crew could tell for sure was that it was a lot bigger than the ship.

"How did we not notice this thing before?" asked Ray.

"With the SRC component offline," began Christie, "if we weren't looking right at it, it could have easily snuck up on us in a short time."

"True," replied Dana, "but something about it isn't right. It appears to be pacing us now, doesn't it?"

"It sure looks like it," said Talvan.

"Maybe it's just in orbit around Alpha Sagittae, like us," said Ray.

"It's impossible to tell," Dana said, moving to her bridge station.

"How long as it been since anyone looked out of the port side of the ship?" asked John.

"I just walked up the port stairs on my way to the briefing," said Ari. "It wasn't there ten minutes ago."

"It's getting closer," said Aldebaran.

"Are you sure?" Talvan asked.

"Just stare at it for a couple of seconds."

Aldebaran was right, the asteroid was creeping toward the Faith. John moved swiftly to the pilot seat and took the controls.

"I'm backing us off," he said.

Those in the hallway joined the others on the bridge. Christie, Dana, Ray, and Aldebaran took their normal stations. Ari, Richter and Talvan watched the asteroid from the rear of the bridge.

"This thing is making me very nervous," said Ari.

"I'll move us away," said John, banking the ship to starboard.

"I'm not detecting any radio transmissions," said Aldebaran. "The object has zero energy signature."

John pointed the ship at Beta Sagittae, and said, "I'm taking us up to ten kilometers per second."

"It's matching us," said Ari.

"Screw this," began John, "we're not in a position to defend ourselves, so safety outweighs curio..."

An instant before John pressed the throttle forward, the ship was rocked by a blue-green energy discharge. The wide, diffuse beam faded rapidly and disappeared ahead of the ship.

"Main engines are back down," said Christie.

"Damn it!"

"It's still gaining on us."

John used the thrusters to rotate the ship around until the asteroid was at their twelve. As the asteroid moved closer, it became evident that they were headed toward the largest crater. The floor of the crater was in a deep shadow.

"I don't see any markings or weaponry anywhere on it," said John. "Ray, give me a burst of thirty-mil into the center of that crater."

"Roger," replied Ray.

The cannon shook the bridge and a tight swath of rounds few forward. The tracers winked out after a few seconds. A moment later, another aquamarine energy discharge hit the ship. This time, the point of origin was clearly the center of the crater.

"Status?"

"No further damage detected," said Dana.

John grunted, annoyed. "I'm at full reverse thrusters and it's still gaining on us. Everybody get to your battle stations."

"My battle station is destroyed," said Richter to no one in particular.

"Ari, Talvan, do you want to man the ventral fifty?"

"With pleasure," Ari said, and patted Talvan on the arm.

The two exited the bridge. John looked over his shoulder at Aldebaran.

"Seth, do you have any insights for us?"

Aldebaran thought for a few seconds, then said, "There were rumors about a race of beings that existed thousands of years ago in the core galaxy that used converted asteroids as ships. One specific story said that a group of pirates had discovered one of these ships, and were using it as a base of operation. That was supposed to be somewhere out around UAS 13520, which, I believe, Christie knows as Tarazed. The asteroids had the potential to be fearsome battleships, but the pirates couldn't get the FTL drives working, so they were limited to sub-light speed. The rumors were hard to believe, considering the incredible amount of power required to move an asteroid anywhere. Given the time frame for the story, that could have been anywhere from eighty to one hundred years ago."

"Tarazed is eighty light years from here," said Christie. "If its been headed this direction the entire time, it could be the same thing."

"Were these pirates ever allied with the Zendreen?" asked John.

"I don't know," replied Aldebaran. "It seems unlikely, since the Zendreen never ventured outside of the Cloud that we know of. That long ago, they were even more isolated than they are now."

"I'd be willing to bet that there's a hangar at the bottom of that crater," said Ari over the intercom.

"I'm not waiting to find out," said John. "If we can't escape from this thing, then I'm going to land us on the rim instead. If there are bad guys in there, hopefully they'll be less willing to attack us in the open."

John began to maneuver. He had the top hat on his joystick set to lateral thrusters, and began tapping it lightly to port, then a few more times downward.

"Maybe this thing is on some kind of autopilot," said Dana. "It could be homing in on us as part of an exploration program, or if it is malfunctioning, it could think we're a friendly and its simply trying to help us dock."

"I hope you're right," said John. "If we can land on it, then we can effect repairs there just as well as adrift."

John's thumb movements on the top hat were becoming longer and more deliberate. There was no apparent change in the Faith's attitude, and the crater moved ever closer. John swore to himself, and held the thrusters down for several seconds.

"It appears to be matching our maneuvers," said Aldebaran.

"No shit! I'm sorry, Seth, I'm getting a little frustrated. Ari, give me a burst across the entire bottom of the crater."

"Roger," said Ari's voice.

The deck rumbled slightly, and a fusillade of fifty caliber tracers drew a nearly straight line through the crater floor. Some of the tracers burned slightly longer than others, giving the observers a sense of three dimensions.

"There's definitely some kind of hangar or hatch down there," said Christie.

"Let's let 'em have it with all we've got," said Richter. "Let them know we mean business."

"I don't think that's a good idea," Dana replied, looking at him. "This thing may have a weapon system we haven't seen yet, and if we suddenly become a more palpable threat, it may try to destroy us. As far as we can tell, it wants us alive."

"For now," began John, "but if we end up in that hangar, our options will definitely decrease."

"That last burst of fire gave me a chance to estimate the size of the asteroid," said Christie, scribbling a long triangle on her scrap paper. "Based on the travel time of the rounds to the surface, I can estimate distance. It also gives me an idea of the diameter of the crater, which I can apply to the length of the entire object. It looks like five kilometers from end-to-end and three across the middle."

The crew waited in silence for several seconds as the asteroid approached.

"Suggestions?" asked John.

"Is there any way we can extrapolate the location of its thrusters?" asked Richter.

"I'm not sure," Christie replied, "if they're disguised on the surface, then only their interaction with some other medium would reveal where they are."

"If we could detonate something on the surface, wouldn't that kick up enough dust and debris to reveal a thruster?"

"We'd have to have a general idea of where the thrusters are to begin with."

Richter moved next to Christie. "If it was up to you, where would you put the thrusters?"

"The most logical places would be easy enough to guess, the only problem is that there may be several small thrusters instead of one big one, spread out over a larger area."

"It wouldn't work anyway," said John. "The only thrusters we'd have a shot at are on the facing side of the asteroid. We don't care about it moving away from us, so blow them up and we accomplish nothing."

"Crap, you're right," said Christie.

"I can see the hangar," announced Aldebaran.

The others turned to look. The outline of a massive opening had indeed become visible within the crater. The rectangular opening was definitely not a naturally-formed feature.

"Maybe if we can identify a power conduit in there," began Dana, "we can destroy it and see if that disrupts the thrusters."

John shook his head, and said, "By the time we're close enough for the exterior lights to work it will be too late."

"Throw a plasma flare in there, then," said Aldebaran.

"Plasma flare?"

"Don't you have the cannon set for plasma flares?"

"I have no idea what you're talking about, Seth."

"The cannon is capable of firing a low power, self-contained ball of plasma. It will burn brightly for about a minute, then extinguish itself."

"The cannons didn't come with an instruction manual," said Richter.

"It's very simple," continued Aldebaran, accessing the computer. "Here, I'll do it right now. All you have to do is adjust the power and the magnetic containment. I'll add a shortcut link later… there you go. Fire when you're ready."

"Wait a minute," said Dana, "I'm still worried that if we damage it, then the reprisal will be more than we can handle."

The bridge entered the shadow of the crater, and John said, "This may be our last chance to escape."

John squeezed the trigger on his joystick. An extremely bright bluish-white sphere shot forward and crossed the threshold of the hangar.

The crew was immediately able to identify the hangar doors. The doors were open halfway, which was more than enough to admit the ship.

"It's got to be at least two hundred meters wide," said Christie.

The plasma ball continued inside the hangar. It revealed nothing but smooth rock and several smaller corridors leading off into darkness. It impacted the rear wall and dissipated harmlessly.

"Did anybody spot anything?" asked John.

The others responded in the negative. The rest of the ship entered the shadow of the crater, casting it instantly into complete darkness. The crew waited impatiently for their eyes to adjust, and Ari apparently got there first.

"The doors are already closing," she said over the intercom.

"Damn it," said John, "don't these assholes know we're in the middle of a fucking war? We don't have time for this shit."

"Whatever this thing has in mind for us," said Ray, "hopefully it won't derail us for too long."

"This galaxy hasn't cut us any breaks yet and I don't expect to get one this time."

There were two slight bumps on the hull. John flipped on the exterior lights and the crew looked out of the windows.

"We've just been hit by two small objects," said Ari. "They look like garbage can lids attached to long cables. They bounced off the hull and now they're just floating there."

"I bet they're magnetic harpoons or mooring cables," said Aldebaran.

"Well, they're not going to work on the Faith," said John, "not unless I deactivate the energy dispersal system."

The crew suddenly experienced an odd but brief light-headedness. Dana identified the likely cause.

"An artificial gravity field has just been activated," she said.

"There are several landing areas on the floor of the hangar," said Ari. "I don't see any activity down there. By the way, the hangar doors are now closed."

"Should we land?" asked Christie.

"No," replied John. "As long as we're floating here we can't be boarded, unless they come to us."

"At least get closer," said Ari, "the lights aren't powerful enough from this distance."

"You mean closer to the landing platforms?"

"Yes."

"Fine by me. I'll take us to within thirty meters."

"I'm detecting trace levels of oxygen and nitrogen," said Christie. "They're rising. Air pressure is also increasing."

"They still haven't done anything overtly hostile," said Dana.

"Yeah, well, they're not exactly rolling out the red carpet, either," John grumbled.

"All I see down here is some equipment," began Ari, "probably refueling apparatus. I can't tell whether or not it has been used recently. There are twenty landing platforms in all, connected by flat pathways. I believe some of the smaller surfaces are elevators to lower parts of the hangar, but I can't be sure."

"Roger that, Ari," said John. "I'm going to explore the rest of the interior. Let me know if something catches your eye."

"I'm definitely thinking we're stuck in an automatic docking procedure," Dana offered.

"Whatever's going on, we're going to have to find a way to get those doors back open."

It did not take long for John to cover every inch of the hangar. A darkened control room was the only other feature he could find. He returned the ship to the hangar doors, and locked the flight controls into hover mode.

"Now what?" asked Ray.

"Now, we wait," John replied. "If nothing happens in the next hour, I'm going to open up on these doors will the plasma cannon."

"I wouldn't bother," said Talvan over the intercom. "I got a good look at those doors on the way in. They're at least ten feet thick and very likely able to withstand anything we can throw at them."

"The atmosphere has stabilized," said Christie. "It's holding steady at twenty percent oxygen, seventy percent nitrogen, and ten percent other inert gases. Ambient temperature is fifteen degrees Fahrenheit."

"Okay, then. We'll wait one hour for a reception committee, and then we'll go looking for answers."

Sixty minutes later, an away team had gathered in the cargo bay. It consisted of Ari, Aldebaran, Ray, and, Richter. John and Professor Talvan were also present, helping the others gear up. John had relented to Richter's insistence that he be allowed to go on the mission after he had demonstrated his ability to use one of the Phalanx rifles despite his bruised arm, and since his head wound had finally sealed itself up. The other two Phalanx rifles were in the possession of Aldebaran and Ray. Ari had chosen an M1A for herself; plus there were various pistols and edged weapons among the group.

John had chosen the landing platform closest to the hangar control room. A hallway led off into the rock wall about twenty-five meters from the platform. The plan was for the team to reach the control room and figure out how to open the hangar doors.

"Are you sure you're up for this?" John asked Richter for the fifth time.

"For the tenth time, yes," replied Richter.

"Good. All right, folks, remember to do a radio check as soon as you're out of sight of the ship. Our units may not be able to broadcast through this rock, but we have to try.

Ari zipped up her jacket, and said, "You got it."

"We'll take care of it," said Ray, putting on a watch cap, "you just concentrate on helping Christie and Dana get the systems back online."

"Yeah, don't have too much fun without me," said John. "I'd rather go with you, but somebody has to stay behind to fix the ship."

"All set here," said Aldebaran, donning his gloves.

"Great. Take it easy out there. Professor?"

Professor Talvan nodded, turned down the cargo bay lights, and pressed the button for the ramp. The four team members took up positions on either side of the ramp. John crouched behind a crate and aimed his M1 rifle toward the exterior.

"Dana, look sharp on that Nineteen," he said.

"Roger," said Dana from the bridge.

Bitterly cold air from the hangar entered the cargo bay, quickly evacuating the warmth from the chamber. The exterior lights illuminated the landing platform brightly, but did not extend far into the nearest hallway. John had placed the ship at a thirty degree angle to the hallway, allowing the ventral gun to cover it. The team swept forward a moment after the ramp stopped moving, cleared all directions, then moved slowly toward the hallway. John kept his rifle sights on the darkness, straining to catch any sign of movement.

A blinding barrage of plasma fire emanated from the hallway. The team was ready for it, and returned fire simultaneously. The sudden exchange of fire turned the tomb-like silence of the hangar into an echoing cascade of noise. Without a word, they began to execute a maneuver called a banana peel, in which one person would fire furiously toward the enemy while the others withdrew, the next person in line repeating the task. John's field of fire was mostly blocked by his friends so he picked his shots carefully; Dana had no such restriction from her angle and let loose with the GAU 19/A. Most of the enemy fire impacted the ship and a few shots entered the cargo bay, but the four team members were able to withdraw without a casualty. Richter was the last one across the threshold of the ramp. He emptied his Phalanx and all but threw it onto his back (his sling rig assured that it would actually stay there), and transitioned to his pistol with a practiced snap.

"Talvan, kill the lights and close the ramp!" yelled John after the clip ejected from his rifle.

Looking over the crate to his right, John failed to locate Talvan. Swearing to himself, he ran over to the ramp control switch and smacked it with his palm. The others continued to return fire from the cover of the cargo bay. John reloaded his rifle and fired eight quick rounds into the hallway. When the ramp closed, he turned off the exterior floods and turned on the interior lights to check on his friends.

"Is everybody okay?" shouted Ray, echoing John's concerns.

"I'm fine," said Ari.

"No injuries here," replied Aldebaran.

"No problem," Richter said evenly. "Scherer, are you all right?"

"Yes," said John. "Professor Talvan, where the hell…" John cut himself off as his gaze was attracted downward. His right foot was planted in what used to be Professor Talvan's chest. "Oh my God!"

The others ran over and added their own expressions of shock. Aldebaran turned away in horror.

"Is everybody all right down there?" asked Dana over the intercom.

"We're fine," John managed to say, almost choking on the words. "How about you?"

"We took fire from three different hallways, as well as one of the larger tunnels. Christie and I drove them back with the fifty and the lasers."

"Roger. Stay where you are and keep your eyes peeled."

"You got it."

"The girls don't need to see this," John said to Aldebaran, turning off the intercom.

"Hell, none of us needed to see this," said Ari. "What happened?"

"I guess he zigged when he should have zagged," said Ray.

"Damn it," said John. "We just lost one of our top technicians."

"He didn't deserve to go out like this," added Aldebaran, his hand over his forehead.

"I hate to sound callous," began Ari, "but we'd better get this body stowed and the cargo bay cleaned up right now. We need to focus on the enemy."

"You're right," John said, and shook his head. "One of Umber's greatest heroes, and he dies on this God-forsaken rock."

"A soldier's only reward is death," said Aldebaran solemnly.

"Let's concern ourselves more with the victory aspect of soldiering right now," said Ray, removing his jacket.

John reactivated the intercom. "Dana, take us back to the geometric center of the hangar and lock down the autopilot. Everybody, meet in the conference room in five minutes."

"I'll take care of the body," offered Ari.

"Me, too," said Aldebaran. "We should give him a proper send-off when we can."

John nodded. "I guarantee it. I'll see you in the conference room in five, okay? We need to figure out what the hell is going on with this place."

Five minutes later, the crew of the Faith was gathered in the conference room. Christie and Dana had just been informed of the loss of Talvan. Christie shed a few tears, and Dana just seemed to be stunned.

"I'm sorry, but we can't dwell on Professor Talvan right now," said John. "I promise we'll do the right thing for him when we have the time."

"There's no justice in this God damned universe," muttered Dana.

"Okay, so we were ambushed. What did we see out there?"

"I never got a look at our actual attackers," said Aldebaran.

Ari said, "I saw figures in the shadows, that was it."

"I was just aiming for the muzzle flashes," said Ray.

"There were four to six figures in the nearest hallway," said Richter. "They were behind hard cover, I think pieces of equipment, three to four feet high. The figures themselves were humanoid, five to six feet tall; beyond that I didn't see anything distinctive. They began falling back in a similar fashion to a banana peel when Dana opened up on them with the Nineteen."

"You saw all of that?" asked John.

"I'm quite certain."

"Christie, Dana, what did you see from your end?"

"Just muzzle flashes," replied Dana. "We traced the shots back to their origin points easily enough. The laser banks were very effective in suppressing them. The enemy shots that hit the Faith had no effect."

"That's about what I saw," Christie said.

"Did anybody get a confirmed kill?" asked John.

The crew shrugged and looked at each other. John smirked.

"It's likely that we hit some of them in the nearby hallway, just from the volume of fire," said Richter, "but I didn't see any of them go down."

"Fine. So what's our next move?"

"We need to be able to find a defensible position other than this ship. They apparently have the advantage in numbers, so we need to draw them into a skirmish that limits their field of fire. I suggest we create a diversion down here and make them think that we're trying for the same hallway. Then, take the ship to one of the upper tunnels as quick as we can and disembark up there. Once the team is on the ground, we can try to work back to the control room while minimizing our exposure to enemy troops."

"That sounds good to me," said John. "Anybody else have a better idea?"

"I think a stealth approach would be best," said Ari softly.

"That's an alternative," replied Richter. "The only problem is that stealth trades firepower for mobility and silence. I don't think we would be able to remain hidden all the way to the control room. We have to assume that they know we're trying to get there, so it will be guarded. The stealth approach could work if we knew of an alternative location to open the hangar doors, but we don't."

"I suggest sending just me," said Ari.

"That's very noble of you," replied John, "but even you have your limits."

"It's time to show you something that the Zendreen left me with. Call it a gift, perhaps. You see, there was a reason other than my charming personality that Captain Calico hired me on to his crew."

Ari withdrew her control device from her pocket, an item none of the crew of the Faith had yet seen. She unzipped her jacket and untucked her t-shirt from her jeans. Those to her right noticed the metallic glint of the cybernetic jack in her abdomen, and the others realized what she was doing when she plugged herself into the device.

"What the hell?" mumbled John.

"The Zendreen discovered a way to allow my cybernetics to interact with the natural electrostasis of my body, and amplify it. They were primarily concerned with light-bending technology like that of our invisibility shield, but also worked to allow light projection from the stasis. I can change my appearance, or become invisible."

Ari demonstrated the latter form of technology by disappearing from sight, leaving only her clothing hanging in space. The crew reacted with appropriate awe, and she returned to view.

"So you have to go out there naked for the full effect?" asked Christie.

"No, my flight suit and boots from the Almagest have been modified to work with the stasis field. It's not quite warm enough for fifteen degrees Fahrenheit, but I'll live. The device also has a built-in transmitter, so we can stay in touch."

"What about weaponry?" asked Richter.

"The way the field works, I can carry simple metal objects as long as the total weight doesn't exceed about one and a half kilograms. That rules out firearms. The handle of my Rakhar battle blade is a synthetic polymer, so I already know that's not going to work. Maybe there's something down in the galley I can take with me, but I should be able to obtain a weapon in the field if the situation calls for it, so I'm not too concerned about it."

"I have something that might work," said Richter, nodding.

"The Tarsus blade?" asked Dana.

"Bingo."

"I'll check it out," said Ari. "For now, I'm going to need a lot of food; I basically need to stuff myself before I go."

"Didn't you just eat a couple of hours ago?" asked John.

"The Zendreen device feeds off of energy derived directly from calories. I used up the last of my available body fat during my last undercover job for Calico, so I'll need lots of food energy available instead."

"There is no way you've got zero percent body fat." Christie said. "You've still got your... girly bits."

"I think I'm at ten percent. Actually, if I go any lower than that I can risk health problems.

Human bodies need some fat to function properly."

"Okay, fine," began John, "somebody get her a double cheese pizza or something. Those of you interested in helping refine our stealth plan, come with us down to the galley. Everybody else, please do your best to get our engines back online. Opening those hangar doors won't do us any good if we can't get away."

"Christie and I will handle that," said Dana. "Aldebaran, we could use your help, too. You're our best surrogate for the Professor in that regard."

Aldebaran nodded. "Unfortunately, yes."

"I'll meet you two down there," said Richter to John and Ari. "I need to go grab Vesper Tarsus' best friend."

12.

In the Zero-G room at the aft of the Faith, Aldebaran crouched by the body of the man who used to be his best friend. Wrapped tightly in two large wool blankets, the corpse was as impersonal as the crew could make it before any further disposal. It was a senseless death for a learned man, one who had endured ten years of occupation by a hostile force only to meet his end at the hands of a random assault, and an exceedingly random "lucky" shot that happened to pass into the cargo bay.

Aldebaran wanted to feel angry, but only sadness came. He had long since forgiven the man for causing the schism that had separated him into Seth the AI and Aldebaran the pirate, and it hurt even more to know that Fugit had never forgiven himself for letting it happen. Still, Talvan had been responsible for so much of the Faith's success, first as the programmer of the long range deep space probe that had housed the orb, and time and time again for several pieces of extremely useful technology. Aldebaran had some access to this knowledge thanks to his time spent as part of the ship, but having never actually linked with Talvan through the orb, he could never have the same level of insight into the Professor's mind as he did with the others.

"I'm so sorry you had to die out here, Fugit," Aldebaran whispered. "We saved Umber, but this was never your fight."

Aldebaran looked up as John, Richter, and Ari entered the room. Ari had changed back into her flight suit, and grasped the Tarsus blade in her right hand. Aldebaran stood up and acknowledged his comrades with a nod.

"Sorry to disturb you," said John.

"Not at all. Just paying the man my respects. What are you doing here?"

"We're hoping that using the airlock won't attract any attention," replied Richter. "Our foes might get suspicious if the ramp lowers for no apparent reason."

"Did you bring a rope? It's twenty feet to the hangar floor from here."

"I can handle it," Ari said. "I'm the bionic woman now, remember?"

Aldebaran shrugged. "You're not entirely cybernetic, you should still be careful."

"I will, Seth." Ari drew the sword and handed the lacquered wooden scabbard to Richter. "Why do I feel like I'm casting this into the sea?"

"You'd better come back," said Richter smiling. "Second Minister Lalande would kill me if I lost the Tarsus blade."

Christie's voice came in over the intercom. "Scherer, this is Tolliver."

"Go ahead," replied John.

"We've got the engines back up."

"Outstanding! Good work. Ari, there's no time to waste."

"I'm ready," said Ari.

Aldebaran worked the controls for the airlock, and the hatch slid open. The exterior door opened a moment later, and chilly air wafted in. Ari moved to the doorway, and smiled at the others.

"Be careful out there, and hurry back," John said earnestly.

"No problem."

Ari calmly stepped off the edge of the outer hatch. She landed on the hangar floor in a wide crouch, barely making a sound. She glanced up to see the exterior door closing, and looked around the hangar. Without the flood lights of the Faith, the area remained almost completely dark.

Her eyes picked up on a few lights sources either down hallways or tunnels, and a few faint fixtures on the sides of the hangar itself. As they'd planned, Ari began moving toward the tunnel adjacent to the tunnel where the ambush had occurred. She moved swiftly and silently, eager to start generating body heat to counter the frigid air. As she approached the entrance to the tunnel she got a sense of relative size, a sensation that had been lost on her during the ambush, and she realized just how huge the hangar really was. Even then it accounted only for a small percentage of the potential space inside the asteroid. Ari arrived at the tunnel entrance, and paused.

"Temerity, this is Ghost, radio check, over," she whispered.

"Ghost, I read you three-by-five, how me?" replied John's voice.

"Lima Charlie, Temerity. I'm beginning my pub crawl. Ghost out."

Ari moved inside the tunnel. The corridor was about ten meters in height and roughly cylindrical. It ran forward about fifty meters before curving to the left; beyond that was too dark for Ari to see. It was also curving away from the hangar control room, which was almost directly above her. However, it appeared unguarded, so she moved forward. The tunnel ended in a large cavern, smaller than the hangar but still enormous. The light level here was almost non-existent. Ari moved to her right along the perimeter, trying not to trip on the metallic debris that littered the floor.

As she made her way through the cavern, it became apparent to her that it had once been some kind of repair shop. There were pieces of heavy equipment in the middle of the area; they were nothing she could identify without more light. She came across a set of double doors.

Next to it on the wall, a control panel with two buttons seemed to indicate that this was an elevator. It was impossible to tell whether or not there was power to the doors, and Ari was reluctant to find out. Surely any movement of doors or lifts would alert their attackers to her presence. She would have to find a set of stairs, or maybe an open elevator shaft that she could scale. The walls of the cavern themselves were too smooth for any climbing attempt. Barring that, she would have to create a diversion and slip into an elevator while no one was paying attention.

Ari stopped moving and knelt down. She thought she heard something, and even though sound carried well in this place, she couldn't tell for sure. A pang of adrenaline hit her, and for the first time she felt slightly afraid. Ari felt like she could face anything with at least one other person backing her up, but stuff like this still made her somewhat uneasy. She controlled her breathing and directed her eyes upward. She noticed that there were clear panels set into the ceiling, and motionless points of starlight were visible through them. She took a step forward, moved her head back and forth, and was able to judge the distance to the ceiling at about two hundred meters.

Ari's sword accidentally impacted a piece of metal. It reverberated up the blade like a tuning fork, and she hurriedly pressed the flat of the steel against her calf to silence it. The echo of the subtle sound bounced around the cavern. Ari held her breath and waited for a response. Almost two minutes later, she began moving again, this time reversing her grip on the sword and tucking the blade behind her back. She continued along until she came across another hallway, this one to her two o'clock. It was hexagonal in shape, with all metal walls, and was dimly lit with a row of soft blue fixtures. It ran only twenty-five meters. Ari moved down it carefully. At the other end was a balcony, and a sight that took her breath away.

An immense open area lay ahead. The floor of the expanse was about five hundred meters below her, and stretched three kilometers into the distance. Before her lay a city, with hundreds of well-defined blocks brightly illuminated by three-orbed street lights and buildings stretching as high as ten stories. Half a kilometer above, a clear dome allowed starlight to enter. Several bridges spanned the area at various heights, each rimmed with what Ari would call Christmas tree lights. It was beautiful, and completely silent. From where she stood, Ari couldn't detect any movement. The city appeared to be abandoned, or at least disused.

Looking to her right, she saw a staircase. It went up to another balcony, so she ascended it. At the next landing a long hexagonal hallway led back toward the smaller cavern before taking a sharp right turn. Again, it was away from the control room, but Ari got the feeling that she was getting closer to something important. She traveled down the hallway, noted a closed door to her left, and made the right turn, continuing for another hundred meters or so. At the end of the hall she found a darker area. As she entered the room, she realized it was an old mess hall. A thin layer of dust covered the several tables and benches, and a shutter covered the aperture to the kitchen. Two empty serving tables occupied one side of the room, and four vending machines sat without power on the other. Beside the kitchen, there was another exit across from the hallway. Ari headed toward it. Through a half-open door she found a staircase leading upward. As she entered the stairwell, her foot dragged across a cord. She looked down, and realized she'd just set off a tripwire. She froze, mouthing every invective she knew to herself. Footsteps almost immediately could be heard both from the hallway and far above in the stairwell. Ari moved swiftly over to the vending machines and pressed herself against one.

"Time to put this technology to the test," she said to herself.

Four figures entered the mess hall from the hallway, immediately spreading out to either side. They were canine humanoids, about five feet tall, wearing fur-rimmed winter clothing and armed with energy rifles. One of the creatures had two yellow stripes around his left arm. A moment later, two more troops appeared from the stairwell. They were similarly dressed and armed, and one of them also had two stripes on his arm. That one was less than three feet from Ari. They waited in the eaves of the room, apparently waiting for their eyes to adjust to the dimness.

A seemingly human woman entered the room from the hallway. She was dressed in a fur-rimmed overcoat and tight-fitting black pants, and wore a pair of goggles on her forehead. The goggles pinned back her short black hair. She had her hands stuck in the voluminous pockets of her coat, so she could have been holding anything.

"I smell scented soap," the creature nearest to Ari said, her translator offering an English version of the unknown language.

"My dear Miriam," began the woman, speaking in the same language, "there are no other exits from this room. You might as well come out."

Ari wasn't about to stand in for this Miriam person, so she stayed silent. After a minute, the woman gestured and the troops started poking around. Ari moved carefully around the creature nearest to her as he inspected her corner. When the one who had inspected the kitchen returned and shrugged his shoulders, the woman donned her goggles and activated them. The eyepieces glowed green, then red, then blue. The woman's gaze rested on the last vending machine.

"Warber, to your left!" she snapped.

The trooper next to Ari spun around with his weapon. Ari caught the foregrip with her left hand and swung her sword in an upward arc. The blade effortlessly cleared three-quarters of the creature's torso and withdrew just as easily. It gurgled and collapsed, and Ari bolted for the hallway, retaining the rifle. The woman realized she could do nothing but dodge out of the way, and did so. Ari sprinted down the hallway at close to twenty miles per hour, and rounded the corner before any of the troops could fire. Two or three of them opened up, the plasma shots impacting the doorway Ari had previously left unexplored. A flash of insight caused her to pause for a second, and she swapped the weapons in her hands. She returned to the corner of the hallway, hefted up the six-pound rifle with her right arm, and sent a barrage of poorly-aimed shots back toward the mess hall. That accomplished, she ducked into the doorway and hid behind the corner.

"Hold you fire, you idiots," one of the troopers said, "Miss Cassie wants her alive."

"That's not Miriam, you fetid, swamp-brained tooth-rot," said the woman. "She's from that ship."

Ari looked around the new space. She was in a fairly well-lit chamber, which had once been a computer station. All of the consoles were dark and dusty. An elevator was at the far end of the room, and the call buttons were illuminated. Ari ran over and attempted to access the lift, but when she pressed the up button, another panel switched on. There were nine keys on it with unknown numbering. She swore to herself and returned to the hallway door. The woman and the troops were still in the mess hall. Ari put her sword on the nearest console and looked at her new rifle. It was two and a half decimeters long, with a tube-style collapsible stock and a stowable-forward broomhandle grip. There was a zero-power holographic aiming device on the top, and it was fed by a battery behind the rear pistol grip. A power meter presented Ari with some undecipherable information. She couldn't even be sure if the rifle had any shots left. Apparently, neither could her opponents.

"Okay," yelled Ari down the corridor. "Now that we've established a few things, let's play diplomats, shall we?"

"I'd almost forgotten what it was like to deal with people who like to waste time," replied the woman. "Sure, why not, I've got all day. How about we start with introductions? I am Commander Cassiopeia, and I'm in charge of this asteroid, which is called Vulture, the last of the great Stymphalian raptors."

"My name is Coma Veronice. My ship is the Reckless Faith. Why have you captured and attacked us?"

"The attack was necessary to display force and relay the important facts; you are outnumbered and we have infinite patience. The capture is simply to scavenge your resources and subjugate your crew."

"Oh, is that all? Gee, maybe we got off on the wrong foot."

"You have already changed that plan, Veronice. By killing Warber, you have gained status in the culture of his people. You must be dealt with as an equal now, and while you may be ally or enemy, you cannot be subjugated. In fact, if you challenge their leader to single combat, and win, you earn the right to mate with the males of your choosing."

"Aren't you their leader?"

"Yes, but my commitment to commanding the Vulture is more important than their social rules, and they agree with me. I am not expendable, insofar as we will not risk control of the asteroid on a simple duel. I can declare a surrogate, however, if you're attracted to the whole unrestricted mating idea."

"Uh, no."

"Our visitors never are. I myself am not compatible genetically, but I had to kill quite a few of my crew's great-great-granduncles to prove it."

"Wow, that's so interesting. Listen, Commander, you have more to gain from my ship and crew as allies than you do as quarry. You are invited to sit down with us and negotiate an agreement; even your violence of action so far hasn't eliminated that possibility."

"It's out of the question, Veronice. Our plan for you goes far beyond anything a potential alliance could gain us. We answer to a higher power."

"Nuts," whispered Ari, then she asked, "Yeah, who might that be?"

"The Kira'To, of course."

Ari suddenly and vividly remembered being on a Zendreen operating table. Her new leg was being installed, and the operation was so routine to the Zendreen doctors that they were mostly talking about something else. Ari was far too drugged-up to care about the conversation, but when the tone turned serious there was something she did remember. The Kira'To were a great concern to the Zendreen, both in the past and currently. However, the Zendreen did not seem to regard the Kira'To as deities. Even still, the very name sent chills down Ari's neck and left her unsettled. She shivered and returned her attention to the present.

"Whether your motives are religious or sexual, or both, my crew won't be taken as long as there's an ounce of fight in any of us."

"Then your ship itself will have to do."

Out of the corner of her eye, Ari noticed more canine troopers show up at the other end of the hallway, at the balcony landing. She swore to herself and activated her comlink.

"Temerity, this is Ghost, over."

John's voice came in with a tiny bit of static. "Ghost, this is Temerity. You're coming in about one by three, over."

Ari spoke slowly and clearly. "I have made contact with the enemy. Negotiations are failing. I am going to try another route, over."

"Say again, all after negotiations, over."

"Negotiations are failing. I am going to try another route, over."

"Roger that, Ghost. Stay sharp, over."

"I will comply. Out."

Ari went over a plan in her head. Only Cassiopeia could see past the invisibility field, as far as she could tell, so if she stormed the group of soldiers on the balcony landing, she might be able to break free. Ari fired the seven remaining shots out of the rifle, discarded it, and retrieved her sword. She was about to run for it when a panel moved in a nearby bulkhead. Ari leaped backward three feet and turned her attention to the panel. The head of a humanoid girl poked out from behind the panel. She looked around the room.

"It's Coma, right?" the girl said. "Come with me, quick."

Ari deactivated her invisibility field. The girl was startled but didn't revoke her suggestion.

"Let me guess," said Ari quietly, "you must be Miriam."

"How did you know that? Forget it, just get in here."

Ducking down, Ari followed the girl. She replaced the panel, and then immediately noticed that the younger woman was wearing a US Air Force N3B parka and blue jeans. She also realized that her translator hadn't added anything to the conversation; the girl was already speaking English, and with a British accent.

The passageway through the panel opened up into a narrow conduit. There was room enough to stand but barely enough to turn around. Ari followed Miriam into the darkness.

"Why are you helping me?" asked Ari.

"We have a common foe, isn't that enough? Come on, I know a safe place."

The conduit widened a little, and Miriam stopped at a ladder. She began to ascend it.

"Wait a minute," began Ari. "I don't have time to go hide somewhere. I need your help."

"I can't help you if we're both dead, and... hey, are you speaking English?"

"Yes, same as you. Are you from Earth?"

Miriam looked crestfallen. "Please, don't you start with this outer space nonsense too."

"Listen to me. Do you want to get out of here?"

"Yes, of course. You met Cassie and those monsters, this is no place for a young woman."

Ari put her hand on Miriam's shoulder. "Then I promise I will get you out of here. But you've got to trust me and answer my questions truthfully, okay?"

"Fine," said Miriam, stepping off of the ladder. "I'm from Earth. England, to be precise."

"How did you get here?"

"I haven't the foggiest."

"How long have you been here?"

"Perhaps a fortnight, maybe more."

"What's your relationship with Cassiopeia?"

"Cat and mouse, basically. I'd rather not find out exactly what her and her contingent have planned for me."

"Agreed. Okay, Miriam, here's the deal. If you can open the hangar doors or show me where I can do it, then you've earned yourself a ride on my ship."

"I can't do it, and I don't know where you might find the controls, but if I had to guess I'd say it could be done from the control room on level five."

"Can you get me there?"

"The only way into that control room is the lift in the room we just left."

"Damn it. Still, I think I can hack the access code with enough time. I have a device that can probably interface with the panel. We'll need a distraction to get Cassie away from there as I'm fairly certain she's the only one who can see past my invisibility shield."

"You really can go invisible? I thought I was imagining things."

"Excuse me for a moment." Ari activated her comlink. "Temerity, this is Ghost, over."

John's voice echoed in her head. "Ghost, this is Temerity. Your signal is slightly better now, over."

"Roger. Listen up. I need the biggest distraction you can give me for as long as possible."

"Roger. I don't think that will be a problem."

"Good, I'll radio you again and tell you exactly when I want you to begin. Ghost out."

"What did they say?" asked Miriam.

"They're going to blow the shit out of something, or pretend to, on my mark. What I need from you is a more local distraction."

"You want me out there with my arse in the breeze?"

"It would help draw Cassie's attention away from that lift. Do you have any weapons?"

"Just my father's Colt," replied Miriam, producing such a thing from her pocket. "I only have five bullets and I'm a terrible shot."

"From here, can you get close to the mess hall?"

"I can get to the set of stairs on the far side."

"Perfect. Go there, announce yourself, take a pot shot at a soldier if you want, and then run like hell. Hide out near the hangar and we'll both get out of here when the time is right."

"How do I know you won't leave without me?"

"Because my captain won't leave without me, and you'll be on board before I get back, that's why. Now, do you think you can do this?"

"Yes. However, Coma Veronice, if I get killed in the process I will be very cross with you."

13.

"I'll give you one chance to get out of here."

The two canine troopers who had been left behind to guard the elevator to the control room looked around in surprise. They glanced at each other, and scanned the chamber carefully. One of them believed he knew from where the voice had come, and motioned to his partner to focus on that area.

"Temerity, this is Ghost. Begin now."

"Miss Cassie wants you alive," the first soldier said. "We won't hurt..."

He was interrupted by a tremendous racket in the distance. The echoes of energy and projectile weapons were not overpowering, but the floor shook with each salvo. Voices on the radios of the two soldiers reported that the Faith was on the move and trading weapons fire.

"I'm serious. Get out of here while you still breathe."

The troopers quickly pressed their backs against each other, and filled every horizontal inch of the room with plasma fire. Almost as soon as they ceased firing, the first one watched his arms fly away from his torso. The second one spun around before his partner could scream, and began firing his rifle. His head slid from his neck without resistance, and the muzzle of his rifle found the abdomen of his friend. The two fell in a wet heap and stopped moving.

Ari deactivated her invisibility field and moved to the control panel for the lift. She fumbled around until she found an access port, then removed the Zendreen device from inside her flight suit. She unplugged it from herself, swooned, and fell down. She pulled herself back to her feet with the help of a dusty chair. Activating a scanner, she waved the device in front of the access port until the plug whirred. The plug seemed to melt slightly, then solidified in a new shape. Ari plugged the device into the access port and began working.

The noise from the hangar resumed again in earnest. Ari wished she could call the ship and hack the panel at the same time, and regretted not being able to take a dedicated transceiver.

The Zendreen device hummed as it translated the unknown characters into its best guess of English. A different kind of dizziness began to creep over Ari. She was ravenous, to the point where she doubted she could use the invisibility field for much longer without more food. As long as she encountered no further (or at least light) resistance on the way back to the ship, she would make it without the tactical advantage.

"I don't suppose you guys have any spare Kibbles," she said to the corpses.

Her device beeped at her in a reassuring manner, and she opened the door to the lift. She also noticed that she had a chance to change the access code, and did so. She unplugged the device and stepped into the lift. There were only two buttons on the panel inside, so she chose the top one. The door slid closed and the car began moving.

"I am going to eat the rest of that Umberian beef stew when I get back. I don't care if I have to shove a gun in someone's face and then lock myself in the galley, that entire bucket is mine. Then I'm going to wash it down with six pints of that ale, or three pints of stout and a bottle of red."

The elevator arrived at the same time as the noise from the hangar once again ceased. The door opened, revealing a recently-used chamber.

It ran twenty meters long and five meters wide, and the far wall was entirely windows onto the hangar from halfway up to the high ceiling. It was much warmer in this room, and Ari felt a bit better upon entering. A quick glance out of the windows revealed nothing; the Faith had apparently gone to the other end of the hangar. There were two consoles powered-up, so she investigated them. Both had access ports identical to the one for the elevator. She chose one and began working.

Figuring out how to open the hangar doors was easy, but figuring out how to delay the act by a certain amount of time was not. John had made it clear that leaving her behind this time was not an option (a notion with which Ari wholeheartedly agreed), and if she couldn't put the doors on a timer, they'd have to resort to a second and far more dangerous maneuver.

Ari navigated through the computer system without any further insight. She plugged her device back into herself and called the ship.

"Temerity, this is Ghost, over."

"We're glad you're still with us, Ghost," replied John's voice. "I read you three-by-five."

"I am ready to open the hangar doors. I could not complete the secondary objectives."

"Roger. We will rendezvous at your location. Any idea how much force we're going to need on those windows?"

"I'd say start with nine-mil and move up from there. Oh, there is one more thing. There's a human girl in need of rescuing; if she's still willing and able she'll be somewhere down on the hangar floor."

"Did you say a human girl?"

"Roger that, I'll explain when we're safely out of here. Just look for her and pick her up. I'm going to try one more time to put the doors on a timer. I will be back online in five minutes."

"Okay, good luck. I'll speak with you then. Temerity out."

Ari terminated the call on her end, and unplugged the device from herself. She swooned and saw the floor heading for her as her vision faded into a black tunnel.

She found herself in a busy street-side café, under a parasol casting a perfectly round shadow from the noonday sun overhead. She sat at a table, and in front of her was a cup of tea. The patrons around her and the people on the street were speaking in an unknown language, but Ari was more concerned with the person seated across from her. She was having lunch with Seth, not Seth Aldebaran but the creepy, androgynous combination of John, Ray, and Ari as Seth had originally manifested himself. He was wearing that same old smile that didn't fit his face, and looked at Ari calmly.

"So I've gone and passed out, I see," said Ari, grasping the cup of tea.

"This is what you would call the past," said Seth.

"My past? I'm pretty sure I've never been to this place."

"Don't you recognize it?" asked Seth, picking up a crepe.

Ari sipped her tea. "It looks like somewhere in the Middle East. Marrakesh?"

"No, this is the City of the Vulture."

"Oh, I see, this is how the city in the asteroid used to look."

Seth drizzled chocolate syrup on his crepe. "This is the past."

"I get it. So is this a factor of my imagination, or is this image being fed to me somehow?"

"The past and future are concepts of your kind, not mine."

"Well, if this is all in my head, I might as well order some food. I'm absolutely starved."

"Look to the Eagle and the Swan to find us. The Vulture is corrupted and lost."

"I'll keep that in mind, Seth. Do you know how to call for the waiter in this language?"

Ari regained consciousness and found herself looking underneath the computer console. There was a skeleton of a small rodent in the back by the wall, along with about a century of dust. She pulled herself up to a seated position and looked around. She had no idea how long she was out. Her stomach growled angrily at her as she carefully stood up. Out of the corner of her eye she noticed the door to the lift closing and a figure standing next to it.

"Hello again," said Cassie. "Veronice, isn't it?"

Ari let her hand wander to the grip of her sword, and smiled. "Commander. I guess my new password didn't slow you down much."

"Not when there's a manual override lever available."

"Of course. You know, I was just thinking about your city down there. It looks like it used to be quite beautiful."

"More beautiful than you could possibly imagine. And it will be that way again."

Cassie took two steps forward, revealing the pistol in her hand. Ari's fingers tensed around her weapon.

"I don't suppose I could talk you into that duel after all," Ari said.

"I didn't notice that you had the blade before. You are a very curious person, Veronice."

"Did you think I was slicing up your dudes with my razor-sharp wit?"

"I surmised you were using an energy blade. How quaint that you are using the original variety. I imagine the choice has more to do with your invisibility field than your desire for any tradition."

"Right on the first part, but I did once study a sister art to the one that governs this weapon."

"Ah, so you are a traditionalist. I count myself as such as well. In fact, my jealousy for your blade is so palpable I would almost trade you your freedom for it."

"Sorry, but it's not mine to give away. I'm only borrowing it from its master."

A bright light hit the windows of the control room. Ari recognized the source as the Reckless Faith. The light dimmed, and she realized she was looking at the top deck, starboard side. Richter was standing in the open airlock, holding a Phalanx. He waved at Ari and indicated that she should take cover. She dove behind a console as he shot out the window furthest from her, which happened to be the one that Cassie was standing behind. Cassie threw herself to the deck as the plastic-coated glass panes popped out and fell inward with a crash. Ari looked up to see Richter leap out of the airlock and into the control room.

Cassie had apparently lost her sidearm, and immediately closed the distance with Richter. Her speed surprised him, and he drew his weapon back. Cassie grabbed the top of the rifle and easily wrenched it from his grasp. She threw a side kick, which he dodged, and the two squared off against each other. Richter drew his knife, and Cassie responded by drawing an expandable baton. She opened it with a snap and the shaft extended a full meter. Ari staggered over with her sword in hand.

"Thanks for dropping in," Ari said to Richter.

Richter nodded to her, then addressed Cassie. "Are you responsible for our capture?"

"The Vulture found you," replied Cassie. "I merely provided some final guidance."

"I'm sure you have a very interesting story, but I'm not the historian of the ship. I only care about you backing off and letting us go."

"I cannot allow you to escape. I intend to stop you from opening the hangar doors."

"Did you pick up the girl?" Ari asked Richter.

"Yeah, we just found her," he replied. "Open the hangar door. I'll take care of this woman."

"Richter, I don't think I..."

Ari keeled over and passed out on a console. Richter swore to himself. Cassie glanced at the Phalanx on the deck and made a rush for it. Richter snatched up the Tarsus blade and met Cassie in the aisle. He kicked aside the rifle as she brought it around, and swung the sword downward. She blocked the blade with her baton and jumped back.

"Open the doors and I'll spare your life," he said calmly.

"Almost seventy years ago," began Cassie, "I began a lifetime commitment to combat training. I had more than my fair share of practical experience in that area, although the last fifty years have left me with no one to fight. I have kept my skills sharp by training with my soldiers, but I have not had the taste of blood on my lips for far too long. If you think you can intimidate me, you are wrong."

Aldebaran appeared at the airlock, holding a rifle. He surveyed the scene with surprise.

"Hey Richter," he yelled across the gap. "You want a hand with her?"

"Only if I lose," Richter called back, smiling.

Cassie lunged forward and resumed the fight. Richter backpedaled at a measured pace, allowing his movements to flow with her attacks, and began to evaluate her potential. Her offense was formidable, and she displayed no fear of being cut. The Tarsus blade deflected the baton without any indication of snapping, and Richter began to treat it more like a wooden weapon than a steel blade that wouldn't withstand the abuse. Still, he avoided full blocks, preferring to side-step and let the baton slide off the blade. He began retaliating, attempting to guide Cassie's weapon in a direction that would leave her open to a quick, deadly follow-up. He found an opening and went for it, only to receive a hit on his left flank. The muscles in his leg spasmed and he stumbled back, again on the defensive. From the corner of his eye he noticed Ari dragging herself to her feet.

"Open the hangar doors!" he said to her.

If Cassie's attack had been harsh before, now it was vicious. She began to circle around Richter in an attempt to head off Ari, who was clearly having a lot of trouble moving along. In the airlock, Aldebaran looked for a shot, but the room was too crowded to risk it.

Cassie had figured out that Richter was guarding his left arm. She pressed her attack on that side of his body, and tried to lock up her baton and the blade several times. She succeeded, and Richter struggled to hold her back with his right arm.

"You would make an excellent addition to my army," she said through clenched teeth.

"We've already got one war to worry about," grunted Richter. "You're just wasting our time."

Richter felt Cassie's balance shift. He pressed the baton in that direction, freed himself from the entanglement, and drew his blade across her abdomen. Cassie looked in shock at the subsequent evisceration and fell on her face. He flicked the blood from his blade and moved to assist Ari.

"So much for taking her prisoner," panted Ari.

"What's wrong with you?" asked Richter.

"I just pushed myself too hard. I need food and rest. Here, help me get to the computer."

Richter did so. Ari worked for a moment and then looked at him.

"Ready?" he asked.

Ari nodded. "All I have to do is press this character here."

"I'll do it. You get on board first. I don't know how violent the depressurization will be from here."

Richter all but carried her over to the destroyed window. Aldebaran put down his rifle and the two men helped each other get Ari across. Richter handed the sword to Aldebaran, retrieved his Phalanx, and returned to the computer console.

"Clear the way," he shouted to Aldebaran. "I may be in a big hurry."

Pressing the key on the screen, Richter watched as the hangar became alive with yellow warning strobes. A klaxon sounded and a voice announced that the doors would commence opening in ten unknown time units. Richter knelt down beside Cassie's body and searched it. He found a couple of unidentified devices and a power cell for her pistol. He glanced around for the weapon but couldn't see it.

"I'm sorry about this. I think we could have learned a lot about each other."

The door to the lift opened, admitting four canine soldiers into the control room. Richter immediately opened fire, felling two instantly. The other two took cover and returned fire wildly. Aldebaran returned to the airlock and provided cover fire as Richter headed for the gap. When he was ready, Aldebaran ceased fire and backed off. Richter emptied his magazine at the soldiers before turning and sprinting for the window. He leaped onto a computer console and bounded across the gap, landing on his injured arm inside the airlock. Almost blind with pain, he spun around to a seated position, pistol drawn, and resumed firing. A moment later the ship pitched away.

"Tell them to wait!" he screamed at Aldebaran. "Somebody needs to keep those assholes pinned down until the doors open!"

Aldebaran relayed this information to the bridge. Richter stood up and exited the airlock, closing the hatches behind him as the ventral fifty turned the control room into slag. He holstered his pistol and helped Ari to her feet.

"John says the doors are opening," said Aldebaran. "It looks like we're going to make it out."

"Is the girl all right?" whispered Ari.

"She's fine, she's down in the galley. The poor thing was ravenous."

"She'd better make room for me down there. I'm hungry enough for Residerian cuisine."

Aldebaran smiled. "Let's not go crazy."

Thirty minutes later, the crew of the Faith minus Ari and John were gathered in the conference room. They were gathered in a semi-circle around Miriam. The young woman was freshly showered and wearing clean sweat pants and a gray Suffolk University sweat shirt two sizes too large for her. She was staring out of the window into space, a half-smile on her face, cradling a steaming cup of tea in her hands. She and Ari had finished a meal together; the latter woman had immediately returned to her quarters to pass out. Christie had been hosting the girl, and had heard some of her story already, but she'd brought her to the conference room to bring the rest of the crew up to speed.

John entered from the bridge, and moved over to the others.

“We're on course for Beta Sagittae, back on our original schedule to rendezvous with Captain Calico,” he said.

“Let's hope he hasn't run into as much trouble,” replied Dana. "John, now that we're clear of that wretched place, I thought you should know something. We lost Talvan as a friend and brother-in-arms, but we also may have lost the ability to weaponize the Vengeance virus. Professor Talvan was the only one who knew how to cultivate it."

"We still have our sample, right?"

"Yes, but without further research or aid, it's not enough to infect even a single Zendra. We also left to investigate the wormhole before he and the other scientists were able to determine a reason for the allergic reaction in some people. Even if we can find a way to cultivate the virus, it should only be used as a last resort. Who knows how it will effect other races?"

“I get your point. I suppose we're lucky none of our people are allergic to it. Anyway, maybe someone on Calico's crew can help continue the research." John gestured at Miriam. "How is our guest doing?”

“She's doing very well,” began Christie. “It sounds like she's been through hell, though.

Only time will tell how well she'll adapt. Miriam, are you ready to meet the rest of the crew?"

Miriam turned around and nodded. "Yes, mum."

"Good. You already know Ari and I. This is John Scherer, commander of this ship. We also have Ray Bailey, Dana Andrews, Chance Richter, and Seth Aldebaran. With the exception of Seth, we're all from the United States."

"Where are you from?" Miriam asked Aldebaran.

"I'm from a planet called Umber back in the Large Magellanic Cloud."

"I guess there's no denying it, then. We really are in outer space. Very well, I'm Miriam Colchester from Romanby, Yorkshire, England. I'm seventeen years old."

"How did you end up on the asteroid?" asked John.

"I wasn't sure at first, but I came to realize that my parents and I were abducted. I don't know if they were murdered, or didn't survive the trip."

"Do you know who abducted you?"

"According to Commander Cassiopeia, it was done by a group called the Kira'To."

"The Kira'To?" asked Aldebaran. "Are you sure?"

"Completely, sir."

"Did you get a look at them?"

"I never saw anyone. Not before the abduction, and when I woke up on the asteroid, the only ones there were Cassie and her dog soldiers. She told me a little bit about the Kira'To, but I was on the run from her and I didn't have many opportunities to chat."

"What do you know about them, Aldebaran?" asked John.

"The Kira'To are a legendary race of extremely advanced beings," replied Aldebaran.

"They could be nothing more than a myth or fairy tale. The stories go that they involve themselves in the affairs of other space-faring races in a very limited fashion, but toward a greater purpose that may or may not benefit the rest of the civilized galaxy. I've never met anyone who claimed to have dealt with them, much less ever seen one."

"My parents were ufologists," said Miriam. "I thought they were stark raving mad, and I only put up with them because they were completely normal in all other areas of our lives and I loved them. However, they had become even odder in the weeks before our abduction. My father claimed to have contact with one or more alien beings, and my mother began to worry that they were in over their heads. On the last night that I remember from Earth, we were awakened in the middle of the night to a bright light in the sky. My parents went out to investigate, and I ran after them when I realized the light wasn't normal. The next thing I knew, the three of us were in a room on the asteroid. They were already... they... I don't know why."

"What was the date of your last day on Earth, Miriam?" asked Dana.

"December 29th , 2028."

"Are the Kira'To capable of transporting people such a vast distance so quickly?" John asked Aldebaran.

"If the rumors are true," replied Aldebaran, "then yes."

"Why, what's the date now?" asked Miriam.

"January 8th," said Dana. "Adjusting for our travel time, 2029."

"What happened after you arrived on the asteroid?" asked John.

Miriam said, "I began exploring and it wasn't long before I ran into those soldiers. They tried to capture me so I ran away. I began to learn the layout of the structure and found a relatively safe place to hide out. I cached supplies and stole what I could from the soldiers. I stayed away from the city, though. That place gave me the creeps. One day I ran into Commander Cassiopeia. She tried to get me to join them, but I refused. I kept to myself and just tried to survive. Then, you arrived. I decided to help Veronice since it seemed like the only way I would ever get out of there."

"You seem remarkably calm for all that you've been through," said Christie.

"You think so? My hands only stopped trembling a short time ago."

John asked, "Were you able to learn anything about the history of the asteroid, or what its purpose was?"

"It seemed obvious that there used to be a large population there. Cassie spoke of trying to return the asteroid to its former greatness. I found children's books here and there, and although I couldn't read them, the pictures told a story. The best I could piece together from them, the society that used to thrive in the asteroid city broke into two factions and eventually wiped each other out. I got the impression that Cassie was a former citizen herself due to the similarities of her clothing to that depicted in the books. Perhaps she's the last survivor of the conflict. I have no idea where the dog soldiers came from, however. I think Cassie might have created them genetically from an original canine source."

"It's a shame we couldn't have met in peace," said Christie. "Everything about this situation is fascinating."

"Was there anything else?" asked John.

Miriam thought for a moment. "Something that Cassie told me stuck in my mind, because it gave me nightmares every bloody night since I met her. She said that the asteroid, which she called the Vulture, was one of three originally. She referred also to the Eagle and the Swan, and called the three... what was it... the Stymphalian raptors, I think."

"The Stymphalian raptors, seriously?" Christie asked, mystified.

"I think so, yes."

"Does that mean something to you?" John said to Christie.

"Hell yes. The Stymphalian raptors were mythical birds from one of the twelve trials of Hercules. They were a plague on the land; something having to do with toxic offal, I believe. In astronomy, they're represented by Aquila, the eagle, Cygnus, the swan, and the constellation Lyra, which was known as a vulture to the Greeks."

"Why would Greek mythology mean anything to an alien woman on an asteroid five hundred light years from Earth?"

"Probably the same reason why she's named Cassiopeia," said Miriam. "She told me that I wasn't the first human brought to the asteroid by the Kira'To. Perhaps, at a time in the past, someone was brought who had knowledge of mythology and astronomical figures. Cassie struck me as a loony, she could have heard these stories and integrated them into her own psychosis."

"You're pretty smart for a kid," said Ray.

"Smart parents, smart kid. So, what about you? How did a bunch of Yanks end up with a ship like this?"

"Blind luck, divine intervention, take your pick," replied John.

"It's a long story," added Christie. "Fortunately we have some travel time ahead of us before the next stage in our mission. I'd be happy to fill you in on circumstances past and present after you've gotten some rest."

"There's something you should know," said John. "We don't have plans to return to Earth anytime soon. You are free to leave the ship when we get where we're going, and make your own way in the galaxy, but this ship is the safest place for you right now. There aren't any other humans operating out here, and without strong combat skills and a disposable income you won't get far anyway."

"Everyone I truly cared about died on that asteroid," Miriam said sadly, and sat at the conference table. "I'm not in a terrible rush to get back to Earth. I'm only afraid that I won't have anything to offer you here. I'd hate to just exist to consume your resources."

Christie said, "Miriam, we are running real short on sympathetic allies out here. If you have the capacity to learn, we can teach you everything you know to be an asset to this crew. You don't need to be big and strong to work the weapons systems, and if you demonstrate aptitude for flying, John and Dana can get you trained up on the stick. Did you have any specific schooling back home?"

"Yes, I was taking college preparatory courses in physics and mathematics."

"That's good, Miriam," said John. "Don't worry. We'll try our best to make this place feel like home. And when we're done with this mission, perhaps we can start researching the Kira'To and these asteroids and find out why you were taken."

"Blind luck or divine intervention," said Miriam softly, sipping at her tea.

14.

Major Pyramis was roused from a sound sleep by an annoying beeping noise. In his groggy state he couldn't immediately identify it, and only after a painful burst of adrenaline hit his heart did he wake fully. Pressing a key in the dark silenced the beep, but replaced it with a voice.

"Sir, this is Lieutenant Brentage," said the voice. "Are you awake?"

"Go ahead, Lieutenant."

"Sir, it's zero-six-thirty."

"I don't recall asking for a wake-up call, Brentage."

"Excuse me, sir, but your meeting with the Freedmen prime minister is in fifteen minutes."

Pyramis sat upright in his bed and turned on his lights. His quarters aboard Freedmen station were smaller than on Hayaku station, but they were still larger than those used by most of his new charges. In either case, freshening up in a hurry would be slightly hindered by the cramped conditions, so he got started right away.

"I thought this was going to be a transmitted call," he said around a toothbrush.

"That's what I meant, sir. Do you want to take the call in your quarters?"

"No, I'll be up in ten minutes. Pyramis out."

Once he'd finished cleaning his face, Pyramis put on a fresh set of underwear and a yet-untouched flight suit (replete with packing creases). The sewing shop had already prepared his name tapes, but he needed to add his new rank himself. He then opened his tiny closet and retrieved the jacket portion of his formal dress uniform, and replaced the rank on it as well. He made a pass over it with a lint brush, then pulled on his boots.

Pyramis exited his quarters, jacket in hand. To conserve power, which was not an issue on Hayaku station, the gravity in the corridors and cargo areas here were set to 1/6th that of normal. He bounded along vigorously, almost hitting his head on the ceiling, unused to the change. It was a quick trip to the double-tiered command center, which was relatively small but still allowed twelve people to operate in comfort. Lieutenant Brentage and several other officers greeted Pyramis formally upon his arrival, and he returned the salute.

"Status report," he said.

"Sir," began the lieutenant, "all systems are operating within established parameters. The squadron is on one hour standby, and all ships report ready to fuel."

"Excellent."

"We've also got the prime minister on the line."

"She's early, but that's fine. I'll take her on monitor eight."

Pyramis put his dress jacket on, which entirely concealed his flight suit from the waist up. He then sat down at one of the rear stations and pulled himself up to the console. Brentage followed him over and spoke to him in a low voice.

"Sir, I hope you don't mind me asking, but did you read the mission summary last night?"

"Yes, I did. Don't worry, I won't let the prime minister freak me out."

Brentage nodded and backed off. Pyramis put on his best manufactured smile, and opened the channel. On the screen in front of him was the image of a thin Hayakuvian woman in her sixties, wearing a flower pattern sun dress and a large, floppy hat. She was smiling, and appeared to be sitting cross-legged on the floor in an unbelievably fecund greenhouse.

"Good day, Prime Minister Calico, I am Major Rafe Pyramis of the Hayakuvian space fleet. I am the new commander of this station."

"Please, Rafe, call me Mother Calico," came the measured response.

"As you wish ma'am. Thank you for agreeing to this call. I would like to formalize our professional relationship, and renew my government's commitment to providing our Freedmen brothers with unconditional protect…"

"Rafe, I understand the need for you to be formal," interrupted the prime minister, "but you should know that we are much more open down here. Many of the men on your station have been happy to take leave under our auspices, and it would be foolish to deny the same to yourself."

"I also understand that you have a vote coming up soon."

"We can change the subject if you wish. Yes, we have a vote coming up. As you are probably aware, the last vote failed by a slim margin. This time, the measure is expected to pass."

"Then our relationship may be very short. I hope that it is a good one, regardless of the duration."

"Indeed. Again, if you and your men need anything, don't hesitate to ask."

"I won't, ma'am. Have a good day."

"Bye bye."

The screen went blank, and Pyramis stood up. He removed his jacket and joined the lieutenant at the command station.

"I see the summary didn't quite prepare you for that, sir," Brentage said.

"She's a trip, no doubt about it," replied Pyramis. "Now, do we have anybody on liberty down there?"

"A couple."

"Recall them. There are to be no further trips to the surface without my express permission. We are too close to a potentially bad situation to remain quite so friendly with the colonists."

"Understood, sir," replied Brentage, then more softly, "I didn't know things were heating up, sir."

"They haven't. It is a formal process to submit a declaration of independence to the central government, but despite 'Mother' Calico's dulcet tones, we can't be sure they will be patient enough to let the process take place."

"If we had just sent spies, we would know if they're just bluffing."

"And if they are, and the spies are discovered, then we look like overbearing fools. We need to let this play out as it will, LT, and there's little point in second-guessing ourselves, especially now."

A young ensign suddenly turned around, and announced, "Sir, we've detected an unknown vessel passing our sensor net."

"Distance?" asked Pyramis, mildly annoyed at the interruption.

"Five AU and closing. Speed is one c. They will be in visual range in forty minutes."

Pyramis sighed. According to his mission briefing, many of Freedmen's ships refused to broadcast an SRC signal, and could only be detected coming and going by the station's remote sensor net, which consisted of one hundred interlinked buoys.

"Send a hail, let's see if they actually care to respond."

"Aye, sir."

To the audible shock of those present, an insectoid face appeared on the main monitor. It had a long, teardrop-shaped green head with large eyes on either side, and a humanoid mouth. It spoke Residerian, according to the computer, a language familiar only to Pyramis.

"This is Lieutenant Commander Valichi of the Zendreen. We come in peace to request mutually beneficial trade with your world."

"What in the holy hell are the Zendreen doing over here in the core galaxy?" asked Pyramis, further surprising his crew.

"I might ask the same thing of you, Umberian. Our information told us that this star system is under the control of Hayaku."

"I am Major Pyramis of the Hayakuvian space fleet. I do not represent Umber or its interests."

"Very well, then I hope you will listen to reason. Major, my people have given up control of Umber and have abandoned the Tarantula Nebula. We have decided to colonize another planet, peacefully. Our information indicated that UAS 1026 contained a suitable uninhabited world, but our scans have just proved that data to be incorrect. We will continue our search for a new home, but we would like to trade for supplies and information first."

"How many are you, Commander?"

"We are not a threat to you, Major."

Pyramis muted the audio as Brentage said, "I'm still only reading one ship."

"Get the squadron ready to launch," said Pyramis, then reopened the channel. "Commander, I will pass your request on to my superiors. You may proceed to within ten thousand kilometers of this station and hold there."

"Understood. We will await your response. Valichi out."

The image disappeared. Pyramis stood up and turned to Brentage.

"There is more going on here than the Zendreen are letting on," he said, "you can be sure of that."

"You'll have to excuse me, sir," began Brentage, "but I don't know anything about the relationship between your people and the Zendreen."

"First of all, I'm as much of a Hayakuvian as you are. Second, all you need to know is that the Zendreen are ruthless war mongers. There is no way they are simply here to trade for supplies. I'll call Hayaku from my office."

The commander's office was one deck below, accessible by a short staircase directly behind the command center. Brentage followed Pyramis to the top of the stairs.

"Sir, I hope I'm not overstepping my bounds, but if you are only concerned with the best interests of Hayaku, then you need to be open to the possibility of neutral, if not friendly, relations with this race."

Pyramis stopped descending the steps, and turned around. "I know, LT. That doesn't mean I have to like it."

On the bridge of the Faith, most of the crew was preparing for the ship's arrival near the colony of Freedmen. Beta Sagittae, up until recently distinguishable only as the brightest star ahead, suddenly began to grow in apparent size. Miriam sat near the rear of the bridge, watching the others with keen interest.

"Drop out of superlume on my mark," Christie was saying. "Three, two, one, mark."

John flipped the appropriate switch on his control panel. Beta Sagittae was directly in front of them, taking up one degree of the field of view.

"How far out are we?" he asked.

"It's impossible to know without the SRC active," replied Dana.

"Finding anything in this solar system is going to be a pain in the ass without the SRC," said John.

"That's an understatement," said Christie. "We don't even know if we're on the ecliptic plane. We could head for the star at sub-light speed and start searching from there, but such a search would take forever. The chances of us running into a planet or another ship at random are, well, astronomical. I never realized just how much telemetry we were receiving from the SRC. We really took it for granted until now."

"What about radio transmissions?"

"There's nothing being broadcast on any frequency our original receiver can detect."

"We could always turn on the VLF transceiver and wait for Calico to find us," offered Dana.

"I don't see any other choice right now," said John. "Go ahead. I might also suggest that we get as close to the star as we can. Hopefully Calico will look for us there first. Either that or somebody from Freedmen will notice us and come by." John flipped on the intercom. "Ray, this is John. Are you and the others still playing poker?"

"Yes," said Ray's voice.

"Either get up here or monitor the bridge from the galley."

"We'll be up after this round."

"Far be it from me to interrupt your game," replied John, laughing. "Take your time."

"I have a suggestion, if you don't feel like waiting for Calico," said Aldebaran, looking over his shoulder from a console.

"By all means."

"It shouldn't be too hard to find a random asteroid. If the technology of the Freedmen colonists is anywhere near the rest of the civilized galaxy, and I use the term loosely, then they'll be able to detect our energy weapons from up to five astronomical units away."

"Five AU from the star is well within the likely radius of a habitable planet," said Christie.

John nodded. "So we approach the star, find an asteroid, and blow the hell out of it?"

"Chip away at the surface," replied Aldebaran, "but yes."

"It sounds like fun, but I'm rather fed up with asteroids right now. I think our best bet is to approach the star and wait for Calico to find us. Until then, we've got to keep trying to reboot the SRC. It drives me crazy to wait while the Zendreen fleet gets to proceed with their plan, whatever it may be, but I don't think brash action is the answer right now."

"I agree. As far as the SRC is concerned, I've been observing Christie and Dana's efforts to get it working. While I don't have anything to add from a technical perspective, I did want to mention that something about the driver files doesn't feel right to me."

"Is it anything you can verbalize?" asked Christie.

"I know it sounds strange, but I think there are too many files. Something in the back of my mind is telling me that there should be ten drivers, not eleven."

"You used to be the computer," said Dana. "It doesn't sound strange at all."

"I never noted the number of drivers before the problem arose," said Christie. "In fact, I don't know how many drivers any of our systems have, come to think of it. If there is an extra driver file in this case, and it's either a duplicate or a corrupted copy, then it would make sense to delete it and reboot the program. Aldebaran, is there any chance you could identify which driver doesn't belong?"

"I'll study them and see," he replied.

"Once we get this problem under control," John said to Christie and Dana, "I want you to take a snapshot of the state of our computer system and create a backup image."

"That will require a new program created from the ground up," replied Dana. "The backup program built into the OS can't accommodate the Umberian components. Writing code isn't my strong suit… Christie?"

"I can handle it," said Ari from the back of the bridge. "That's one advantage I still have over you two. No offense."

"None taken. You wrote the code for communicating with the orb in the first place, I trust you won't have a problem with this."

"Good," said John. "I know better than to ask you how long it will take, but please get right on it.

"It's this one," Aldebaran said, looking at his monitor. "Lqr14m02. There should be lqr14m01, but not 02."

"Are you sure?" asked Ari, approaching his station.

"Almost. Still, there shouldn't be any harm in renaming it and rebooting the program. In fact, if I'm right about the extra driver, we can apply that strategy to all ten of them."

"Give it a shot," said John.

It did not take Aldebaran long to rename the file and access the SRC component. Immediately, the system resumed functioning. Everyone on the bridge expressed some form of relief or pleasure.

"Good call, Aldebaran," said Dana.

"I'm scanning the solar system now," said Christie. "I'm receiving astronomical telemetry, as well as an IFF signal from the Hayakuvian station orbiting Freedmen. There's no sign of the Almagest or any Zendreen ships, but we're still on the edge of the solar system, at about 40 AU."

"I'm calling up a diagram of the system," said Dana.

An overhead view of the solar system appeared on the heads-up display. Christie described it to the others.

"This is Beta Sagittae's system. We are at Lat 40 relative to the star's equator, which gives us a nice view of the ecliptic plane. Let me render the orbital paths… there we go. The planets are as follows, outermost first. Beta Sagittae IV is a gas giant at 17 AU, with two major moons and thirteen minor satellites. B Sag III is a larger gas giant at 6.1 AU, with three major moons and almost two dozen minor satellites. B Sag II, Freedmen, is a rocky world at 1.3 AU. There are no natural satellites, only the Hayakuvian station. B Sag I is a rocky world at 0.25 AU, and is very similar to Mercury. The star itself is an unremarkable G-type."

"Call Calico on the encrypted channel," said John.

"Roger," said Aldebaran.

A moment later, Captain Calico's image appeared on John's monitor. The 'Gest's bridge and some of its crew were visible in the background.

"Hello, Commander Scherer," he said. "I see you have resolved some of your technical problems."

"After a rather annoying distraction back near Alpha. I'll tell you about it later. What's your location, Captain?"

"My ship and I are currently headed to Hayaku. I believe you'll find the Zendreen fleet somewhere in the Freedmen system."

"What happened? Why did you break off pursuit of the fleet?"

"The fleet is in no condition to go back into deep space, Scherer. Freedmen is their only possible destination. I am on my way to appeal for help directly to the Hayakuvian central government."

"All right, Captain. I'll defer to your judgment on this one. We just arrived at Beta Sagittae, so we'll scout out the location and condition of the fleet, and wait for your word."

"If you're not content to just sit around for another day and a half, I might suggest that you proceed to Freedmen and see if you can find out the current state of the colonial independence movement. It may have some bearing on Hayaku's willingness to help us oppose the Zendreen."

"Doing so might steal your thunder, Calico. Not that I'm unwilling to make first contact here."

"I meant talking to the colony directly. I have an older encrypted frequency that they might still be monitoring. If your invisibility shield is functioning, you can try contacting them without the Hayakuvians knowing you're there."

"It's worth checking out."

"Fine. I'm sending you the frequency information now. Don't mention me unless absolutely necessary."

"Aren't they going to be curious as to how we obtained the encrypted frequency?"

"Tell them you once worked with Janish Revelnik. He's a former colonist who left around the same time I did, and ended up as a shuffler in the Nursery of the Gods."

"Janish Revelnik. Got it. Good luck with the central government, Captain. We'll wait for your report."

"Calico out."

John turned his chair around and looked at his crew.

"Does anyone else find Calico's actions a bit fishy?" he asked.

Christie hurriedly scribbled something on her scrap paper as the others looked at each other.

"You're not upset that he changed his course without checking with you first, are you?" asked Ari. "We were out of contact for awhile, he has every right to make a change if it's best for the mission."

Christie thrust her paper toward John, who accepted it absent-mindedly.

"I don't know," he replied. "There was just something odd about his demeanor."

John glanced down at the paper. In addition to several complex equations that were already present, Christie had scrawled, "Are you sure you want to discuss Calico's motives in front of Ari?"

"I don't think now is a good time to second-guess Calico's commitment to this mission," said Aldebaran. "I would simply assume that he is operating off of the best course of action as he sees it."

"Yeah, I'm probably just being paranoid. Call it left-over angst from our dealings with the SUF."

"Hey guys," said Dana, "I'm detecting several ships broadcasting Hayakuvian IFF signals departing the station. They're headed toward the third planet."

"I'd bet dollars to doughnuts they're on their way to intercept the Zendreen fleet. I'll take us in for a closer look."

John put the piece of paper in his pocket, swiveled his chair around, and resumed piloting the ship. He brought the ship up to 500 c, crossing the distance in just over thirty seconds.

"There they are," said Christie, punching the image up on the HUD.

The Zendreen fleet was in orbit around Beta Sagittae III, a pale gray-orange sphere with a thin ring. The ring illustrated a planetary axis of about 20 degrees. Christie zoomed the image into an area next to the ring, and the larger Zendreen ships could be seen.

"I count fifteen ships," began Dana, "including the battleship and four remaining cruisers. Their operational status is unknown."

"I wonder where the other four ships got to," said John.

"Here come the Hayakuvians."

John nodded. "Let's listen in on the conversation."

"Roger," said Aldebaran.

The Hayakuvians were piloting several single-seat fighters. They executed a gravity whip around the planet, and settled into a far orbit. A moment later a transmission was received, and translated into English.

"This is Lieutenant Yavil with the Hayakuvian Space Fleet. We are here to observe you. We do not intend any hostile action. Your request for trade has been forwarded to our central government. Please be patient as we await a response. Thank you for your cooperation."

A few seconds later it seemed obvious that the Zendreen weren't going to reply.

"I guess we missed an earlier conversation," said Aldebaran.

"Apparently," replied John. "So they're trying to trade with Hayaku, or at least with Freedmen."

"I'm sure that the squadron of fighters is analyzing the fleet as we speak. If they don't deem the Zendreen a threat, I don't see why they wouldn't open up peaceful trade with them."

"Then we need to convince them that they'll become a threat eventually."

"Whether it's true or not?" asked Christie.

"Plot me a course to Freedmen. I want to end up on the opposite side of the planet from the station."

"Excuse me? Answer my question, John."

John sighed. "Yes, whether it's true or not. As Professor Talvan said, they could become a threat at any point in the future."

"Can I talk to you alone for a minute?"

"Fine. Dana, please plot the course and take over for me. Put us in geosynchronous orbit when we arrive."

"Roger," said Dana.

John and Christie stood up and entered the conference room.

"I want to be clear about what we're talking about here, John," Christie said immediately.

"We need to convince the Hayakuvians and/or the colonists to reject the Zendreen, and hopefully to attack them."

"If they don't deem the fleet to be a threat, just how do you plan on convincing them?"

"I'm not sure. Hopefully Calico will have a better idea. If not, maybe we can draw the Hayakuvians into a conflict by other means."

"That's what I was worried about. John, don't you think that's crossing the line?"

"What line? Our goal is to prevent the Zendreen from reaching Earth, isn't it?"

"Not at the cost of Hayakuvian blood. Not if we have to use some sort of subterfuge to get them to fight."

"I can't believe you're equating Hayakuvian life with human life."

"And I can't believe you aren't!" snapped Christie. "We don't have the right to weigh one life over another!"

"Are you seriously suggesting that we let the Zendreen fleet reach Earth?"

"No, I'm saying we need to find willing allies. We need to show the Zendreen that several peaceful planets are united against hostile action, and will respond with appropriate force if necessary. Without knowing the Zendreen's ultimate intentions, anything else would be unethical."

"And if we're wrong, Earthlings wake up one morning to Zendreen orbital bombardment. Look, I didn't mean that I wanted Hayakuvians to die, but we're talking about a few Hayakuvian casualties versus tens, if not hundreds of thousands of humans. Maybe even the entire planet, we don't know what they're capable of doing if they're desperate."

"I will not accept that trade-off. If we want to retain the moral high ground, we have to find a way to stop them without a manufactured war."

John sighed. "I'm sorry, Christie. I'm just really getting pissed off at these frigging bugs."

"Just now? Come on, let's see what the colonists have to say. Hopefully we'll get some good news."

Ten minutes later, Dana had placed the Faith in orbit around Freedmen per John's instructions. The planet appeared to almost completely covered in clouds, including three striated bands that circled the entire planet at the equator and both tropics. Breaks between these bands revealed either blue-green oceans or brown-gray land mass. Freedmen station was orbiting at 30 degrees latitude, so the Faith was parked at negative 30. Dana had made her distance ten thousand kilometers, and the ship happened to be along the circadian threshold. A few artificial satellites twinkled in the setting sun. On the bridge, Dana locked down the flight controls and stood up. John took her place.

"Are you ready to transmit?" he asked of Aldebaran.

"Just say the word," the Umberian replied.

"Open the channel. Attention Freedmen colony. This is Commander Scherer of the independent trade vessel Reckless Faith. We seek mutually beneficial trade in goods and information. Please reply."

A moment later, the visage of an older Hayakuvian woman appeared on John's monitor. She looked rather plain except for the garland of fresh flowers in her hair.

"Welcome, stranger," she said, the translator kicking in a split-second later. "I am Mother Calico, prime minister of this colony. We are always open to new trade alliances; however, I must inquire why you chose to contact us on this frequency instead of opening a channel with the large, impressive station orbiting our world."

"Gossip in this sector implies that Freedmen colony has asserted its independence over the Hayakuvian government. We believe that there is more profit to be had in dealing with you, as we have little to offer a larger civilization like Hayaku."

The prime minister's smile waned slightly. "I see. The rumors are correct, Commander. Freedmen has introduced congressional articles of independence against the Hayakuvian government, not two days ago in fact. However, Hayaku has approved the secession, but not the particulars of such matters as revenue and defense. We are willing to trade with you, but be aware that if Hayaku becomes aware of the relationship, they may demand taxes from you to which they believe they are entitled. Therefore, please be aware that the climate is unsettled in the vicinity of the Great Arrow and plan accordingly."

John nodded. "Understood. Shall we meet on the surface to discuss trade?"

"It would be my honor to host you, Commander. If today is good for you, I happen to have some spare time in an hour."

"That definitely works for me," replied John.

"I am sending you coordinates for a rendezvous. Commander, please do not be alarmed by the anti-matter cannons that you will find near the landing area. They are for our own protection. Also, we would appreciate it if you left any projectile or energy weapons aboard your craft during our meeting."

"Naturally, Prime Minister. We'll see you..."

"Please, child, call me Mother Calico."

"Okay, Mother Calico, we will see you in one hour. Scherer out."

The transmission terminated. John turned around and looked at his friends.

"Well that was decidedly odd," said Dana.

"I wonder if she's any relation to Captain Calico," said Aldebaran.

"For all we know," replied John, "Calico is the Hayakuvian equivalent of Smith or Jones."

"And yet, Calico asked us not to mention his name."

"There are any number of very good reasons for that," said Christie. "We don't know much about his history in this part of the galaxy."

"Did you notice that she called this area the Great Arrow?" asked Dana.

"Yes. More evidence of an earlier human presence in this area, perhaps?"

"The galactic core is on the other side of the arrow, it could have been named by visitors from that direction," said John. "Now then, who's coming with me?"

"I'll go," said Aldebaran.

"Me, too," added Christie.

"Hell, count me in," said Dana.

"I'd like to keep the contingent small," said John. "Three people should be fine. If you guys need to flip a coin or something, be my guest. I'm exercising commander's fiat, however, so I'm definitely going. Honestly, if we're not going to be able to carry, I'd like my best hand-to-hand fighters with me. With Richter injured, that leaves Aldebaran and Ari."

Dana laughed. "Wouldn't your best diplomats be better?"

"Behind every good diplomat are several mean, ruthless bastards."

15.

In his quarters aboard Freedmen station, Major Pyramis stared in shock at his computer console. He had just received a set of orders, encryption level five, for his eyes only. He was tempted to execute a back-trace, or at least contact Commander Ballard to confirm that the order was legitimate. He read the words again carefully, hoping that the message would somehow change the second time through.

HAYAKU SPACE COMMAND/ OFFICIAL ORDERS/ ENC-KEY-5B

MAJOR RAFE PYRAMIS, COMMANDER, FREEDMEN STATION

YOU ARE HEREBY ORDERED TO OBSERVE THE ZENDREEN FLEET AND GUARD FREEDMEN STATION ONLY. DIRECT ACTION AGAINST ANY ZENDREEN SHIP IS FORBIDDEN EXCEPT FOR DEFENSE OF THE STATION. NO ACTION IN DEFENSE OF THE COLONY OR ANY COLONIAL VESSEL IS AUTHORIZED. YOU ARE ORDERED TO WITHDRAW YOUR SQUADRON TO THE STATION AND AWAIT FURTHER ORDERS. AGAIN, NO DIRECT ACTION AGAINST ANY ZENDREEN VESSEL IS AUTHORIZED.

MAJOR GENERAL THADDEUS FELMIO

COMMANDER BREIT BALLARD

As the initial shock wore off, Pyramis thought better of questioning the orders. There was no evidence that the order might be a mistake, and encryption level five was foolproof. Any reply to his query would take two hours because of the distance back to Hayaku, so there was no point in a hasty missive.

Pyramis exited his quarters and headed to the command center. He had to disseminate the order to his lieutenants, but he didn't know them well enough yet to solicit their opinions about the situation. He sighed, and wished he still had Mert's council available. He paused outside the hatch to the command center, and leaned against the bulkhead to think. Far from feeling slighted for being left out of the loop, Pyramis was only concerned with the heart of the reason behind his new orders. The central government had agreed to sanction Freedmen's Articles of Independence, so it could simply involve a trade agreement between the colony and the Zendreen. To intervene now, whether it be for the collection of taxes or for any other reason, would be inappropriate. From a diplomatic perspective, if the newly-liberated colony needed help, they would have to ask first.

Pyramis entered the command center. He hoped that he was right, since the implications of a more complicated explanation would be both infuriating and horrifying. Even if it was as simple as a trade agreement, he feared that the Zendreen would reveal themselves to be the same belligerent force they had been back on his home planet. There was far too much trust being thrown around at this stage for his liking.

"Report," he said.

Lieutenant Brentage stood up. "Sir, the squadron has finished scanning the Zendreen fleet."

"Good. Recall the squadron, Lieutenant, and proceed with your briefing."

"Yes, sir. The Zendreen fleet consists of fourteen vessels. There is one fully-armed battleship and four cruisers in varying conditions of readiness. All five of these ships are capable of carrying dozens of fighters but we have been unable to determine if any fighters are actually present. The remaining nine vessels are support ships of various types, and run the gamut from well-armed to completely unarmed."

"Threat assessment?"

"Even without any fighters, the fleet could easily destroy our squadron and this station. I would highly recommend that we request at least one battle group to be dispatched here immediately, just in case they're planning on attacking us."

"Lieutenant, it is command's firm belief that the Zendreen do not intend any hostile action against this station. Therefore, no reinforcements will be forthcoming."

"Let me guess," began Brentage, "since Freedmen colony has achieved its independence, they're going to let them deal with the Zendreen."

Pyramis nodded. "Correct."

"That sounds like a rather naked attempt on our part to get the colony to reveal its defensive strength. Since I doubt they stand a chance against the Zendreen without our help, I bet command is hoping that they'll come crawling back, hat in hand, begging for our fleet to intervene."

"Lieutenant, you would do well to curtail too much speculation. I am more inclined to believe that the colony has opened up trade relations with our new visitors, and Hayaku is remaining neutral out of deference to the democratic process."

"I hope you are right, sir."

"I'd better be. We have been forbidden to take action against any Zendreen vessel unless for self-defense. Now you know as much as I do, so please don't ask me for more information."

Brentage looked surprised. "As you say, sir."

Pyramis sat in his chair and grumbled to himself. As if the circumstances of his first command weren't bad enough, now something interesting was happening and command had tied his hands. A moment later he realized there was one more thing he could do without violating his new orders.

"Lieutenant Brentage, open a channel to the colony. I want to talk to the prime minister."

"Aye, sir."

Brentage motioned to the communications officer, who did as the major had instructed. After almost a minute the young ensign spoke.

"Sir, we've received a reply from the surface, text only. It says, 'Call back in an hour, child.' Sir."

Pyramis sighed. "Fine, let the old bat come down from whatever she and her house are smoking. If they're not aware of the threat from the Zendreen, they're going to be in for a sobering surprise."

In the galley aboard the Almagest, Captain Calico and most of his crew were enjoying a hot meal together. The two absentees were Bugani, who was working in his laboratory, and Railyn, who was minding the bridge. The mood at the table was lively, although Megumi seemed preoccupied with something. The others were enjoying the last of the fresh vegetables they'd picked up on Misrere Prime, as well as something savory that Knoal had thrown together.

The captain was reserved, as usual, but allowed himself to joke around a little with his crew. He was relieved that the raid on the Zendreen medical vessel had been successful, and that nobody had gotten themselves shot.

"Everyone, we're arriving at Hayaku in a few minutes," he announced. "Take your time finishing up dinner, if I need anyone sooner I will call you. See you on the bridge."

"Good luck with the Hayakidians," said Gueyr.

Calico stood up and headed for the lift. He had neglected to leave himself enough time to talk to Bugani; he wanted to check on his progress in the lab. They may not have had the best equipment, but Bugani had insisted it was up to the task. However, Calico's curiosity had no bearing on the speed of the research, so he had to be patient.

"Hello, Cap," said Railyn as his superior arrived on the bridge. "You have good timing. We've dropped out of superlume and we're approaching Hayaku Prime."

"Sometimes good timing can compensate for a lack of command ability, my friend."

Railyn turned around, and said, "Huh?"

"Just kidding. Now then, if I remember Hayaku right, we should be receiving a hail from the fleet any second now."

A light began flashing on Railyn's console.

"Timing again?"

"I'll take it in my room."

Calico entered his private office. He poured himself a cold cup of yutha, sat down, and turned on his monitor. He was greeted by a Hayakuvian military officer, apparently stationed planetside. The man was middle-aged, and looked bored.

"Welcome to the Hayakuvian system," the officer said. "Since you are not broadcasting an

IFF signal, please state your… oh, you're one of us."

"I was born on Hayaku, yes," replied Calico. "I'm Captain Farril Calico of the freelance vessel Almagest. I'm here to warn you about a possible threat from a race of insectoids who call themselves the Zendreen."

"You're here for altruistic reasons? Why do I think this conversation will end with you asking us for money?"

"Oh, I'm not going to argue that I'm here to make a profit. However, I believe the best chance of that is to start with the truth, and the truth is that there's an entire fleet of belligerent aliens headed toward the Freedmen colony."

The image on the monitor suddenly changed to a different man. The replacement was of much higher rank, and was framed by a window into space behind his desk.

"Captain Calico, this is Major General Felmio of the Hayaku Space Fleet."

Calico sat up straight. "What happened to the other guy?"

"You are dealing with me now. Mister Calico, our records show you served in our military forty-five years ago."

"I did my two years, like every young man."

"Time has been kind to you, it would seem."

"I've spent more than my fair share of space travel in ultralume. Sir, this isn't about me. I'm here to warn you about a threat to the colony on Freedmen."

"Our records show that you were also married to Anya Calico, is that correct?"

Realizing he was no longer in control of the conversation, Calico became slightly nervous.

He tried to look relaxed, and sipped from his cup. "What of it, General?"

"Where have you been for the last thirty years?"

"The Large Magellanic Cloud, making a living as a registered mercenary."

"What make of ship is that?"

"It's a Residerian-Z'Sorth Conglomerate cargo vessel, modified for a more active lifestyle. General, it seems you are already aware of the presence of the Zendreen fleet. I have a great deal of information about that race that you should hear."

"Are you on good terms with Anya Calico?"

"I haven't spoken to her in thirty years! Why are you more interested in our relationship than the Zendreen?"

"Forgive me, Mister Calico. Go ahead and tell me about the Zendreen."

Calico paused, flustered. Anya had always been a very strong-willed woman, and a fervent advocate for Freedmen's independence. Was it possible that she'd done something stupid, and become a fugitive? Calico resolved himself to find out, but from other sources. He could barely contain his frustration at General Felmio's method of questioning, and diverted his energy into a summary of Zendreen history. He started with the ancient supernova of Sanduleak which had caused the Zendreen's migration within the Large Magellanic Cloud, then described their attempt to integrate themselves into the sub-galactic community, and ended with a three-minute version of the Umberian war and the aftermath. The general raised an eyebrow upon hearing of the wormhole, although Calico left out the tidbit that it might have been generated with Umberian technology. He also chose not to mention the

Vengeance virus specifically, instead attributing the Umberian victory to a more conventional rout by a combination of underground fighters and freelance mercenaries.

"That's a fascinating story," said the general after a moment of reflection. "It sounds like the Zendreen took quite a pounding. How can you be so sure that they aren't interested in a peaceful relationship with Hayaku?"

"If they are truly that desperate, see if they'll agree to an unconditional surrender and disarmament."

"But we are not at war with them. Such a demand would be ridiculous."

"Sir, I have not mentioned the Zendreen's incredible fecundity and rate of reproduction. While they may not pose a threat now, it wouldn't take them long to get back up to strength given a hospitable environment."

Without warning the transmission terminated, leaving Calico looking at a blank screen. Before he could utter anything about this, the ship lurched violently. He leaped up, his cup of yutha bouncing off of his rising knee and impacting the bulkhead. He burst out onto the bridge before the ceramic shards had even hit the deck.

"I'm already moving," said Railyn, his voice raised.

"What the hell?" roared Calico, almost cut off by another hit.

"It's a squadron of Hayakuvian fighters. We're already outrunning them."

"How did they get the jump on you?"

"I didn't know they were going to attack us!"

"Get us into superlume, now."

Railyn did so. The ship jumped to 800 c in a split-second.

"Anywhere in particular you'd like to go, sir?" asked Railyn.

"Set a course for Freedmen." Calico looked at a nearby console. "Shit. Just those two blasts took out half our systems. They meant to destroy us, not scare us off."

"Did the conversation really go that badly?"

"It was an ambush, Railyn. I don't know what's going on here, but it's not like my countrymen to try to kill an otherwise peaceful visitor."

Megumi's voice came in over the intercom. "Everything okay up there, Cap?"

"Get everybody up here," replied Calico. "Gueyr, can you hear me?"

"Roger," said Gueyr's voice.

"I need you to get down to the engine room and plug in the overdrive device."

"Aye, sir."

"I'm not sure the ship can take the strain right now," said Railyn. "The secondary power grid is offline, which means if the primary fails…"

"The overdrive blows us up," interrupted Calico. "I'm well aware of that. That's why I need you to work with Gueyr to make sure all the power is routed correctly. This is exactly the kind of emergency that the overdrive is for, so we're damn well going to make it work."

"Do you want to call the Reckless Faith?" asked Railyn, locking down the autopilot and standing up.

"I'm going to wait until we're a few light years out, I want to minimize the chance of the Hayakuvian fleet intercepting the signal." Calico kicked the nearest chair. "Damn it. Scherer, I hope you got a warmer reception out there."

In the cargo bay of the Faith, John, Aldebaran, and Ari prepared to disembark. Richter, his left arm in a sling, stood by jealously. Dana was still on the bridge, having just brought the ship down through some rather turbulent cloud layers, and Christie and Ray continued to labor away somewhere on fixing a series of minor computer glitches. Miriam stood by, eager to breathe the air of an alien world.

While still in the air, the crew had observed the city to which they'd been called. The cloud layer had ended at about fifteen thousand feet, giving them an excellent view of the landscape. The city was on an dirt island, bare of any visible vegetation. The structures and streets of the city took up almost the entire island, which was at least ten square kilometers. The streets were paved with large flagstones, and the buildings were either white granite or something similar, and although none of them exceeded five stories in height the net effect was incredibly impressive. Canals were as prevalent as roads throughout the city, and it was obvious that they were used just as much for transportation as for conveying water.

The largest building was at the center of the city, and resembled the Parthenon except it was six-sided and divided into rings. The Faith was expected to land in a huge square in front of the building, so they didn't get a good look inside the rings, but they appeared to contain courtyards and flower gardens. There wasn't a hint of technology visible from the air; all of the citizens going about their business were dressed as they pleased, which was quite casually, and the primary means of transportation, other than the water-borne gondolas, seemed to be bicycles.

"One minute to landing," Dana said over the intercom.

"Scherer," said Aldebaran, "you still haven't told me how you plan on synthesizing more of the Vengeance virus now that Talvan is dead."

"Are you implying that we should ask the colonists to do it for us?" replied John.

"It would obviously be to their benefit if the Zendreen are planning an invasion, assuming, of course, that they're not allergic to it themselves."

"I'll bring it up if necessary. I'd rather not jump from a simple warning to an attempt to get them to fight in the very first conversation. Revealing we have such a virus would also raise too many other questions."

"Understood."

Dana had expressed concern about landing in the middle of the square, which was busy, but as the ship approached the people made way for it.

“Good luck,” Dana said. “You can lower the ramp when you're ready.”

“Roger,” said John, nodding to Richter.

Richter pressed the appropriate button and the ramp lowered. A warm breeze ushered in a pleasant aroma. There was a large crowd gathered several yards from the ship, and an individual easily recognizable as Mother Calico stood a few feet from the end of the ramp. She was wearing a flower-patterned sun dress, and had traded the garland on her head for a straw hat. John and Aldebaran both thought she was a little too old to pull off the outfit, and all four crewmembers would have agreed that it was very odd garb for the prime minister of anything except a gardening club. John strode forward to meet her.

"Commander Scherer, welcome to Freedmen colony," said Mother Calico, kissing John on the cheek as soon as he was in range.

"Thank you, ma'am," he replied, offering his hand. "This is Seth Aldebaran, my purser, and Coma Veronice, my master-at-arms."

Mother Calico kissed Aldebaran on the cheek and planted one right on Ari's lips. John thought he caught Richter stifling a laugh back in the cargo bay.

"Come with me, please," the prime minister said.

The older woman led the three crewmembers across the square to a large fountain. The fountain was a brass representation of a nude couple gazing satisfactorily into the sky. There was fruit and wine ready for them on a picnic table. The crowd seemed more interested in the Faith than the visitors, although some had followed them over to the fountain. John noticed that the water cascading over the figures in the fountain was much quieter than it should have been, and didn't interfere with conversation. The four sat down at the table at Mother Calico's gesture.

"I wish you could have come during a sunny day, rare as they are," she said. "This city is a wondrous sight in such a glow. Alas, the weather patterns are very predictable."

John's natural reaction was to look upward, and he noticed that the skies appeared much like they do on Earth right before a vigorous thunderstorm. Absent, however, was any accompanying wind.

"Your city is beautiful nonetheless," he said.

"Thank you, child. Please, eat and drink. If you should chance to stay longer, you will find these the least of our offerings."

The crew needed no further bidding and gladly sampled the food. The wine was possibly the best in the galaxy, and John immediately hoped they could vacation here sooner than later.

"Prime Minister," he said, "let's get down to business. We are indeed here to trade; however, we must also warn you of a possible threat to your colony."

"If you refer to the alien fleet that is orbiting Fletch III, we have been observing them. They have chosen to open trade relations with Hayaku. Since our independence from Hayaku has just been legitimized, we must deal with them separately. My council and I are currently waiting to determine the exact nature of the agreement between the aliens and Hayaku before contacting them ourselves. And please, call me Mother."

"Mother, those aliens call themselves the Zendreen. They are a belligerent insectoid race from the Tarantula Nebula in the Large Magellanic Cloud. We have just been successful liberating a planet from their grasp, and now, having returned to a nomadic state, they are seeking resources and possibly a new homeworld. While it is possible that they will trade with Freedmen and Hayaku in a peaceful manner, their propensity for waging war should not be ignored."

"I assure you, we are not ignoring them. Our diplomatic courtesies demand that if they approach us in peace then we shall respond in kind. I do not doubt your concerns, child. I can see that you are sincere."

"Then heed our warning well, and be prepared for the worst."

"We most certainly do. Now then, let us talk trade. Please start with your needs."

"Very well. Aldebaran?"

Aldebaran swallowed a gulp of wine, and nodded. "Mother Calico, thank you for your hospitality. Our ship is in need of repair. Most of these repairs we can take care of ourselves, and for that we need only a safe body of water to place her while we work. We would also like to trade for fresh provisions and non-perishable medical supplies."

"I see. Anything else?"

"As far as the last category," began Ari, "if you have an osteogenerator we'll buy it."

"I'm afraid those are too valuable to give away in trade, my dear. If you have an immediate need our doctors will assist you, naturally, but you can't take it with you."

"I understand. Other than that, we're simply talking about antibiotics, dermaplasts, et cetera."

"I believe we can offer those. What can you offer us?"

"I'm almost embarrassed to propose it, considering the demeanor of your society, but the most valuable thing we can offer you is weaponry."

"Do you seriously think that a society such as ours can exist without a strong defense?"

There was quite an edge to the prime minister's reply, and Ari smiled.

"Do you have a need for projectile weapons?"

"Small arms or vehicle weaponry?"

"We have both available. Our weapons have been shown to couple well with energy discharges, whether it be amplified photons or superheated plasma. By themselves, our small arms are effective against lightly armored humanoids and insectoids, and are particularly effective against energy dispersal armor. Our articulated guns and cannon are very effective in ground attack roles and in atmospheric combat, and have been shown to have excellent range in zero-g. Any purchase would include full schematics as well as specifications for manufacturing ammunition. All of our weapons are available for a live-fire demonstration."

"Interesting. Our squadrons of atmosphere-only defenders might benefit from such weapons, but I doubt we would have much use for your small arms. Anything else, my dear?"

The crew's radios began to beep softly. John and Ari silenced theirs, and John motioned to Aldebaran to take the call. He arose and walked a few meters before replying.

"Sorry about that, Mother Calico," said John. "We have a lot of important repairs to take care of right now, and two of our experts are here at this table."

"It matters not one whit, child" replied the prime minister.

"Commander," said Aldebaran. "Andrews says there's a call from… our mutual friend. It's an emergency."

John stood up. "I'm sorry, ma'am, but I have to take this. Please make arrangements with my associates for trade items, and arrange a demonstration if you please."

Mother Calico nodded, and John walked at a fast pace back to the ship. Richter and Miriam were still standing at the top of the ramp, and a couple of young female colonists were nearby, acting coy toward Richter.

"Back so soon?" he asked.

"Calico's calling us, priority one," said John, ascending the ramp.

John crossed to the computer station and powered it up. He accessed the communications system, only to remember he couldn't route the call manually from that console.

"Andrews, this is Scherer," he said into the intercom. "I'll take the call in the cargo bay."

"Roger," Dana replied.

"Captain Calico, this is Commander Scherer, can you hear me?"

"I hear you," said Calico's voice. "What's your status?"

"We've made contact with Mother Calico, the prime minister of Freedmen colony. We've warned her about the Zendreen fleet and we're attempting to open up trade rela…"

"Did the prime minister give you her first name?" Calico asked, interrupting.

"No. Do you think you might be related?"

"Forget it, it's not important. Listen, Scherer, we've been ambushed by the Hayakuvian space fleet for no apparent reason. We're on our way to Freedmen at top speed and we'll be there in ninety minutes."

"Ninety minutes? Did you get a new ship while you were over there?"

"We have an emergency overdrive device that can boost our speed past 800 c. This is definitely an emergency. Whatever you do, don't trust the Hayakuvians. Are things going well with the colonists?"

"So far. Captain, you have no idea why the Hayakuvians attacked you?"

"None whatsoever. The conversation was going fine, relatively speaking, then whammo, a squadron jumps us. We barely got out of there with our hull intact. I'm not an idiot, though. This has something to do with the Zendreen fleet, my ex-wife, or both."

"Do you suspect that your ex-wife is the prime minister?"

"Anything's possible, Commander. We'll discuss it further when I arrive; we shouldn't keep this channel open for much longer. In the meantime, keep on eye on the Zendreen. At this point they could be up to anything."

"Understood, Captain. Hey, do you want me to reveal your existence to the prime minister?"

"No, if it's Anya, I want to save that satisfaction for myself."

"Okay. Good luck, then, I'll see you soon. Scherer out."

John terminated the call, and turned to look at Richter.

"Is it possible that Calico fucked up?" Richter asked.

John shrugged. "I'm not sure. I doubt it. He seems too cautious for that. I'm going to see if I can get more information out of Mother Calico, not the least of which is her first name. I'd like you and Ray to prep the ship for a possible demonstration of our slug-throwers. We may be replicating either one for the colonists."

"Are you sure you don't want to break atmo and observe the Zendreen fleet?"

"Not before we're done here. See if Dana can access a satellite for a real-time view of the system, although I doubt any of them are unencrypted. Our only other option is to contact the Hayakuvians ourselves and play dumb, and at this stage I can't imagine they'll buy that act. Our presence is too much of a coincidence by itself."

"I agree. We'll take care of those things, Scherer. Good luck with 'Mother' Calico."

John nodded, and returned to the fountain. The clouds had become deeply corrugated, but much brighter between the folds, and a slight, pleasant breeze had kicked up. At the picnic table, Aldebaran and Ari were calculating relative values of goods with the prime minister.

"Is everything all right, my dear?" asked Mother Calico.

"Mother," began John, "you said that your colony had recently declared independence from the Hayakuvian central government, correct?"

"I said that they'd recently recognized our articles of independence. We declared independence several years ago."

"I understand. In any case, what is the current status of your relationship with them?"

"Child, surely you would rather save such serious conversation for a later time, would you not?"

"I'm just trying to understand your relationship, in case we should choose to trade with them."

In an almost condescending tone, she replied, "Suffice it to say that we pretty much leave each other alone."

"What about the orbital platform?"

"We are hoping to purchase it from Hayaku before too long."

John smiled. "Are they amenable to that?"

"For the right price."

"Of course. Mother Calico, there is something else I wanted to ask you. We were referred here by a former colonist by the name of Jarvis Revelnik. He mentioned that he knew one Anya Calico, that wouldn't happen to be you, would it?"

"I knew a Janish Revelnik, many years ago."

"Yes, that's it, Janish. Nice guy, he's a successful freelancer back in the Cloud."

"I'm glad to hear it. He was a very skilled fighter pilot, I was sorry to see him go."

John nodded, then said, "How are things progressing between us?"

"Mother Calico is willing to give us everything we need in exchange for two each of our Earth weapons systems," said Aldebaran. "Provided she is satisfied with the demonstration."

"There is a large inland lake on the southern continent that will be perfect for both of us," Mother Calico said. "There are several derelict ships and two abandoned oil drilling platforms that we use for aerial gunnery practice. It is also calm enough for you to place your ship there for repairs. I will accompany you on your ship if you don't mind."

"That won't be a problem, Mother," said John. "When do you want to accomplish this?"

"Can you do it immediately, dear? I don't have anything more pressing right now, and it is so hard to find spare time these days."

"That works for me. Just give me five minutes to brief my crew and we'll depart. Ari, stay here and work out the particulars of the trade, we'll be back for you soon."

"No problem," replied Ari, then to the prime minister, "Ari is a nickname in our language for master-at-arms."

"I see," said Mother Calico.

John and Aldebaran turned around and walked back toward the ship. When they were out of earshot, John spoke.

"I wish Ari would figure out which name she likes best, and stick with it."

"What's going on with Calico and the Almagest?" asked Aldebaran.

"The Hayakuvians are hostile to him. We don't know why just yet. He's on his way here as fast as he can. Turns out he's got some sort of emergency overdrive device that can boost his top speed, so he'll be here in ninety minutes. Listen, when we're done with the weapons demonstration we need to make fixing the dorsal gun room a priority. We may not be able to fix the gun, but we need to patch up the hull ASAP. There's trouble brewing in this star system and we need to be able to face it without a frigging hole in the ship."

"Do you think we can trust the prime minister?"

"Right now, Seth, we have no choice."

16.

"I'm sorry, Major Pyramis. Mother Calico is not available right now. I am Second Minister Zuben, and I can speak for the prime minister."

Pyramis frowned at his monitor, and leaned back in his chair. The older male colonist on his screen seemed genuinely apologetic, so he resisted the temptation to respond with feigned annoyance.

"Very well, Second Minister," he replied calmly, "I have contacted you to inform you that I have been ordered not to interfere with the affairs of either the Zendreen or Freedmen. However, I have no further details. Please, if you are able, describe your relationship with the Zendreen visitors."

"Major, the colony has not had any contact with the Zendreen as of yet. However, since I have you here, I would like to know the nature of Hayaku's relationship with the strangers."

"I can't get into specifics right now, but the relationship is peaceful."

"That is fortunate for all of us."

Lieutenant Brentage gestured to get the attention of Pyramis. The major nodded at him and spoke to Zuben.

"Sir, do you mind if I mute the channel for a moment?"

"Not at all," replied Zuben.

"Major," began Brentage, "the squadron reports that the Zendreen fleet is on the move."

"Speed and heading?"

"They're moving out at one-tenth c, bearing toward Freedmen."

"Understood. This doesn't feel right to me, Lieutenant."

"You got that right, sir."

Pyramis returned to his monitor and pressed a key. "Second Minister Zuben, the Zendreen fleet has just lifted anchor and is headed your way. They will arrive in approximately seven hours. I can't send my squadron after them, but we will continue to track them with long range sensors. Good luck."

"Thank you, Major. Peace to you and yours. Freedmen out."

"Order the squadron back to the station," Pyramis said to Brentage.

"Aye, sir," replied the lieutenant, and passed the order on to his ensign.

"Lieutenant, a word please."

Pyramis stood up and headed to the rear of the control room. Brentage joined him. Pyramis stroked his chin and considered his words carefully.

"I have this sneaking suspicion that the Zendreen are about to attack the colony, and Hayaku is complicit," he said after a moment.

"I get that feeling, too," replied Brentage. "They wouldn't move out the whole fleet just to open up a diplomatic relationship. I don't see anything we can do about it, though. Our orders are quite clear. If they attack, we get to watch the pretty colors."

"Is there any chance whatsoever that the colony could put up a fight?"

"It's doubtful. Freedmen has lots of natural resources but a limited industrial capacity."

"The Zendreen must be going there to trade. There is simply no way that our leaders would sit back and let the colony, their own blood, get wiped out."

"Are you sure about that, sir?"

"I refuse to believe anything else."

"Sir, I find it hard to believe that you weren't exposed to a great deal of anti-colonial sentiment at your former assignment. I was under the impression that it was the prevailing attitude among military personnel back home."

"There was some dissent, yes. However, you know how much is scuttlebutt and how much is true. I can whine about the uppity colonists all day long, that doesn't mean I'm going to let them all die."

Brentage lowered his voice even more, and said, "I heard rumors that the upper echelons were, in fact, that hard core about it. It might be possible that the military is acting contrary to the wishes of the central government."

"Hey, LT, I enjoy a good conspiracy theory as much as the next guy, but that's beyond ridiculous."

"And yet, here were are. If you want to put your career on the line by going over Commander Ballard's head, go for it, but even if you're right it will be too late to save the colony."

"Maybe. At the very least I'm going to confirm the validity of that order. Perhaps I'll get new orders, or clarification, at least."

"I think that's the best course of action, sir."

Pyramis nodded. "I'll be right back. Let me know if anything changes with the fleet."

"Aye, sir."

Turning around, Pyramis exited the command center and headed for his quarters. His temper was rising, and he tried not to misplace his anger with Brentage. He hated feeling helpless, and even more so to be manipulated. While it was never his place to question his orders, for the most part in his military career, they at least made sense. He began to think about some of the conversations he had with colleagues regarding the situation, wondering if there was a constant subtext that he somehow missed. It seemed crazy that anyone would take normal anti-colonial sentiment and turn it into mass murder, even if it was another party performing the act.

Pyramis entered his quarters and turned on his computer console. He hadn't yet eaten lunch, and his typically voracious appetite reminded him of it. Even something this frustrating couldn't distract him enough to allay hunger, and he grabbed a protein drink out of his mini-fridge. He popped the top and took a swig as he checked his messages.

There was indeed a new set of orders waiting for him. His adrenaline spiked as he read it.

HAYAKU SPACE COMMAND/ OFFICIAL ORDERS/ ENC-KEY-2A

MAJOR RAFE PYRAMIS, COMMANDER, FREEDMEN STATION

ALL FLEET PERSONNEL ARE HEREBY ORDERED TO BE ON THE LOOKOUT FOR THE INDEPENDENT VESSEL ALMAGEST, COMMANDED BY CAPTAIN FARRIL CALICO. IT IS A TEN-DECK CRUISER, HEAVILY ARMED, AND KNOWN TO BROADCAST TRANSMISSIONS IN THE 500 MEGACYCLE RANGE. IT IS CONSIDERED TO BE A ROGUE VESSEL. ALL FLEET CRAFT ARE ORDERED TO REPORT ANY SIGHTING OF THIS VESSEL, AND IF OVERWHELMING FORCE EXISTS AGAINST IT, AUTHORIZATION IS GRANTED TO DESTROY. IT IS BELIEVED TO BE HEADED TOWARD THE FREEDMEN SYSTEM ALTHOUGH IT COULD APPEAR ANYWHERE. AT NO TIME IS DIRECT CONTACT WITH THIS VESSEL OR ANY OF ITS CREW AUTHORIZED.

MAJOR GENERAL THADDEUS FELMIO
COMMANDER BREIT BALLARD

Pyramis swore to himself and closed the file. It was just another piracy alert. He opened a new text message and thought about exactly what to send back to Commander Ballard. He chugged the rest of his drink angrily and sighed. None of this made any sense. There was no doubt in his mind that the central government would want to defend Freedmen. His adoptive culture was simply not that cruel.

With his heart pounding in his chest, Pyramis decided what to do. He shut down his console and headed back to the command center. Lieutenant Brentage approached him, looking inquisitive.

"We've received new orders," Pyramis said, loud enough for all present to hear him. "We are to defend the Freedmen colony against all hostile forces with complete resolve. We will continue to observe the Zendreen fleet, but we will attack them the instant they deploy any combat resources. If that occurs, Central Command will reinforce us. Any questions?"

"Sir," said Brentage, "if command believes that an attack is possible, why haven't they dispatched reinforcements already? The fight could very well be over by the time they get there."

"That detail has not been communicated to me. I surmise that command does not wish to antagonize the Zendreen if their intentions are indeed peaceful."

"Unless the colonists have many more ships than they've let on, our squadron isn't going to make any difference in an all-out battle."

"You're underestimating us," replied Pyramis, grinning. "Besides, our jockeys are itching for a fight, you know that."

"Can I talk to you alone, sir?"

"Of course. Ensign, relay the new orders to the squadron."

The ensign nodded. Pyramis and Brentage moved into the hallway, and the lieutenant closed the hatch. Pyramis scratched his head and looked at the younger man.

"Sir, this is a rather abrupt departure from our previous set of orders, don't you think?"

"So it would seem."

"I'm sure you wouldn't mind if I had our communications technician confirm the validity of the transmissions."

"Both messages were for my eyes only. They contained additional information not relevant to the immediate situation and are not subject to review."

"That's a good thing for you, sir."

Pyramis folded his arms across his chest, and said, "I'm not sure I like your tone, Lieutenant Brentage."

"I'm just saying that it's fortunate that command agrees with you, philosophically speaking."

"Indeed. Lieutenant, we need every available fighter out there in case the Zendreen start trouble. Since you're not a pilot, I'm going to need you to command the station while I join the squadron."

"As you say, sir."

Pyramis opened the hatch, and said, "Defending the colony is the right thing to do, Lieutenant."

"Oh, I know, Major. There's just often little difference between right and dead."

On the surface of a gray lake, a rusty freighter suddenly shook as a barrage of 30mm rounds impacted the hull. The Reckless Faith swooped over the riddled craft and the ventral fifty-caliber guns raked the deck. On the bridge, Prime Minister Calico clutched the back of the pilot's chair as Dana pulled back on the stick for another pass. Her two male aides seemed equally queasy from their seats at the rear of the bridge.

"Did you see the Nineteen-A on the monitor, Mother Calico?" asked John, seated to her right.

"Yes, dear, I did," she replied. "Your inertial control systems aren't perfect, I noticed."

"The added stress on the anti-gravity system during atmospheric flight can cause lateral g-forces like that during more extreme maneuvers. You get used to it."

"Speak for yourself," said Ray from the opposite console.

"Since you obviously enjoy the experience," said the prime minister to John, "I invite you to try one of our atmosphere-only fighter craft during your visit. In fact, I was hoping you could assist our engineers in integrating your weapons systems into those fighters."

John smiled. "So you're happy with the demonstration? You don't want a closer look at the damage?"

"I'm well familiar with what projectile weapons can do to those old ships. Your weapons are clearly adequate for our needs."

"The ship is listing heavily to port," said Ari from the ventral gun room.

"Perhaps the thirty millimeter is even more powerful than I surmised."

"The GAU 8 isn't meant to sink ships," replied John. "At least, not of that size. The freighter was probably ready to go and we just added the final touch."

"Even still, I am satisfied. Commander Scherer, please put your ship down on the west side of the lake. Our mobile repair team is already on the way to assist you with your hull breach."

"We should be able to repair the damage ourselves, but we will definitely take advantage of your team if need be. Thank you."

Dana leveled the ship and headed west. Mother Calico directed her to the precise spot, marked by a modern marina. Crews of fishing vessels and the occupants of recreational sailboats watched the Faith come in, with a few children on the latter boats waving in greeting. Coastal birds screamed in protest and made way as Dana brought the ship in. The prime minister pointed to a dock with a gangway capable of reaching the airlock.

"Ari, retract the ventral gun and seal the hatch," said John into the intercom.

"Roger that, Scherer," came the reply, then a moment later, "Gun system is secure."

"Initiate water landing procedures," John said to Dana.

Dana looked over her shoulder. "You never went over any specific procedures for a water landing."

"Uh. Well, just take us in nice and easy, and bring the waterline to the top of deck two. Then you can deactivate the anti-gravity system."

"Understood."

With a soft touch, Dana maneuvered the ship. When they reached the surface of the water, she switched to an exterior camera view to further guide the vessel. There was a rather disorienting sensation as she deactivated the anti-gravity field, and the ship settled into the water without a bump. A crew on the dock lined the gangway up with the airlock door.

"Somebody better get back there and help tie us off," John said.

"I'll go," offered Ray, standing.

"Thanks. Dana, better lock out the ramp controls in case somebody forgets that it's submerged. Knowing my luck it'll probably be me."

"No problem," replied Dana.

"Once that's done, shut down the emergency force field and all non-essential systems. Set the air exchangers to vent mode, we might as well air out the ship while we're planetside. Prime Minister Calico, shall we move to the conference room to discuss the particulars of our trade?"

"Of course, dear," replied Mother Calico. "This way, please. Ari, Aldebaran, meet us in the conference room."

John, the prime minister, and her aides exited the bridge to the next room, passing Miriam, who had just extricated her fingernails from the underside of her chair. John offered seats to the contingent, but only the prime minister accepted.

"Your daughter is very beautiful," she said as her aides flanked her. "You and Coma must be very proud of her."

John paused as he began to sit, and looked at Mother Calico with confusion. The woman's eyes grew wide for a moment, and she smiled apologetically.

"I'm sorry," she said, "am I wrong about the girl's heritage?"

"Completely," began John, settling into his chair. "In fact, neither Ari or I are old enough to be her parents."

"Curious. The resemblance is striking, especially to Coma."

Ari and Aldebaran entered the conference room from the lounge area. Aldebaran sat down as Ari noticed the attention of the others.

"What?" she asked.

"The prime minister thinks we would make good parents," said John, smiling.

"Maybe with different mates on different planets," Ari replied with sarcasm.

If John hadn't been distracted by a thousand other things, he might have been insulted by the comment. Instead, he nodded vacantly and returned his attention to his guests.

"Now then, Mother Calico, shall we discuss the terms of our exchange?"

Oblivious to any discussions of her genetic background, Miriam excused herself from the bridge and wandered down to the galley. Richter was there, getting himself a glass of water. His face was smudged with grease and he smelled of copper solvent. He smiled sincerely, if briefly, and swallowed the liquid rapidly.

"What happened to your hand?" the girl asked, referring to the two missing fingers on Richter's left hand.

"We got into a bad scrape a few weeks ago. I'm lucky I didn't get off worse."

"It looks like it healed up well enough."

"The Umberians have excellent medical technology."

"You were cleaning guns?"

"You mean just now? Yes, this is the perfect time to do maintenance on the fifty cals. Those are in a turret on the belly of the ship. We used to have a top turret as well, but it was destroyed during our last space engagement."

"I have a pistol that needs cleaning," said Miriam shyly. "Do you know how to take apart a Colt 1911?"

"Christie told me you had a pistol on you when we picked you up. Between that and your perfect English your story seems to check out."

"I'm sure it seems quite daft to you."

"Look around you. This ship is all about making the impossible possible. Anyway, yes, I can field strip a 1911. Did you father teach you how to shoot it?"

"Yes," said Miriam proudly, then more muted, "but I'm not very good. Besides, I only have five shots remaining."

"We have plenty of forty-five, thanks to Ray. In fact, my pistol is the same model."

"I'm far more interested in, what did you call them, the fifty cals?"

"Come with me, I'll show you the ropes."

Richter put his empty glass on the counter and moved to the stairs. He opened the hatch in the floor and climbed down the ladder into the cargo hold. Miriam followed him and closed the hatch after her. Continuing into the corridor, Richter opened the door to the ventral gun room and ushered Miriam inside. Richter had yet to reinstall the GAU 19/A machine gun into its mount, and the heavy barrels lay beside the receiver. Between the weapon, the ammo cans, and the computer equipment, there was almost no room left.

"Have a seat," Richter said, motioning to the computer station.

Miriam squeezed past the older man and sat down. The computer station was equipped with six monitors, and joystick and rudder pedals in addition to the standard keyboard and mouse.

Richter moved the mouse to wake up the console and leaned against the back of the chair.

"Just interrupt me if you have any questions," he began. "This is the control station for the ventral turret. The weapon is a GAU 19/A machine gun installed in a fully articulated, remote control turret. When the weapon is in its mount, the hatch in the floor will be open; that's how you would reload it. Don't worry about that right now, I'll just teach you how to operate the software. On the desktop, click on the icon labeled 'weapon system.' Good."

A targeting reticle and a little icon of the ship appeared in front of a black background as Miriam followed his instructions. A dialog box appeared, which Miriam read aloud.

"Turret retracted. Switch to virtual mode?" she recited.

"Click yes."

A simulated starfield appeared in a panoramic view on the monitors. The hull of the ship loomed over the top portion of the screens.

"Grab the joystick and put your feet on the rudder pedals," continued Richter. "The pedals control your horizontal axis and the stick controls the vertical. Try it out."

Miriam did so. The image spun as she brought the turret through its full range of motion. The icon of the ship in the upper right hand corner indicated where the weapon was pointing relative to the ship. She brought the reticle back to the twelve o'clock position and smiled.

"What do all these buttons do?" she asked.

"First of all," replied Richter, "if you look to your right you'll see a switch mounted below the desk. That's the master arm switch. If we were in live mode, you'd have to move that to the up position. That light will come on to confirm that the weapons are hot. Next, look in the upper left hand corner of the screen. You'll see that it currently says 'fifties.' If you press key number four on the joystick, it will change to 'fifties and lasers.' In this mode, the laser systems will fire in tandem with the fifties if they have a shot; however, since the laser emitters are on the sides of the ship they can only fire in tandem up to thirty degrees of declination relative to the horizontal axis of the fifties. Go ahead and hit the key. Good, now rotate the barrels downward. You can see that once you pass a thirty degree angle, the word 'lasers' changes from green to red. If that wasn't obvious enough for you, the fact that the lasers stop firing should be. Press the key again to switch to lasers only."

Miriam followed his instructions. The field of view changed, and the message in the left corner changed as well.

"Port lasers," she read aloud.

"Correct. Press it one more time to switch to the starboard lasers. Good. One last press will bring you back to the fifty-cal only. Now, when you're in tandem mode, the primary trigger will fire both weapons if they both have a shot. The secondary trigger, which is right here, will fire the fifty only. The tertiary trigger, directly above that one, will fire lasers only."

"Why have separate modes if each trigger does the same thing?"

"It's just to give the user more flexibility."

"Oh."

"Now, the starboard lasers are damaged and we may not be able to repair them, so if necessary I will remove them from the selection. Hopefully we will be able to get them back online."

"Is there a practice mode?" Miriam asked hopefully, looking over her shoulder at Richter.

"There sure is. Dana and Christie programmed a engagement simulation based on our fight with the Zendreen defense satellites. Follow the root menu and you'll see it."

"Okay."

The door opened and Christie stuck her head inside the room.

"Here you are, I've been looking all over the place for you," she said.

"What's up?" asked Richter.

"Dana and I have made an exciting discovery. We want to address the crew."

"I take it John is still meeting with Mother Calico."

"Yes, but we can fill him in when he's done. Everyone else is meeting in the galley."

"Miriam, would you rather stay here and try the simulation, or join us in the galley?"

"I would like to try the computer, please," Miriam replied earnestly.

"Sure thing. Come upstairs when you're done."

Richter left Miriam to her virtual enemies and followed Christie to the galley. Dana and Ray were seated at the table, enjoying a beer. No sooner had they exchanged greetings and sat down when John, Ari, and Aldebaran came downstairs.

"Done already?" asked Ray.

"Yes," replied John. "Pour me an ale and I'll tell you how our discussion came out."

"I got it," said Aldebaran, opening a cabinet.

John stood at the head of the table and leaned forward, resting his hands on the surface. He took a deep breath, and spoke.

"We are providing two Avengers and two Nineteens for the colony. A transport vehicle is being dispatched to the pier. When it arrives, we will use the matter replicator to synthesize the weapons systems directly onto the transport vehicle. We've also been asked for 2500 rounds of 30mm and 5000 rounds of fifty-cal, and technical schematics for each weapon system and ammunition type. We may encounter some problems downloading the information to the colonists' computer system, so I'd like Christie, Dana, and Ari to handle that portion. Thanks." John accepted the ale from Aldebaran, took a swig, and continued. "In exchange for these weapons, we are receiving food, medical supplies, and engineering assistance to repair the ship."

"That hardly seems like a fair trade," said Ray.

"I have also pledged our assistance should the Zendreen decide to threaten the colony. This may entail enlisting the help of their scientists to replicate the Vengeance virus, and/or some of us making ourselves available to pilot their atmosphere-only fighters if we can't get the Faith back in the air before things heat up."

"Don't they have enough pilots of their own? And how did the prime minister feel about the virus?" asked Dana.

"I haven't told her about the virus yet, and I don't know if they have enough pilots. But they currently have more fighters than they do pilots, so we might as well take them up. Plus, we have experience fighting the Zendreen in space engagements."

"What's your tactical assessment of the colony's defensive capabilities?" asked Richter.

"Based on what the prime minister told me, they can just barely repel an attack by the Zendreen. However, her body language betrayed a lack of confidence in her words, so I'm not so sure. Getting the Reckless Faith back up to full capacity will be essential to that effort."

"I think we should ask for help with the virus now," began Aldebaran. "Waiting until the Zendreen make a move could be too late."

"As I said, I only want to employ the virus again as a last resort. We still have yet to ask Calico if any of his people can help us with the cultivation and I'd rather keep it between us. In any case our priority is getting the Faith back in action. How are the repairs coming along?"

"As well as expected," replied Ray. "Once we patch the damage to the hull we'll be able to break atmo. Repairing the starboard laser banks should be possible if we cannibalize the Talvanium from the rear cannon. Since we have a larger source of raw material, and if we have enough time, we can even synthesize a new dorsal turret. I also think that we can synthesize and install another forward-facing Avenger, and/or add forward facing fifty-cals, if you think you can enlarge the nose section."

"I don't have a lot of confidence that I'll be able to program the matter replicator to do that, not without the assistance that the orb provided us the first time around."

"In that case, you should find our news to be of great interest," said Christie, smiling.

"Remember you asked me to do a complete inventory of what we can replicate?" asked Dana. "When I did, I found a new addition."

Dana activated the nearest console and brought an image up on the wall-mounted plasma screen. The replication inventory was displayed, along with a familiar item. John read the description with surprise.

"Quasi-actualized Intraspace Quantum Grid? We can replicate a new orb?"

"So it would seem," replied Christie. "We only need a small amount of Talvanium, which would reduce the yield of the starboard lasers by an inconsequential amount."

"What about an AI?"

"It wouldn't have one," said Aldebaran. "By itself, the orb will allow us to do all of the things we used my orb for, but it will be a passive device. It is capable of being programmed with an artificial intelligence, but considering what happened to me I doubt you'll be able to find a willing volunteer for the process."

"Never mind the fact that the only facility for doing so was destroyed," added Dana.

"Even as a passive device, the orb has too many advantages to be ignored."

"Great," began John, "let's do it. I'll get started on redesigning the forward section to accommodate a second Avenger. Now that we can replicate ammo on demand I don't really see the advantage of adding any fifty-cals, though. Dana, Christie, get started on the orb. We have about an hour until Captain Calico gets here and I'd like to be finished with it before then."

Christie and Dana nodded and exited the galley for the cargo bay.

"I wish Talvan was here to see this," said Aldebaran. "He'd be very proud."

"What about reinstalling the rear-facing Avenger?" asked Richter.

Ari shrugged. "It wasn't articulated, so it was very rare that I had a shot in actual combat. I assume everyone else who used it had the same experience."

"True, but it's better than nothing. Scherer, do you think you could design a new rig to make an articulated rear gun?"

"Not without substantially redesigning the aft section," replied John. "I don't have enough time for that. It would be much easier to install a couple fifty-cals using a B-17 or B-29 tail gun configuration, but I don't think it is a priority right now. If something really dangerous gets on our six we can always pitch to give the other guns a shot, or yaw the whole damn ship around and bring our best weapons to bear."

"We're ready to replicate the orb," said Christie over the intercom.

"We should do a complete shut-down and systems reboot after the orb is in place," said Ari.

"Good, let's get started," said John.

"Hold on a second," said Richter. "Miriam, this is Richter. I need you to shut down your simulation for now."

"I'm sort of in the middle of it right now," Miriam's voice replied.

"I'm sorry, it has to be now. Meet me in the galley and you can tell me how you like it so far."

"Okay."

"I think she'd like to see the new orb put in place," said Richter, standing.

"I think we all would," said John.

"I'll meet you in the orb room, then."

John, Ray, Ari, and Aldebaran exited the galley for the orb room. The cold room was quiet, as always, and seemed preternaturally vacant since the destruction of the original orb.

Ray said, "Did Mother Calico tell you anything about their atmosphere-only fighters?"

"Not really," replied John, "but I'm itching to try one out."

"I hate to say it John," began Aldebaran, "but unless things go very much against the colony, fighters of that type aren't going to be very useful."

"What do you mean?"

"If the Zendreen attack, they're going to use orbital bombardment to target as many of the colony's military resources as they can find. Only after they're done pounding the surface will they send in an invasion force. We should hope to force off the fleet well before that happens."

"I see."

"What about the Vulture?" asked Ray. "Did she have any information on it or the other two asteroids?"

"No, unfortunately not."

Richter and Miriam entered the room, and John activated the intercom.

"Go ahead with the replication, ladies," he said.

"I still don't understand what I'm supposed to be looking at," said Miriam.

A beautiful dance of green light emanated from the center of the room, sparkling like an infinity of emeralds, and a pellucid orb the size of a volleyball appeared. The others smiled with satisfaction even as Miriam recoiled in horror.

"It's all right," said Richter, "I'm sorry if that surprised you."

"Get that thing out of here!" Miriam screamed.

"Miriam, this is just part of our computer system, it's nothing..."

"Can't you feel it? It's just like them!"

"Richter, get her out of here," said John.

Richter nodded, and escorted Miriam back into the galley. Ari and Aldebaran looked at each other.

"She's not wrong," muttered Aldebaran.

"Something is definitely not right about this," added Ari.

A new voice filled the room, ostensibly from the intercom system, but with much more timbre and depth.

"Where am I?" the voice asked.

Everyone instantly recognized the voice. Only John was able to push past his confusion and identify it, and he did so with a combination of shock and contempt.

"Byron Sterling?"

"Everyone but John and I needs to get off the ship right now. Get those technicians down from the dorsal turret and onto the pier."

Aldebaran spoke with an authority and intensity that only Ari had ever heard, and he spoke with such veracity that no argument was raised. The others exited the orb room without a word to him. When they had gone, John and Aldebaran looked at each other and shared a stern expression.

"Byron, can you hear me?" asked Aldebaran carefully.

"Yes," said the voice, still loud and deep in tone. "I don't understand what's happening."

"Do you know who I am?"

"You're Aldebaran the space pirate. Have I been captured? Am I on some sort of life support?"

"Byron, this is John Scherer," John said. "Can you tell us what you see right now?"

"I'm surrounded by light," Byron said, clearly quite scared.

"Can you determine how many light sources there are?" asked Aldebaran.

"I think so. There are at least a dozen of them... with colored strings extending from them in all directions."

"Good, that's good. You need to relax, Byron, everything is fine. Can you tell me the last thing you remember?"

"Arianna Ferro shot me in the head," Byron replied with a hint of anger.

"Okay. Just relax now, Byron. You were right, you're on life support, but everything is going to be okay. Don't concentrate on any of those points of light too hard or you may give yourself a headache. You might also fall in and out of consciousness, but don't worry, that's normal."

"All right, but why am I talking to you?"

"You've been unconscious for a long time, Byron," replied John. "Aldebaran and the crew of the Reckless Faith have forged an alliance."

"Okay."

"Just relax, Byron," said Aldebaran. "We'll let you know when your condition changes."

Aldebaran gestured at John, and the two men made their way to deck one and off the ship. It was a beautiful sunny day on this part of the planet, and a warm ocean breeze met them as they crossed the gangway onto the pier. To the left, colonial officials kept curious locals at a distance, and to the right the crew of the Faith waited impatiently. The sounds of marker buoys and sea birds created a peaceful background hum.

John and Aldebaran approached the crew, the latter man gesturing for everyone to proceed further down the pier. Miriam was sobbing into Christie's lap as the two sat on a bench, and they did not come with the group.

"What the hell is going on?" asked Ari, still blinking in the bright light.

Aldebaran said, "I don't understand exactly how it happened, but Byron Sterling is now the resident entity inside the new orb."

Various expressions of shock were expressed by the crew, replete with creative invectives, and John held up his hand for silence.

"He must be super fucking pissed," said Richter.

"The first thing he thought was that he is on some kind of life support," said John. "We played along and I don't want to disabuse him of that notion until we know how to proceed."

"Is he in control of the ship?" asked Dana.

"Not at the moment," replied Aldebaran. "Based on what he described, he is currently in sort of a diagnostic mode. If he figures out how to navigate the quantum grid, he'll realize he has control over almost every aspect of the ship. If that happens, we'd better hope he doesn't begrudge us for what happened or he could very easily harm us or damage the ship."

"Why don't we just remove the orb from the ship?" asked Ari.

"Or put a bullet in it?" added Richter.

"It's too late for that," said Aldebaran. "He's already networked in with our Earth computers. Removing him or deactivating him could irreparably harm the network, the programs, and the database. The only way to safely get him out of there is to have him willingly shut himself down, which will require an honest explanation of what's going on. It would sound a lot like suicide to him, so I doubt he'll go along with it."

"How do we know it's really him?" asked Christie, approaching with Miriam clinging to her side.

"Maybe it's a new AI that just assumed some parts of his personality and memory," said Dana.

Aldebaran frowned. "We can't know how much of Byron is there until we know how this happened in the first place."

"Do you have any guesses?" asked John.

"I do. When the Reckless Faith was captured, I, as Seth the AI, had gone into system defense mode. It's a mode that was meant to protect me from outside hacking attempts, while at the same time still providing essential ship functions. I did not have the authority to initiate any process that could harm the crew, but I could try to prevent my programming from being compromised. Unfortunately, the only person in the universe who had any inkling of how to circumvent the defense mode was on the ship: Aldebaran the pirate. Initially upon boarding the ship, I, I mean Aldebaran, attempted to reconstitute himself with the orb using the same AI integration protocols that merged Seth with the orb in the first place. This attempt failed because the process requires a quantum grid field stabilization device found only on the Umberian System Way Station. However, those protocols could have still been running when Byron was shot and killed. Theoretically, his personality and memories could have been stored locally on the Faith, ready to be loaded as an AI into an orb. Since the original orb was destroyed when I reconstituted myself back on the Way Station, nothing would have happened. The data could have gone undiscovered, or misinterpreted, until a new orb became available. If I'm right, as soon as the new orb was created, the program loaded what it thought was the right data: Byron."

"But Byron was never merged with the original orb," said John. "How did his pattern..."

Aldebaran shook his head. "He was, John. He tried it between the time he stowed away and when he revealed himself to the rest of the crew. He was only merged for a few seconds; he didn't like the experience at all, but it was long enough."

"How come you never mentioned this before?" asked John angrily.

Aldebaran folded his arms across his chest. "Excuse me, John, it was never relevant before now."

"Byron may have been a son of a bitch," began Dana, "but this may not be a disaster. Maybe being killed sort of... tempered his personality."

"One thing is absolutely certain," replied Aldebaran. "Arianna, you can't go back on board the ship until we've sorted this out. Unless we can figure out a way of getting Byron out of there in a hurry, it is inevitable that he will figure out how to navigate the quantum grid. He will gain the ability to sense and identify everyone on board the ship. Your presence will doubtlessly be a serious hindrance to patching up our relationship with Byron."

"I agree," said Ari.

John said, "So our options are to try to get Byron to be a cooperative and functional AI, or to figure out a way of removing him?"

Aldebaran nodded. "Yes."

"Is having Byron as the AI really even an option?" asked Christie, somewhat irked.

"It's the easiest solution, and our best chance to keep the ship operating at full capacity."

"I think you should listen to what Miriam has to say before you make up your minds."

Everyone turned to look at the girl. She wiped the tears from her face and pushed her bangs back behind her ears. She sniffled and looked at the others sheepishly.

"I don't know who this bloke Byron is," she said, her voice wavering, "but there is definitely some sort of connection between that orb, as you call it, and the Kira'To."

"What are you basing that opinion on?" asked John.

"I know it sounds silly to base what I think off of an emotional reaction. I only hope that you understand that whenever I've had contact with the Kira'To, or whatever thing may go by that name, there has been a certain feeling attached to it. Creepy, doubtlessly, but also like someone is looking right through your head and at the back of your skull. There's also a sense that someone or something is about to speak, like knowing you've just walked into a surprise party."

"Never mind being scared out of your wits," added Christie.

"I'm fairly certain those emotions are my own."

John nodded. "Without knowing more about the true nature of the Kira'To, we can't draw any conclusions as to your reaction to our new orb. I suppose it is possible that the Kira'To are beings that are similar in composition to the quantum grid somehow, and that's why you're getting a similar feeling from the orb."

"Yes, but..." Aldebaran began to say. "When the orb was synthesized, I felt something quite like what Miriam described. However, I also felt a very distinct malevolence, something that was very much wrong for something so familiar to me. I may not be the best judge of such things, as I've never stood on this side of a functional orb before. I assume if any of you felt something like that when I was Seth, you'd have mentioned it by now."

"We were terrified when we first met Seth," said Ray, "but it was our own reaction. Once we started interacting with you, the negative feelings dissipated and we felt nothing but a thrilling curiosity."

"Isn't it simply possible," said John, "that Byron is unconsciously harboring feelings of intense anger for being murdered in cold blood, and you both picked up on it?"

Aldebaran nodded. "Yes, of course. And who would be best able to pick up on that but Ari and I?"

Ari stuck her hands into her pockets and turned away from the group. John crossed to her side and put his hand on her shoulder.

"You felt it too?" he asked softly.

"Of course," Ari replied morosely.

"Whatever we're going to do," said Richter, stepping forward, "we need to do it soon. We don't have much time before the prime minister's transport vehicle is going to arrive for the weapons, and the Almagest is going to be here soon."

"Aldebaran," said John, "is there really any point in trying to keep Byron fooled into thinking he's on life support?"

Aldebaran crossed his arms and shook his head. "No. He's probably already started exploring the quantum grid. Better to tell him the truth and work on getting him to cooperate."

"Who has the best chance of that?" asked Dana. "None of us were exactly chummy with the kid."

"A neutral and honest person like Miriam is our best shot."

"Bullocks," said Miriam, kicking a seashell. "Count me out."

"I think I was the closest thing that Byron had to a friend," said John. "I think I always treated him fairly."

"I agree," said Christie. "He has the best chance of earning Byron's trust."

"Will he be sufficiently distracted for us to replicate the weapons?" asked Richter.

"Maybe," said Aldebaran. "The worst that can happen is that he won't authorize that action."

"Good," said John. "Christie, Dana, as soon as I begin my conversation with Byron, I want you to go to the cargo bay and replicate those weapons. Put them on the pier where they can be easily loaded onto the transport vehicle. Miriam, Ray, I need you to get Friday and Tycho off of the ship for now, I'm worried that their receptive minds will be confusing to Byron or that he may intentionally or unintentionally harm them. Ari, Aldebaran, wait here for the transport vessel and help coordinate loading the weapons. If we can't do it, I need you to explain the situation to the colonists."

"What if Byron won't cooperate and we can't get rid of him?" asked Dana.

"Then we're screwed."

In the virtual world of the quantum grid, Byron was getting to know the finer points of the ship's waste reclamation system. He'd taken Aldebaran's advice to heart, but had found the scintillating points of light irresistible. He chose one at random, and ended up looking at a technical schematic. The image seemed to fill his entire view no matter which way he looked. He was getting used to perceiving his surroundings without the handy reference point of his own body, but was now starting to feel panic as he realized that he couldn't figure out how to back away from the schematic or return to the place of many lights from where he began. It was then that he felt John's presence, and a moment later, his voice.

"Byron, can you hear me?"

"Yes, John."

Byron's words seemed to issue forth from the center of his forehead, or so it felt, since he couldn't lift a hand to feel his face. As soon as John spoke, a point of light appeared in the corner of the schematic. Byron concentrated it and was relieved to find himself back at his starting point. One point of light looked particularly interesting, and a purple string leading from it pulsed invitingly. Following it put him in the orb room, regarding the area from an upper corner. The view was distorted like a curved security mirror, and he recognized John standing by the aft hatch. The purple thread floated in the corner of his view and led back to the orb itself. Despite his confusion, Byron felt at ease here.

"Do you know where you are?" asked John.

"I'm aboard the Reckless Faith."

"That's correct. Byron, I have bad news for you, I'm afraid."

"That doesn't particularly surprise me, but go ahead."

"We were unable to save your body. You now only exist as a stabilized consciousness aboard this ship. I'm sure that you'd rather have your body back, but I hope you realize that our only choices were to place you in the quantum grid or let you die."

"What does it mean to be a stabilized consciousness, John? I seem to be able to move around in here."

"You remember Seth, our AI system?"

"Of course."

"You are now what he was. Seth was part of Aldebaran the pirate, the missing part of his soul that he was looking for. He was able to reconstitute himself with Seth the AI after you were shot, thus giving us the opportunity to place you in the quantum grid aboard the Faith."

"I feel like a lot of time passed between those two events."

"Yes. You were held in stasis for several weeks."

Byron had a strong desire for John to place his hand on the orb. A bright green thread appeared between John and the orb, waving like a clothesline in a gentle breeze. John obviously reacted to something, and Byron sensed that there was an outline of a hand on John's side of the orb.

"For some reason I have the feeling that it would be a lot easier for me to understand you if you put your hand on the orb," he said.

"Yes, if I do, we'll be able to share a much stronger link. However, it's too soon for you to try something that advanced. Right now you need to learn how to exist inside the quantum grid."

A new feeling inundated Byron, and he struggled to process it. A moment later he realized what the feeling meant, and the information came to him intuitively.

"Christie just replicated two each of the GAU 8 and GAU 19 weapons systems," he said. "That was a very odd feeling."

"Yes, we're right in the middle of a mission. That's why it is essential that you start learning how to navigate our systems."

"What function will I be serving here, John?"

"At first you will simply assist us in monitoring the ship's systems. As your familiarity with the quantum grid increases, you will be able to monitor and control all of the systems simultaneously, which will greatly increase the efficiency and effectiveness of the rest of the crew."

Even before John had finished speaking, Byron was overcome with excitement and happiness. The opportunity he had just described sounded great to him. Then, suddenly, he was hit with anger. The opposing feeling was so strong that he gasped out loud. He vocalized the first thing that came to mind.

"Why would I want to do that?" he asked, his voice heavy with spite. "You held me as a prisoner. Ferro murdered me!"

"Ari is no longer a member of this crew. As for the death of your body, Byron, I'm sorry. Nobody wanted you dead. We had our differences, sure, but nobody would have killed you. Even Ari was under the control of Aldebaran the pirate when she attacked you. Byron, you can't forget the circumstances that led to your severely curtailed privileges aboard the ship. You never earned the trust necessary to be a full member of this crew, although I firmly believe that you were well on your way. I never believed that the original seven crewmembers ended up together just by accident. You have the chance to live up to your full potential now, and honestly, we need your help."

Byron more cautiously kept his thoughts to himself this time. After a few seconds he spoke again.

"Who's on the ship now?"

"Myself, Ray, Richter, Dana, Christie, and the reformed Seth Aldebaran. There's also a girl named Miriam that we picked up a little while back. Listen, Byron, before you decide anything further, I want you to access the ship's log that Ray's been keeping. Read about everything that's happened since you were shot and let me know if you're still angry with us. I can help you find it, or I could just read it to..."

"I want to talk to Christie."

"If you agree to help us, you'll have plenty of time to talk to whomever you please."

"Either I talk to Christie, or I follow some of these points of lights until I find the life support system and start pushing buttons."

"I'll go get her. Byron, while I'm gone, think about this. It was my decision to place you in the quantum grid. Not everyone on board agreed with that. Christie was never your biggest fan, you know that. Still, after everything that's happened, we ultimately decided that you deserve a second chance. At least that much she agreed with."

"What was your other choice?"

"To let your consciousness disappear."

"No, I mean for running the ship's systems. You said Seth became part of Aldebaran. So what happened to the ship?"

"By then we were able to duplicate most of the Umberian programming with our Earth computers, but it was never the best solution and proved to be highly problematic. Using you to replace Seth was the most logical fix. Once you get used to your new job, our odds of succeeding in the upcoming mission will dramatically increase. We need your help."

"I still want to talk to Christie."

"Do you mind if I ask why?"

"Get Christie in here or I kill everyone."

"Poke around a little bit more and you'll find that we're currently planetside. Everyone else is off the ship right now. If you want to subvert the ship's systems you will only harm yourself. I'll let you talk to Christie, but you need to promise not to disrupt anything. That includes the repairs to the dorsal turret that are going on right now."

"Agreed."

In the busy main hangar on Freedmen Station, Major Pyramis was just strapping himself into his fighter when Lieutenant Brentage called him.

"Pyramis."

"Sir, a ship is approaching. We're being hailed."

"Identity?"

"Captain Farril Calico of the Almagest."

Pyramis almost dressed down the lieutenant until he realized he had never passed on the alert from his superiors. It was an embarrassing oversight, but it would probably never be discovered. Chalk it up to the privileges of command, he thought wistfully.

"Put him through to my Stylus," he said.

"Roger."

An obviously Hayakuvian man appeared on Pyramis' monitor.

"Captain Calico, this is Major Rafe Pyramis, commander of Freedmen Station."

"Major, I sincerely hope that you are not deaf to reason. Please hear me out before you launch your fighters."

"Captain, whatever actions caused you to be flagged as a rogue vessel are none of my business. Consider yourself fortunate that I am too busy to attack your vessel as I have so been ordered. If you do not exit this system, however, you will leave me no choice."

"The only thing I did to piss off Hayaku Central Command was show up and try to warn them of the arrival of the Zendreen fleet at Freedmen! Since when are you guys in the habit of killing the messenger?"

"What do you know about the Zendreen activity?"

As succinctly as possible, Calico told Pyramis what had happened up until that point, notably leaving both his opinion and speculation out of the narrative. Pyramis nodded at the conclusion.

"If what you say is true," began Pyramis, "then CentCom has no intention of intervening against the Zendreen. My second-in-command speculated that this may be a move to force the colonists to abandon their bid for independence in exchange for military protection, now I suspect he is correct."

"If that's true, then why destroy my vessel? What's the worst I could do other than try to convince the colonists of the same thing?"

"You said your name is Calico, right? What's your relationship with the prime minister?"

"Of Freedmen? None that I know of. What's his name?"

"Her name is Anya Calico."

The captain leaned back in his chair and sighed. "She always had dangerous ambition. Yeah, I know her, Major. It's possible that General Felmio wanted me dead because I might have undue influence over her."

"Is she your mother?"

"Ex-wife, actually. I've been mucking about in the Nursery of the Gods lately; time dilation explains the age difference."

"Is it possible that Felmio wanted to eliminate you simply to get rid of one more Freedmen ally?"

"I suppose, but I am only one ship."

"General Felmio may be many things but he is not an idiot. One ship can make all the difference."

"Perhaps. Major, am I wrong that the only reason you're entertaining this conversation is because you disagree with CentCom?"

"This sector of space is my responsibility and I reserve the right to converse with whomever I please. My orders are to defend the colony if the Zendreen attack."

"Why would you be ordered to defend the colony if CentCom is holding out for a deal?"

"That's above my pay grade, Captain."

"You can't possibly have more than one squadron on your station. How much good can you expect to do without backup from the Hayakuvian main fleet?"

"We can show the colony that Hayaku will still back them up, if they agree to abandon their independence. Captain, there is far too much speculation flying around in this conversation. It's inappropriate for me to be discussing it with you at all."

"Unless Hayakuvian weapons technology has grown at an exponential rate since I left, one squadron will hardly even slow down the Zendreen fleet. Aren't you concerned that CentCom is going to sacrifice you just to fool the colony?"

"I'm hoping to cause a standoff, not a skirmish. If we show the Zendreen that we're willing to fight, then that gives the colony time to capitulate to our demands."

"I'm sorry, Major, but that doesn't make any sense. If the Zendreen attack the colony then they will roll right over you long before reinforcements can arrive."

"I have yet to evaluate the offensive capabilities of the Zendreen fleet. It's possible..."

"No, it's not. Take my word for it, the fleet will kick your ass in the time it takes to write your two-paragraph obituary."

Flustered, Pyramis was at a loss for words. A simple lie to his lieutenant to buy time had turned into a huge mess. He knew he could change his mind and tell Brentage that command had told them to stand down, but the evidence for a conspiracy against the colony was overwhelming. He had hoped that his squadron would be a deterrent against the Zendreen fleet; now he wondered if he had the right to sacrifice his own men for his philosophy.

"I know you have no reason to believe my side of the story," said Calico. "I appreciate that you have been willing to at least listen to me. There should still be enough time to contact your superiors for clarification. I respectfully suggest that you do so."

"I believe I will. And because there is a possibility that you were wrongfully attacked, I will leave this encounter out of it. I assume you will be heading to the colony next?"

"Yes."

"Good. If need be I will contact you there. Just know that if CentCom is indeed using this opportunity to force the colony to abandon its bid for independence, then this may be our last conversation."

"I understand. Good luck, Major. Calico out."

The screen went back to a display of the Stylus' systems. Pyramis groaned in frustration.

"I have no idea what I'm doing," he said to himself.

Lieutenant Brentage came back on the channel.

"Sir, you have a message from command coming in, encryption level five," he said.

"Put it through to me," Pyramis replied.

"Respectfully, sir, that's a violation of protocol. Encryption level five communications must be opened on a secure terminal."

The inconvenience of returning to the command center was far outweighed by the possibility that the new message could solve his problems, so Pyramis removed his helmet and opened the cockpit.

"I'll be back in a few minutes," he said to the hangar chief, and headed to the nearest lift.

Pyramis removed his pressurized flight gauntlets during the ride up. Brentage met him as he entered the command center.

"I've put the message through to the terminal in your office," the younger man said.

"Thank you, Lieutenant."

Pyramis was surprised when Brentage followed him into the office, and even more so when the lieutenant drew a pistol and pointed it at him.

"Don't do anything stupid, sir."

"I take it you've been monitoring my communications," Pyramis said as he attempted to disguise a painful rush of adrenaline. There was something in the lieutenant's bearing that easily convinced the major that physical resistance would be deadly.

"Command was kind enough to raise my clearance level from four to five. I got the message about an hour ago. I took the liberty of reading all of the level five communications that this station has received since you got here. I had suspected that you were going against the general's wishes, so it was nice to have those suspicions confirmed."

"Have you reached the same conclusion as I? I think it's rather obvious that command is preparing to let the Zendreen have their way with the colony."

"It does seem that way, Major. However, I am not prepared to commit treason just because I disagree with command."

"Military law allows commands to be disobeyed under certain circumstances. Regardless of the political relationship between Freedmen and Hayaku, ordering us to stand by and do nothing in the face of a hostile alien invasion is just plain wrong. I simply cannot believe that parliament would allow that to happen. I'm convinced that the military is going ahead with this plan without the consent of the government."

"There's no shortage of military officers who disagree with Freedmen's bid for independence."

"As we both well know. Are you one of them?"

Brentage lowered his pistol slightly. "My opinion is irrelevant."

"And yet, you chose to confront me alone. Why haven't you called for the captain of the watch?"

Brentage sighed, and tapped his pistol against his leg. "Here is what's going to happen, sir. You're going to call off the patrol. Then, you're going to get into your Stylus and leave the station. I'll report you as a deserter, or you can submit your resignation first and be guilty only of theft of military property. I am not willing to let you throw the entire squadron into a suicide mission, but if you want to kill only yourself, I'll do you the courtesy of looking the other way."

"Why not put the question to the squadron? I think two or three pilots would come with me."

"Don't push your luck, Pyramis. If I let more than one pilot get away then I lose my plausible deniability. I am not willing to throw my career away over this damn quagmire."

"How does letting me go benefit you?"

"What do you care?"

"Pure curiosity, Lieutenant."

"I get to sleep with a clean conscience. Now get out of here before I change my mind."

18.

"I'm really not comfortable with this."

On the busy pier next to the Reckless Faith, Christie folded her arms across her chest and frowned at John. Behind them, the newly-replicated weapons systems were being loaded onto an anti-gravity sled for transportation to Freedmen's nearest airbase. A Freedmen technician approached the pair, ignoring John's gesturing to him to wait.

"We're almost done fixing the dorsal turret," he said, grinning.

"Good, keep at it," said John. "We're still dealing with other problems right now."

The technician returned to the ladder leaning against the hull. John took Christie's arm and walked her a few feet further away from the others.

"You know as well as I do that we need Byron to cooperate with us right now," he said. "I don't think he can harm you, and I don't think that's what he wants."

"What does he want to do?" asked Christie, frustrated. "Gloat? Bitch? What's the point?"

"Whatever his motivation, you need to mollify him. I know it's going to be humiliating, but tell him what he wants to hear."

"Won't he be able to sense any insincerity? He won't be expecting me to be friendly."

"You may be right. Just use your best judgment. And don't forget that he doesn't need to know that Ari's with us."

"I understand."

"Good luck."

Christie nodded, and crossed the gangway into the airlock. Immediately upon boarding the ship she could feel a presence, and the sensation raised the hair on her neck. She tried to keep her mind calm as she made her way to the orb room. She entered the chamber, and felt stark fear at the sight of the new orb. After a few moments of silence, an outline of a hand appeared on the sphere.

"Byron?" she asked.

"Put your hand on the orb, Christie," said Byron's voice.

"Can't we talk here? Why did you want to see me, Byron?"

"I'm having a lot of trouble adjusting to this form. It would be easier if we could meet in the virtual world."

"Do you know what you're doing? Seth needed a considerable amount of practice before he could effectively run a simulation."

"I have something easy in mind. Don't worry, I've got a handle on it."

Christie swallowed and moved forward. The room melted away as she touched the warm surface of the orb, and she found herself in a familiar place. She was in the Derne Street Deli, a restaurant nestled between the buildings of Suffolk University in Boston. She was seated by the window, and a lightly toasted tuna sub with provolone cheese was on the table in front of her. It was all very familiar, except that the deli was deserted and the street was devoid of pedestrians or cars. The sub smelled wonderful, so Christie indulged in the penultimately useless act while in a sim: she took a bite. It was then that she noticed Byron standing by the counter, sporting the less-toned body he inhabited before finding himself exiled to the cargo hold of the Faith. In fact, he was wearing the same mock turtleneck sweater and sport jacket he preferred while attending

Christie's class. He seemed vibrant and his eyes flashed behind his glasses.

"Not a bad job, eh?" he asked.

"You got the tuna sub right, that's for sure," replied Christie.

"It was one of my favorites, too, although I preferred American cheese."

Despite her previous animosity toward Byron, Christie felt herself at ease in this environment. Still, it was impossible to forget the current situation. She took another, smaller bite of her sandwich.

"Did you remember to order a cup of Earl Gray for me?" she asked, invoking a simple simulation technique that worked well with Seth.

"I suppose I did," replied Byron, producing one from the counter behind him. He picked it up and sat down at Christie's table.

"You got me alone," she said, sipping the tea. "I'm the only one aboard the ship right now. Why did you want to talk to me?"

"Is Scherer telling the truth about my situation?"

"Yes," said Christie, putting a tremendous amount of faith in the answer.

"Seth had the memories of everyone who ever came into contact with the orb, correct?"

"It certainly seemed that way."

"Either he did or he didn't."

"I'm sorry, I'm not being glib; just empirical. It's most likely that he did, yes."

"Is this orb different from Seth's?"

"I don't believe so. It's too early to tell. You and I will have to work together for several days to determine..."

Byron interrupted her. "I've been able to access some of my own memories well enough, but the only ones of yours that I can find are the ones when we were together."

"Is exploring my memories really a priority for you right now?"

"Perhaps not, but I need to understand my capabilities and limitations."

"You might find it more instructive to have Aldebaran be your guide."

"I'll worry about that later. Right now I want to talk to you."

The light in the deli dimmed appreciably. Christie's sandwich suddenly changed color and she realized it had aged a few days. She pushed it away in disgust along with an unexpectedly empty tea cup.

"Why don't you concentrate on something a little bit easier, like your dorm room?" she asked.

"I'm not sure that will make any difference. I can't quite... concentrate on this place."

The deli faded away entirely and the pair found themselves on a busy city street. The buildings had a distinctly middle-eastern look, and the people who mingled past them were dressed in robes, hoods, and four-cornered hats. The noonday sun shined brightly above. An outdoor café was nearby, and a free table seemed to beckon them over. Christie immediately recognized the scene from a recurring dream that was bothering her, and her adrenaline rose in her chest.

"Where the hell are we?" asked Byron. "Is this a city you visited at some point?"

"I don't know where we are," replied Christie.

"I feel very strongly that this is your memory, not mine."

"This is a dream, not a memory."

"Or the memory of a dream?"

"Maybe. Let's worry about that later."

Byron shrugged and sat down at the table. Christie joined him, not without trepidation. She noticed a root beer float with vanilla ice cream at her setting.

"I sense that this place is very important, are you sure there's something you're not telling me?"

"It's impossible to know exactly what's going on with this place, so let's just concentrate on why you asked me here."

"Fine. I want to know how you really feel about me."

"My past feelings are irrelevant now, Byron. Your body died. How I felt about you personally is no longer relevant either. I consider the slate to be clean and I intend to judge you entirely on your future actions."

"Fair enough. I still want to know."

"I already told you. We could have been friends, and we were never going to be anything more. The decisions you made leading to our fight with the CIA had a very negative impact on our relationship, as they did for the entire crew. Some of us were willing to give you a second chance. John was your greatest advocate. I still believe you could have redeemed yourself if Ari hadn't... you know."

"I'm in love with you, Christie."

"You're infatuated with me, Byron. You can't be in love with me. Even if we wanted to we could never satisfy an essential condition of love, which is to be together. You need to accept that your life will never be the same, and our relationship will never be anything more than professional. We saved your soul by integrating you into a new orb, and you have the responsibility to the rest of us to help run the ship."

Byron reached for Christie's hand, and she drew away.

"You never let me participate in the simulations," he began, "but I heard about them. I know perfectly well that if you want to be with me, we can be together, in a reality of my creation."

"How can there be any future in that?"

"Don't belittle me, Christie. You know as well as I that orb simulations are all about the present. Forget about that for now, though. What if I make time with me a condition of my service?"

"I beg your pardon?"

"What if I insist that spending time with me, in this place, is a condition of my employment as an AI entity?"

"You should want to do that out of a sense of responsibility, honor, and damned human decency."

"That's a pretty hilarious statement coming from someone who stood by while a member of her own crew murdered me."

"You can't pin that on me. You can hardly even pin it on Ari, considering the circumstances."

"Just answer the question."

"If you refuse to help us, then you'll be removed from the system. If that happens, I have no idea how limited your consciousness will be. You might even be unconscious as long as the orb is disconnected. Weigh that possibility against simply treating me like a peer instead of a marionette. We got along just fine without an orb and we can just as easily pack you in Styrofoam and put you in the hold until you come to your senses."

"You're holding something back. Your words aren't ringing true. It doesn't quite make sense, either. What was it that John said to me..."

Byron trailed off and appeared to shimmer. Christie felt like she was losing a grip on her composure.

"Byron," she began, "try to concentrate on the fact that you have a second chance here."

"What's he doing here?" Byron asked sharply.

Christie looked around despite knowing that Byron meant someone in the orb room.

"Christie, is everything okay?" asked Ray's voice.

"I'm fine, Ray," Christie said into the air. "Byron and I are just working a few things out."

"Get him out of here," said Byron. "I insist on talking to you alone."

"He can't hear us. I'm not even sure that I spoke aloud just now."

"I don't care. Tell him to go away."

There was a violent flash of light and Christie found herself back in the orb room. Ray caught her as she lost her balance, and stood her back up.

"We need to talk outside," she said to him.

"Here, put your arm over my shoulder," said Ray.

"I know what's going on," said Byron's voice as Christie and Ray made their way through the galley. "You can't get rid of me. You're stuck with me. That explains some of what John said to me. Tell me I'm wrong!"

Christie and Ray doubled back upon reaching deck one and headed aft.

"You're not going anywhere," Byron said ominously.

Fearing that Byron might lock them in, Ray increased his pace to a trot, almost dragging the unfortunate Christie along with him. The airlock doors remained open, however, even after the pair crossed the gangway onto the sunlit pier.

The utility vehicle and weaponry were gone, as was the curious crowd, replaced instead with the smaller form of Prime Minister Calico's personal transport. Mother Calico and two of her aides stood with the rest of the Faith's crew. Ray and Christie approached, blinking in the daylight, and Christie nodded toward the prime minister.

"Please tell me you've made progress," said John.

"Byron has made a romantic relationship with me an imperative of his employment," she replied curtly.

The prime minister and her aides reacted with surprise, but their expressions were lost on Christie. John's anger was unmistakable.

"Son of a bitch," he muttered. "Any signs he's taking control of the ship?"

"Many. John, I need more time with him."

"We're out of time. The prime minister has just informed me that the Zendreen fleet has begun assuming an orbital posture. If you can't get Byron to cooperate, then we have no choice but to destroy the orb, restart the computers, and hope for the best."

"Have the Zendreen made a threat?"

"Yes, child," replied Mother Calico. "Freedmen is preparing for a battle. Your ship may only be one of two hundred, but it is one of the most powerful."

"Prime Minister," said one of the aides, "there's a call coming in you're going to want to take."

"Very well. Commander Scherer, do what's best for your crew, even that means sitting out the fight."

"I will, ma'am," replied John.

The prime minister and her entourage returned to the transport ship. The crew looked at each other grimly.

"Dana, Aldebaran and I have been discussing a third option," began Ari, "assuming Ray isn't on board with sharing Christie with our resident Lazarus."

"I'm all ears," said John.

Dana said, "Once we successfully integrated our Earth-based servers with Seth, he took advantage of the extra storage capacity they offered and began using our Random Access Memory to help process orb simulations. It was only a boost of a few percentage points but it was worth it. In fact, Seth was able to apply an essential aspect of quantum grid processing technology to our own network, enhancing it beyond anything we could have done on our own. Even after the original orb was destroyed, those enhancements remained. What this means is that there are two kinds of orb simulations that have the potential to shift Byron's consciousness entirely onto our Earth network. If Christie engages Byron in one of these types of simulation, then we can safely shut down the network without worrying about any cross-technology errors or destroyed hardware."

Christie blushed. "But the two types of sim you're talking about are combat and..."

"Fight him or fuck him," said Ari.

"How did you discover this?" asked Ray, also clearly embarrassed.

"It was by accident, I assure you," replied Dana.

"Relax," said Richter, jabbing Ray with his elbow. "There are entire communities devoted to the love of stuffed animals."

Christie shook her head. "There is no way I am willingly going to touch Byron, real or virtual, with anything less than a ten foot sanitized pole."

"Don't worry about that," said Aldebaran. "If you engage Byron in combat to a sufficient level then we can accomplish the same thing."

"How in the world am I supposed to do that?"

"You have more control over the sims than you might think. When I was running them as Seth, I relied on information from your minds for the majority of the images and sensations that you were experiencing. Now, obviously you can't kill Byron in a sim. However, to place himself in a sim, he has to play by all the same rules that you do. He'll feel adrenaline, fatigue, and pain, if you can manage to force them upon him. It will be during that time that we can isolate him."

"What if he doesn't feel like fighting? Even if I'm guiding the sim, he can still quit any time he wants."

"True. You need to make him want to hurt you."

"It sounds like I'd be a better candidate for the job, then," said Ari.

Aldebaran shrugged. "Yes, but I doubt he'll allow you into a sim in the first place. It has to be Christie."

"I'll do it," said Christie. "I'm quite sure I can piss him enough to make him attack me. How should I do it? Give myself a gun and start shooting at him?"

"The more personal, the better."

"There ain't nothing more personal than a knife in the ribs," said Richter flatly.

"Just so everyone is clear on the concept," began Dana, "if we're successful at this, then Byron will cease to exist. Essentially, we'll be killing him again. Is everyone on board with that?"

"I'm beginning to feel a lot better about doing it the first time," said Ari.

Christie headed toward the gangway. "He's going to kill himself. He just doesn't realize it yet."

In his office adjacent to the bridge, Captain Calico's hands tightened around a new ceramic mug. One of Freedmen's supernumeraries had just informed him that the prime minister was about to take his call. He found himself much more nervous than he'd anticipated. There were a number of conflicting emotions resurfacing in him, not the least of which was that someone he ultimately cared about was in the path of an invasion fleet.

Mother Calico's image appeared on his monitor. Even though he'd prepared himself for how Anya might have aged, to actually see her was a shock. There was no mistaking her for his ex-wife and the mother of his deceased child, but the older woman he saw on the surface of the planet was much thinner, and there was something in her eyes that he'd never seen before.

"Anya," he said quietly.

"Farril," Anya replied, a soft smile on her face. "I wish your return could have come at a more peaceful time."

"How are you? I mean, not counting the belligerent aliens encircling your home."

"I am very well. Time has been very kind to me. My fortune has been boundless, even when current circumstances are considered. And you, Farril?"

"Time, by its fickle nature, has left me virtually untouched."

"I should say so. You look exactly the same as when you left."

The captain's heart rose in his chest. Anya may have been hiding an insult inside a compliment, and if so, it stung him. He chose his words as to mitigate that possibility.

"My anguish is dull compared to when we last spoke. Seeing you is bittersweet, as it brushes away that tarnish."

"I was unfair to you. I can only blame the same anguish for that. I forgave you as soon as that transport ship went light. I hope you were able to forgive yourself not to long after."

"I never truly did."

Anya's smile disappeared. "Farril..."

"Forget it. We have larger problems right now. What has the Hayakuvian Central Government said to your request for military backup?"

"Nothing. We haven't requested it."

Surprised, Farril took a moment to reply. "Then either you've decided to let the colony be destroyed, or your defensive capability is far beyond what the Hayakuvian military believes it is."

"I would hope it would be obvious to you that we have no intention of submitting to the Zendreen."

"You should know that there is evidence that Hayaku Prime has allowed the Zendreen to proceed unimpeded. Is there really that much opposition to colonial freedom?"

"If true, it would not surprise me. The distance between us creates a convenient excuse for their inaction. Did you try to warn them?"

"That's how I got roped into this mess. I was speaking with a general when I was attacked."

Anya absent-mindedly twirled a strand of her hair. "It is unlikely that the Hayakuvian central government would withhold military aid if we had indeed asked for it. I find it humorous that if there is a conspiracy within the military toward inaction that they just assumed we'd come hat in hand begging and desperate for their help."

"Why? Have you made an effort to hide your true defensive strength?"

"Of course," Anya said casually. "Besides, it's no secret that there are high ranking members of the military who disagree with Freedmen's bid for independence."

"And you'd like nothing more than to prove yourself by routing the Zendreen."

"It would be convenient."

Farril gestured at his monitor. "Anya, that is easier said than done. Right now I'm watching the fleet set up for a major assault. I'm not a military tactician but I'd estimate you're going to need at least five cruisers and three hundred fighters, and that would only gain you a stalemate."

"I have faith in my people, Farril. I've also taken the liberty of scanning your ship, and I would be honored if you would join the defense of my home."

"We're not at full capacity, but I'm ready to assist you as much as I can. Do you have any idea what the Zendreen hope to gain here?"

"They sent us a message not too long ago. They claim they're going to take resources and move on, but we've been warned that they're actually planning on colonizing the planet."

"I take it you've been conversing with Commander Scherer and his lot."

"Yes. I suspected you two knew each other after he mentioned Janish Revelnik. How is old Nicky anyway?"

"In a Rakhar prison, unfortunately. Shuffling without a license in former Empire territory."

"How sad. I hope Megumi Rukitara met a better fate."

"She's my first mate, actually, and she's fit as a phoenix. Anya, I know you're not going to discuss your defensive capabilities with me over the radio, but do you really have the resources to repel the Zendreen?"

"It won't be easy, but yes. Farril, I know the battle is imminent. There's a mission briefing in ten minutes, and I'd like you to attend in person. I'll send you the coordinates."

"Will you be there?"

"Of course."

"Then I won't miss it. Speaking of Commander Scherer, has he and his crew pledged the Reckless Faith to the defense of the colony?"

"Yes, but they're having a serious problem with their computer systems and the ship is deadlined on the surface. They may have to sit this one out."

"If I know Scherer, he won't like that one bit. Perhaps if there's time I'll send my engineers to assist them with their problem."

"Time may be too short for that. I'll see you at the briefing, Farril."

Nine minutes later, Captain Calico and First Mate Rukitara found themselves standing in a marble hallway in one of Freedmen's impressive capitol city buildings. A parade of young fighter pilots, male and female, had been trickling into a nearby auditorium since they'd arrived. Calico didn't know exactly how many there were, but it didn't seem like enough. Again, Farril was nervous about seeing Anya in the flesh, and wondered whether a hug or a simple handshake would be appropriate. After all, she was the senior leader of an entire planet. As he considered this his eyes fell on a male pilot he actually recognized.

"Major Pyramis?" he asked the man.

"Captain Calico," replied the younger man. "I'm not surprised to see you here."

"I am to see you! Did you go AWOL or something?"

"I've resigned from my position. They're going to have to bill me for the advanced tactical fighter craft I took with me on my way out the door, however."

Farril laughed. "Fantastic! From what I can tell, we could really use even one more guy out there who knows what he's doing."

"Are you going to introduce me to your companion?"

"Sure. Major Pyramis, this is Megumi Rukitara, my first mate."

"You look as dangerous as you are beautiful," Pyramis said to her.

"You're Umberian," Megumi replied. "How did you end up all the way out here?"

"My parents thought it a better place to raise their son than under the heel of the Zendreen."

"Life is not without its little ironies," said Farril. "We'd better get in there, the briefing is about to start."

The others nodded and the trio entered the auditorium. Captain Calico took note of a sign indicating the maximum capacity of the room on the way in. The large chamber was set up as an amphitheater, and a large monitor took center stage. The room was supposedly limited to three hundred occupants; Farril estimated only about two-thirds of the seats were taken.

"I hope this isn't everyone," he muttered as they found a place to sit.

"If they have cruisers," began Megumi, "then those crews are probably aboard."

The amphitheater was dimly lit, the only light issuing from pellucid white bas-relief sconces spaced every eight feet along the walls and framed with black marble panels. Each sconce depicted what appeared to be important events in the history of the colony. On the stage, a Hayakuvian man in a black flight suit stood up in front of the monitor and motioned for silence.

"For those of who don't know me, I am Second Minister Zuben," he said. "I will be briefing you on the order of battle."

Farril looked around for the prime minister, and noticed her sitting in the front row. An image of the planet appeared on the monitor, along with animation of both the Zendreen fleet and colonial resources.

"As we speak," continued Zuben, "the Zendreen fleet is preparing to assume orbit. We have counted the following ships: one battleship, four heavy cruisers, and ten support vessels. We have been informed that the larger ships are carrying fighters, but their number is unknown. Based on pre-orbital approach vectors, we have projected the following paths."

Zuben pointed a remote control at something, and the image on the monitor changed to show several bands encircling the globe.

"The heavy cruisers are most likely targeting the following strategical assets for orbital bombardment: the Marikal power station, the Basilisk power station, Colonial Heavy Industries, and of course, the capitol city. The battleship is not targeting anything specific that we can tell."

"The path of the battleship takes it right over the Reckless Faith," said Mother Calico.

"They must really have a score to settle with our guests," replied Zuben.

"Remind me to ask them about that, my dear," said the prime minister quietly. "Now, please continue."

Zuben cleared his throat. "Yes, ma'am. Now then, pilots, assuming these orbital trajectories remain consistent, the first target will be the Marikal power station in approximately two hours. Next will be Basilisk thirty minutes later, then CHI fifty minutes after that. This city will be in range in four and a half hours."

"What about the Reckless Faith?" asked Farril.

"They have nine minutes," answered Anya, having done the math in her head.

Zuben folded his arms across his chest. "Sir, with all due respect to your friends, we can't devote any resources to protecting one ship. Surely you realize that."

Farril nodded, and said, "I can at least offer to evacuate any of Scherer's people, just in case."

"Of course."

Farril pulled out his communication device, and began to send a text message to John.

"Please continue," said Megumi.

"Now then, the most obvious course of action is to attack the cruisers in the order of the threats. However, several of the support vessels appear to be preparing for a landing. If so, they probably contain enemy infantry. Now, dismounted infantry by themselves don't pose much of a threat. What is of interest here are the support vessels themselves. If we can capture them, then we can use them as weapons against the cruisers and battleship. If we're right, the Zendreen will be expecting a high-altitude skirmish with the large ships as our main targets.

If we keep the fight near the ground, then we can ensure the utilization of all of our atmosphere-only fighters."

"Only sixty percent of their fighters are space-capable," whispered an astonished Farril to Megumi as he read the information on the central monitor.

"And they only have two hundred and seven fighters in total," replied Meg.

"They're either stupid or brave," added Pyramis.

"So," continued Zuben, "here is our plan. All of our space-capable fighters will attack the cruiser targeting the capitol. The remaining fighters will split up and attack five of the support vessels. However, their goal will be to help capture those ships, not destroy them. Then, five brave volunteers will pilot them near to the larger ships and overload their stardrives. If any of the larger vessels survive that, our fighters should be able to finish them off. Any questions?"

Most of the pilots raised a hand. Zuben pointed at a young female.

"Are we basically sacrificing CHI and the power stations?" she asked.

"Yes. Those facilities are being evacuated now. Hopefully at least one of them will be saved by our efforts, but they're acceptable losses. Next?"

"How exactly are we going to capture the support vessels without damaging them?" asked a male pilot.

"You don't need to worry about that; the fighters are only meant to keep any enemy escorts busy and to protect the ground troops. Then you need to escort the captured ships into position for the engine overload. Next?"

"Those volunteers, it's a suicide mission, right?" asked a middle-aged woman.

"Unfortunately, yes. We just don't have enough force for a stand-up fight. Fortunately five volunteers should be easy to find, since virtually every unmarried man and woman in the army offered to go. Next?"

"Will the escort fighters be able to escape the overload blast in time?" asked a muscular, balding man cradling a capable-looking projectile rifle.

"Chief Correia, it is good to see you again. All I can tell you is that the fighters will need to cover the approach of the support vessels for as long as possible. Once detonation is certain they will obviously need to exit the vicinity at top speed."

A wave of grumbling washed over the crowd.

"In other words, you're likely screwed," Megumi whispered to Farril.

"Some die or everybody dies, it's not a tough decision," he replied. "It just seems unnecessary..."

"My Stylus could seriously damage a cruiser if I overloaded the engine," whispered Pyramis, "but I'm rather fond of being alive."

Farril stood up. "I'd like to suggest an alternative."

"This is not a forum," began Anya, "but since you are an off-worlder who has offered to fight on our side, I will listen to your idea. Please introduce yourself to the Air Corps."

"I am Captain Farril Calico of the independent vessel Almagest. The prime minister and I are blood relatives. Prime Minister, Second Minister, while I deeply respect your decision to fight this battle without the assistance of Hayaku, I cannot agree with it considering the circumstances. How can you ask your brave young men and women to sacrifice their lives before all options for peace have been exhausted? My proposal is this: enter into negotiations with the Zendreen to buy time, and I will return to Hayaku and make an appeal directly to the civilian government. Even if the military is against it, they won't be able to stop me from informing them. Then at least we'll know the decision of those who truly hold the power, barring of course an overt military coup."

"Cap, we can't risk using the overdrive device again without at least a few hours of repairs," said Megumi quietly.

"Captain," began Pyramis, "all outside communications with Hayaku are screened by the military. You couldn't get a message past them without landing on the planet, and the defensive net is too strong for you to seriously expect to slip past. I'm awed by your offer on our behalf, but it's just not realistic."

"I didn't know that the military screens all incoming radio traffic," replied Farril. "Times have changed since I called Hayaku home."

"Unfortunately, yes."

"We appreciate the offer," said Anya, stepping onto the stage. "If we had time, perhaps a diplomatic envoy could be dispatched to Hayaku. That is not our disposition, however. We must prove to Hayaku, and especially the military, that Freedmen is capable of providing for its own defense. Only then will we truly gain our independence."

Farril looked into his former wife's eyes. He smiled as he remembered the firebrand he'd married, though time had turned her red hair to silver.

"I understand," he said. "I just have one question: do we have any idea what the infantry elements are targeting?"

Zuben said, "They're most likely going to target our airbases. Now, if there are any other questions specific to the mission, talk to your squadron leaders. Lieutenants, you will receive your squadron assignments immediately following this mission. Everyone else, gas up your fighters and begin engine shakedown. That's all."

The pilots stood up and began talking amongst themselves. Farril's communicator beeped.

"Scherer replied to my text message," he said, reading the screen.

"Yeah?" asked Megumi. "What's he say?"

"Fuck me."

"What?"

"No, that's what he said: 'Fuck me.' See?"

"That's an odd expression," said Pyramis, "but considering the circumstances, I think I understand the sentiment."

"Let's hope he can get his ship in the air soon. Pyramis, good luck out there, I'll keep your freq on commo. Rukitara, I'll catch up with you. I'm going to have a word with Anya for a moment."

"You aren't still trying to change her mind, are you?" Meg asked.

"I should have remembered that's impossible. No, this is strictly personal."

19.

The Pigeon Cove Quarry in Rockport, Massachusetts was not something that most people would consider romantic, but certain past experiences for Byron had provided him the proper context to think so. It was for those reasons that he chose to simulate a picnic for Christie there, imagining a warm summer night and a beautiful starlit sky to compliment the rocky environment. The motionless water created a perfect mirror of the celestial sphere, and in shallower water somewhere nearby hundreds of small frogs endeavored toward romance of their own. Christie's compliance with the fantasy was all part of the plan, but she found herself exposed to a side of Byron that was not entirely objectionable. Still, the food, wine, and Byron's charming demeanor didn't deter her from her mission, as no level of good will on his part could make up for his transgressions. However, she was fair-minded enough to accept that perhaps, in another life, she could have warmed up to him.

"Christie, this is Dana."

Dana's voice rang out in Christie's head, as clear and strong as if the other woman was seated beside her on the blanket. Byron, who was talking about his orb discoveries, refilled Christie's glass and showed no sign of hearing anything other than his own voice.

"If you can hear me, brush your hair back over your left ear."

Christie did so, earning her a renewed smile from Byron.

"Good. I hate to distract you, but listen carefully. Ari and I discovered a way to open a secure audio/video channel with you. Byron should not be able to hear us, and we are watching you on a monitor on the bridge. You should also know that Byron has locked the doors to the orb room, so we're not going to be able to get you out of there until you complete your mission. If you understand, scratch your nose. Good. Now here's the really important part. The Zendreen battleship is targeting the Faith for orbital bombardment and will be in firing position in seven minutes. I suggest you move forward with the plan now."

Christie drank from her glass to conceal her anxiety. She took a deep breath and imagined Richter's combat knife in her left hand. As it materialized, Byron leaned in and kissed her. The leather handle of the knife was cool in her palm and Byron's soft touch was like melted chocolate on her lips.

"That was wonder..." Byron started to say.

Standing up, Christie kicked Byron in the chest. He splayed backward onto the rock, scattering the contents of the portable cooler. The bottle of wine rolled off the ledge and hit the surface of the water half a second later. Byron leaped to his feet with remarkable agility and cried out in surprise and disgust.

"What the hell?" he added.

"You didn't seriously think that I'd go along with this bullshit, did you?" asked Christie, pointing her knife at him.

"I thought you might extend me some trust!"

"We're beyond trust by now. The least you could do is die with dignity."

Christie slashed Byron's arm, opening up a three-inch laceration. He stepped back and put up his fists, grimacing.

"You mean something more dignified than letting Ari splatter my brains across a boulder? Anyway, how do you expect to kill me in here?"

"I'm sure going to enjoy trying."

Christie resumed her attack. This time, Byron was ready. His defensive moves were unpolished, but effective, and she realized that doing any significant damage was going to be more difficult than she first thought. Christie's own hand-to-hand training was meager, especially in comparison to Richter and Aldebaran, and Byron had apparently absorbed some of the knowledge resident in the orb. He reinforced this by successfully implementing an arm bar and knocking the knife to the ground. Christie stomped on his shin and broke free.

"Hurts, doesn't it?" he sneered, squaring up.

"You tell me."

The fight had progressed into the woodline. Christie picked up a branch and broke it across Byron's arms. He was unable to conceal how much this hurt, and backed off.

"Son of a bitch!"

"That's the general sentiment."

Christie decided that if she couldn't best him with quality, she'd go for quantity. She set upon him with a flurry of blows, some of which made contact, and managed to mash up at least one of his testicles with her knee. She drove him back toward the ledge before he regained his balance.

"You seem to forget who's in charge here," he wheezed, and spun around.

The four-foot long hardwood staff he suddenly wielded caught Christie in the ribs, and she doubled over in pain. She struggled to breathe the simulated air as her eyes involuntarily teared up.

"You know," he panted, "this might actually be good for our relationship. If we can't be lovers, at least we can be sparring partners with a genuine emotional connection."

"Damn you, Byron. After all this, you think this is just a game?"

"Isn't it? Nothing that happens in here matters. At least not to me."

Christie rose up quickly and threw a handful of dirt into Byron's face. He stumbled back and she wrested the staff from his grasp. She hit him as hard as she could in the side of the head, and he collapsed.

"That did it," said Dana's voice. "Just keep him isolated for a few more seconds and we'll..."

Ari's voice interrupted her. "He's evacuating all the air from the orb room."

"Don't distract her! Christie, kick his ass!"

Byron pushed himself onto his side. He brushed the blood from his face and looked at Christie.

"This might kill you, or it might keep us together for eternity," he said, grinning.

"I'll take my chances," she replied, and brought the staff down one last time.

"God damn it, Dana, get this door open!"

Ray slammed his fist again on the hatch to the orb room. Richter put his hand on his shoulder in a vain attempt to calm him down.

"I got it, I got it," said Dana over the intercom.

Ray almost dislocated his own shoulder opening the hatch. A rush of wind accompanied the men into the room. Christie lay motionless on the floor beneath the orb. Ray rushed to her side and Richter turned his attention to the bank of computers against the wall.

"Server number nine!" said Dana urgently. "Now!"

Richter drew his pistol and thoroughly destroyed the selected machine. A moment later, Ari entered the chamber.

"Couldn't you have just unplugged it?" she asked.

"She's not breathing!" yelled Ray.

Richter holstered his weapon and knelt by Christie. He grasped her wrist.

"No pulse," he said, "Ari, get the AED. Ray, start rescue breathing."

Ray put his mouth against hers as Richter cut open her shirt. It didn't take Ari long to retrieve the Automated External Defibrillator from the galley. She set up the device rapidly, referring to its simple diagrams for guidance.

"Initiating systems restart," said Dana.

"What's going on down there?" asked John.

"Christie's crashing," replied Richter. "We may have to shock her."

Making no attempt at modesty, Ari placed the paddles on Christie and waited for the machine to diagnose the problem.

"Her heartbeat is all over the place," Ari said.

On the bridge, Dana kicked the panel at her feet in frustration. She took a deep breath and continued to work at her station. John wiped off his brow and looked at Aldebaran, who was double-checking Dana's efforts.

"One minute," John said quietly.

Miriam, who was outside minding the animals, called in on the radio.

"John, this is Miriam," she said. "The Almagest is here. Tycho is going bonkers, I think I need some help restraining him."

"I'll go," said Aldebaran. "I'm not doing any good here anyway."

Aldebaran exited. John looked skyward and saw dozens of ships glittering in the setting sun. Combat had yet to be initiated, but it was obvious which scintillating point of light was the Zendreen battleship. It was moving in a straight line opposite the horizon, and was headed directly for them.

"Scherer to all crew," said John, activating the ship-wide intercom. "I want everyone to evacuate to the Almagest. Dana, that includes you. I'll continue to work on the reboot."

"I'm not going anywhere," Dana said tersely.

"That's your choice. Richter, get Christie and the others on board the Almagest."

"Christie's dead, John."

Richter's announcement stunned the crew into silence. John stared at his console in shock. Dana put her hand over her mouth as if to stifle a scream. John pushed past his emotions and spoke.

"Get her over to the Almagest, Chance. They may have more advanced medical equipment."

"John, this is Ari. We don't have enough time to carry her up three decks and out to the 'Gest."

"God damn it, Ari, just try!"

"She's right," said Richter. "Even I can't carry her that far that quickly."

The lights on the bridge immediately went to 100%, and the hum of the ship's engines filled their ears.

"All systems just came back online!" said Dana.

John vaulted over the side of the pilot chair and grabbed the controls. He sealed the airlock and brought the ship roughly out of the water.

"Captain Calico, this is Scherer," he said into the radio. "As soon as Aldebaran and Miriam are on board, break atmo and prepare to dock with us in low orbit. We have a critical casualty to move to your ship."

"Roger," replied Calico, "I'm just closing up our ramp now."

"The Zendreen battleship will be in firing range in ten seconds," said Dana.

"It doesn't matter anymore," said John, and pushed the throttle to the firewall.

The ship rocketed upward at over four thousand miles per hour, clearing the atmosphere in seconds. John's monitors showed him that the Almagest joined the Faith a few seconds later.

"Scherer, this is Calico. I hate to say it, but docking maneuvers are impossible right now. We'll be sitting ducks for too long. How bad is your casualty?"

"She's already dead," John replied with frustration, "but only for a few minutes. I was hoping that you might have better medical equipment on your ship."

"I do, but we'll have to find somewhere to hide on the surface to transport the crewmember."

The Zendreen fleet, almost indistinguishable from the starfield at that altitude, began trading fire with the colonial fighters. Space and the upper atmosphere of the planet lit up with colorful energy discharges. At the moment, none of it was aimed at the two ships. Richter entered from the corridor and stood next to John.

"Do you have any idea where would make a good landing site?" asked John after glancing at Richter.

The signal from Calico's ship crackled with interference from the battle, and his voice sounded further away.

"I'm sorry, but we don't really have time for that. I need to brief you on the order of battle and get started on my objectives. We need the Faith as a combat vessel, too. We have razor-thin margins of error for this defense to work, Scherer. If you order me to land with you then we may be able to save your friend. We might also compromise the entire mission."

"You can't possibly expect me to make that kind of choice!" yelled John.

"Wait one, Captain," said Richter, and muted the radio connection.

"We have to try and save Christie," John said to Richter.

"Captain Calico is right. We have a greater commitment here. Christie is just one person. She's gone, John, and even Calico's equipment might not be able to bring her back. We need to concentrate on the task at hand. You're angry, I'm angry, so let's get in this war and get some fucking payback."

John took a deep breath, and nodded his head. He wiped off his brow and got back on the radio.

"Calico, this is Scherer. What's our plan of attack?"

"One of the cruisers is targeting the capitol city. We need to assist the fighters assigned to attacking it. In fact, they probably won't be able to stop it without our help, so let's not dawdle."

"Okay. Let's get in the war. Shall I take point or do you want to..."

"The Zendreen battleship is sending a wide band broadcast," interrupted Dana.

"Let's hear it."

A Zendra speaking Residerian was heard, and a moment later it was translated into English.

"This is Commander Lithilkin of the Zendreen. We are prepared to fire on several critical targets, including your capitol city. Order your fighters to stand down and we will discuss terms of a ceasefire."

"Let's hope the prime minister answers on an open channel, too," said Richter.

The two sides stopped trading fire, and a moment later Richter's wish was granted.

"This is Mother Calico of Freedmen Colony. I am prepared to listen your terms; however, you should know that my people will never submit to an invasion."

Ray and Ari entered the bridge. Ray's face was smudged with tears, and he wore a taut expression. Ari looked exhausted.

"Where's..." whispered Richter.

"I put her body in cold storage," replied Ray, his voice hoarse.

"Here are our terms," said Lithilkin. "Several lightly-armed support vessels will be directed to your largest sustenance repositories. We will take as much of your shelf-stable supplies as possible, as well as several thousand gallons of potable water."

"That's it?" asked the prime minister. "Commander, such a request is hardly worth going to war over."

"You will also deliver the ship known as the Reckless Faith to us."

"Son of a bitch," said John.

"I have no way of controlling that ship, Commander. Even if I could betray an ally, the crew of that ship is free to make their own decisions."

"Get me in on this conversation," said John to Dana.

"Roger," Dana said, working at her console. "You're live."

"This is Commander Scherer of the Reckless Faith. Are you really willing to risk the potential loss of several ships, or even the failure of your resupply mission, just for an act of revenge?"

"I should ask you the same thing, Scherer," said Lithilkin, "except in your case, it is the lives of thousands of colonists. If you don't surrender to us, we will attack, and from where I'm sitting I don't see much of a chance that we'll lose the engagement."

"I will not ask you to surrender yourself," said the prime minister. "Commander Lithilkin, please listen to reason. We will gladly give you all of our shelf-stable stores and water to avoid bloodshed. However, your assessment of our defensive capabilities is wrong. If you insist on a fight, you risk the destruction of your fleet."

"Scherer. Give up your ship now, or we attack. You have two minutes to decide."

"The signal has been terminated," said Dana. "Mother Calico is hailing us."

"Let her wait a minute," said John, then to the crew, "Okay, folks. This is where ideology meets reality. Is anyone here willing to sacrifice their lives or this ship to prevent open warfare?"

"Scherer," began Richter, "you can't trust the Zendreen to peacefully take the food and water if we surrender. Besides, we've got an entire wing of fighters ready to stand beside us. If they're willing to fight, then let's give 'em hell."

"Richter speaks for all of us," said Dana. "We also have a greater commitment to return to Earth alive someday."

"You're not seriously considering offering yourself, are you?" asked Ari.

"No," said John, "but I thought I might make the gesture, just to seem magnanimous."

"Then why are you asking the rest of us?"

"I just don't want to look like an asshole."

"You can't help that, John," said Christie.

Christie's voice rang out, as clear as if she was standing in the center of the bridge, but with an added layer of bass and vibrato that could only have come from one place.

"Christie?" asked several of the crew, astonished.

"Are you..." gasped Ray, trailing off.

"Yes," she replied calmly. "I'm inside the orb. Sorry it took so long for me to find my voice. I had to accept the shock of losing my corporeal body, as well as learn to navigate the quantum grid."

"So you know that your body is dead?" asked Ari.

"I watched you and Ray work on me. I am very sorry to say that your efforts were futile. I realized I was the only one who could get the ship's systems online, so I remained inside the orb until I discovered how to accomplish that."

Ray said, "So you could have returned to your body?"

"Yes, but we'd all be dead. I did what had to be done."

Sinking into a nearby chair, Ray began to cry again, but this time out of joy. "I'll take you any way I can, Angel."

"Your body is on ice," began John, "so we may yet be able to restore you if we can find advanced enough medical care. For now, I'm thrilled to have a cooperative AI back on board. Are you up to this fight, Christie?"

"Hell yeah, John," she replied. "I wish you could feel what I feel right now. It's like being able to see and understand every aspect of the ship at once, without really thinking about it. I'm even receiving feedback from the crew's minds that I can only begin to comprehend."

"That's very cool and somehow disquieting at the same time. For now, we have some alien thorax to kick."

On board on the Almagest, Doctor Trewler made his way from the medical bay to the galley. He was tapping on his PDA and ignoring the faint sounds of the ship's weapons systems. He knew better than to bother the captain during a combat action, and there was no rush to pass on the new information he'd just received. He wanted to talk to the newest arrival on board first anyway, a girl named Miriam whom he had yet to meet.

He found her in the galley at a computer console, a small feline curled up in her lap. She'd figured out how to access a video link to the bridge, and was watching the battle unfold with great interest. She looked up as Trewler stepped into the chamber.

"Miriam, isn't it? I'm Doc Trewler, the physician aboard the Almagest."

"Nice to meet you, sir," she said, immediately returning her attention to the screen.

"Wasn't there one other from the Faith that came aboard with you?"

"Yes, Seth. He's in the loo right now."

"Do you mind if I ask you some questions?"

"What about?"

Trewler pulled up a chair and sat down. "I hate to pry into your personal life, but Arianna Ferro was never very forthcoming about her past during her time on this ship. I was hoping you could fill me in on her past, at least up until you saw her last."

"Ari? I only just met her a few days ago."

"You'll excuse me if I find that hard to believe."

"I beg your pardon?" asked Miriam, turning to face him. "Earth is a big planet, we don't all know each other down there."

"Whenever someone boards the Almagest, our computer screens them for pathogens. This includes a DNA profile. I apologize if you find this intrusive, but it's for the safety of the crew. If you were sick you could compromise all of us."

"Are you accusing me of something?"

"No, I just find it incredible that you wouldn't know that Ari is your paternal sister."

"What?"

"I mean I know that you both had the same father. There is an obvious physical resemblance as well. Am I to believe that you didn't notice that either?"

Miriam stood up, ejecting her cat to the deck. "I'll take that as a compliment, but no, I didn't know. In fact, unless your tests can be independently verified I find them quite suspicious."

"Why would I fabricate them?"

"I meant that you made a mistake."

"Impossible. This is well-proven scanning technology. I suppose I could believe that you've never met. I've seen some pretty amazing coincidences in this galaxy before."

"This would be well beyond amazing, Doctor, considering that Ari and I came to the Faith by entirely different means."

"Oh?"

A door opened on the other side of the galley, and Miriam's other friend entered. He was leading a well-groomed canine and smiled at Trewler.

"I can't stand being a spectator in a scrum," he said.

Trewler gaped in shock at seeing the man, and turned to face him squarely.

"Aldebaran?" he breathed hatefully.

"Oh, have we met?" asked Aldebaran.

"Sette Al Deb'aran, Follower of the Seven. We have indeed met."

Trewler deftly pulled a pistol from the small of his back and pointed it at him.

"What's this?" asked Miriam, backing away.

"You probably don't remember me," Trewler began, "but maybe you'll remember my ship. Tell me, you bastard, how long has it been since you raided the Percheron?"

"Almost exactly five years," replied Aldebaran evenly.

"So tell me why I shouldn't kill you right now!" screamed Trewler.

"I won't. You would have every right to kill me for what I did."

"Gentlemen, please," said Miriam, "I don't know what happened between the two of you, but now is not the time to settle it."

Trewler lowered his weapon slightly. "You're right. The captain wouldn't appreciate it if I killed you without consulting him first. I'm confident, however, that he'll raise no objection when he finds out who you really are."

The ship shuddered as energy weapons impacted the hull nearby.

"I won't fight you," said Aldebaran. "I'll even submit to being detained in your brig until the captain has time to deal with us."

"Fine. Slowly unholster your weapon and put it on the..."

Trewler collapsed instantly as Miriam hit him over the head with a metal chair.

"Thank you, Miriam," said Aldebaran, collecting Trewler's weapon, "but this will only delay the inevitable. I'll have to settle this before we return to the Faith."

Miriam said, "Why can't we just tie him up and hide him somewhere?"

"The first thing the captain is going to do after the fight is over is take account of his crewmembers. Even if this guy's primary responsibility is washing windows, his absence will be noticed."

"He's the ship's doctor."

"Shit. Even worse."

"What did you do to piss him off so much?"

"I used to be a pirate."

"No way! You mean like, a pirate in space? A space pirate?"

"Yes. It's not something I'm proud of..."

"That is so cool!"

A tremendous crash shook the ship, and a nearby serving station fell over. A warning klaxon started up, accompanied by flashing red lights.

"I'll address that very incorrect notion later, Miriam! Right now let's get this guy to the medical bay and ourselves and the animals to a safer place."

Aldebaran gathered up the lithe form of Trewler easily as Miriam grabbed the dog's leash and scooped up the cat, the latter of whom was unusually resigned to that mode of transportation.

“What was it he called you?” asked Miriam.

“Sette Al Deb'aran. It's the old Umberian transliteration of the Follower of the Seven, a figure from Umberian history and my namesake.”

"Aldebaran, Terror of the Tarantula Nebula," said Miriam, smiling.

He looked at her grimly. "That's exactly what they used to call me.”

20.

In the glittering sky high above Freedmen, Pyramis watched with concern as the Almagest took a hard hit from one of the cruiser's plasma cannons. Calico's ship was taking turns with the Reckless Faith executing attack runs on the massive enemy craft as Pyramis and several colonial fighters provided cover from the Zendreen's single-seat Stingers. He'd been assigned to Green Squadron during the hasty pre-mission briefing, accompanying eleven sarcastic and fatalistic youngsters currently hurling themselves at the enemy with almost suicidal abandon. The Zendreen had the advantage of numbers, but the Green Meanies, as they called themselves, were superior in both armament and skill. Their exuberance was kept in check by Chief Correia, whose leadership was probably the only thing that kept them alive after the first merge. Pyramis and his robust craft were worthy additions to the rabble, and he had been accepted as one of the team immediately.

In the nascent fight, he'd already sustained several direct hits from the Stingers without serious damage, although he knew a single shot from the cruiser would spell certain death. It was for this reason that all of the colonial allies were staying in the thick of things, as at least for the moment the cruiser was avoiding firing too close to its own fighters.

Between the chaos of the melee and the lack of radio discipline it was almost impossible to take in the big picture. Pyramis was content, as much as one could be, to concentrate on each problem as it presented itself. He had precious little real combat experience in his Stylus, and he had to rely on simulator training and luck to score hits on the fast-moving Stingers. Despite what the

Zendreen did to his people, it was too far in the past and too far removed from this place for Pyramis to feel a present anger toward them. Instead, he mostly felt frustration, since the entire conflict seemed to be nothing more than an act of revenge. If they truly only needed food, water, and other basic supplies, committing themselves to a fight of this scale was beyond foolish.

However, Mother Calico's response made sense to him. She had no reason to trust Commander Lithilkin's promise that the Zendreen were only interested in humanitarian aid (for lack of a better term). Even without the Reckless Faith as a pawn between them, allowing the Zendreen to land supply vessels unopposed would only open the colony to a more devastating surprise attack. Fighting them now was the best option. The wing commander for Green Squadron had mentioned that even a worst-case estimate of the size of the Zendreen ground infantry wouldn't be enough to seize more than a handful of objectives, and maintaining an occupation force was out of the question. That left orbital bombardment as the only true threat.

"Green Squadron, this is Green One," crackled Pyramis' radio. "The battleship has diverted to assist our target. ETA for firing range is five minutes, all units acknowledge, over."

Pyramis swore to himself as each of the squadron members called out in order. He added his own acknowledgment as Green Thirteen, and checked his energy reserves. His weapons carried a ridiculous number of charges, but the battleship was known to carry dozens of fighters. He might actually survive long enough to run out of ammo.

"Green Thirteen, this is Green One. You are being tasked out to the Almagest. Standby to connect with them, over."

"Roger, Green One," Pyramis replied. "Standing by. Good luck, Chief."

"Major Pyramis, this is Captain Calico," said a new voice.

"Captain, I am at your disposal."

"Good, listen up. We need more fire concentrated on the cruiser. We need you to form up on us and follow us in on our attack runs. Our gunners will cover your six; how do you copy?"

"Good copy. I will comply, Captain. Out."

Pyramis located the Almagest on his Heads-Up Display, and peeled off to join them. Almost immediately two Stingers diverted to follow him. He visually located the Almagest and swooped in on its five o'clock. As he arrived, an impressive swath of plasma fire from the larger ship passed over his cockpit and vaporized the Stingers. There were some ugly black scorch marks on the Almagest, but so far it didn't appear to have suffered decompression anywhere.

Pyramis rolled his ship to the left as Captain Calico set himself up for an attack from directly above the cruiser. He knew that his counterpart was facing the dilemma of damage versus unpredictability. Ideally each attack run would target the same area on the enemy vessel, but the volume of fire and number of Stingers made that impossible, or at least a very bad idea. It was very fortunate that the cloaked Reckless Faith was forcing the cruiser's frustrated gunners to try to extrapolate its position based only on incoming fire. Pyramis was currently quite jealous of the Faith's invisibility shield, although at least now he had the Almagest backing him up.

"I'm sending you telemetry," said Calico. "Concentrate all of your fire on that point."

"Understood," said Pyramis, checking his HUD for the new information.

"Fire!"

Pyramis squeezed the trigger. At the same time, all of the Almagest's forward-facing weapons and her articulated turrets fired on an otherwise unremarkable section of the cruiser's hull. There was an unimpressive flash as the weapons impacted, and it wasn't until the ships peeled off and passed the cruiser that the full effect was evident.

Looking over his shoulder, Pyramis realized that their shots had traveled completely through the cruiser and blown through the ventral hull. A new source of fire emanated from space, presumably from the Reckless Faith, and impacted the exit breach at almost the same angle. The cruiser silently bent like a pine cone struck with a hammer, and stopped firing. Friendly fighters continued to chip away at it until the order to find a new target came through over the radio. Pyramis was sure the younger pilots were disappointed by the lack of a spectacular explosion.

Chief Correia came in over the radio. "Green Squadron, this is Green one. We have been ordered to attack the cruiser at the following coordinates... hold on, I'm receiving new orders from Central Command... the remaining cruisers and battleship are withdrawing to a much higher orbit. Five support vessels have entered the atmosphere along with at least two hundred fighter escorts. All units are to divert to attack the support vessels. Stand by for our precise target, over."

Pyramis consulted a computer-generated image of the battle's participants. The moribund cruiser was still listed as a target; he decided not to delete it from the register since it was possible, however unlikely, that it could still pose a threat before the fight was over. Orders for Blue and

Yellow Squadrons were apparently sent, as those vessels headed for the atmosphere. Pyramis noticed that the Zendreen support vessels were already a few hundred feet above the surface of the planet. Not knowing the location of any of Freedmen's critical assets other than the capitol city, the targets of the ships remained a mystery to him. He suspected that the delay in assigning Green Squadron a target was due to CentCom failing to understand the Zendreen's ultimate strategy. Mother Calico had no reason to trust Commander Lithilkin's word. Regardless of their intent, destroying the support vessels would soon become less important than stopping the troops they doubtlessly carried.

A glut of new data came across Pyramis' screen. The atmosphere-only fighters had engaged the Stingers, and it was immediately obvious that the craft, despite being heavily armed, stood no chance against the well-armored Zendreen vessels. Pyramis watched with muted horror as scores of Freedmen fighters were destroyed within seconds of convergence. If they were to hold off the enemy, the task would fall to the now badly outnumbered space-capable fighters.

At last Correia's voice echoed inside his helmet. "Green Squadron, this is Green One. Our target is marked on your screens. The ship has already landed, so our task is to cover the Reckless Faith, which has been tasked out for ground attack. All units acknowledge transmission, over."

Pyramis took a deep breath as he calculated the best re-entry trajectory, and pointed the Stylus at the planet.

___

On the bridge of the Reckless Faith, John sent a message to Central Command agreeing to the new orders, and reduced speed for atmospheric re-entry. The ship had lasted through the fight with the cruiser without any significant damage, and the crew was feeling pretty good about themselves. Ray and Richter had been manning the laser systems from the bridge gun stations, since so far the fifty-caliber turrets had been kept in reserve. Ari, much to her chagrin, had been manning the sensors and relaying pertinent information to the others. Dana, as usual, was monitoring both incoming communications and ship status, although the latter duties were pretty much redundant with Christie's omnipresent eye on the same thing. This left John free to concentrate on flying and operating the plasma and projectile cannons.

"What about the Almagest?" asked Dana from her station.

"They're going to do ground attack as well, but in another location," replied John.

"I hope Aldebaran and Miriam are doing okay over there."

The ship began to ignite the atmosphere as it plunged downward. Bright orange flame licked rearward from the nose.

"How's our invisibility shield holding up, Christie?" asked John.

"Obviously it's compromised at the moment," Christie replied, "but we'll be safely hidden again in a few seconds."

"Good."

Richter said, "I suggest we utilize the fifties during this next engagement."

John nodded. "I agree. Ari, Richter, man the dorsal turret. Ray, Dana, take the ventral."

"It is definitely my turn to take the trigger," said Ari.

"Far be it from me to hog all the action," Richter said, standing.

"Are you going to be all right?" Dana asked John.

"I'll be fine," John said. "I've got Christie watching over me."

The others exited the bridge. John guided the ship toward the designated area, which was on the night side of the planet.

"The fight is not going well for the colony," said Christie.

"We'll do what we can," said John. "Christie, get me infrared, and a topographical overlay once we're within ten kilometers."

"No problem."

The screen in front of John lit up as Christie engaged IR imaging. A few seconds later, a unobtrusive series of lines appeared as well, clearly marking the terrain. There was no question that a supply ship was in the general area, as the sky buzzed with aerial combat.

"Listen up, people," John said into the intercom. "It's not going to take those fighters long to notice us once we start engaging targets on the ground. Green Squadron is on its way to support us, but expect contact to be heavy. I may have to call a ceasefire if we start getting pounded."

"There's the supply ship," said Christie.

The ship glowed like a beacon thanks to the Faith's enhanced optics. It was perched halfway down a tall cliff, under a large overhang, either in hover mode or attached to the rock face by mechanical means. At the bottom of the cliff, in a forest clearing, lay a small cluster of buildings. Dozens of Zendreen troopers were rappelling from the ship onto the roof of the largest building, a structure of about thirty meters in height. They were using energy tethers rather than physical rope, which disappeared as soon as the troopers touched a solid surface. The soldiers were trading a small amount of fire with friendlies on the ground, but so far they were proceeding virtually unopposed. In the sky overhead were several Stingers; at the moment there were no friendly fighter craft to be seen.

"Ask CentCom to find out if those ground units have any sort of IFF indicators," said John, banking above the scene. "I don't want to fire too close to them."

"Roger," said Christie. "You should also be aware that the operating manual for the plasma cannon indicate a minimum safe radius of one hundred meters for atmospheric discharge. In fact, you'll probably vaporize those buildings if you use it."

"All right, then. What about the laser banks?"

"They don't have any concussion impact, assuming, of course, you don't shoot anything explosive on the ground. John, Central Command is reporting that ninety percent of all friendly ships have been destroyed."

"Damn it! Any good news?"

"The Zendreen ships in orbit are attempting to jam all friendly radio traffic. CentCom doesn't think they'll be able to compensate against it for much longer."

"I hate to say it, but this operation is looking like a bust. Everyone, we may have no air support. That means we only get one attack run before we get swarmed by enemy fighters."

"Did I hear right?" asked Ari. "We lost ninety percent of our defense force?"

"So it would seem."

"I hate to be the voice of doom, but this fight is over. We should withdraw before the

Zendreen figure out a new way to circumvent our invisibility shield."

"You're not shirking away from a fight, are you?" asked Richter.

John said, "I'm not withdrawing until we've done as much damage as possible. Here's the plan. I'm going to pass low and slow over those buildings. Ray, I need you to take out as many ground troops as possible. Then I'm going to destroy the supply ship. If for some reason the fighter ships haven't detected us, we'll do another ground attack. Then we'll link back up with the Almagest and plan our next move."

"Roger," said Ray, "ready when you are."

John brought the ship down to less than one hundred feet above the forest canopy. He reduced his speed to one hundred and fifty miles per hour. In front of him, the supply ship moved away from the cliff and began to rise.

"Did they detect us?" he asked.

"I don't think so," replied Christie.

"It doesn't matter. Hold on, slight change of plan!"

John pointed the nose toward the enemy vessel, and opened up with both cannons. The bridge shook with the almost unbearable noise of the weapons systems discharging. The supply ship immediately exploded, blanketing the ground with flaming wreckage. Ray needed no further cue, and began firing on the troops. John spun the ship around on the Z-axis to allow his friend the maximum amount of enfilade. Above, the Stingers descended, looking for the source of the attack.

"Cease fire, cease fire," said John. "Christie, contact the Almagest and tell them we need to meet."

"The signal is being jammed," Christie said.

"Try the VLF transceiver."

A new fighter craft appeared, cutting a swath through the enemy ships. Some of the Stingers peeled off to pursue it.

"I'm receiving two replies on the VLF channel," began Christie. "One of them is Calico, the other is Green Thirteen."

"Put through the last one," said John, destroying a fighter that wandered in front of him.

"Are we in a cease fire or what?" asked Richter.

"Reckless Faith, this is Green Thirteen," said a new voice. "What's your status?"

"This is Commander Scherer. We're okay, and yourself?"

"This is Major Pyramis. My squadron leader and I are the only ones left and we've been cut off from CentCom. What are your orders?"

"We can't stay here, Major. Follow me out and we'll try to figure out what to do next."

"Understood. We'll be right behind you. I think we can tag a few more of these bastards."

"Don't take any unnecessary risks. Scherer out."

Christie said, "I've lost the signal with the Almagest."

"Damn it. We'll try to regain contact with them once we're away. Hold on, everyone, we're breaking atmo."

"John, look."

High above, a larger ship was streaking across the sky, leading a trail of fire and debris. John zoomed in on his display and identified it as the Almagest.

"Oh, my God."

"They've sustained critical damage," said Christie, unable to hide her emotions. "It looks like they're attempting a controlled descent."

"Pyramis, this is Scherer," John said urgently. "I need you to help me cover the Almagest's landing. If they survive, we'll immediately begin a rescue operation for the crew."

"I will comply, Scherer," replied Pyramis.

John pointed his ship at the stricken craft. "Hold it together, Calico."

"I don't care where you get it, Gueyr, I need more power to the flight controls."

Captain Calico's voice was calm, even as the Almagest seemed ready to shake itself apart. In the medical bay, Aldebaran and Miriam held on to a piece of bolted-down equipment as they breathlessly listened in on what was surely a desperate scene on the bridge. Doc Trewler lay strapped to a gurney nearby, oblivious to the crisis. A man named Railyn clutched a broken arm on the other side of the bay, and tried to control his breathing. Tycho and Friday huddled under another gurney. Aldebaran softly took a terrified Miriam by the shoulder, and caught her eye.

"Listen to me, Miriam," he said evenly. "We're going to crash. I need you to understand that when we stop moving, we're going to have to get Trewler out of here as quickly as possible. I can't do it alone, I'm going to need your help. Are you going to be able to do that?"

"I..." stammered the girl.

"Miriam! Are you with me?"

"Yes."

"Good. Protect your head, this will be over soon."

Miriam did so by nuzzling her head into Aldebaran's chest. He embraced her tightly with his free arm, and looked back up at the flickering console. The good news was that the ship had survived the devastating heat of atmosphere re-entry. The bad news was that their velocity was still too fast for a safe landing. Despite his reassuring words, Aldebaran had little faith that anybody would be walking away from the crash. Calico and someone named Megumi were working feverishly to slow the craft, and communicated with Gueyr, who was trying to keep things patched together from the engine room.

Part of Aldebaran wished he was on the bridge, feeling what Calico could feel. Despite his extensive experience piloting a ship, he'd never had to deal with an emergency landing outside of a training simulation. Still, what is abnormal tells a competent captain as much about what is going on as what is expected, and only a cool head could be trusted to compensate. He was long past the point of feeling fear at his possible death, instead feeling only frustration for not having any control over the situation. He was far more concerned for Miriam's safety. She was the only one of the Faith's crew thrust into the conflict by sheer accident.

The medical bay was filled with the roar of wind as Calico opened the cargo bay one deck below. Aldebaran knew the captain was trying to create as much drag on the fuselage as possible in order to augment the failing anti-gravity systems. For now, there was nothing more for him to do but to rest the side of his face in Miriam's soft hair and hope that the universe owed him one more favor.

21.

The Almagest cut an ugly gash into the rocky surface of Freedmen, tracing a dark brown furrow for five hundred meters before cartwheeling several times and coming to rest mostly upright at the edge of a canyon. From above in the Reckless Faith, it was hard to imagine that anything that size could be thrown about with such force; it looked more like a child's toy had been held to a flame until smoldering and then scornfully tossed across a beach. That the ship did not immediately explode was the only relief the spectacle offered, and John was preparing to land nearby before the Almagest had even stopped moving.

The horror of what had happened shocked the crew into an unusual silence. John jumped when a voice came in over the radio. He steadied his grip on the stick and answered the call.

"Go ahead, Major Pyramis," he replied to the query.

"The Almagest going down was impossible for the Zendreen to ignore," said Pyramis. "Some of the fighters over here have broken off to investigate the crash site. You may want to delay any rescue efforts until they've departed."

"That won't work if they intend to capture prisoners."

"Those are single seat fighters. Unless a larger vessel shows up, you won't have to worry about that."

"John, look," said Christie.

Christie took the liberty of zooming John's display onto the wreckage. A Residerian that John recognized as Knoal had just crawled out of a smoking breach in the hull, and was struggling to stand up.

"Major, get over here and provide us cover," said John, "I'm not waiting. Christie, are you detecting any survivors?"

Christie said, "I'm reading an unusual source of radiation from the Almagest. One of their reactors may have been compromised. It's interfering with my ability scan for life signs."

"How dangerous is it?"

"Short term exposure won't be a problem, but it's also creating interference with our invisibility shield. The closer we get to the crash, the less likely I'll be able to maintain a flawless illusion."

"Give me a number."

"One hundred meters if you want to play it safe."

"Fine. Listen up people, we're going to need everyone out there in case we have to run litters. Everyone gather up the CLS kits, the stretchers, and rifles, and meet me down there. Christie, once we're on the ground, I want you to take the ship up and keep an eye on things. We'll call for evac as soon as we can."

"Understood."

"Christie, you have the controls."

"I have the controls."

With that confirmation, John slid his chair away from the console and stood up. He grabbed his jacket, exited to the port hallway, and took the stairs to the cargo bay. The first to arrive, he accessed the nearest console and resumed watching the crash site. Shortly, the others emerged from the armory, laden with gear. Richter hesitated at the top of the stairs.

"Scherer, which weapon do you want?" he asked.

"US Rifle, M1, caliber thirty."

Richter disappeared briefly to retrieve the requested item. Ari and Ray were already carrying stretchers, which were folded up for transport, and Dana held one of the medkits. She also carried a M1A rifle, as did Ray. Ari carried the Phalanx, and when Richter came down the stairs he was carrying both a M1A and John's Garand. He also had the other medical kit. He handed John his rifle and a shoulder bag of clips as he joined him at the console.

"May I?" he asked, pointing at the screen.

John moved out of the way. Richter called up an overhead diagram of the area and spent a few seconds reviewing it. John loaded his rifle.

"This is not going to work," he said to John gruffly. "There's no cover out there. We have to assume we'll be spotted by those fighters immediately, and it will take us at least thirty seconds to get to the ship."

"They'd have to be pretty hot shit to fire on us that quickly," said John.

"Maybe, but how long will it take us to get our casualties back on the return trip?"

"Good point. Christie, are you listening?"

"Of course," said Christie.

"Get us as close as possible to the Almagest. We'll have to take the chance of the Faith being detected. If you do get spotted while we're out there, feel free to fire on the enemy."

"Understood. We're moving again. I'll have you fifteen meters from the bow in ten seconds."

"Good," said John, then turned to face the crew. "Since the Faith will be right there, we might as well make the cargo bay the casualty collection point. Everyone ready?"

"All set," said Ari.

"Deploy the ramp at your discretion," said Christie.

John hit the button to open the ramp. The bay opened, admitting a cool evening breeze. The Almagest towered in front of them, eerily silent save for the crackling of some flaming debris. Knoal lay face down in the dirt five meters ahead. Ari, Dana and John took up defensive positions as Ray and Richter began to evaluate the casualty. Above, Pyramis traded shots with his foes, the reports echoing softly between the two ships. Determining that Knoal was still alive, for the moment, the two men struggled to load the heavy Residerian onto the stretcher and moved him into the cargo bay.

"The guy's gotta weigh four hundred pounds," grunted Ray, lowering the stretcher.

"He's got some first and second degree burns," said Richter. "Christie, does he have any internal injuries?"

"I'm not familiar with his cybernetics," replied Christie, "but everything appears to be in order."

"Think he'll survive another few minutes on his own?"

"I guess so."

Richter and Ray retrieved the stretcher and wrapped the man in a blanket. Moving swiftly back outside, the team located the hatch from where Knoal had come. They entered the murky corridor. Emergency lights shined dimly from recesses in the bulkheads. Panels and supports had been torn away from the superstructure, littering the deck, and a few shorted wires spat sparks intermittently. Ari located a console and attempted to access it. An image appeared, flickering. She smacked the wall next to the screen, and the image cleared up considerably.

"Most systems are offline," she began. "There is a radiation leak, but there's no additional information about it."

"Can you scan for life signs?" asked John.

"I'm detecting five people. Two are on the move, three decks above us. The other three are on the bridge. I don't have any information about who they might be."

"Should we split up?" asked Dana.

"Not until we've collected the two survivors closest to us," said Richter. "Then we can have one or two of us escort them back to the ship while the rest of us continue to the bridge."

"Sounds good," said John. "Let's hurry."

The group continued down the corridor. The interior of the ship was a jumble of wires and twisted metal. Every several seconds, the hull shuddered with disconcerting vibrations.

"Ari, we're counting on your knowledge of this ship to navigate this mess," said John.

"Don't worry," Ari said, "I made it my business to know the layout. Unfortunately this is going to take a while if we don't find a working lift."

"Would you trust it if we did?" asked Ray.

"Probably not."

John activated his radio. "Christie, this is Scherer, radio check, over."

"I am reading you four by four, over," replied Christie, the transmission crackling but stable.

"Good. Keep an open channel. We're detecting five life signs but it's going to take some time to investigate all of them. Have you been able to reach Aldebaran?"

"Negative. John, a few more enemy fighters have shown up. I'm not sure Pyramis is going to be able to keep them away for much longer. If they figure out what's going on..."

"I know. We'll be quick. Standby."

The team continued into a cluttered stairway and ascended three decks, pausing only to clear larger pieces of wreckage from their path. Upon arriving at deck six, they found the hatch to the corridor jammed, open only three inches. Two pairs of hands were trying to open it from the other side.

"Hello!" said John into the darkened gap.

"Scherer, thank the core," said Aldebaran.

"Are you all right?"

"I'll live. I've got Miriam and the animals here with me. Think you can help us get this door open?"

"Of course. Richter, Ray, get on this hatch with me."

The other two men joined John at the door, and together with Aldebaran they strained against the mechanism. The door moved about half an inch.

"Get out of the way, you bunch of chauvinists," said Ari, slinging her rifle.

The others stepped aside. Ari grasped the door and the frame, and pushed. There was a snap, and the hatch groaned open. Miriam stepped through, carrying the cat, and was followed by Aldebaran, who had the dog by the leash. Aldebaran's face was covered in blood; Miriam looked fine. Ari reached for her medical kit.

"That can wait," Aldebaran said. "Just get Miriam out of here."

"You're both going back to the Faith with Dana," began John, "and I don't want any argument about it. We can handle the evacuation. Are there any other survivors?"

"We haven't run into any. There were two fatalities in the sick bay."

"Damn. Who were they?"

"A Misrerian and Doctor Trewler."

John nodded, and activated his radio. "Christie, this is Scherer. We've found Aldebaran and Miriam; Dana's bringing them out now."

"Roger," replied Christie through a bad transmission. "Be advised I am reading you two by three."

"Understood. The rest of us are continuing to the bridge, over."

"John, I hate to rush you, but there's a larger Zendreen vessel coming in."

"Perfect. Hold them off if you have to, we'll do the best we can. Scherer out."

"Once you get to the bridge," said Aldebaran, "look for an emergency hatch from that deck. It will save time if we pick you up there."

"Good idea. Dana, get going. We'll see you back on board."

Dana nodded, and began to lead Aldebaran and Miriam down the stairs. Miriam paused next to Ari.

"Who is your father?" she asked.

"What?" replied Ari, confused.

"Your father's name, what is it?"

Richter said, "Miriam, you need to get out of here."

"I have to know," said the girl, her eyes flashing. "Come across with it, Arianna."

"I am your father," said Ray deeply.

"Ray, shut up," Ari said. "Gabriel Ferro. Why do you want to know?"

Miriam smiled wistfully. "Incredible. I'll tell you when we get back."

The trio disappeared down the stairwell. The others began ascending again, this time as quickly as their surroundings would allow.

"What was that all about?" Ray asked Ari.

"My father moved to England after the divorce," she said, hopping over a fallen conduit. "Maybe Miriam and her family knew him."

"Concentrate on getting us to the bridge," said John, moving a loose panel.

Finding the next flight blocked, the team backtracked to another stairwell. The power had failed completely on this deck, so they drew their flashlights. The darkness only added more time to their journey. Fortunately the next set of stairs had suffered less damage, and they were able to quicken the pace. After a few minutes they reached the door to the bridge, which was in no better condition than the rest of the ship. Captain Calico and Megumi were attempting to lift a large beam from Gueyr. It had pinned his left leg to the deck.

"Scherer, thank Verruct," Calico said, clearly exhausted.

The vessel shook with the impact of energy weapons. A transmission from Christie was blocked out by the noise. John guessed at the intended message.

"Captain, we are officially out of time," he said. "The Zendreen are trying to finish you off."

"Everyone get on this damned beam," grunted Megumi.

Together, the five allies tried to move the debris. Even with Ari's help they were barely able to budge it. After exchanging much vituperation they fell back, panting.

"Get out of here, Cap," said Gueyr.

"There's another option," said Richter, looking at Ari.

"Do it," said John. "Captain, is there an emergency hatch nearby?"

Calico nodded. "There's one off my office. I might need a hand opening it."

John and Calico exited to an adjacent room. Ari removed a tourniquet from her bag and applied it to Gueyr's femoral artery at the groin. Richter drew his sword. Megumi grabbed Gueyr's hand and squeezed it.

"Shit, this is going to suck," Gueyr said, closing his eyes and turning away.

"Can you do it in one try?" asked Megumi.

Richter let out a brief, sharp cry and brought down the blade. Megumi and Ari immediately pulled Gueyr away from the wreckage as the young Kau'Rii screamed.

Fresh air wafted into the bridge as John and Calico re-emerged. The sound of weapons fire accompanied them, several decibels higher than it had been.

"The hatch is off," said John, grimacing at Gueyr's wound. "Christie, can you hear me?"

"I got you," said Christie's voice.

"Bring the ship around and open the ramp. We're ready to evacuate."

"I'm not leaving without the rest of my crew," said Calico.

"Railyn and Trewler are dead," said Ari. "Knoal is already aboard the Faith."

"What about Bugani?"

"Internal sensors didn't read any other life signs."

"You can't trust the sensors after that landing! I should at least check his lab."

John said, "Captain, listen to me. We can't hold off those fighters and a larger ship is on the way. If you go looking for Bugani you're just going to get yourself blown up."

"That's my choice to make," Calico said, picking up a flashlight.

Ari finished placing Gueyr on a stretcher, moved over to Calico, and grabbed his arm.

"The ship is trashed," she began. "It will take you at least ten minutes to get down there. Never mind that if Bugani was in his lab when we crashed, then he was most likely killed by flying equipment."

"You don't know that. Let go."

"Farril, please. I don't want to lose you."

"Don't let these bastards win, Calico," said Richter.

Calico kicked a panel. "Damn it."

"We don't have time for this!" yelled John.

"All right, all right, I'm coming."

Richter and Megumi picked up the stretcher, and the crews headed for the emergency hatch. Christie had guided the Faith into position, and the ramp to the cargo bay was only eighteen inches from the hull of the Almagest. Everyone made their way rapidly aboard even as Christie began firing on targets with the port laser and the top turret. Aldebaran was in the bay, holding a bandage to the back of his head and keeping watch over Knoal.

"We're all here, close the ramp," said John.

"Roger," said Christie.

"Pyramis, this is Scherer, do you copy?"

"I hope this is good news," Pyramis said, his voice strained. "My squadron leader just went down."

"We are out of here. Break atmo and meet us in high orbit.

"I will comply."

Richter and Ari set Gueyr down next to Knoal and began to work on them. Calico kneeled next to his men and offered to help. The others headed for the bridge, arriving just in time to see the Almagest explode. John brushed by an astonished Miriam as he took the pilot chair. He took control and guided the ship into high orbit. They were not pursued.

"Scherer, this is Richter. We need to get Gueyr to a bona fide hospital as soon as possible."

"Freedmen Station is his only hope," said Calico. "We need to contact Pyramis and have him get us permission to dock."

"What's going on?" asked Miriam. "Did we lose the battle?"

"The Zendreen are still jamming all but the VLF channel," said Christie. "I can't account for any other ships beside ourselves and Major Pyramis."

"There is little doubt in my mind," said John, wiping the sweat from his forehead. "The Zendreen have won this round."

One hour later, Ari was sitting with Ray in the galley on board the Faith, enjoying a beer. The ship was docked with Freedmen Station, and the wounded had been moved to the medical bay. Calico and Megumi had boarded the station to keep their injured comrades company, as had Richter with Aldebaran, although the latter pair were none too pleased about having to leave their weapons behind.

John and Dana had excused themselves after docking to take badly-needed naps, and they snoozed peacefully in their respective quarters. Miriam did the same in the lounge. Ray hadn't intended to sleep, but sat passed out across from Ari at the dining table. Friday was asleep, too, curled up in her lap. Christie was telling Ari about things that had happened to the crew of the Faith in her absence, and seemed to be taking the loss of her physical body well enough. Ari was only paying so much attention to her.

In order to secure medical aid for the injured, Major Pyramis had to turn himself over to his people. Pyramis had conversed with his lieutenant on an open channel, undoubtedly so that the others could understand exactly what had happened. Only then had the scale of Hayaku's betrayal become apparent. Ari had no way of knowing what would happen to the major now, but she and the others knew they could never properly repay him for his help.

Ari was sad about a number of things, enough so to make her shed tears when she thought she was alone. She was sad for Calico, who didn't deserve to lose his ship, and for Gueyr, who didn't deserve to lose his leg. She was sad for Railyn, Trewler, and Bugani, with whom she'd become friends. She was more confused than sad about Christie's predicament. Preserved as part of the ship was certainly a better fate than death, but Ari wasn't sure how she would feel about losing her body if the situation had been reversed. There was also the possibility that it wasn't really Christie in there, but only an almost perfect copy, and the ramifications of it were too much for Ari to think about.

Despite all of this, Ari couldn't get herself to feel bad about the colonists on Freedmen. The Zendreen couldn't sustain an occupation, so even after getting their asses kicked, at least the colonists knew that the Zendreen would eventually leave. The Faith and her allies were powerless to do anything else anyway.

As far as Ari was concerned, there were only three unresolved issues. One, what to do next. Two, what to do with the survivors of the Almagest. Three, what the hell was Miriam going on about back on the planet?

Still oblivious to the fact that Ari was tuned out, Christie only stopped talking when John and Miriam came down the stairs from deck one.

"Feel better?" Ari asked John.

"Yes, thank you," said John, retrieving a mug from the cabinet. "Miriam, want a beer?"

"Sure, why not?" said Miriam, sitting at the table.

"How are things going on the station?" John asked.

"Nothing has changed since you went to sleep," replied Christie.

"I guess no news is good news. What about from Freedmen?"

"The Zendreen are still jamming radio transmissions, so no news there either."

"How are you doing, Christie?"

"Myself? This is incredible, John. I wish you could see what I see. It's... exhilarating. I've never felt so alive."

John sat down and passed a mug to Miriam. "Ironic. I'd still rather have you in physical form."

"I'd like to be able to do both. My body is on ice, who knows, maybe with the right technology..."

"So," said Ari to Miriam, leaning back in her chair. "How do you know my father?"

Ray woke up, wiped the drool from his chin, and blinked. Dana came downstairs and greeted the others before heading to the fridge.

Miriam sipped from her glass and looked at Ari. "The doctor on board the Almagest told me something very interesting. He did a genetic profile on you, did you know that?"

"No, but it doesn't surprise me."

"He says we're paternal sisters. That's why I asked you for your father's name. My father changed his name after he moved to England.

Before he was Gabriel Colchester, he was a US citizen named Gabriel Ferro."

"I don't believe it."

"What are we talking about?" asked Dana, chewing on an apple.

"I'm only telling you the facts," said Miriam." I'm not attempting to explain it."

John said, "I don't believe it either. It's simply incredible that the two of you could have met up out here. What are the odds?"

"They're too high. The Kira'To must've had a hand in it."

"Wait a minute," Ari said. "First of all, the genetic test could be wrong. Maybe the equipment that Doc Trewler was using wasn't properly calibrated for humans. Second, if we share the same father, then why did he never mention me to you?"

"Did he ever mention me to you?"

"Well, I... last time we spoke on the phone, he told me he'd fathered a girl with his new wife."

"He must have told you the name of that girl."

"He did, but I honestly don't remember."

"That's pretty callous, even for you," said Ray.

"Hey," Ari said, standing up, "I don't get to choose what I remember and what I don't."

"So your father never mentioned to you that you had a half-sister," said John to Miriam. "Why would he hide that from you?"

"My father was very secretive about his past," replied Miriam, sipping from her mug. "He never told me anything about his life before moving to the UK. I only found out what I did by rummaging through the old foot locker he kept in the attic. It was full of memorabilia from his time in the United States Air Force. At first I thought it might be his father's stuff, but I researched the gear I found there and determined that most of it was of the type only issued after 1994. It had to be his."

"Like what?"

"There was a uniform in there that was three-color desert camo."

"She may be right," said John to the others. "The military switched from six-color to three-color desert camo in the mid-nineties."

Ari folded her arms. "That does fit with when my dad was in."

"We could find out for sure if we went back to the asteroid," said Christie.

"I think we blew our chance to make friends with those guys," Dana said.

"I find this situation far more disturbing than I do amazing," said John. "I agree that the odds are too great against this being a coincidence. The Kira'To must have some knowledge of our existence, and they decided to get Miriam and her parents involved for some reason."

"But Miriam ended up on that asteroid before we came through the wormhole," said Ray.

John nodded. "That's what I find most disturbing."

"What if the Kira'To and the Zendreen are working together?" asked Christie.

"The Zendreen might have anticipated that the wormhole would attract our attention, but they couldn't have been sure that we'd follow them through. Hell, they tried everything to prevent us from doing just that. Even if the Kira'To were able to anticipate our run-in with the Vulture, why transport relatives of one of our crewmembers there?"

"Leverage," said Ari. "If they weren't able to stop us using force, then perhaps they thought we'd back off in exchange for my father and sister."

"Which makes the Kira'To ruthless as well as incredibly powerful," said John, frowning. "Also, if we're so damn important to them, why haven't they attempted to contact us themselves?"

"I think they may have, John," said Christie. "Some of you had that funny feeling when Byron showed up inside the new orb. They could have seen an opportunity to communicate at that point and tried to use the orb as a kind of transmitter. Byron's presence might have prevented it."

"Either that or they're responsible for Byron showing up entirely," said Ray. "We never did get a satisfactory explanation for how his essence got stored."

"I wouldn't feel so disturbed about the Kira'To's meddling if it hadn't cost my parents their lives," said Miriam. "In fact, why would beings powerful enough to transport people across hundreds of light years allow them to die at all?"

"Maybe they fucked up," said Ari. "Nobody's perfect."

"That's not all," said Christie. "I've had some very vivid dreams that the Kira'To may have had a hand in. They always occur in the same weird city..."

"In an outdoor café?" asked Dana.

"Yes! You've had them, too?"

"Once, yes, before we even left Earth."

"That long ago?" asked Ray.

Christie nodded. "That city also appeared in one of the orb simulations with Byron. Maybe it's a Kira'To city."

"I had the same dream," said Ari, "only I know where that city is. It's on the Vulture."

"Whoa," said Dana, shivering, "that sent chills down my spine."

"Son of a bitch," said John. "These people may have been keeping tabs on our entire journey, and that alone I suppose I could live with. But if they're working with the Zendreen, and fucking with us to boot, then that's totally unacceptable."

"What do you think you could do about it?" asked Miriam.

"Regardless of whether or not any of this speculation is true," began Christie, "it seems that the next logical step would be to contact the Kira'To. I have a very strong feeling that we may be able to do that from the Vulture."

"How?" asked John.

"I don't know, but if they haven't contacted us directly, maybe we need some sort of device or medium to do so. I get the feeling such a thing might be present on the Vulture."

"Christie may be onto something," said Ari. "Cassiopeia spoke with authority about the intentions of the Kira'To. I thought she was just plain crazy, but maybe not."

"Cassiopeia is dead," replied John. "I suppose we could try to make peace with those soldiers. With working engines, we can always simply leave if they won't cooperate."

"Or we could go in hot. I don't think there are that many of them left."

John thought for a moment. "I know I'm supposed to say something about preventing a fight, but I'm sick of half-measures. For once I agree with you on that option. One thing is for sure, we're all exhausted and we still haven't solved our Zendreen problem. I think we should get some food and rest and approach the problem fresh. At the very least, Aldebaran and Calico should be part of this discussion."

Ray asked, "What do you intend to do with Calico and the other survivors?"

"If they don't choose to stay on the station, they'll be welcome to travel with us. If we ever get this mess wrapped up, then we might be able to accommodate any transportation requests they have."

Ari said, "If I know Captain Calico, he's not going to want to go anywhere until the Zendreen have left Freedmen."

John nodded. "I'm not inclined to abandon Freedmen to the Zendreen either. In fact, we can't afford to lose track of the fleet as long as they're still a threat to Earth."

"It seems to me," began Christie, "that the best way to eliminate the Zendreen as a threat is to get Hayaku to turn against them."

"I agree. That's why I'm eager to discuss our options with Major Pyramis."

Ray said, "From his conversation with Lieutenant Brentage, it doesn't seem like he's in any position to help us right now."

John stood up. "Maybe not, but Brentage did let us dock for medical aid. I'm going to find out. Dana, could you get a meal going? I'll be back soon. The rest of you can eat, sleep, or do both. Ari, I'd like you to come with me."

"You bet," Ari said, standing.

John exited the galley to the orb room as Ari drained her glass. Miriam stood up and walked up to Dana.

"I'll help," she said. "Ari, will you come see me when you get back? I have a lot of questions about our father."

Ari laughed lowly as she headed for the door. "You and me both, sister."

"All set. Try not to let things fall on your head anymore."

In the medical bay on board the station, a doctor had just finished stitching up the back of Aldebaran's head. It was relatively quiet in the clean, bright room, contrasting the frenzy that had been going on in the adjacent operating room. Richter stood nearby, leaning against the bulkhead. He smiled.

"Advice we all should follow," he said.

"I'm fine," said Aldebaran, standing up. "We should get back to the Faith."

Captain Calico entered. He was smiling as well, but looked exhausted.

"How are your people?" asked Richter.

"Gueyr will be fine," Calico replied, "and he'll be a lot happier once we get him a quality cybernetic replacement. Knoal has been stabilized, but he'll have to stay off his feet for several days. His burns will also have to be tended to, but we can do that easily enough aboard the Faith."

"And yourself?" asked Aldebaran.

"I just lost my ship and half my crew. I'm still pretty pissed off."

Aldebaran nodded. "I know the feeling."

"We still haven't been formerly introduced."

Richter stepped forward. "Captain Calico, this is Sergeant Jack Smith."

Calico shook Aldebaran's hand. "Don't I know you from somewhere?"

"I doubt it," replied Aldebaran. "I was stuck on Umber for ten years."

"That must have been hard."

"Actually, the Zendreen were fair and reasonable, as far as fascist invaders go. They just wouldn't frigging leave."

"What are you going to do now?" Richter asked Calico.

"I'm still technically under the command of Scherer," began Calico, "although I've long since given up on ever going back to Umber to get paid. Still, a contract is a contract. I only wish I still had a ship to offer him."

"I think Scherer will let you out of the contract if you want."

"Do you have any other assets?" asked Aldebaran.

"I have a rainy day deposit on Misrere Prime, but again, it's not worth the expense of getting back there to access it. All my platinum is currently under thirty thousand tons of burning slag."

"Why is platinum so valuable?" asked Richter. "Can't anyone just replicate it?"

"Oh right, I'm sure someday someone will invent a practical matter replicator. Until then, rare metals will still have value."

"Umber did," said Aldebaran proudly.

"No shit? No wonder General Zeeman offered gold and uranium as payment for my services."

"Actually," began Richter, "the only working replicator in existence is on board the Faith."

Calico looked at Richter in disbelief for a moment before replying. "How much platinum do you think you can replicate?"

"Theoretically, an unlimited amount, if we have enough source material. There's always a rate of attrition in the exchange between the source material and the desired output. The Umberians gave us a giant block of lead to use for that purpose, but it's already doing a fair impression of Swiss cheese due to our needs."

"Excuse me?"

"I mean there's very little left."

"Oh. But, given enough lead, you can replicate platinum."

"Correct."

Calico shook his head. "If you ever get sick of starting fires all over the galaxy, you can retire quite nicely."

"At the very least we might be able to buy you a new ship."

"That would be a lot of platinum."

"Christie would know exactly how much source material we'd need."

"For what?" asked John, entering the medical bay from the corridor. Megumi was at his side.

"Hello, Scherer," said Calico. "Thanks again for pulling our asses out of there."

"No problem. How's your crew doing?"

"As I was just telling the others, Gueyr will be fine. There shouldn't be any complications, but he'll be on crutches until we can get him a prosthetic. Knoal's recovery will be much slower, however. Lieutenant Brentage has offed to let him stay here until he's better."

"Good news. What did you want to replicate?"

"Platinum. If you can really replicate enough of it, I could use some compensation for my losses."

"Hell yeah," said Megumi.

"I don't think that will be a problem, but we may not be able to access enough source material until we've resolved our Zendreen problem."

"Do you have a next move in mind?" asked Calico.

"I'd like to have a meeting with everyone on board the Faith to discuss it. First, I've requested an audience with Major Pyramis. I'm going to see him now, and I'd like everyone here to accompany me. Aldebaran, are you good to travel?"

"Yup," said Aldebaran.

"Good."

"Megumi," Calico said, "would you please get Gueyr and Knoal onto the Faith?"

"No problem, Cap," replied Megumi.

The others moved into the corridor, and were met by a Hayakuvian corporal. The young NCO gestured and the group followed him. After a brief walk and elevator ride, they entered a large conference room. Wide windows encircled half of the room, offering a beautiful view of the solar system. Major Pyramis and Lieutenant Brentage stood at the far end of a long table, flanked by two guards on either side. Brentage motioned for his guests to sit down.

"I hope you don't mind if my friends are here for this," said John, taking a chair.

"Not really," said Brentage.

"I understand Major Pyramis has been detained."

"You already know that he violated orders and took a Stylus without authorization. I have no choice but to deliver him to Central Command, or my own career will be over. If you are the professional that the major says you are, I won't expect you to try to change my mind."

"Lieutenant, my only mission is to eliminate the Zendreen's ability to wage war. Since Hayaku has chosen not to intervene when they could have done so easily, that makes you de facto allies of the Zendreen. Technically, that makes us enemies. I don't see things in such black and white terms, and since you allowed us to dock, I sense that neither do you."

"It would be far more accurate to say that I allowed you to dock because any hostile action on your part would be suicidal. From the moment you entered the range of this station, powerful weapons were trained on your ship. Obviously I asked you to leave your small arms on board your ship so that you couldn't attempt anything stupid."

"You also don't have any orders to refuse a request for medical aid," said Pyramis.

"Respectfully, Major, you'll have your chance to speak. Commander, the most I can do in this case is remain neutral. It is in the spirit of diplomacy that I'm allowing this forum at all."

John said, “I understand. But you must also understand that the Zendreen can't be trusted. While they may not be in a position to threaten Hayaku right now, if you continue to support them, passively or otherwise, then they may regain enough strength to threaten you in the future.”

“Just because you and the Zendreen aren't the best of pals doesn't mean they're mindless warmongers. I know my history, Commander Scherer. The Zendreen honored the terms of their non-aggression pact with the Solar United Faction for the ten years that they were in control of the Umberian system. Even if they were to double or triple the number of their warships, they would still be no match for Hayaku.”

“It was easy for the SUF to enforce that pact because the Zendreen weren't powerful enough to take them on,” said Pyramis.

“That just reinforces my point, sir. We all know that the Zendreen don't have the manpower to maintain an occupation of Freedmen. What the colony lacked in aerial defenses they make up for with the size of their infantry. If they stick around too long, the colonists will simply reorganize their forces and counter-attack.”

“Couldn't they just bomb the crap out of them from orbit?” asked Richter.

"If there's one thing that the history of the Rakhar Empire taught us," began Calico, "it's that orbital bombardment of an entrenched enemy is usually futile."

"I'm not privy to the agreement into which Hayaku entered with the Zendreen," said Brentage, "but I'm sure that orbital bombardment of the colony was off the table."

"It isn't just for the sake of Umber that we've so tenaciously pursued the Zendreen," said John. "When they took their fleet through the wormhole, they brought themselves within striking distance of the home planet of myself and most of my crew."

"And a few dozen other inhabited planets. Look, Commander, I understand your problem. Hayaku needed to prove to the colonists that it was far too soon for them to govern themselves directly..."

Calico said, "So you're going to sit there and tell us, with a straight face, that the military isn't acting without the permission of the Hayakuvian government?"

"To propose otherwise would be preposterous."

Pyramis was livid. "Damn it, Lieutenant, how can you say that?"

"Because I don't have the luxury of an opinion anymore," Brentage yelled back.

"Gentlemen, please," said Aldebaran, bringing quiet to the group. "Thank you. Lieutenant Brentage, are you under orders not to allow a third-party ship to travel to Hayaku?"

"No," replied Brentage morosely.

"Then it seems to me that we can get to the bottom of this easily enough. The Reckless Faith doesn't need your permission to go to Hayaku, nor will we compromise your neutrality by doing so."

"Perhaps you haven't been paying attention," Calico said, "but the military attacked my ship when I started asking questions."

"Then we go straight to the government," said John.

"That won't work either."

"The military will never allow you to contact the government without going through them," said Pyramis.

"He's right about that," added Brentage.

John said, "The Reckless Faith has a very good invisibility shield. We can probably sneak past any defensive net."

"You don't get it," said Pyramis. "The government probably has no idea that the military is conspiring against the colony. If you contact them directly, they'll simply refer you to the military anyway."

"They won't even listen to what we have to say first?"

"Not unless you happen to contact a member of the ultra-left Social Reform Party. Even then it would take some time for the word to get out, and that would only cause weeks of debate in parliament, followed by a formal investigation into the military, and so forth. Meanwhile the Zendreen are long gone."

"Commander Scherer," said Brentage, "If you want to continue your fight against the Zendreen, that is your decision. You should follow them when they leave and forget about Freedmen and Hayaku."

"I'm not satisfied with that answer," said Calico.

"I can't accommodate your dissatisfaction, Captain."

"Kiss my ass, can you accommodate that?"

"Relax, Calico..." John began to say.

An incoming message grabbed the interest of Brentage, and almost simultaneously John received a transmission from Christie. Brentage listened to his message privately as John did the same.

"John, this is Christie," her voice said. "The Zendreen have stopped jamming radio traffic on Freedmen, and the fleet appears to be preparing to break orbit."

"Roger, standby," he replied, then to Brentage, "Can I assume your people are telling you the same thing?"

"That the Zendreen are on the move?" asked Brentage. "Yes."

John stood up. "Then it seems our business here has concluded. I'm sorry we couldn't reach an agreement."

"I'm sorry the Zendreen chose Freedmen as a resupply point. Some things are simply out of our control."

"There is something else before we go. I know Pyramis traded his freedom for the medical aid of our wounded. However, turning him over to you, after what he did for us, is unacceptable."

Brentage stood up. "I already told you, it's his career or mine. There is no third option."

"Never say that with a ninja in the room. Ari?"

There was a violent blur as two of the guards across the table seemed to smash their heads together. The other two guards were also rapidly knocked unconscious, and Aldebaran and Richter easily disabled the corporal. Ari deactivated her personal shield and relieved the lieutenant of his sidearm.

"You'll never get away with this," Brentage said, astonished.

"God, how I've waited for someone to use that line on me," said John, smiling.

"You don't have to do this," said Pyramis. "I'm willing to accept the consequences of my actions."

"Even when you know the military is in the wrong?"

"I was hoping to be able to plead my case to my peers. There was never much hope of changing anything, but I thought I'd try."

"We can still leave you here if you want."

"Hell no."

"Good, let's get moving. Brentage, you're coming with us to ensure our safe departure from this station."

Brentage let out an impressive string of invectives, but did not resist. The others each grabbed a weapon from the fallen soldiers.

"We should contact Mother Calico and see how they made out," said Calico.

"Of course," replied John. "We can't dally for too long, though. If we lose sight of the fleet then we're back to square one."

The group entered the hallway, which was empty, and headed for the lift. Ari kept her captured pistol firmly in the lieutenant's back.

"I don't know what you hope to accomplish by trailing the Zendreen fleet," said Brentage. "You said yourself that your home planet doesn't stand a chance against them."

"We may have one more trick up our sleeve," said John quietly. "And you won't have to worry about Hayaku, Lieutenant. We are done with your planet."

22.

"Bless you, child, you still live. And you brought my dearest Farril back to me as well."

The bridge of the Reckless Faith was crowded with old and new allies alike. The only ones not present were Lieutenant Brentage, who was locked in the cargo hold, and Knoal, who was still too banged up to participate. The ship was taking a slow fly-by of Freedmen, giving the crew a few minutes to talk to the prime minister before continuing on after the Zendreen fleet.

The visage of Mother Calico was on the main viewscreen. She was wearing yet another flower-pattern sun dress and appeared no worse for wear. She was smiling, but she also had sadness in here eyes. John sat in the pilot chair, flanked by Captain Calico and Ari, and the prime minister could also see everyone else standing behind them.

"Anya," began Farril, "I'm relieved you survived the invasion."

"The Zendreen weren't lying about their intentions," Anya replied. "They took control of several supply points just long enough to load up and get back into orbit. They never did fire on any of their initial targets. They never even got near the capitol."

"I'm sorry the aerial defense failed."

"It is a tragic blow, to be sure, but if the Zendreen stay away it won't take us long to rebuild."

"I'd be more worried about Hayaku moving in, under the guise of providing the colony protection."

Anya frowned. "If the central government thinks this setback will quash our commitment to remaining independent, they are wrong. Still, playing along for the short term may be our best strategy."

"Excuse me, Prime Minister," said John, "we don't have much time if we intend to follow the fleet. I need to know if you had any further contact with the Zendreen commander after the invasion began."

"Yes, my dear."

"Did he give you any indication where they might be headed next?"

"Why would my enemy volunteer that information?"

"They're new to this part of the galaxy, ma'am. I had hoped they'd ask you for a recommendation for an uninhabited planet."

"Please excuse me, child, I misunderstood your question. The commander demanded that we provide our astronomical database. I consider it quite likely that they intend to use that information to look for a new home, or at least a place to safely rest."

"Did you give it to them?"

"I didn't have to. Once I suggested the Vulture, the commander terminated the transmission."

"What?" exclaimed John loudly. "Why would you volunteer that information to them?"

Anya's eyes flashed and she replied testily. "Based on what you told me, Commander Scherer, occupying that asteroid wouldn't pose a threat to anyone."

"Oh, shit!" said Ari.

"Did I say it wasn't a threat?" asked John, livid.

"If I recall correctly," said Anya, standing, "you called it 'derelict'."

"Scherer, take it easy," Farril said evenly.

John sighed. "I'm sorry, Prime Minister, but I did not adequately relay to you the potential threat that control of that asteroid could pose. If the Zendreen ever get it running at full capacity again, whether it be next week or next year, no one will be safe. Not even Hayaku."

Anya returned to her seat. "Then, my dear, if your ship is faster than the fleet, I suggest you get there first."

"Yeah, I think that's good advice."

"Commander Scherer, thank you for your help, even though we lost the battle. You and your crew will always be heroes of Freedmen. I hope you can dissuade the Zendreen from taking control of the asteroid. Somehow I think you will find a way. Farril, I hope you will come see me soon."

"You can count on it," replied Farril.

John closed the channel, and swiveled his chair around to face the others.

"I can't believe she told them to go to the Vulture," said Dana.

"She's right," John replied, shaking his head. "I didn't tell her about the full potential of the asteroid."

"You can't let them get control of that place," said Miriam.

"I know. We have to get back there ahead of the fleet."

"What are we going to do when we get there?" asked Ray.

"Make friends with the canine soldiers, and get them to activate the defensive systems," said Ari.

"Good luck with that," Dana said.

"Apparently I gained some status among them as a warrior. With Cassie dead, maybe we can exploit a power vacuum."

John nodded. "That may be our only option. I doubt they'll talk to us otherwise.

Christie, can you extrapolate the location of the Vulture?"

"I can give you a search area based on all known variables," replied Christie, "although it is possible that the asteroid is capable of velocities exceeding that which we've observed."

"What did you tell Anya about the location of the asteroid?" Farril asked John.

"Just that we encountered it within 40 AU of Alpha Sagittae," said John.

"The Zendreen probably have a good idea of what they're looking for," Dana said. "Remember, we came out of the wormhole together almost on top it. We should assume they scanned it before they left."

"That would explain their eagerness to follow Mother Calico's advice."

"I think we need to consider another, simpler explanation," said Richter.

"Oh?"

"I know what Richter is going to say," said Aldebaran.

Richter looked at Aldebaran knowingly, then said, "We've assumed that the Zendreen chose Alpha Sagittae either because they needed a star of that type to create the wormhole, or because of its proximity to Earth, or both. But what if they already knew about the Vulture?"

Aldebaran nodded. "It's possible. They could have been trying to reach it the whole time, but had to stop off somewhere for supplies first."

John said, "The more I know about this whole mess, the less I like it. It only points to more meddling by the Kira'To."

"So the Kira'To told the Zendreen to go to the Vulture?" asked Miriam.

"We already guessed that they might be allies," Ray said.

John furrowed his brow. "The Vulture may have been their ultimate goal, but it changes nothing. If there's any way we can prevent them from occupying it, we have to do so. Agreed?"

There were no objections. John turned his chair around to face the viewscreen.

"Christie, how long will it take the fleet to get to the search area?" he asked.

"If they go at top speed," began Christie, "just under three and a half days."

"Good. Get us there in twelve hours. That will give everyone enough time to rest and recuperate. If we're fortunate enough to make peace with the current residents, we can use the rest of the time to help them restore as much of the asteroid's defensive systems as possible. At the very least we can warn them."

Farril said, "Commander Scherer, thank you for your hospitality."

"It seemed the least I could do for you. Ray, do you want to find a place for our guests to sleep?"

"Someone might as well make use of my quarters," said Christie.

"Are you sure?" asked Ray.

"It would be silly to do otherwise."

Ray gestured to Pyramis, Farril, Megumi, and Gueyr, the last of whom was on crutches, and led them through the conference room into the lounge area. Knoal slept peacefully on one of the three couches.

"Well, there are two more comfortable couches in here," said Ray, "and there's the couch in the galley. We have a spare mattress in the cargo hold, but as long as Brentage is down there we should let him use it. I guess you four can draw straws for Christie's room."

"No need," said Farril. "Gueyr can take it."

"I'll be fine out here, Cap," said Gueyr.

"This is not up for debate. The rest of us can deal with these couches better."

The ship shuddered as it entered superluminal flight. A moment later John and Richter entered from the conference room.

"We're on our way," said John. "I wish I could offer you better accommodations."

"This will be fine," said Megumi.

"I hate to impose further," said Farril, "but we could use some food."

"I was headed to the galley next," John said. "You're welcome to join me."

Pyramis turned to John. "Can I talk to you alone first?"

"Sure. Ray, do you mind?"

Ray shook his head, and motioned for the others to follow him downstairs. John and Pyramis entered the conference room. Both men were visibly exhausted.

"I wanted to talk to you about Lieutenant Brentage," Pyramis said, leaning against the table.

"It looks like we're stuck with him for now. I don't know how we're going to return him to the station without putting ourselves at risk."

"It's too bad we don't still have my Stylus. I'd simply let him fly it home."

"Major, if you have concerns about the way he'll be treated..."

"No, it's not that. I want to try to convince him to work for us while he's here. I haven't known him for very long, but he's a very reasonable man. I also don't believe he would stab any of us in the back if we let him out of the hold."

"I've gone down that road before, Major Pyramis, and it has only led to trouble. Besides, he has no reason to cooperate with us. What does he have to gain by helping?"

"He's a military officer, Commander Scherer. It will drive him crazy to sit in the hold during a mission of any kind, regardless of whether or not he's invested in it."

John sat down at the head of the table. "I understand that you feel like you owe Brentage. I am also appreciative of the medical services he offered us. However, I don't feel like I can extend that gratitude as far as letting him roam freely on the ship."

"All right. At least let me fill him in on what's going on."

"Fine. Take Richter with you. I don't want him to get any ideas."

"Thanks, I will."

Pyramis exited to the lounge area. John leaned back in his chair and closed his eyes. He might just as easily fall asleep here, but his bed was only a few paces away. After a minute, he forced himself to stand and walked to his quarters. The sounds of a meal being prepared and pleasant conversation wafted up from the galley and followed him down the corridor, ceasing when he closed the door to his quarters. He hoped that such hospitality would help ease the loss suffered by Calico and his crew, if only temporarily.

John brushed his teeth and washed his face. There were dark circles under his eyes, and he looked to himself many years older than his chronological age. Too much had happened in too short a time for his conscious mind to process. Eight hours of sleep would help, but even as John flopped heavily into his bed, sleep did not come right away. The specter of the Kira'To was gnawing at him like heartburn. John deeply hoped that it was a bunch of bullshit, but the collective dreams of his crewmembers was powerful evidence of some sort of yet-to-be understood influence. That the Kira'To could have been behind the scenes manipulating their fate betrayed John's ordered view of reality, tenuous though it might have been. Still, all he had to do was glance out any window to be reminded of the vastness of the galaxy, and his own very small place therein.

Despite these disturbing things, John was bothered most by what had happened to Christie. If the Kira'To were indeed somehow responsible for Byron's presence, as Ray had speculated, then that made it personal. He raged against that possibility until it pushed him into unconsciousness.

It was a perfect replica of Christie's Somerville apartment, although Ray would have to take her word for it. In the virtual world of the orb, all senses were accounted for, and the first thing he noticed was her perfume. It was a subtle scent he hadn't encountered for weeks, as she'd run out shortly after their arrival in the Tarantula Nebula. Christie herself emerged from the bedroom, and her beauty seemed to exceed any level Ray had ever appreciated while she was in corporeal form. She smiled in that easy way that he loved so much and walked up to him.

"What do you think?" she asked.

"You're gorgeous," Ray replied.

"Thank you, but I mean the simulation."

"It seems flawless to me."

"I figured for my first attempt, I should choose a place that made me feel completely safe."

Ray embraced her and they kissed. He brushed her hair back from her face.

"I wish I had met you back in college," he said.

"As long as you're wishing, you should wish that I still had my body."

"Trust me, it's on the list. Are you sure you have time for this?"

"We're on autopilot for the next twelve hours, and Dana agreed to keep watch on the bridge. I mean, I could keep part of my consciousness on the operations of the ship, but that wouldn't be fair to you."

They kissed again. Ray began to cry.

"I thought I'd lost you."

"Shh. I'm not going anywhere."

Ray suddenly laughed. "You know, I wonder if Richter and Ari are finally going to seal the deal tonight."

"I doubt it. I took a peek. Her heart belongs to someone else. Now, do you want to talk about other people all night?"

"Hell no."

On the bridge, Dana was leaning back in the pilot chair with her feet up on the console. She had agreed to watch over the bridge while Christie took a break, but that didn't mean she couldn't catch some sleep at the same time. There wasn't anything that could happen that wouldn't sound an audible alert, and Dana was rightly confident that such a tone would wake her up no matter how deep her sleep.

Dana mulled over recent events in her mind. She had forgotten all about her dream of the city on the Vulture until it had been brought up, but now those images were fresh and troubling. She suspected that she and John were of like minds when it came to sizing up the Kira'To; the possibility that they were involved on some level was beyond frustrating. She did not know, however, if John felt the same creeping terror that she did about returning to the asteroid. It was a fear to which Miriam readily admitted, but the girl remained stalwart about doing so.

Dana's own fears were far less justifiable, although no one aboard would fault her for having them.

In past missions, curiosity had mitigated fear. When the missions involved combat, the impalpable fear of the unknown had been replaced by the palpable fear of death. The latter state had become like a familiar song to Dana, but no matter how many times it was played, it never got any easier. Dana was grateful that she could draw strength from those around her. The others had become seasoned adventurers, and knew how to remain calm in the face of disaster. Richter and Aldebaran were particularly level-headed, although John had recently become almost as steely.

Dana's thoughts dwelled on Aldebaran. Having overcome his initial imbalance after reconstituting himself with Seth the AI, he had become a good friend. That he shared Dana's memories was no small part of that. It was easy to forget that they hadn't known each other their entire lives. She could rationalize that, but it was a different emotional connection that she found more compelling. When she thought of Aldebaran in a fashion sympathetic to the tragedy in his life, she experienced an emotional state indistinguishable from a crush. Dana figured the feeling would pass in time. It would certainly be better to keep it to herself for now.

Dana drifted into dreams, and hoped that the Kira'To would stay out of them.

An hour later, only three people were left in the galley. A liberal amount of alcohol had been consumed by almost everyone during the previous meal, leading to a quick exit to their respective beds or couches once the effect took hold. Pyramis was no exception, and snoozed fitfully on the nearby couch. Calico and Ari remained awake. Calico was never a big drinker, and tonight was no exception. He was still nursing his second stout. Ari imposed no such restriction on herself, but an inexplicable reserve of energy was overcoming the sedative effect of the alcohol. The conversation after the departure of the others had centered around Calico's guilt over the crash of the Almagest. Ari offered the obvious but necessary assurance that he did everything he could, and it was a miracle they didn't all die. After that topic had lapsed into a few minutes of silence, Ari changed the subject.

"Did you know about Miriam and I?" she asked.

"I don't understand," replied Calico.

"Doc Trewler told me that she and I are paternal sisters. We were able to confirm it with Professor Talvan's equipment."

"You're putting me on."

"I wouldn't do that to you, Farril. Not right now, anyway."

"So you had a sister you didn't know about, that's a surprise enough by itself. The two of you ending up on the same ship hundreds of light years from your home planet, that's quite a shock."

"Do you think the Kira'To have a hand in it?"

"Anything that I could say about that would be pure speculation. After all of my experience and travels, I've learned never to assign to chance that which could be explained by design. However, coincidences do occur. For you and Miriam, either is possible."

"If it's not a coincidence, it opens up a rather disturbing collection of possibilities."

"Maybe. Although..."

"What?"

"Did you ever think that whomever is responsible for your union did it out of benevolence?"

"That would mean that someone out there cares about us, which I find more incredible."

"You mean other than the people on this ship?"

"Of course, Farril, I didn't mean to imply otherwise."

"Don't worry about it, Coma. So, you have the same father. Have you had a chance to talk to her about it?"

"Oh, yes, we've spoken at length about Master Sergeant Gabriel Ferro aka Gabriel Colchester. In a nutshell, my father divorced my mother after I left for college and moved to another continent. For reasons unknown to either of us, he changed his surname from Ferro to Colchester. He remarried, and had Miriam. Thanks to the effect of time dilation and the wormhole, we end up only twelve years apart in age. He and his new wife were ufologists, or people who are obsessed with unidentified flying objects and extraterrestrial alien life."

"That must be rather popular on your planet."

"No, not at all. Anyway, unlike most ufologists, they actually had contact on some level with aliens. The nature of their relationship was never clear to Miriam, only that it consumed their lives in the weeks leading up to their abduction. I'm reserving judgment on whether these beings were the Kira'To of galactic legend or something else entirely."

"Let's hope there are some answers to be found on the Vulture. How are the two of you getting along? She must trust you at least well enough to share your cabin."

"I don't think there's a trust issue there. She tries to play it cool, but I can tell by the way she hugs me... she's grateful for being rescued."

"You're a nice person to be rescued by."

Ari laughed. "Thanks. Maybe invisible assassin isn't my true calling."

Calico drank from his glass. "What do you want, Coma?"

"To kick ass and chew bubblegum..."

"Seriously," interrupted Calico. "I never doubted your resolve to serve on my crew, and I never attributed your zeal for the job to anything other than genuine drive. Now that the Almagest is gone, what do you intend to do? I mean, assuming we don't all get killed trying to defend the asteroid."

"I'm not sure. Stick with the Reckless Faith, I suppose. You?"

"First of all, I'm going back to Freedmen to see how I can help with the reconstruction there. They'll also need people who know the truth about the collusion between the Zendreen and the Hayakuvian military. Soon, though, I intend to take a freighter to a more populated system and use the payment that Scherer has promised me to buy a new ship. I won't be happy if I'm not a freelancer. Coma, you will always be welcome on my crew. If you decide to come with me..."

"I'll keep it in mind, Farril. I'm just not really the long term planning type."

Farril smiled. "That you are not. Still, think about it. When I find good people I hate to let them go. Speaking of which, I'd better check on Knoal and Gueyr, if I can stay awake long enough. Shall we call it a night?"

"You can call it a pink elephant for all I care."

"You should get some sleep, too. We still have our work cut out for us."

"I'll be ready."

"Dana, wake up."

Dana did so and almost fell out of the pilot chair. She turned to see Richter standing next to her, smiling. He had a cup of coffee in his hand.

"Is that for me?" she asked, rubbing her face.

"No, it's for me," replied Richter. "I'm relieving you."

"How long was I out?"

"Six hours. I figured you'd want to get some sack time in your own bed."

"Thanks. Where is everyone else?"

Richter sat at the next station. "Sleeping. I was, too, until about fifteen minutes ago."

Dana stood up, stretched, and yawned. "Excuse me. I'll take you up on that offer. Just make sure I'm up before we make contact with the asteroid."

"Of course. Hey, how are you holding up?"

"I'm fine. I'm just sick of all this fighting. Watching the Almagest go down was the most horrifying thing I've seen since we left Earth. If Miriam or Aldebaran had been killed, I don't know... Well, I have no idea how do deal with something like that."

"Aldebaran knows what kinds of risks we take living this life, but it's his choice. Miriam, she didn't get to make that choice, so I'm much more worried about her being involved in all of this."

Dana crossed her arms. "I agree. You hit on another point there though, Chance. Living this life? What does that mean? The Reckless Faith hasn't had a clear mission statement since we liberated Umber."

"Once we went through that wormhole, our mission changed from defending Umber to defending Earth. As long as the Zendreen are the greatest threat to Earth, everything we've done has been the right course of action."

"I know. I just wish we could have found a diplomatic solution."

"The Zendreen have never indicated any willingness toward diplomacy."

"Except with Hayaku, but only because..."

"Exactly," interrupted Richter. "Only because they're too weak to oppose them. That's the bottom line, Dana. Our only choices are to mount a constant defense against the Zendreen, or destroy them utterly. As much as I'd like to do the latter, we don't have enough force. Whether or not we can deny them the Vulture, our next step will be to bolster Earth's defenses. If they actually do capture the asteroid, all the more so."

"I've always thought we should return to Earth and introduce humanity to Umberian technology."

"I know. It's a logical progression. Fuck the Prime Directive."

Dana laughed. "Exactly. Anyhow, I'm too zonked out to have a serious discussion right now. Have fun."

"Sleep well."

Dana exited the bridge. Richter moved to the pilot chair and sipped his coffee.

"Good morning, Richter," said Christie's voice.

"Hello. I was wondering where you were."

"I'm everywhere and nowhere, or where I care to be, depending on how you look at it."

"I suppose you don't need to sleep."

"No."

"Has the thrill worn off yet?"

"Thrill or shock? Either way, yes, but I'm far from being bored. I have access to all of Umber's archives, both historical and technical. What time I haven't spent keeping this ship running I've spent reading up on those. It's a nerd's paradise."

"I never took you for a nerd," replied Richter.

"Oh, I'm a total nerd. I'm just also a girly girl."

"A girly girl who can shoot better than some Marines I've known."

"Flattery will get you nowhere. Listen, Richter, I couldn't help but overhear the conversation you just had with Dana. Do you think we really have the right to commit genocide against the Zendreen?"

"I wouldn't phrase it like that, but they are our enemy, and as long as they continue to be our enemy, our goal should be to destroy them utterly. If they fight to the last man, or creepy insectoid thingy, then they'll commit suicide by our hands."

"What if they rebuild their forces and become a threat again?"

"Then they'll find a massive fleet of willing allies ready to stop them."

"So at some point, we return to Earth and build more ships."

Richter crossed his legs. "Sure, why not?"

"I'm not sure we have the right to disrupt the lives of so many humans. Even the United States government couldn't keep a project of that size a secret."

Richter laughed. "As long as a single Zendra draws breath, they know about the presence of Talvanium on Earth. I don't see the Earth being left alone to progress at its own pace as long as such valuable material is there."

"Are you suggesting that the only way the Earth will be truly safe is to kill off the Zendreen?"

"Not at all. Regardless of who knows or cares about the Talvanium, anyone else is liable to wander by and take an interest in Earth's other nice things. Knowing how dangerous the galaxy really is, I think we have an obligation to share this technology with humankind. Subjugation or destruction at the hands of either the Zendreen or a yet unidentified threat is hardly worth prolonging our innocence."

"What about the pride in making technological advances without help?"

"Did you invent the M1A?"

"You mean the rifle? Of course not."

"Yet you have no trouble using it to defend your life."

"Okay, I take your point. By the way, that reminds me. Remember that you were complaining that we were all out of ammo for your M4?"

Richter finished his coffee. "Yeah. Without a representative cartridge to scan, we were stuck."

"You once read a reloading manual for that cartridge, do you remember?"

"I remember reading the manual, but I don't remember the technical data."

"Ah, but you do. That's the beauty of having unrestricted access to your memories, Chance."

"That's more disturbing than it is positive."

"You trust me, don't you?"

"Implicitly, Christie; I was just being glib. I'm not ashamed of anything I've done, certain auto-erotic activities in my teen years notwithstanding."

Christie laughed. "I'll remember not to look there. Anyway, I can replicate as much five-five-six as you need. Well, a few hundred rounds, anyway. We're actually running out of lead as source material. We're going to have to be more selective in what we replicate until we get more."

"At least I'll get my M4 back in service. The Phalanx is a great weapon but I think someone else might benefit from it more in a real pinch." Richter stood up. "I'm going to get more coffee. When I get back I'd like to go over with you everything we already know about the asteroid."

"Okay. With your permission, I'd like to access your memories of your time there."

"Fine with me. Although..."

"What?"

"When you access memories, can you also register emotions?"

"As I interpret the data, the two are one and the same."

"Hmm. I guess I don't need to tell you how I really feel about combat, then."

"You're a classic warrior. I suppose if I had just met you, I might be shocked."

"That reminds me. I'm sure you recall the incident in the galley between Byron and Ari back during transit, right?"

"I've been meaning to talk to John about that. Seth was running a program that we couldn't identify, but I'm familiar with it now. It was an experimental program meant to detect murderous intent. It was unreliable at best."

"And in this case?"

"It's impossible to tell."

"You don't have to sugar-coat it, Christie. We both know Ari had it in for Byron."

"Are you running it right now?"

"No. Do you think I should?"

"I don't. There isn't anyone on board right now that we can't trust. If that situation were to change, I might feel differently."

Christie sighed. "I'm not sure I'd feel comfortable trying to play everyone's conscience."

Richter laughed. "Given our track record, a little benevolent oversight couldn't hurt."

23.

Six hours had passed, and the mood on the bridge of the Faith was calm, though those present were well aware of the urgency of the task at hand. The crew and guests were rested and fed, and the ship had arrived at the Vulture. Finding the asteroid had been easy, as it was right where it should have been barring any course changes. The mission briefing that had concluded five minutes earlier had been simple as there was only one viable plan: make contact with the canine soldiers and hope they were open to a truce. Plan B involved trying to take the asteroid by force, which seemed unwise by any reasonable measure. John had ordered the crew to battle stations, although so far the ship remained hidden behind the invisibility shield.

John sat in the pilot chair. To his left were Ari and Calico, the latter of whom was manning the station formerly occupied by Christie. To his right were Aldebaran and Ray. Miriam and Gueyr sat at the rear of the bridge. Dana, Richter, Megumi, and Pyramis were manning the guns, while Knoal had been moved into the conference room (a not inconsequential effort) so he could at least watch the proceedings via the monitor there. Pyramis had also convinced John to let Lieutenant Brentage listen in on the bridge via an audio link, but with strict orders not to interrupt them.

It had been agreed upon that Ari should initiate contact with the asteroid. John nodded at her.

"Any time you're ready, Ari," he said.

Ari pressed a key on her console. "Residents of the Vulture, this is Coma Veronice. If you can hear me, respond. There are matters of great import which we must discuss."

About twenty seconds passed. Ari was about to try again when a reply came through. She and Miriam immediately recognized the language and tone.

"Why have you returned here?" the voice asked.

"It's one of the canine soldiers," Ari said to the others, and then into the radio, "I have come to warn you of a race of aliens that seeks to capture your asteroid."

"We are quite capable of defending ourselves, thank you."

"Read him this," Christie said to Ari, feeding some data to her screen.

Ari examined the information. "Our sensors indicate that only three percent of your power system is active. I only see one plasma turret online. The force that seeks to capture the asteroid consists of a battleship, four cruisers, and numerous fighter craft. You can't hope to repel them with one turret."

"What makes you think," began the voice, "that all of our systems are powered up right now?"

"Okay, maybe they aren't. You should still listen to us. After what happened between us, you must realize that we wouldn't return here unless there was something greater than either of us at stake."

"And what might that be?"

"Are you familiar with the Zendreen?"

"The playthings of the Kira'To? They're the aliens you're so worried about?"

"They are far more than pets. It is our assessment that they are capable of taking over the Vulture, and if they do, they'll use it to wage war with anyone they wish. Now, maybe you don't care about the rest of the galaxy, but I'm sure you'd rather not abdicate control of your home to the Zendreen."

"So, your philosophy is that the enemy of my enemy is my friend?"

"Exactly. We're willing to put aside our differences in order to fight the Zendreen."

"You might feel differently if you hadn't escaped us. We might be willing to discuss this with you further, but first you must agree to a trade."

"I'm listening."

"Do you have any dermaplasts?"

"Yes, actually. We just picked them up."

"Bring us three dermaplasts and we will honor a truce. I cannot guarantee, however, that we will agree to help you fight the Zendreen."

"Agreed. You should know that our ship is fully operational, unlike the last time we met."

"I'm sending you coordinates for an airlock. Normally I'd invite you into the hangar, but you destroyed the control room on your way out."

"Coordinates received," said Christie.

"Understood," Ari said. "Is there anything else we can get for you?"

"Until the truth of this matter is known, we will deal only with you, Coma Veronice. We will admit only you and the dermaplasts."

"Fine. See you soon."

Ari terminated the connection, and turned to face the others.

"I don't like it," said John. "They might kill you and take the dermaplasts."

"I don't think so. Cassie told me that I'd earned a certain level of respect for killing her soldiers in single combat. I think I'll be fine. Then again, she may have said that sarcastically."

"Take your personal shield, just in case."

Ari smiled. "Oh, of course. I'm also hoping Richter will let me borrow the Tarsus blade again."

"You're not going to be able to conceal that unless your shield is activated," said Richter over the intercom.

"I don't care. If they don't like it they can shoot me."

"Great," said John. "Aldebaran, grab three dermaplasts and meet Ari and I in the Zero-G room. Everyone else, keep your eyes on your stations. I don't want any surprises. Christie, begin docking procedures."

"You got it," replied Christie.

John stood up, and followed Ari through the conference room and into the lounge area. Richter was waiting there with the Tarsus blade, and handed it to Ari.

"I should go with you," he said, "but I understand this is only the first step."

"You're so sweet when you're protective," said Ari.

"How's it going with Megumi?" John asked Richter.

"Good," Richter replied. "She's one tough cat, but I can tell she's pretty upset over losing her shipmates. She feels particularly guilty about what happened to Gueyr. Still, mastering the gunning station posed no challenge to her."

"Let's just hope we're not trading shots with the asteroid."

Richter grunted affirmatively, and returned to the gun room. John and Ari passed by the crew quarters and entered the Zero-G room.

"Are you sure you're up for this?" asked John.

"Is that a serious question? I'll be fine, John."

Aldebaran entered with the dermaplasts, which were sealed in sterile foil. He handed them to Ari.

"Captain Calico gave me a very hard look when you called me Aldebaran," he said.

"Oh, shit," said John. "I forgot about your alter ego."

"If he didn't jump up and kill you immediately, consider it a good sign," said Ari.

"I think he just knows about my former reputation," replied Aldebaran. "If I'd wronged him personally, I think he might have done just that."

"There's no sense pussy-footing around the issue," John said, putting his hands on his hips. "We'll talk to him about it after this."

The ship jostled slightly, and Christie came in over the intercom.

"We're docked," she said. "I'm reading a pressurized atmosphere against the outer door."

"Good luck," said John.

Ari nodded and opened the inner door. She stepped into the airlock and allowed the inner door to close. There was a hissing sound and Ari's ears popped as the pressure normalized, and the outer door opened. She found herself face-to-face with one of the canine soldiers, the cold air wafting his distinctive smell forward. He was holding a plasma rifle, but had it pointed at the deck. He glared at Ari with opal eyes, and motioned for her to come ahead.

"No introductions?" she asked, stepping forward.

"You can call me Shedir," the soldier replied flatly. "Keep moving."

Ari shrugged and went on ahead. The airlock opened up into a larger chamber, and the pair was met by three more soldiers. Besides minor variations in their clothing and weaponry,

Ari couldn't tell them apart. The group proceeded into a corridor, two in front of her and two behind. The corridor met the same description as the other parts of the interior she'd seen, but this one was more brightly lit. The soldiers said nothing as they led her through a series of hallways. Ari struggled to keep the way back to the airlock known, which was a difficult task without any distinctive landmarks. After ascending one set of stairs and descending another, she lost track. Ari swore to herself but realized the soldiers were taking a circuitous route on purpose. After a few minutes, the group entered what was obviously a medical bay, and much warmer than the corridors. Only one bed was occupied, and Ari was surprised to see by whom.

"Cassiopeia," she said.

The other woman was clearly in very bad shape. Although her abdomen was covered up with a sheet, tubes snaked from underneath to two different machines. She had an IV stuck in her arm, and was very pale, but her green eyes still flashed with life. Ari noticed that without her goggles on, the woman was strikingly beautiful.

"I didn't think I'd see you again, Coma," Cassie said, her voice coarse.

"Same here," replied Ari. "Your guys must have got you out of the control room pretty quick to save your life."

"They acted heroically. Without further aid, however, I am doomed."

"My lady," began Shedir, "she has brought dermaplasts which should bind your wounds."

"I can see that," Cassie replied politely. "Coma, I will need your delicate hands to apply them, so I hope you know what you're doing."

Ari said, "I'm willing to help you but we need to talk about the Zendreen first."

"Ah yes, the Zendreen. I find it hard to believe that the lapdogs of the Kira'To have achieved their own space fleet, let alone enough power to pose a threat to anyone."

"I don't know where you got your information, but you are way out of date. The Zendreen have been a force to reckon with for at least ten years. It's a long story, Cassiopeia. You need to trust me when I tell you that they're a real threat to this asteroid."

"Very well. Your mere presence here supports your assertion. What do you hope to accomplish?"

"I need to know everything about the defensive capabilities of the asteroid. The guy I talked to over the radio told me that only a fraction of your power relays were online. Is that true?"

"Mostly. Those that are not online are..."

"My lady," Shedir interrupted. "Please, respectfully, how do we not know that the Zendreen are not in allegiance with Veronice and her ship? This could be a trick to get us to reveal ourselves before the attack."

"Shedir, I do not think she would come here in person if that were the case. If the Zendreen really do have a battleship and four cruisers, they would just fire on us until the Vulture was dust. I believe this is a legitimate offer for help. However, I am still waiting to discover exactly how."

"We have several crewmembers who are highly skilled technicians," said Ari. "If you need assistance repairing the defensive systems of the asteroid, we may be able to help."

"I understand. Apply the dermaplasts, then we will see about the rest."

"Fine. Lucky for you, these things are pretty much idiot-proof."

"By the way, what was the name of the man who bested me?"

"Chance Richter. Don't feel bad, he's a highly trained warrior."

"Are you mates?"

Ari laughed. "Not really."

Cassie smiled weakly. "Then I look forward to meeting him again."

Thirty minutes later, several members of the Faith and six canine soldiers were gathered in a frigid cafeteria almost identical to the one where Ari had first met the strange creatures. Cassie had survived the application of the dermaplasts, and was stable. She had lost consciousness during the procedure, so Shedir was speaking for her. Everyone on both sides was heavily armed, but so far nobody had made any threats, overt or otherwise. John had just finished introducing all of his people, so Shedir reciprocated.

"I am Shedir," he was saying. "This is Caph, Achird, Tsih, Ruchbah, and Segin."

"Thank you for meeting us in peace," said John. "Here's the situation. The Zendreen fleet will be here in about three days. We have until then to repair as much of the asteroid as possible. Dana?"

Dana stepped forward, doffing her knit cap. "Hello. Our Doppler neutrino scanners have revealed much about your home. We know only one of six reactors is currently online, and that the majority of power transfer conduits are damaged and not functional. We may be able to repair most, if not all of them. The question is whether or not we have enough time. We should concentrate on getting the plasma turrets near the main hangar online first, seeing as it's the asteroid's weakest point right now. Ideally, we can find a way to close the hangar doors as well.

All of that will require bringing at least one more reactor online. Of course, to accomplish any of this, we're going to need access to your computer system."

"Very well," said Shedir. "Access to any terminal will be initiated by myself or one of my men. At no time will any of your people be allowed to access a terminal without oversight."

"That may limit the speed at which we can make repairs," said Ari.

"It is the only arrangement I'm comfortable with. You have yet to prove this isn't an elaborate attempt at sabotage. Besides, I have enough men to accompany each of you."

"True," said John. "We'll be traveling in at least pairs anyway."

"What if we can't repel the initial attack?" asked Ruchbah, rubbing his ear.

"Then we set up choke points and fight them inside," said Richter. "Given the possible number of foes, let's make sure it doesn't come down to that."

"There are other tricks we can pull as well," said Aldebaran. "Vent certain areas to space, deactivate the artificial gravity, erect force fields, et cetera. Still, we could run out of ammo before we kill enough of them to make them change their minds."

"At least it will be more interesting than chasing a defenseless girl around all day," said Caph.

"Come over here and say that," spat Miriam, drawing her pistol from her parka.

"Save it for the enemy," Megumi said to her calmly.

"Miriam, would you rather wait back on the ship?" asked John.

Miriam turned red, but put her pistol away. "No."

"I didn't think so. Listen, we all need to put aside what happened between us. I understand you were only trying to survive when you captured our ship. I hope now you see that you have more to benefit from an alliance with us. If we can effect these repairs, you'll be in a much better position to sustain your way of life."

"Time will tell," said Shedir.

"If all is agreed, we'd better get started. We have a lot of work to do."

Thirty minutes later, John, Pyramis, and Miriam were standing with Shedir and Caph at Cassie's bedside. She had just regained consciousness, and having been briefed by the canines, offered no objection. Physically, she looked much better, and was sitting up in bed.

"My teams are already starting a close evaluation of your compromised systems," John was saying. "Miriam and I had some questions for you, but first, this is Major Rafe Pyramis. He has a request for you."

"Ma'am," said Pyramis.

"Go ahead, Major," said Cassie.

"We found something interesting in one of your auxiliary hangar bays. Do you know to what I'm referring?"

"The Umberian ship, I imagine."

"That's right. An Umberian Mark Nine twin-seat fighter, to be precise."

"I suppose you're wondering how we came to possess it?"

"Yes, but more importantly I'm hoping you'll let me try to make it operational again."

"It was heavily damaged. The two Umberian men inside fought valiantly to escape us. I am sorry to say that we were forced to kill them when they exited the craft."

Pyramis huffed angrily. "Who the hell are you people?"

"Come now," replied Cassie coolly, "do you chastise the lion for killing the goat? Or the fox for taking the goose? This is what we are, the Vulture of Stymphalis."

"Do you mind if we repair the ship?" asked John.

"It is yours to pursue."

"Thank you. Major, why don't you get started on that?"

"Fine," said Pyramis tersely.

Caph escorted Pyramis from the medical bay. John pulled up a chair and sat down. Cassie smiled at him.

"And I suppose you want to know about me," she said.

John nodded. "You, this asteroid, your men... Miriam's parents. Everything."

"Very well, I will start from the beginning. The Kira'To commissioned three asteroid cities, one of their Great Experiments, to travel through the core galaxy and seek their fortunes. Each of the three had a different mission statement, a philosophy that was strictly adhered to by the inhabitants. The idea was to see which of the three could sustain itself for the longest time. Ideally all three would last indefinitely, but as you can see, the Vulture is close to failure."

"Ari told me that you mentioned philosophies of diplomacy, exploration, and conquest."

"Yes, but the Vulture's impetus was more passive than simple conquest. It was one of independence, with new residents being obtained by opportunity rather than pursuit. Occasionally, the Kira'To would find a need to infuse the population with fresh genetics, and would bring new residents directly here. Unfortunately, not everyone survived the transportation process."

"How can such advanced beings make that sort of mistake?" asked Miriam, her voice trembling.

"Your planet has always been a great distance from us, more so now than in eons past. There are closer choices, but none offer the most compatible genetic sources."

"I was brought here just to mother children for your city?"

"Ostensibly, your father was meant to mate with your mother and myself. You may have been meant as a test bed for my own genetic research on my soldiers, who are currently not compatible with us."

"How disgusting."

"Yours is the typically narrow-minded attitude of our recent arrivals. However, I would not have let my men mate with you until I was sure of my work, and that is still a few months off. By then you would have been open to the idea."

"I'm glad you'll never have the chance to brainwash me."

"What a curious expression. No, Miriam, I would have let your parents talk you into it."

"Let me get this straight," said John. "You're saying the Kira'To have been taking people from Earth to supplement the population? How long has this been going on?"

"Four and a half thousand of your years."

John leaned back in his chair, astonished. "How many humans have been taken?"

"I was never an official historian, but I believe around seven hundred over the years."

"Wars have been fought over lesser slights," said Miriam.

"You have no capacity for violence against the Kira'To. I am not trying to insult your people, it is just a fact. Besides, most of those taken went voluntarily. What little warning I received about your parents indicated that they were willing to serve my masters."

"You make them sound like gods," John said flatly.

Cassie raised her eyebrows. "How do you define a god?"

"Any god I might believe in wouldn't screw up and kill Miriam's parents. But forget about that. How do you communicate with them?"

"The Kira'To impart their wisdom through dreams. They have not been seen for a thousand years."

"What are they supposed to look like?" asked Miriam.

"Their image has been known to drive men mad, so I remain satisfied that I have no idea."

John said, "How do you think they'd feel about the Zendreen taking over this asteroid?"

"There has been no message by prophecy or lore that could answer that question, which by itself hints upon an answer."

"You've lost me."

"I mean without any hint that it might happen, I can only conclude that it will not."

John shrugged. "By that logic we could sit back and do nothing."

"I am certainly not advocating that. The Kira'To help by degrees, not in totality."

"Even so, the next time you take a nap, ask for a battalion of United States Marines."

"I wouldn't ask those monsters for a sodded shilling," Miriam said scornfully.

"I have no way of initiating contact," said Cassie. "I am sorry."

"You put a lot of faith in what seem like ambivalent and arbitrary beings," said John. "I prefer to put my faith in determination, teamwork, and a shitload of firepower."

"At least there's one thing we agree on," said Shedir.

"How about you guys?" John asked him. "What's your story?"

"My soldiers were originally mere companion animals," Cassie answered. "My great-grandfather began an ambitious plan to genetically modify them. The work took so long that it was only completed by his son. After a hundred generations, we succeeded in making them sentient. Interestingly enough, that same generation lived for forty years. It was as if self-awareness alone was enough to inspire longevity. Unfortunately, even though genetic experimentation continued all the way through my family to myself, we never succeeded in breaking that forty year average."

"Was it always your plan to make them into soldiers?"

"No, but they are natural warriors."

"What happened to the rest of the humanoids?" asked Miriam.

Cassie sighed. "Fifty years ago, a faction of residents rebelled against the core philosophy of the Vulture. There was an uprising. The side of righteousness prevailed, but at a very high cost. Only ninety canine soldiers and myself survived. Since then, a lack of proper medical supplies and provisions whittled my men down to a handful. There is, in fact, only one fecund female canine remaining, and she has almost reached the end of her reproductive period."

"So even though you would have been much better off asking those you encountered, like us, for help, you still tried to take us by force?

Surely you realize that your best chance of survival would have been to contact us in peace?"

"If I violate the philosophy of the Vulture, then all who died in the uprising would have died for nothing."

John nodded. "I admire your resolve, even if I don't agree with it."

"Thank you."

"So how old are you, then?" Miriam asked.

"Seventy-two. My research has also yielded methods of extending youth, although time will tell if it also extends life itself."

"How 'bout the dermaplasts?" asked John.

"I should make a full recovery. I should also be able to walk around in another day or two."

"Good. We're going to need as many people working on these repairs as possible. Miriam and I are going to start on reactor two. With Christie coordinating the technical data, we're hoping it won't all be Greek to us."

"The Greeks? They were, according to historical records, some of the most cooperative humans brought here. In fact, the Kira'To were inspired by their legends in much of their nomenclature."

"Including the asteroids. We were wondering about that."

"Which peoples were the least cooperative?" asked Miriam, managing a weak smile.

Cassie furrowed her brow. "A certain race was so disagreeable that they chose to fight to the death rather than submit. The name escapes me, but I do remember that they asked if they were in a place called Valhalla. When we said no, they attacked with great fury."

John and Miriam laughed.

"Vikings," John replied. "You do not want to piss off Vikings."

24.

Three days later, John sat alone in the conference room aboard the Faith. He was waiting for the rest of the crew to arrive for yet another progress report. He nursed an already-cold cup of coffee and puffed on his pipe. He'd snagged a two-hour nap recently, which was better than nothing, but like everyone else, he was running on fumes.

John was most concerned for Christie. Even though she claimed not to suffer from fatigue, she was single-handedly dealing with the brunt of the repair effort. Almost every malfunctioning component in the systems they were trying to restore had to be scanned and analyzed. Christie's mastery of the scanning technology was impressive, but she was limited by her own ability to understand the results. Occasionally, a component could be replicated or repaired without understanding its intrinsic nature. Unfortunately, the majority of items required not just a detailed diagram but also knowledge of its workings, a problem that was delaying progress significantly. That Cassie and her men couldn't provide much insight was also retarding the mission to the point of frustration. So far their most useful contribution had been raw material for the Faith's replicator.

The teams began to filter in over the next several minutes. John had capitulated and allowed Brentage to assist them, as the enormity of their task made his participation more attractive than leaving him to consume oxygen in the hold. Aldebaran had offered to partner with him as a neutral party, and the two had made an effective pair. They arrived first. Next, Richter and Ari, Ray and Dana, Calico and Megumi, and lastly John's partner Miriam, entered and exchanged small talk. Pyramis had elected to participate via radio, as he was close to repairing the Umberian ship, ironically the best progress of all projects so far. What made the ship worth so much attention was not for defense of the Vulture, as it was hardly a match for the Zendreen fleet, but for the future, if they survived. An additional design to offer any future Earth space fleet would be invaluable. The cold fusion engine aboard the Mark IX was older and slower than the one on the Faith, but much smaller and required less Talvanium to build. At the very least, it could help cover a quick exit for the crew if they had to abandon the Vulture to the enemy.

Another somber task had been finding Miriam's parents and moving them to the cold storage room aboard the Faith. A proper burial was planned for later. Ari had displayed nothing but stoicism at seeing her father's body, but John worried about how she was really effected by it. Still, any mourning by her or Miriam would have to wait.

"If everyone's ready," John said, "let's begin."

"Where's Cassie?" asked Richter.

"She's resting," replied Miriam.

"I'm surprised she's done as much as she has," said Richter. "And Pyramis?"

"Putting the finishing touches on the Mark Nine," said John. "Christie, are you with us?"

"Of course," said Christie's voice.

"Good. Richter, why don't you start us off?"

Richter nodded. "Our part of this will be simple. The number two reactor is, uh, reacting, at ten percent. Ari and I were unable to repair any of the primary power conduits, so even if we could get more power out of it, we couldn't get it to any relevant systems. We can keep at it, but if the Zendreen are still on schedule, we're fucked."

"Wonderful," said John sarcastically. " Aldebaran, Lieutenant Brentage?"

"We were able to restore all of the communication relays," replied Aldebaran. "There shouldn't be any transmission dead zones remaining."

"That's good! Ray, Dana?"

"We were able to get two more plasma turrets up," said Dana. "That's it. The others had parts that were so old that they crumbled into dust when we touched them."

John shook his head. "All right. Captain Calico, Megumi?"

"We were able to repair most of the power conduits from the number one reactor," said Calico. "That means we've been able to restore power to the hangar bay you shot up during your first visit. We also restored the emergency force fields on the entire northern hemisphere of the asteroid."

"That's a very good thing," John said, "because Miriam and I were only able to repair two of the three blast shields over the city. If the Zendreen attack that particular dome, the force field may be the only thing to prevent them from using it as an entry point. Is that it? Does anyone have anything else to add?"

The room was silent. Ari stood up and moved to the coffee machine.

"We need more time," she said.

"That's not going to happen," said Christie. "I've just detected the fleet emerging from superlume. They're five AU out and heading directly this way."

"Shit," said John. "We have less than forty minutes."

"Scherer," began Richter, leaning on the conference table. "We need to accept the fact that it is inevitable that the Zendreen will get boots on the ground. We may be able to hold them off for a couple of hours, but without more power to the shields and more weapons, they're going to find a way in."

"Richter and I have been going over defensive scenarios," said Aldebaran. "Things look grim. If we could be sure where the Zendreen will make entry, we could mount a defensive plan that will inflict massive casualties on their infantry. Even then, without knowing how many we're facing, we don't know how long we could hold them off. If they make entry at two or more points, however, there's no way we can fend them off."

"What about offering them an obvious point of entry, and trying to defend that?" asked Ray.

"That might work, but there would be nothing stopping them from coming in a second way, which, once casualties start to mount, they most certainly would."

"So any way you slice it," began Ari, "the Zendreen win?"

"It looks like they're going to win this round," said Richter. "We could always seek out allies and return with more force, but the only three options right now are die, get the hell out of here, or..."

"Or what?"

John sighed, and looked at Aldebaran. "Christie, Richter, Aldebaran and I have been working on another option. Based on what we know about the reactors, even the ones that aren't online, it may be possible to set charges and force them to overload."

"All six reactors overloading at the same time would destroy the asteroid," said Dana.

"Cassie's never going to go for that," said Ari. "She told me her omega plan is to mount a continuous guerrilla campaign against the Zendreen. She's confident she and her men can avoid capture for years. I have my doubts about that, considering their supply issues... Anyway, Cassie will not sanction this place being destroyed."

"That's only half the plan," said Christie. "The explosion would likely destroy the Zendreen fleet as well. Since none of us want to commit genocide, I came up with a solution." A diagram of the asteroid appeared on the wall-mounted monitor. Christie displayed animation of what she described. "There are dozens of emergency vents for each reactor. They're all interconnected, as you can see. To destroy the asteroid, we would have to close all of the interior and exterior hatches for the vents. However, if we keep these particular hatches open, the resultant explosion would send the asteroid along this trajectory through space, just as if we'd fired its thrusters. If my calculations are correct, the asteroid would be captured by Alpha Sagittae's gravity well, turning it into a permanent satellite of that star. The Zendreen wouldn't be able to weaponize it, and hopefully with a new home, their scorched earth campaign would end."

"Wouldn't the Zendreen just be able to repair the reactors?" asked Miriam.

"The reactors will be destroyed completely. They'd have to start from the ground up, and with their own technology. The engines they use in their battleship and cruisers aren't nearly powerful enough to break the orbit we'd establish, and it would take them years to build new ones. Never mind the fact that they'd have to open up peaceful trade with nearby systems just to get the fuel they need. Short of genocide, we think this is our best option."

"What about deploying the Vengeance virus?" asked Ray.

John said, "Even if we could synthesize enough of it, this is a space station. All they'd have to do is vent the atmosphere one section at a time and repressurize it."

"The Zendreen likely have a vaccine against the virus anyway," said Calico.

"How do you know that?" asked John, surprised.

"After we came through the wormhole, we captured a Zendreen fighter pilot whose crippled ship was in range. When we offered to return him to the straggling medical frigate, he killed himself, leading us to believe that the frigate was one of the plague ships. We raided the ship, an easy task since the crew was either dead or dying from the virus. We obtained a sample of the virus, and were able to confirm that several of the other ships had remained clean, thanks to careful screening of all persons coming aboard. We were also told by several dying Zendra that they had successfully implemented a vaccine against the virus, but that it was only effective for individuals not yet infected, and could not save those already stricken."

"You did all of this while we were repairing the Faith?"

"Yes. By the way, our doctor was working on replicating a new version of the virus, but all that work was lost with the Almagest."

"Shit. Well, we appreciate the effort anyway."

"How long will it take to rig up the reactors?" asked Ari.

"Hold on a second," said Dana. "None of this would have been possible without

Cassiopeia's cooperation. Destroying the reactors would betray her trust."

"It can't be helped," replied John.

"It also can't be done without her consent. We'd have to kill or incapacitate our escorts. Don't even try to justify that to me, John."

"Fine, I won't. I'll just have to get Cassie to see things our way."

"She won't respond to coercion," said Richter.

John nodded. "That's not what I had in mind."

Twenty minutes later, Richter and Ari were standing outside of Cassie's house, an apparently modest abode in the center of the sprawling City of the Vulture. Stars glittered through the dome high above, as did the three-lobed streetlights and illuminated walkways. Navigating the deserted and sepulcher-quiet streets had been a challenge, even with a map uploaded to a PDA. The city gave Richter the creeps, something he would only admit to Ari anyway, and he kept his recently-reloaded M4 carbine at the low ready.

"I still think this is a dumb idea," he said to Ari, keeping his eyes on the street.

"Cassie obviously likes you," Ari replied. "And I think John is right about her true vulnerability. Besides, she's pretty hot, don't you think?"

"She may also be completely nuts."

"Aren't we all? Come on, this is our only option left other than sticking a knife in her back."

"I know."

Richer turned and looked for a doorbell or a similar device. Finding none, he knocked loudly on the hardwood door. There was no reply. Richter shrugged, and found the door open.

"Good luck," said Ari, smiling coyly.

Richter rolled his eyes and entered the building. The foyer immediately opened up onto a balcony, and two curving staircases led downward from either side. Below lay a large open area, what was obviously once a bathhouse. A six-sided pool emitted lazily-wafting steam from the warm water into the freezing air. Small bluish-white lights illuminated the area from a hundred sconces. Red lights somewhere beneath the water created a purplish hue on the ceiling in an ever shifting pattern. Richter was surprised to see Cassie emerge from the water in the nude. She pulled her hair back from her face and looked up at him.

"Welcome," she said.

"This is got to be some sort of setup," muttered Richter.

"I had to wait for the external dermaplast to be absorbed before I could take a bath," Cassie said, slipping back beneath the water. "It's heavenly to be so clean again."

Richter descended the stairs on his left. "We have a problem, Cassie."

Cassie swam over to the edge of the pool. "Surely it can wait until after you've joined me."

"The Zendreen fleet will be here in as little as twenty minutes. Our teams have failed to adequately repair the asteroid. We won't be able to hold them off."

Grabbing the edge, Cassie smoothly pulled herself out of the water and walked up to Richter.

"Can you hand me my robe?" she asked.

Richter looked to his left and noticed a green robe hanging on a hook behind her. Richter reached past her, catching her gaze as he did so. He handed it to her with a half-smile and held her hair up while she donned it. The dermaplast had almost completely erased the scar from their earlier encounter.

"You can't seriously be considering going into hiding," he said. "I've seen what you have to deal with here. You simply don't have the resources to hold out for very long, even if you can successfully raid the Zendreen a few times. You need to accept the fact that your only hope for survival is to come with us."

"Are you giving up that easily?" asked Cassie, grabbing a towel.

"Of course not. We have a plan, but you're not going to like it."

Cassie dried her feet, and put on a pair of slippers. "You want to destroy the Vulture."

"We could, but as far as we know this is the last of the Zendreen race. Since we're not willing to commit genocide..."

"Excuse me?" she asked, drying her already freezing hair.

"We're not willing to commit genocide. Our ethical code is against it."

"Curious, but irrelevant. The Kira'To would intervene before they let you do that."

"How?"

"I don't know. Anyway, what's the other option?"

"Christie believes that if we overload the reactors with certain emergency vents open, that we can destroy the propulsion capabilities of the asteroid while making it a permanent satellite of Alpha Sagittae."

"Interesting. Chance, may I call you Chance?"

"Fine."

"I can't abandon my home, even if all seems lost. Still, I might help you with your plan if you subsequently donate as many supplies as you can. That, and something else."

"I'm listening."

Cassie stepped up to Richter. "Stay here with me. It has been far too long since there was another humanoid male on board. Can you honestly tell me that doesn't hold some appeal to you?"

"It does. I'll consider it. First, I need to know: have you told us everything you know about the Kira'To?"

"For the most part. Everything currently relevant, anyway."

"Wouldn't you like to find out more about them?"

Cassie headed toward the back of the room, and gestured for Richter to follow. "I would, but it is not my place to demand such things from them."

"Commander Scherer has offered to help you find one of the other Stymphalian Raptors. In fact, most of the crew wants to follow up this mission with one to find either the Swan or the Eagle."

Cassie and Richter entered a much warmer room that looked like a kitchen. Richter took off his watch cap and ran his fingers through his hair. Cassie poured herself some tea and offered a cup to him.

"A fascinating endeavor, to be sure."

"If either of those asteroids are still flourishing, they might be willing to help you bolster your forces and mount a campaign to retake this one from the Zendreen. You might not be abandoning it forever."

"Do you really have the resources to provide for all of my men?"

"It will be cramped quarters for awhile, but yes. We've already discussed turning our Zero-G room into a barracks bay."

Cassie embraced Richter, an awkward pose considering all of his gear.

"And you and I?"

"You'll just have to wait and see."

Leaning in, her lips brushed his just as a radio call came in.

"Richter, this is Scherer, over," his radio squawked.

Richter rolled his eyes. "Perfect timing, as always. Go ahead, Scherer."

"The Zendreen fleet is taking up an attack posture. What's Cassiopeia's decision?"

"Well?" Richer asked her.

"Let's do it," she replied wickedly.

"Good. Get geared up and I'll meet you out front. Scherer, the mission is a go."

"Roger," said John. "Captain Calico has prepared charges for us. Report here for your team's assignment."

"Richter, this is Christie. The battleship is taking up a synchronous orbit above your position."

Richter grunted. "Shit. Roger that, Christie. Cassie, how are you set for weapons?"

"I have a plasma rifle in the other room," Cassie said, moving to another door.

"Hurry up and meet us outside."

Richter turned and ran back to the main entrance. Ari met him and immediately directed his attention skyward.

"Damn, they're close," she said.

Above, the massive hull of the battleship had already filled the entirety of the transparent dome, blocking out the stars.

"Christie, this is Richter. How long will the force fields hold if they fire their main bombardment weapon?"

"Not long," replied Christie. "You'd better get out of there."

A wide blue beam swept down from the hull and began crossing the dome. It illuminated the force field and caused a beautiful pattern of energy eddies as it moved from left to right.

"It looks like a scanning device," said Ari.

The beam disappeared briefly, then reappeared as a small oval centered over the dome. The oval widened until it covered the entire aperture. Then, a bright green bolt shot down and dissipated the force field instantly. The green bolt repeated in brief blasts until it had bored a small hole through the dome. A loud roar accompanied the rush of air as the atmosphere began to vent, then almost as quickly the pressure seemed to normalize. Richter screamed into Cassie's house.

"Cassie! We are leaving!"

Several small ships emerged from a bay and began moving one by one through the hole. The whine of engines filled the city as the ships spread out. Cassie appeared at the door, clutching a sturdy rifle, and looked up in shock. She keyed her radio and called for Shedir as Richer and Ari received a transmission of their own.

"Richter, this is Scherer, what's your situation, over?"

Richter had to yell over the noise of the ships. "An assault force is landing in the city! We're getting out of here now, but don't count on us to help plant the explosives!"

"Understood," replied John. "We'll divide them up among us and get to work."

"I've ordered my men to help us escape the city," said Cassie. "Damn these defilers!"

Richter readied his rifle. "Fine, just get us out of here."

Cassie donned her goggles. "Follow me."

They began to move. The ships disappeared behind buildings. Richter had counted seven of the craft, which were about the size of coach buses. As they made their way through the maze of buildings, at least a dozen fighter craft also entered through the hole and began skirting the city. One of them spotted the trio almost immediately, and bore down on them.

"Cover!" shouted Ari.

The team pressed themselves up against a nearby wall as bright yellow energy bolts streaked down. The shots kicked up ancient dust and took chunks out of buildings on either side of the street. The ship brought a strong gust of wind in its wake as it passed a scant ten meters above, and all three allies resisted the urge to return fire.

"We need to get off the streets," said Ari.

"Is there an underground path to the edge of the city?" asked Richter.

"Yes," replied Cassie, scowling at the damage. "The nearest entrance is three hundred meters in this direction."

"Good. Let's move."

Cassie took the lead and they sprinted down a side street. As they rounded a corner, they ran almost headlong into several Zendreen soldiers, lightly armored but heavily armed. There was a brief but furious exchange of fire before Richter and Ari ducked into an alley on the left side of the street, and Cassie into one on the right. Richter leaned around the corner and continued engaging targets. Ari reached into her thigh pocket and withdrew a large package of peppermint candy. Richter ducked back under withering return fire.

"Displace, nine o'clock..." he began to say, then looked at Ari in surprise. "What the hell are you doing?"

"Gonna need energy," Ari mumbled around five of the candies.

Before Richter could object, Ari handed him her rifle, drew the Tarsus blade from his belt, and activated her invisibility device. Across the street, Cassie fired on targets. Richter gave her the arm signal for cease fire, realizing a second later that she couldn't know what it meant. Fire in their direction ceased, and he risked a glance around the corner. He couldn't see Ari, but he could see her handiwork. First confused and then terrified, the Zendreen soldiers descended into chaos as their limbs and thoraxes seemed to magically separate from each other. Three managed to get together and began falling back in a semi-organized fashion, sweeping the street with desperate fire, until one's head popped off. The other two turned around and ran as fast as they could in the other direction. Richter grinned; Cassie was simply astonished. A moment later the smell of mint announced Ari's presence, and she deactivated the invisibility device. She popped more mints into her mouth with one hand and shook Zendreen viscera from her arm.

"Did any of them touch you?" Richter asked.

Ari crunched and munched. "No, but I'm immune from the toxin anyway. They had to do that just to work on me."

Cassie ran across the street. "Keep that up and we won't need my men."

"I can't," said Ari, taking a swig from her canteen. "I use more energy than I can replace. Don't count on me to keep doing that."

"We need to keep moving," Richter said.

"I never thought I'd be glad to see that blade again," said Cassie. "I'm still quite jealous..."

Cassie cut herself off, staring agape down the alley. Richter and Ari turned to look and their conscious minds stopped working.

A six-year-old girl was walking toward them. The girl was translucent and glowed a soft, pale blue. She was dressed in a robe, and was reading a book. She seemed to ignore the others and walked into the street, then disappeared.

"What the flipping fuck was that?" breathed Richter.

"A ghost?" whispered Ari.

"I don't know," said Cassie quietly. "I've never seen anything like that in all my years."

"Look."

Out in the street and on balconies, ghostly figures of adults and children flickered in and out of view. They appeared to be going about daily business, oblivious to either the trio or any of the Zendreen craft.

"They're dressed like my people," said Cassie in wonder.

"Are they the Kira'To?" asked Ari.

"I don't think so. I'm not sensing anything at all from them. They're just images."

"Maybe they're holographic projections or something," said Richter. "Christie, this is Richter. We're experiencing a strange phenomenon here in the city. Are you reading anything on your end?"

"Nothing other than the Zendreen incursion," Christie replied over the radio. "What's going on?"

"Images of people, specters, or something."

"What? I mean, energy readings are fluctuating wildly, I can't account for absolutely everything. What are they doing?"

"Just walking around and ignoring us, really."

"Weird. Take what distractions you can get, Richter, things are heating up elsewhere. I'm trying to reestablish the force field over the dome but you'd be wise to keep moving."

"We've got more soldiers headed this way," interjected Ari.

"Roger. Stay in contact, Christie. We're on our way."

25.

In the cold Zero-G room aboard the Reckless Faith, the remaining crewmembers rapidly finalized the six explosive devices intended for the Vulture's reactors. The devices had been constructed from Calico's memory, and consisted of a binary explosive, a detonator, and a timer. A remote detonator would have been ideal, but there was worry that the Zendreen would jam the signal. How long it took for the slowest team to plant their second charge would determine the duration of the countdown.

Pyramis entered from the corridor. He'd finished repairing the Umberian Mark IX, but it had been decided not to launch it until everyone was ready to evacuate. The explosives were stuffed into rucksacks, and John began to designate teams.

"Okay," he said. "Fortunately, the reactors are clustered together within walking distance, so if we don't run into too many Zendreen soldiers we should be able to set all the charges in an hour or so. Calico, Megumi and Pyramis will take the first two reactors. Aldebaran and Brentage will take the next two. Myself, Ray and Dana will take the last two. Once we're all in place, we'll set the timers based on the return time for my team. This will require leaving at least one person at each reactor to coordinate the timers."

"Or we can just backtrack and set the timers accordingly," said Calico.

"I'll leave that up to each team to decide. Is everyone clear on their assignment?"

"What about me?" asked Miriam.

"We could run into Zendreen soldiers. You'd be better off staying here."

"Bullocks!"

"You don't have to like it. You can help Christie and Gueyr coordinate things from the bridge."

"Miriam can come with Brentage and I," said Aldebaran.

Miriam grinned and looked at John, who shrugged.

"Fine," he said, "if you want to take responsibility for her, she's yours. All right, is everyone clear on their assignments?"

"Rock and roll," said Dana.

"Are all of our guests clear on the operation of the M1A and Phalanx?" asked John, referring to the borrowed rifles that Calico, Megumi, Pyramis, and Brentage carried.

"They're pretty straightforward machines," replied Calico, who still possessed his personal sidearm as well.

"You remember those ads on the 'net about ten years ago, right Cap?" asked Megumi, posing with her Phalanx. "You know, 'A Phalanx is a girl's best friend'."

Calico nodded, and smiled.

"I remember as well," said Aldebaran. "The Umberian military almost picked up a contract for them about twenty years ago. Didn't it show a diminutive Kau'Rii female, too?"

"Yeah, and the ad copy was priceless. 'It can be a lonely galaxy for a girl and her problems. For less than a thousand credits, get yourself a personal escort that rides light and speaks with authority. Available in seven hot colors'."

"Were they marketed to males, too?" asked Ray.

"Of course," replied Aldebaran. "I seem to recall an ad depicting a Rakhar in a formal suit wearing infrared goggles about to slaughter a dinner group."

“Uh huh,” said Megumi. “The caption was, 'The life of the party'.”

“How perfectly messed up,” said John. “Christie, what's our status?”

“Several smaller ships are still attempting to breach airlocks at other locations,” Christie replied. “I don't think any of them have succeeded. Luckily they don't appear to be blasting at installations indiscriminately. There is still no sign that they've detected the Faith.”

“Good. We're departing to set the charges now. Keep us apprised.”

“Roger.”

“Richter, this is Scherer, what's your status, over?”

“Scherer,” said Richter through a bad transmission, “we are experiencing heavy contact. Cassie's men have linked up with us and we are attempting...”

The transmission trailed off, and John said, “Say again, all after attempting, over.”

“Attempting to fall back to the tunnels! Over!”

“Roger that, Richter. We are beginning our mission. Stay in contact.”

“Wilco, buddy. Out.”

“I hope they make out all right,” said Miriam.

“If anybody can survive that, it's Ari and Richter,” said John. “All right, mount up, let's get going.”

Everyone grabbed their gear. The airlock was already open, so it didn't take long for the three teams to exit into the asteroid. The corridor was brightly lit, but only for the first fifty meters. Lighting thereafter was much more sporadic. Dull concussions could be heard, too far away to identify, and occasionally they were strong enough to shake dust loose from the ceiling. The group paused at the first intersection. John's first reactor lay somewhere to the left; the other two teams were going right. They wished each other good luck and separated.

John went first, followed by Dana, and Ray and his shotgun covered their rear. The uncomfortable cold typical of the interior persisted, as no power could be spared to heat it any further. While the humans had been prepared for harsh weather, some of the best gear had to be loaned to their visitors. Miriam was the most fortunate with her Air Force parka, an item that John was still kicking himself for not bringing, even if he would have just loaned it out anyway. As it was, both he and Ray had made sacrifices in warm clothing and were each wearing one less layer than they would have preferred. At least they had hats and gloves. Dana herself remained toasty in her Navy-style pea coat and homemade knit cap.

"I hope you know where you're going," Ray said after a minute.

"Well enough," John said, tapping his rifle stock.

The corridors were numbered with a system understood by only the canine soldiers, so John was relying on a hand-drawn map. The team made several turns and descended a few staircases. The area they were in was devoid of any primary function, as far as they could tell, and was originally either individual crew quarters or spare storage. This added to the difficulty of navigating, as no one corridor stood out from another.

"We should be dropping glow sticks at each intersection," said John, "but I know its a bad idea with the enemy running around."

"Christie's available if you need her," said Ray.

"I know."

"Hey, Ray?" asked Dana.

"Yeah?" Ray replied.

"How are things going with you and Christie? I don't want to pry, but I'm concerned."

"For whom?"

"Both of you."

Ray nodded, keeping an eye on their six. "It's going to be an adjustment. Christie is handling it pretty well, but I'm concerned that she's just suppressing her true feelings for now. Of course, she thinks the same thing about me."

"Are you right?"

"For myself, I've been up front about how I feel. Christie remains as real as any of us, Dana."

John held up his fist and motioned for the others to be quiet. A blue light was coming from a side corridor. The team readied their weapons and spread out. The light grew stronger, and a figure stepped out. It was a man wearing a robe and a four-cornered hat. His bespectacled visage was buried in a large book, and he took a right turn toward the group. The figure itself was the source of the light.

The trio was shocked into silence as the man walked forward, ignoring them. It wasn't until he passed by that they noticed he was translucent. When he passed Dana, she jumped, and stifled a scream with her hand. The figure faded and disappeared.

"That must be one of those ghosts Richter mentioned," whispered John.

"It ignored us," said Ray.

"No," squeaked Dana. "It looked right at me just as it passed."

"Are you sure?" asked John.

Dana's voice trembled. "Completely. He met my eyes for a full second."

"What the hell is going on here?" mumbled Ray.

"Maybe they're some sort of warning."

"As long as they leave us alone," said John. "we can't let them distract us from the mission."

The others nodded, and the group resumed moving forward. After a few minutes, the corridor opened into a larger area. A bridge led across a void into darkness. The trio examined the smooth rock walls as they stepped out onto the span. The dull echoing of distant explosions was slightly magnified in the chasm.

"Uh, this is supposed to be it," said John.

Even though John and Ray were carrying powerful tactical flashlights, the white beams were not powerful enough to reach the floor or ceiling of the chamber. Looking around for any clues, the team made their way across the bridge. Another corridor led away at the other side. John sighed in frustration as Ray removed a chemlight from his pocket. It was one of the bright orange lights; once activated it would last for one hour. Ray snapped it, shook it up, and tossed it over the side of the bridge. It fell for a few seconds before bouncing off a surface and coming to a rest. It was too dim to illuminate anything, but gave them an idea of the depth of the chamber.

"It's got to be at least two hundred meters to the floor," said John.

Ray activated his radio. "Christie, this is Ray. We're at the specified location. We don't see anything but a gigantic cavern."

"Hold on," replied Christie. "Let me look more closely."

"Roger."

"Okay, the reactor is directly below you. There should be an elevator shaft a few meters down the corridor on the far side."

"Great, we'll look for it. Ray out."

"What are the odds that the elevator is working?" asked Dana.

John smiled. "I'd say about a million to one."

Finding the lift did not take long. The door had been frozen open a long time ago, and offered a dizzying view into a dark, seemingly bottomless shaft. Again, Ray cracked a chemlight and tossed it down. This time, it simply disappeared into the gloom. Flashlights pointed upward revealed a similar picture.

"There's a ladder running down the side," observed Ray.

"I wouldn't trust that thing to hold an anorexic lemur," said Dana.

Ray grabbed the nearest rung and shook it. "It seems solid enough."

"Do we have time to go back for some rappelling gear?"

"Maybe," said John. "I think it will hold me, though."

"Why risk it?" asked Ray. "I'll run back to the ship and grab the lines."

"Let me just try..."

John stepped out onto the ladder, which immediately buckled in half a dozen places. John slipped out of Ray's reach and tumbled into the shaft, uttering a panicked yelp. Ray screamed and grabbed again, to no avail.

John fell. He only had time to consider the irony of falling to his death when compared to the far more colorful ways in which space could kill a man, before he felt his center of gravity shift. He shined his flashlight around, and realized he was still speeding along the shaft, accompanied by pieces of the doomed ladder, but no longer felt the tug of gravity keeping the pace. He twisted his body around until he could reach the rock wall and kicked out. This effort rewarded him a trip to the opposite side, where he painfully impacted another section of the ladder. John tried a few times more and eventually stopped his forward movement.

"Damn it, I'm such a fool," he spat as he slowly floated to one of the walls.

"John!" yelled Ray from above.

Looking up, John realized the shaft had a slight curve to it, putting Ray and Dana out of sight from his current location.

"I'm okay!" John shouted back. "There's no artificial gravity past the entrance!"

"So it was just your momentum that carried you down?"

"Yes. There's still the natural gravity of the asteroid, but the force is almost negligible."

"What do you see?"

"There's another door just down from here. It looks like it's open about an inch."

John bounded easily toward the door. An orange glow further ahead caused his heart to leap into his chest before he realized it was just the chemlight. As he approached the top of the door, he felt his inner ear shift again. He was able to stop himself before wandering into the area that, like the one above, had full gravity. There was nowhere to grab onto except the old ladder.

"Fool me once," muttered John as he grabbed the ladder.

This section of the ladder hadn't degraded as much, and bore his weight. He descended until he was next to the door and forced it open. His flashlight revealed the floor of the large area.

"This is it," he shouted up the shaft. "You should be able to safely come down if you watch your initial footing."

"Roger," said Ray's voice.

John held his flashlight up and waited. Two minutes later, Ray and Dana came into view, treading lightly.

"Be careful," began John, "the section near the doors has normal gravity."

"So we gathered," replied Ray, dragging his feet to slow his movement.

"Ugh, just seeing you standing there makes me nauseous," groaned Dana.

After some acrobatics, the trio was reunited on the floor of the chasm. There were several large pieces of equipment, layered in decades of dust, and a twenty meter tall monstrosity that could only be the reactor.

"We thought we'd lost you, John," said Ray, shaking his hand.

"You and me both. Now let's get these charges set and move on to the next one."

According to Cassie, the design of the reactors would guarantee a release of antimatter no matter where the charges were placed, but the ideal location was the primary inflow junction. After a few minutes of searching, however, the team was unable to find anything that met Cassie's description.

The reactor looked more like a steam engine than high technology. Brass gauges, still gleaming, and green copper pipes abounded. Everything was meticulously labeled in the indecipherable text of the original inhabitants. John chose a confluence of several large conduits and began preparing the explosives.

"I can't say I have no sympathy for Cassie," said Dana. "It's a shame to destroy something like this."

"Just imagine the Zendreen using it to nuke Pennsylvania," replied Ray.

Their radios crackled to life. "John, this is Christie."

"Go ahead," said John.

"I'm reading at least three Zendreen troopers somewhere in your area. I'm afraid I can't give you more information than that. There's a lot of interference from the superstructure."

"Copy. We'll keep our eyes open."

"Look," whispered Ray, pointed back toward the elevator shaft.

Glowing energy tethers had descended from far above, drifting lazily as if in a slight breeze. The three tendrils were spaced about ten meters apart and cast a weak blue glow on the surrounding equipment.

"Spread out," whispered John. "I'll initiate fire."

"Are the charges ready?" asked Dana.

John nodded. "Yes."

"Then let's just move on to the next reactor."

"We can't risk the Zendreen finding the explosives," said Ray.

"Spread out," said John, "and wait for all of them. Be aggressive, we don't want to give any of them a chance to call for help."

Dana and Ray nodded, and the team took up positions. Without their flashlights, the area felt all the more empty and cold. Dark shapes soon appeared on the energy tethers, slowly descending. The light cast by the tethers was sufficient to identify only three Zendra. As soon as they touched the floor the tethers disappeared. John raised his rifle and squeezed the trigger.

A violent but brief volley of fire dropped all three insectoids before they could respond. The team remained hidden for a few minutes before inspecting the bodies.

"Nice head shot," John said to Dana.

Dana grinned. "Thanks."

John slung his rifle and activated his radio. "Christie, this is John. Do you detect any further Zendreen activity in this area?"

"Negative," replied Christie. "In fact, I think most of the ground troops are heading toward the city."

"Good news for us, bad news for Richter's crew."

"What about the other demo teams?" asked Ray.

"They haven't encountered any resistance," said Christie. "Three out of four of the other charges have been set."

John nodded. "Good, let's get going. Keep us updated."

Dana screamed in pain. One of the Zendra had grabbed her leg. Ray blasted it three times with his shotgun, swearing. Dana sank to the ground, grasping her calf.

"Let me see," said John, grabbing his flashlight.

Dana's pant leg was torn open, and a nasty scratch had begun to seep blood. She grabbed the medical kit from her backpack.

"How do you feel?" asked Ray, kneeling beside her.

"It definitely got me," Dana said, swooning.

"No, I mean..."

"That's what I mean!"

"Just try to relax," said John. "Every kit has auto-injectors. Ray, decontaminate the wound with rubbing alcohol. Sorry, Dana, this is going to hurt like hell."

Dana coughed, vomited, and passed out.

"Shit," said Ray, clearing her airway. "The poison is effecting her much more rapidly than it did Richter."

"I can see that. Decontaminate her leg, I'll handle the atropine."

John pulled the first of two auto-injectors from a small olive drab pouch. He removed the safety cap and placed the business end against Dana's outer thigh. The needle made a snap as it easily pierced her pants, and hissed as the drug was injected into her bloodstream. He repeated the process with the diazepam. Ray donned latex gloves and started dumping alcohol on the wound. John bent the needles back on themselves and stowed them, then checked her pulse.

"Should I use the whole bottle?" asked Ray.

"Just soak the whole area. Her pulse is steady. We may have caught a break."

"Yeah, but can we wake her up?"

"We can't count on her regaining consciousness any time soon. We need to evac her to the ship."

Ray spread the alcohol up and down Dana's leg. "I can carry her back by myself, but I'm going to need help negotiating the elevator shaft."

"With gravity activated near the doors, I'm not sure both of us can do it without rope."

"I agree."

John keyed his radio. "Christie, have you been following this?"

"Yes," said Christie. "I wish I could do something."

"You can. Somebody needs to return to the ship, grab the rappelling gear, and link up with us. Is there anyone available who can accomplish this more rapidly than Ray or I?"

"Pyramis has split off from his team to recover the Mark Nine, since Calico and Megumi insisted they could handle planting their last charge. There's an airlock at the top of the area you're in, so theoretically, he could retrieve the rappelling gear and meet up with you the soonest. The problem is whether or not he can accomplish all of that without being detected by Zendreen fighters."

"That sounds completely nuts, Christie. Ray and I will figure out a way on our own."

"That will significantly delay the setting of the last charge," said Ray. "I'll guard Dana while you set the charge, and when you get back the two of us will get her out of here one way or another."

"It may not be as dangerous as you think," said Christie. "The Mark Nine has an earlier form of invisibility technology. It's not nearly as efficient as ours, but it may be enough to keep Pyramis safe temporarily."

"Fine, I'll leave it up to him," began John. "Let him know what's going on and call Ray when you get an answer. Either way, I'm leaving for the last reactor now."

"Roger, out."

John stood up. "The alcohol is supposed to neutralize the poisonous enzymes instantly, but keep those gloves on while you dress the wound."

"I haven't forgotten," said Ray, removing a field dressing from the kit.

"Can I borrow your shotgun?"

"Are you sure you won't wait until I can go with you?"

"Time is on the side of the enemy. I'll be okay. If Pyramis shows up, don't wait for me. I'll set the timer on this charge."

Ray handed his Remington to John, along with a shoulder bag full of ammo.

"Just pretend you're Gordon Freeman."

"I do that anyway. Slugs still in the outer pocket?"

"Yes. I'm also still staggering slugs and buckshot in the weapon. Your first round is a slug."

John tightened the sling on his M1, and shouldered the shotgun.

"Wish me luck."

"I thought you didn't believe in fate."

"I'll take whatever help I can get, Ray."

Five minutes later, John was well on his way to the next reactor. Fortunately for him, the confusing portion of the directions had ended, and all he had left to do was follow one of the power transfer conduits. The ease of the route did not make the cold, dark corridor any less terrifying, however, and John shivered as he clutched the stock of the shotgun.

Christie was too busy coordinating other aspects of the mission to keep him company, even if she was just a radio transmission away. John resisted the urge to manufacture a reason to call her. It was the first time in as long as he could remember that he felt alone. Still, he took a small measure of comfort that the horrible act of mowing down scores of mind-controlled Umberians had been far worse. He managed a slight smile before he remembered the ghostly images wandering the asteroid, and his fear returned anew. He would rather run into a squad of Zendreen soldiers than meet up with one of those specters at the moment.

Even though it reduced his own situational awareness, John decided to switch to Richter's frequency. He immediately became an audience to an apparently intense firefight, although so far Richter and Ari were still communicating calmly. He heard what could only be Cassie's plasma rifle discharging, and thought he could hear the woman swearing at something.

The conduit opened up, and John recognized the last reactor. He put his radio back on his team frequency, and rested in the quiet for a moment. His shoulder ached from impacting the shaft wall, and his fingertips were numb with cold. He found an attractive place to set the charge, and removed it from his rucksack. He looked at his watch. It had taken him thirty minutes to get down here from the time his team left the Faith.

"Christie, this is John," he said into his radio.

"Go ahead."

"I'm at the last reactor, but I'm not sure how much time to put on the charge."

"All other teams are standing by to either set their timers, or backtrack to their first charge, depending. Pyramis has retrieved the rappelling gear and he's going to use the airlock above the reactor to lift out Dana and Ray. The only problem is whether or not Ari, Richter, and Cassie can break free from their engagement in time to return to the ship."

"I was worried about that," replied John. "Our best case scenario was to have everyone off the asteroid before the charges went off, but will the city itself take any damage once the reactors go?"

"The city, and most of the habitable portions of the asteroid should survive the detonation."

"That's not reassuring enough. I think we should set the timers, then converge on the city to help expedite their evac. If we can't, hopefully we'll survive the explosions."

"Let's make sure it doesn't come to that, John."

"I agree. Okay, inform the others that I'm setting the time for forty minutes. On my mark, three, two, one, mark." John set the timer, and tucked the charge out of sight behind a panel. "I'm on my way back to the first reactor. If Ray and Dana are already evacuated, then I'll take the long way back to the ship. Scherer out."

John turned around, and barely hid his surprise as his flashlight illuminated someone. He instinctively put the front sight of his shotgun on the figure even as he realized it was not the enemy.

"Commander Scherer," said one of Cassie's canine soldiers.

John lowered his weapon and clipped his flashlight to his jacket pocket. "I'm sorry, I can't remember your name."

"Tsih. Cassie sent me to back you up."

"Fine. I just have to set the timer on one more charge, then I'm heading to the city to join the fight. It will be good to have someone watching my back."

"Indeed. It was a lonely trip down here. I don't know the fastest way to the other reactor, though."

"It's down this conduit," said John, moving forward.

John's head flashed with light and overwhelming pain. He collapsed to the deck, and rolled on his back. Tsih had struck him with a baton, a blow that would have knocked him out if it hadn't glanced off the stock of his M1. John tried to bring the Remington to bear, but Tsih was upon him. They locked up, each trying to gain control of the shotgun.

"What the fuck are you doing?" gasped John.

"This is my home," growled Tsih. "If you destroy all of the reactors, I will never be able to rebuild them."

"This isn't what Cassiopeia wants!"

"She allowed her feelings for people like you to cloud her judgment. She and the others can abandon this place if they desire, but I will never give up my home without a fight."

John struggled against Tsih, to no avail. The canine's hand was over his own on the forward grip of the weapon. John managed to find the slide release lever and pulled down, ejecting the chambered round. Freeing his right hand, he unclipped his flashlight and jammed it butt-first into the chamber. Tsih wrenched the weapon free, the motion closing the bolt. As John hoped, the flashlight stopped the next round from loading. Tsih tried to fire the weapon, and cast it aside as the trigger did nothing. John scrambled backward and drew his Beretta.

Tsih moved like a demon and grabbed the pistol. Again, they locked up in a struggle for the weapon.

"God damn you!" yelled John.

John ejected the magazine from his pistol, and squeezed off the round in the chamber. The shot missed Tsih's head by an inch, but the slide sliced open his palm. The creature roared and swiped curved claws at John's face. John blocked the blow and earned two gashes on his forearm. He managed to get his foot in Tsih's stomach, and kicked him off.

John scrambled to his feet. With practiced speed, he loosened the sling on his M1 and whipped the rifle from his shoulders. He hit Tsih in the face straight-on with the butt of the weapon, a devastating strike that broke the soldier's jaw and knocked out several of his teeth. John swung back around, deactivated the safety, and unloaded the rifle into the mutineer. Tsih was dead before the empty clip hit the ground.

Checking the back of his head for blood, and finding none, John reloaded the M1 and retrieved the other weapons. His forearm hurt, but wasn't bleeding too badly. His unprotected ear had gone deaf.

"Christie, this is John."

"Go ahead."

"Is there any way you can account for all of Cassie's soldiers? I just had a run-in with one who didn't care for our plan."

"I take it you changed his mind."

"Into several distinct pieces, yes."

"There would have to be some aspect of the canine soldiers that differentiated them chemically from the other sentients on the asteroid, otherwise I won't be able to determine who's what."

"Why not just scan for Tycho?"

"Huh?"

John rubbed his head. "Scan Tycho, establish a baseline, then scan the asteroid."

"That just might work."

"I don't care where they are, as long as none of them are anywhere near the reactors. This one intended to deactivate the charges."

"Understood... okay, I'm reading fifteen canine life signs, all of them are in the city."

"Thank God. Let's hope it was just this one that got too big for his britches."

"Uh, hold on. Fourteen, thirteen, twelve... John, I don't think the fight is going well for them."

John began moving down the conduit. "Tell everyone to converge on the city once all the timers are set, except for Brentage and Miriam. He needs to escort her back to the ship, and I won't take no for an answer."

"She's not going to like that."

"Tough shit. I'm getting a bad feeling about this entire mission. Anyway, I'll let you coordinate the action. Scherer out."

John examined his wounds again, grimaced, and sprinted down the conduit.

It was uncomfortably warm for the Rakhar aboard the Zendreen cruiser. Thel Maktar, fifth in line for the Lordship of Maktar, unzipped his jacket as the noiseless elevator car ascended. He kept his discomfort from his escorts, who had remained silent since their initial introductions. Thel did not expect to stay long on the alien ship, and that would be just fine with him.

The elevator arrived on the bridge. It, like the rest of the ship, was nothing like Thel expected of an insectoid race. Bright, clean, and with curved, orderly architecture, only the excessive warmth made the visit uncomfortable for a man like Thel. He had heard rumors that Zendreen latrines were abominable, but he had no intention of ever seeing one.

The bridge was a flurry of activity. This was not a surprise to Thel, since he got a good look at the action on his way in. A particularly tall Zendra approached him, waving off two supernumeraries who attempted to follow. Thel's translator kicked in immediately as the strange creature began to speak.

"I am Admiral Kiveech," it said.

"Thel Maktar," he said in basso profundo. "Are you sure you don't want me to come back another time? You look like you're in the middle of something right now."

"This operation is almost complete. Anyway, I need you to depart as soon as possible. Assuming, of course, you want the job."

"I read the description. There is a great deal about the mission that I do not understand.

However, I realize I don't need to comprehend every aspect of it in order to successfully complete it. I will take the job, for fifteen percent on top of what you've offered."

Kiveech didn't flinch. "Agreed."

"There is one potential problem. Honor demands I admit it before disembarking."

"Regarding the devices?"

"Indeed. I do not possess the surgical skills to implement them in the manner you've prescribed."

"I anticipated that problem," replied Kiveech, glancing at nearby monitor. "Not many mercenaries are also surgeons."

"I am an independent contractor. If you need a wider set of skills you should approach a guild. My former guild, the Black Crest, might offer you a competent surgeon in addition to humble operatives. They will also demand a far greater fee."

Kiveech picked up a plastic box from a console and handed it to Thel. "These are the devices. There are an equal number of accessories that allow them to be installed externally. This will allow you to complete your mission even if surgical implantation is impossible. However, the disadvantage should be obvious."

"If the subject is overpowered, the device can be easily removed."

"Precisely. I recommend you secure a surgeon locally upon arrival, and safeguard him until other devices can be implanted."

"You assume these people are capable of such a procedure. The coordinates you gave me do not correspond to any known civilization."

"They are at least capable of complex surgical procedures. I leave it up to you to find the best candidate."

Thel accepted the box. "It will take me ten days to get there at maximum cruising speed. I will depart as soon as my financial institution confirms the first payment."

"I approved the transfer on your way up. Good hunting, Mister Maktar."

26.

"They're all dead."

Inside an ancient two-story galleria, coated with dust, Cassie, Richter, and Ari took cover behind a counter and caught their breath. The remaining canine soldiers had been across the street, and had remained behind to cover the humanoids as they sprinted across to the galleria. Zendreen troops had obliterated the other building with a portable rocket, with obvious results, thus leading to Richter's pronouncement.

"Curse these interlopers," muttered Cassie, removing her goggles and wiping her brow.

"We don't have much time before they figure out where we went," said Richter, examining his recently-acquired plasma rifle.

Ari tried to reload her M1A, and fumbled with the magazine. Richter moved to her side.

"Damn," she mumbled.

"Are you all right?" asked Richter.

"I'm exhausted. I need food. I certainly can't use the Zendreen device again today."

"We only need to cross three more blocks. Can you make it?"

Ari grinned. "I should ask you the same thing."

Gesturing, Ari pointed out the blood running down Richter's left arm and the chunk of flesh that had been seared away from his right calf.

"It's nothing serious."

"Tell me again why you wish to leave any of these foul creatures alive," said Cassie.

Richter and Ari's radios crackled. "Richter, this is Christie, over."

"Go ahead," replied Richter.

"I have good news and bad news, which do you want first?"

"Is this a trick question?"

"The good news is that Calico, Megumi, and Aldebaran have finished planting their charges and are on their way to help you get out of the city. The bad news is that I haven't been able to successfully interface with the Vulture's emergency ventilation subsystem."

Richter sighed, annoyed. "Can it be done locally?"

"That's what I need to find out."

"Wait one, over. Hey Cassiopeia, is there somewhere we can jack into the asteroid's central computer?"

"I vow to take seven Zendreen for each of my soldiers lost today," Cassie said, her eyes closed.

"Hey! Pay attention!"

"I heard you, Praetorian. The best place would have been the control room, but you destroyed it."

"It seemed like a good idea at the time. Anywhere else?"

"There's an old console in a restaurant near here. If your people can download the specifics to the PDA, then I should be able to take care of it."

Richter nodded. "Christie, this is Richter, did you catch that?"

"Roger," said Christie. "I'm sending you the information now."

Checking the PDA, Richter handed it to Cassie. She accepted the device and studied the information. She looked confused.

"You don't have to memorize it," said Richter.

"I know," said Cassie softly.

"Come on, let's hope we can sneak out a back door without being noticed."

Richter helped Ari to her feet, and the trio moved toward the other end of the galleria.

"Many years ago, these shops sold health and beauty products and services," said Cassie.

"Any food?" asked Ari.

"Would you really want to eat anything you could find?" asked Richter.

"You've never been this hungry," said Ari sincerely. "I feel like I haven't eaten in three days."

"There are food caches in places," began Cassie, "but nothing in the immediate vicinity."

"I hear plasma-roasted Zendra is quite delicious," said Richter, grinning.

Ari smiled wanly. "Well, I know it won't kill me."

Cassie led the group through a first-floor shop to a small exterior door. Out on the galleria floor, there was a series of small explosions. Several ceiling tiles fell, and a display case toppled over.

"Here they come," said Richter.

Cassie tried in vain to clear some plaster dust from her goggles, then shoved them into her thigh pocket. "The alleyway is clear."

"If they haven't surrounded the building yet, we just might make it."

The team moved swiftly into the narrow alley. The city had grown quiet without any targets for the Zendreen troops and fighter craft, although the latter still circled above. The alley opened onto a curved street, one of the few that hadn't been confined to the grid pattern that dominated the city. The trio waited for a chance to cross without being spotted from above. The fighters weren't allowing much of an opening.

"Okay, after this one," whispered Richter.

A fighter passed overhead, then jinked away. Richter sprinted ahead, followed by Ari, then Cassie. They stumbled into a storefront across the street and waited. Ari gulped for air.

"I can't keep this up much longer," she gasped.

"We'll get you out of here," replied Richter.

"The restaurant should be halfway down this block," said Cassie.

"Let's keep moving."

The trio emerged from the building just in time to be noticed by Zendreen soldiers down the street. Richter laid down a brilliant swath of cover fire as the women ran ahead. As they'd been doing for most of the fight, they leap-frogged ahead one by one and covered each other in turn. Ari's aim with her rifle remained as deadly as ever, although the effort was obviously taxing her greatly. Fortunately for her it did not take long for them to reach the restaurant.

Ari stopped short upon reaching the building, and for a moment it appeared that she didn't want to go inside. Richter grabbed her arm.

"What the hell, Ari?" he asked.

"This is it," she replied in hushed tones. "This is the café from my dream."

The outdoor seating area of the café was enclosed by a waist-high wrought iron fence, and the tables and chairs were of the same material. The frames of umbrellas remained above some of the tables, the fabric long since rotted away. A lone teacup rested on one of the tables, a dusty testament to a happier time. Richter dragged Ari inside. The interior was mostly a mess, but coffee machines and carafes were still arranged neatly behind the counter.

Cassie tossed a cabinet aside and found the console. She tinkered with it for a moment and cursed.

"No power?" asked Richter, keeping an eye on the street.

Cassie shook her head. "No. I'm going to have to go downstairs and see if I can reconnect it to the grid."

"Hurry up, we can't hold this position for very long."

Cassie nodded, and disappeared into the back. Ari turned a fallen chair upright and sat down wearily. Almost immediately one of the legs gave way and she collapsed to the floor, swearing. Richter ran over and helped her up.

"Damn this place," she said.

Two Zendreen soldiers burst into the room. Richter and Ari were caught completely flat-footed. He only had time to place himself in front of Ari before one of the soldiers fired. The shot caught him in the right side of his chest, burning away the ceramic plate of his body armor and scorching his skin. He gasped in shock and pain and fell to one knee. Ari brought her rifle up but she knew she'd be too slow.

"Drop your weapons," said one of the soldiers, according to their translators.

Richter had already released his grip on his rifle, and Ari threw down hers.

"It's her, all right," the other soldier said. "You. Female. Come with us."

"Go fuck yourself," Ari replied.

The first soldier aimed a device at Ari. "It's not working."

"If you're trying to activate the mind control thingamajig, your fellow bug-fuckers never had a chance to install it. However..."

Ari activated her invisibility shield. Richter used the momentary distraction to draw his pistol and deliver two shots each to the soldiers. They fell and did not move.

"Ari?" he asked.

Richter searched the floor until he found Ari, recumbent and motionless. He fumbled around again, locating the cord for her device, and unplugged it from her torso. She reappeared, out cold.

"Ari! Come on, babe, you've got to wake up."

His most recent injury was not life-threatening, but it hurt like hell. Richter tried to hoist Ari's limp form onto his left shoulder and failed. He painfully rose to his feet and moved to the rear doorway.

"Cassie!" he shouted into the darkness. "I need your help!"

There was no reply. Out on the street, plasma fire erupted. It was returned with projectile weapons, and a few seconds later three humanoids ran into the café. Richter lowered his pistol in relief.

"I want to complain to the manager," said Calico. "The service here is awful."

"Captain, thank God," wheezed Richter.

Megumi and Aldebaran took cover on either side of the door, and continued to trade fire with the Zendreen. Calico moved over to Ari.

"How bad is she?" he asked as he knelt.

"She's unhurt, just exhausted," Richter said. "She used her invisibility device one too many times."

"And you?"

"I'll be fine, I'm just too messed up to carry her."

Calico easily gathered Ari into his arms. She stirred and came around.

"Farril?" she murmured.

"Can you hold on to me?" Calico asked.

"I think so."

Calico transferred Ari to his back, and she wrapped her arms and legs around him.

"We're not going out the same way we came in," said Aldebaran urgently.

Cassie emerged from the back and barely acknowledged the new arrivals before turning her attention to the computer console.

"Is there another way out back there?" Calico asked her.

"No," she replied curtly, activating the console.

Richter passed his plasma rifle to Aldebaran, who immediately used it with enthusiasm. Errant shots from the Zendreen continued to slam into the storefront. Megumi seemed to be genuinely enjoying herself, firing her borrowed Phalanx rifle with grim efficiency.

"We can't hold them off forever," Megumi said.

"If they figure out we're trapped in here," Richter began, "they're just going to destroy the whole building."

"Christie, this is Calico. Is there anyone else available to help us out?"

"Captain," replied Christie, "John and Ray have finished loading Dana into the Mark Nine. I can divert them to the city, but it's going to take them at least ten minutes."

"There's going to be a pile of smoking rubble here in ten minutes. Any other ideas?"

"Standby, I'll think of something."

On the bridge of the Faith, Gueyr and Knoal were helping Christie stay on top of things. Seated at consoles, their injuries weren't slowing them down, although Knoal was still feeling horrible. The two colleagues were in the middle of a meal when things got busy, and their consoles were littered with half-eaten meals and forgotten glasses of ale. Lieutenant Brentage and Miriam entered from the corridor, and joined the other two at their stations.

"How's it going?" asked Miriam, removing her parka.

"The charges have been set," said Gueyr, "but we're on the verge of losing control of the situation in the city."

"What else can we do?"

"Scherer and Bailey are on their way down there."

"Don't you have some sort of matter transporter?" asked Brentage, opening a bottle of water.

"Yes," replied Christie's voice, "but it can't transport living matter."

Brentage slugged down half the bottle. "What happens if you try?"

"It would be fatal, certainly. There has to be enough redundancy in the target matter to compensate for subatomic variables."

"Why not transport the Zendreen, then?"

Christie paused before replying. "That's not a bad idea. I'll have to deactivate the safety protocols, and it's going to get pretty messy in the cargo bay, but it might work."

"This I have to see," said Brentage.

"Richter, this is Christie. How far is the largest concentration of enemy soldiers from your location?"

"About fifty meters," replied Richter through a terrible transmission.

"Roger. I am going to try to use the matter transporter as a weapon. Let me know if anything happens on your end."

"Copy that!"

Christie relayed information on her efforts to Gueyr's console. She was able to call up a crude overhead diagram of a portion of the city, and represented Zendreen soldiers as red blips.

"Do you want to check it out?" Brentage asked Miriam.

"Okay."

Brentage and Miriam exited the bridge to the corridor, and descended the stairs to the cargo bay. Miriam approached the console and activated the intercom to the bridge.

"Safety protocols disabled," said Christie. "Attempting transport now."

A beautiful swirling pattern of green light appeared in the center of the cargo bay. The image of a Zendreen soldier appeared, the insectoid form frozen as it reloaded its plasma rifle. The energy field dispersed, and for a moment it looked like the ant-like alien was fine. A moment later it collapsed into a clear, uniform pile of yellow-green goo.

"Christie, it worked!" said Miriam into the console. "It was sodding disgusting, but it worked!"

"Good, I'll keep it up," Christie said.

Over the next two minutes, more Zendreen appeared and dissolved into gelatin. After the third one, the frozen soldiers appeared to be panicking, and by the fifth transport they were obviously trying to run away. The pile of organic matter spread out like Jello across the floor, threatening to cover most of the cargo bay deck.

"Christie, this is Richter," crackled the intercom. "The volume of fire has decreased significantly. We're going to make a run for the edge of the city."

"Got any Cool Whip?" Miriam asked Brentage.

"Everyone's aboard. Pyramis is moving away in the Mark Nine."

Gueyr nodded at Christie's announcement. Ten minutes had passed since Christie's nasty surprise, which had effectively routed the Zendreen assault on the café. The allies had encountered little resistance in their return to the ship. John, Ray, and Cassie entered the bridge from the conference room.

"Time check?" John asked.

"Two minutes until detonation."

John sat down at the controls. "I'm taking us to the edge of visual range."

The massive form of the asteroid disappeared as John guided the ship away. Several of the Zendreen ships stood between it and deep space.

"I assume we're still successfully hidden," said Knoal.

"We should be fine."

"You look like crap," Gueyr said to John, looking at his wounds.

"Trust me, I'd rather be unconscious right now. It's Richter and Dana I'm more concerned about."

John maneuvered slowly between the much larger enemy ships, then turned the Faith around to get a look at the asteroid. Two of the cruisers were still firing at the far side, and another had apparently docked in the southern hemisphere. The battleship remained parked over the city.

Richter entered the bridge, his tattered t-shirt removed and his wounds hastily dressed. The plasma burn on his chest looked bad. Calico and Megumi followed him in, no worse for wear.

"You should be resting," John said to Richter.

Richter leaned against Knoal's chair. "I don't want to miss this."

"How's Dana?"

"She's asleep. Her vital signs are stable."

"I'm detecting something strange," said Christie. "There's a lot of interference, but it appears that all of the emergency vents have just closed."

"That's impossible," said Cassie. "Show me."

Christie called up the data on a nearby computer screen. Cassie looked at her PDA in confusion.

"Who gave that command?" asked John.

"It wasn't me."

"The Zendreen, maybe?"

Cassie cursed so creatively the translator was stumped. "It would be suicide. We all know what will happen if those explosions are contained inside the superstructure."

"We shouldn't have trusted her to program the venting sequence," said Megumi.

"Meg, shut up," said Calico.

"I don't want the Vulture to be destroyed!" shouted Cassie. "Commander Scherer, get me back there now."

"There's less than a minute before the charges go off!" John said, gesturing at the screen.

"Forget it," said Christie.

Cassie grabbed John and tried to pull him out of his chair. The others intervened and Calico and Ray held her back.

"Damn you!" she screamed. "How do I know you didn't close the vents?"

"We may not be saints, but we're sure as hell not murderers," said John, straightening his jacket.

"Detonation in five, four, three..."

Christie calmly counted down the seconds. Cassie strained mightily against her restrainers and screamed in protest. The asteroid silently began to shake, then cracked along several large, dark faults. The diameter of the asteroid appeared to collapse by a tenth, and for a couple of seconds nothing changed. The Zendreen ships not docked started to move away.

"Oh, no," said Christie. "John, look at these readings."

"Damn it!" John muttered, leaping into the pilot chair. "Pyramis, this is Scherer! Get the hell out of here!"

"I recommend at least one eighth AU," said Christie.

John pushed the throttle forward, and crossed 12 million miles in a few seconds. He spun the ship around.

"The Kira'To may curse you for this," spat Cassie.

"They can get in line," said Richter.

A pinpoint of light almost as bright as Alpha Sagittae appeared, then winked out. Christie displayed sensor readings on each of the bridge consoles. Radiation along the whole spectrum spiked, then dropped back to normal levels.

"It should be safe now," she said.

John said, "Pyramis?"

"I'm not reading his ship."

"Keep looking. I'm taking us back."

John brought the Faith back to the former position of the asteroid. A dark cloud of dust was all that remained. Wisps of gas began to glow as the solar wind passed through. As they drew nearer, some larger pieces of debris became visible.

"Anything?" John asked softly.

"Nothing," replied Christie. "The asteroid and the fleet have been vaporized."

"There were three cruisers that may have been able to jump to superlume," said Calico.

"I've got them. It looks like they were on the edge of the blast."

John brought the ship to Christie's readings. Three burning hulks drifted aimlessly, two venting gas and the third almost broken in two.

"Grim," said Richter.

"No life signs," said Christie. "There isn't a single chamber that hasn't lost pressure."

"Keep scanning," John said, standing. "You have the controls. Let me know the instant you find Pyramis or anything else."

"Roger. What are you going to do?"

"I think Queen Cassiopeia and I need to have a chat." John gestured to Ray and Calico, and the three men brought Cassie into the conference room. "I'll handle this, guys."

"You sure?" asked Ray.

John nodded, and the other men left the room. Cassie glared at him.

"Aren't you afraid I'll harm you?" she asked.

"No. Well, maybe a little. I wanted to do you the courtesy of a private conversation, although I'm sure everyone would like to know what the hell just happened."

"I already told you, I don't know. I wanted the Vulture to survive, even if it fell into enemy hands for some time."

"Is it possible that the Zendreen tried to open all the vents, to mitigate the damage of the explosives, and messed up the command?"

"If they found a working computer console, then that's possible, but they'd have to have been aware of the explosives."

"I think one of your men tipped them off."

"Preposterous," Cassie said angrily.

"You think so?" asked John, livid. "You see these wounds? Tsih was responsible for them. He ambushed me at the second reactor. He almost killed me!"

Cassie started to reply, then let the air out of her lungs. She leaned against the conference table, discouraged. "Tsih disappeared soon after the assault began. I assumed he'd been killed. He was my problem child, Commander, and he had some discipline issues, but I never thought he'd disobey a direct order."

"Forget it. I'm fine with the idea that the Zendreen accidentally caused their own demise. Just look me in the eye and tell me you had nothing to do with it."

Cassie did so. "I am blameless, Scherer. The Zendreen may well have killed themselves. There is, however, another possibility."

"What's that?"

"The Kira'To may have closed the vents."

John folded his arms. "I thought you said the Kira'To were the benefactors and protectors of the asteroid."

"They were, but they may have been unwilling to let it fall into the hands of the Zendreen."

"Didn't you say the Zendreen had also received help from the Kira'To at some point?"

"That was a long time ago. Unfortunately, there wasn't much information about that relationship in the Vulture's archives."

"It's a shame those archives were destroyed. I'm sorry."

"I downloaded a portion of them to this device," said Cassie, holding up the PDA. "Perhaps some information remains after all."

"John, this is Christie," crackled the intercom.

"Go ahead," said John.

"We've found Pyramis. He's okay, but the propulsion system of the Mark Nine is offline. He's requesting to dock."

"That's good news." John smiled at Cassie. "Prepare to have him brought into the cargo bay. Any sign of Zendreen survivors?"

"Nothing. I have no doubt, John. The Zendreen are toast."

27.

The monastery sat high on a hill overlooking a large lake in the southern hemisphere of Freedman, an area at the peak of autumn color. The white granite structure was trimmed with alabaster and gleaming copper, and shined like a beacon in the late afternoon sun. A warm breeze offered one last taste of summer, in contrast to the bright orange and red of the surrounding foliage.

The main courtyard of the largest building was busy with activity. The order had an unusually large number of guests that day, not the least of which was the prime minister herself. Dinner was being prepared, to be served at long tables in the courtyard, and although the gathering had the appearance of a celebration, the mood was considerably more reserved.

John Scherer stood at the entrance to the courtyard, underneath a heavy portcullis that looked like it hadn't been used in decades. He smoked his pipe and grasped a bottle of mead. His view of the shimmering lake was partially blocked by the hull of the Reckless Faith, parked nearby over the veranda. The sun, Beta Sagittae, had just set behind the ship, causing the outline to glow like an incandescent lamp.

Megumi approached John, and leaned against the stone wall. She took a pull from her own bottle of mead and considered the view.

"Are we getting started?" John asked her.

"Not yet," Megumi replied, looking back into the courtyard. "The monks don't want you to leave Calico's payment here, so we'll have to do the transaction somewhere else. Anyway, they've finished discussing the matter, so I'm sure they'll have us sit down soon."

"Fine, I'm hungry."

"It's a funny tradition, isn't it? Drinking straight out of the bottle."

"I'd just be refilling my glass every five seconds anyway."

Megumi smiled. "Now you're on my frequency, Commander. You seem preoccupied, though."

"There are a lot of unanswered questions," said John, looking at Megumi.

"Come on. Do you really think the galaxy is worse off without the Zendreen?"

"The ends can't justify the means. But I'm not going to lose any sleep over it. My own planet is..."

John trailed off. Meg stood next to him and stared at the lake.

"You were going to say safer?"

"Uh huh. That was before I had to deal with the Kira'To."

"There's still no proof they were involved in any of this, or if they exist at all."

John drank from his bottle. The mead was flavored with coriander and had a hint of cloves. He got two more puffs out of his pipe, and tapped out the bowl on the heel of his boot.

"Something brought Miriam and her parents to the asteroid. We're also clueless as to the nature of those ghosts that appeared during the raid."

"Yeah, but it's quite a stretch from a couple of unexplained events to shadowy, omnipotent puppeteers."

"Maybe."

Dana emerged from the Faith, shielding her eyes from the brightness as she descended the ramp. John waved at her and she somewhat unsteadily approached.

"Feeling better?" asked Megumi.

"Yeah, I guess," Dana replied.

"Did Christie fill you in on our circumstances?" asked John.

"Yes. I can hardly believe the asteroid was destroyed."

"You're not the only one."

"So, we're the guests of Prime Minister Calico?" Dana asked, looking at the tables. "Christie told me the Hayakuvian military is in control of the planet."

"Yes, but they don't know about this meeting. The prime minister has been ordered to stay here until further notice. She's infuriated to be so marginalized, of course."

"The military is here under the guise of protection," began Megumi, "but they're not fooling anyone."

Dana nodded. "You have to admit, the colony is rather exposed right now."

A cloister bell sounded twice from somewhere within the monastery. A glance into the courtyard revealed about a dozen monks emerging from unseen corridors, laden with food. The contingent from the Reckless Faith appeared from the cathedral, led by Prime Minister Calico and two of her aides. Richter waved at John and company.

"Let's get some grub," said Megumi.

John and Dana followed a staggering Meg back into the courtyard. John made a mental note of those present and noticed some discrepancies.

"Where's Ray?" he asked.

"He chose to spend this time with Christie on the ship," replied Dana. "You don't think Mother Calico will be offended, do you?"

"I don't think she ever met her, so no."

"What about Cassiopeia?"

"I don't know."

They approached the tables. An impressive assortment of meat, vegetables, and pastries had been arranged for the guests. An additional bottle of mead had been placed at each seat. John let Dana and Meg sit down, and walked over to Richter.

"This mead is frigging incredible," said Richter, smiling.

"Where's Cassie?" asked John.

"I don't know. She was moping in the back of the sanctuary while the prime minister was giving her speech. Oh shit, you didn't want me to keep an eye on her, did you?"

"No, she's not our prisoner. I thought she might have more information for us, so I hope she comes back before we leave."

"Maybe she's just not in the partying mood."

"Yeah, I don't feel much like celebrating anything either, Richter. Still, it was nice of the prime minister to host us."

"You'll feel better after about half a bottle of this stuff."

John nodded, and took note of the seating arrangements. While most of the guests had seated themselves, the chair next to Anya was being reserved by one of her aides. When he looked at him, the man gestured for John to take it. John was more interested to see that Ari had placed herself between Farril and Gueyr. His stomach grumbled at him, so he accepted the seat from the aide. Almost immediately, Anya stood up. She hoisted her bottle up, and spoke.

"This dinner is in honor of the Almagest, her crew, and those aboard who gave their lives in defense of Freedmen Colony. Their names will be recorded along with our brave sons and daughters who died in the skies of our home. Let no one ever forget their sacrifice."

Everyone stood, and the sentiment was echoed by several people. Everyone took a swig from a bottle, including the monks, although Farril also cast his face downward and closed his eyes.

"To Doc Trewler and Bugani!" yelled Gueyr.

"To Railyn!" added Knoal exuberantly.

There was another round of drinking. John could already feel the mead working on his empty stomach.

"Let us sit down and enjoy this meal," began Anya, "as our departed friends would want us to."

Once everyone had returned to their seats, Anya gestured ahead. John tore into a loaf of bread nearby, and munched on a piece while those around him filled their plates. He looked over at Ari. She was sampling a braised hunk of meat, and caught John's eye. She raised her eyebrows and grinned stupidly at him. John rolled his eyes in response, then noticed that there were two people not yet seated. Behind Ari, near a fountain of granite cherubs, stood Pyramis and Brentage. Anya followed his gaze.

"Will your friends be joining us?" she asked.

"Eventually," mumbled John around the bread. "It looks like they're working something out."

"Are you sure you won't reconsider?"

Pyramis leaned against the fountain. Brentage crossed his arms and regarded him seriously.

"I have been exceedingly polite so far, Major," he said. "However, I can't forget the circumstances that put me here right now. I cooperated during the assault on the asteroid because I agreed with the mission and there was no point in wasting time in Scherer's cargo hold. I continue to treat you with respect because I sympathize with the colony's point of view. But now, I have no excuse. I have to go back to my post. I will lobby on your behalf, but we both know that your actions will be considered treason no matter how convincing I manage to be."

Pyramis sighed. "I know. I want you to tell them the truth about what happened. I have no intention of turning myself in. I only ask that you keep my location a secret until the Reckless Faith departs."

"So you're going with them?"

"I might as well. The invitation is there."

Brentage and Pyramis shook hands.

"Make sure we don't meet again, Major," said Brentage. "Next time I'll have no choice."

Pyramis nodded. Brentage turned and headed out to the veranda. He looked at the Faith for a moment before descending a stone staircase and disappearing from sight. Pyramis approached the tables and took the only remaining seat, which was next to Aldebaran.

"Where's he going?" he asked after swallowing.

"He's walking to the nearest Hayakuvian garrison."

"Isn't that more than ten kilometers from here?"

"It was his choice," said Pyramis, grabbing some steamed greens. "I guess he wants some time to himself."

Miriam leaned around Aldebaran, and said, "Are you sure he won't send his mates here looking for you?"

"Yes."

"I hope you're right," said Aldebaran. "The last thing we need right now is another confrontation."

"Did you get the Mark Nine fixed?" asked Miriam.

Pyramis said, "Yes. It's a fine ship. I wish I could keep it, but I'm not that selfish."

"Didn't you just tell Brentage that you were coming with us?" asked Aldebaran.

"You have very good hearing. Yes, I lied to him. I intend to stay here and help rebuild the damage from the attack. They're going to need experienced combat pilots to start training a new round of recruits. Prime Minister Calico asked me to stay, and I agreed."

"We'll miss having you on our side, Rafe."

"Thanks, Seth! Now pass me some of that roast creature, I'm starving."

Forty-five minutes later, the feast was over and the monks had made short work of the leftovers. The last traces of twilight were fading from the sky, and most of the guests had stumbled back to the Reckless Faith to sleep off a legendary bout of drinking. Despite the initially somber mood, good mead (and a bottle of something stronger that had made the rounds) had dulled the pain of recent losses. On the veranda, the few souls who had either paced themselves or possessed an unusually high constitution shared in some Umberian cigars left over from the last wine-and-dine session. Alpha Sagittae glittered like a gem in the eastern sky, obscured occasionally by passing cirrus clouds. The slight breeze had changed direction and carried the smell of candles from the courtyard to the veranda.

John stood between Ari and Calico. He zipped up his jacket to ward off the evening cool, and puffed on his cigar.

"This is a great cigar," he said.

"What time tomorrow do you want to synthesize my payment?" asked Calico, looking at his cigar with indecision.

"We're not on a tight schedule. Whenever you please. Listen, Calico, Ari, there's something you need to know."

"We're listening," replied Ari, and picked an errant piece of tobacco leaf from her lips.

"Last night I held a meeting with Ray, Christie, Richter and Miriam. We want to go back to Earth before we begin searching for the other asteroids. Megumi wants to come with us. Aldebaran is on board for whatever we do, of course."

Calico puffed. "Megumi doesn't need my permission to go with you, John."

"She said the same thing. I'm talking about you, Ari. I've been avoiding asking you this..."

"I'm sorry, John," said Ari quickly. "I'm not ready to rejoin your crew."

John took Ari's hand. "You must realize, after everything we've been through, that there's no ill will between us."

"It's not that. I know you and the others have forgiven me."

"Then what?"

Ari faltered and pulled away. She looked at Calico, then at John. Her expression was almost fearful.

"I'm in love with Farril."

"You are?" asked Calico, genuinely shocked.

"Do you really love me like a daughter?"

Calico blanched. "Of course I do!"

"Then what should I do?"

"You should work this out," said John, stepping back. "Ari, you don't need to justify your decision to me."

"Well, that's my answer. I'm staying with Calico. Look us up when you get back into the area."

"We might not be coming back this way. We'll be following the clues, what little we have."

Ari smiled sadly. "In that case, tomorrow may be goodbye."

"Maybe. Until then, I'll leave you two alone. I'll tell Christie to leave the light on for you."

"Thanks," said Calico.

"Goodnight, John," said Ari.

Reeling, John wandered up the ramp and into the ship. When he disappeared from sight, Ari turned toward Calico.

"Before you say anything," he began, "I want you to know that I never wanted you to think that loving me was a condition of your membership on my crew. I accepted your affection because it seemed to make you happy. It made me happy, too, but for different reasons. You strongly resemble my daughter before she died."

"Really? The prime minister wasn't too impressed by me."

"Not physically, Ari, I mean personally. After I rescued you from the Zendreen and got to know you, I figured maybe I had a second chance to have a daughter."

"You should have told me. I thought you might be open to a romantic relationship. At least now I understand some of our more awkward exchanges."

"No kidding."

Ari hugged Calico. "Perhaps it would be simpler if I just say that I want to stay with you, no matter what happens."

Calico held Ari at arm's length. "I wish it was that simple. You are welcome to remain with us, but you need to know that I can never return your affection in the way that you most desire.

You need to seriously consider how that will effect our relationship."

Ari's expression fell. "So that's it? You're just going to take the high road and call it good?"

"What other choice do you leave me? If you want to continue traveling with us, that's the way it has to be."

"I thought I'd finally found a place that offered unconditional acceptance," Ari said, turning around.

"Except that you can't make romance a condition of that acceptance. You're already like family to me. Honestly, I'm astonished that you continue to ignore the fact that John seems willing to provide you precisely what you want so badly."

"I can't overcome my guilt over what I did to him any more than you can overcome your guilt for what happened to your daughter. I'm not saying that to be hurtful, I only want you to understand the depth of my feelings."

Calico jammed his hands into his pockets and looked out over the lake. "Damn it. I can't take the high road, Coma. We've both been fooling ourselves here, in different ways. You are not my daughter, and you never will be. Perhaps our relationship would have been healthier if I'd never made that emotional connection with you."

Ari folded her arms and turned back toward Calico. "Do you think we can try to start over, then?"

"I don't know."

"What would you say if you really were my father?"

"You just acknowledged that John and the others have forgiven you. If you were my child, I would tell you to go to him. Tell him how you really feel and I bet you'll find what you're looking for."

"You think so?"

"I've only known Scherer for a short time, but even I can see how much he cares for you."

Ari smiled. "You may be right. I'll sleep on it. Tomorrow you'll know my decision."

Calico hugged Ari. "If you stay with me, I promise I'll treat you like my equal. If you go, I'll miss you."

"Me too."

"Dear God, you scared the hell out of me."

Cassie gave John a half smile. He'd almost bowled her over on his way up the stairs to the bridge. She was sitting on the stairs, in the dark, holding a bottle of mead. She was wearing a pair of Christie's blue jeans and one of Dana's college t-shirts, which presented her in sharp contrast to her original vestments. Her short black hair was also free around her ears, and she seemed human for the first time.

"I'm impressed you got that old fighter working again," she said, referring to the Mark IX in the cargo bay. "I tried myself, after its crew was taken."

"I have some very smart people on my crew. Where have you been? I was wondering if we'd ever see you again."

"Pathetically, this is the only place I have left to go."

John frowned. "That can change if you want to be an asshole about it."

"I was referring to myself. Fate is not without a sense of irony."

"I'm not sorry you didn't get your way, but I am sorry you lost your home. Come on, let's talk on the bridge."

Cassie stood up and ascended the stairs. John followed her onto the bridge, which was empty. He checked one of the consoles and looked nonplussed.

"Something wrong?" she asked, sitting across from him.

"Christie has listed her status as 'dormant.' I assume that means she's resting, although she had previously indicated that she didn't need rest."

"Maybe she hit her limit," replied Cassie, removing the stopper from her bottle.

John realized his cigar had gone out, and he fished around in his pockets for his lighter. As he brought the cigar back to life, he noticed that Cassie's bottle was full.

"How many is that for you?"

"This is the first one. On the Vulture, we ran out of alcohol so long ago... I didn't think it wise to drink alone."

Cassie drained a third of the bottle. John sat down at the next station.

"You might want to take it easy with that stuff," he said.

"The others tell me you have decided to look for the Eagle and the Swan."

John reached for the bottle and Cassie gave it to him. "That's right. I find the possible involvement of the Kira'To in the affairs of humans to be unsettling. That's why I'm hoping you can still provide us with some insights. In fact, you are welcome to come with us in the search if you want." John took a drink, and handed the bottle back. "We're stopping at my home planet for a little bit of an overhaul, first. There's only one problem."

"Oh?"

"Some of us aren't convinced you have no ill will toward us for what happened to the Vulture."

"Don't worry, I'm not going to stab you in the back."

"Normally, Christie could verify how you really feel, but as I suspect you already know, your mind is closed to her."

"Amateurish fumbling, like two virgins in a hammock."

John laughed. "How descriptive. Still, if you would be willing to submit to her, it would go a long way towards trusting you. Otherwise, we'd have to severely restrict your access to the ship, as we did on the way back from Alpha."

"Fine, wake her up."

"Not right now. I don't think she wants to be disturbed."

Cassie took another long swig of mead, and asked, "Are we the only ones awake right now?"

John visibly tensed up. "Calico and Ari are right outside."

"Relax, Commander. If I wanted you dead I would have killed you three minutes ago. Tell me, though, which of these women belong to you?"

"The women on my crew are my equals, not my property."

"But you are not mated to any of them?"

John folded his arms. "No. Why do you ask?"

"I just find it curious that a man of your station wouldn't take the company of a woman. Are you a gelding?"

"No, I'm not a fucking gelding, and apparently our culture has different rules about 'mating' than yours."

Cassie smiled. "I beg your pardon. I was going to suggest Miriam, but she seems rather taken with the Umberian."

"Then that's Aldebaran's problem," said John, blushing slightly.

"Then there's Arianna, whose intentions mystify me. She has shown affection for you, Calico, and Richter. Has she made herself available to all the males on board?"

John stood up. "Absolutely not. She's had feelings for each of us, just at different times. And before you ask, our relationship is none of your business."

"Very well."

John dropped his cigar on the floor and stamped it out. "Now, I'm off to sleep. Are you going to stay here or take advantage of the rooms the monks offered?"

"I would like to stay here, if you don't mind."

"Then come with me."

John threw the cigar in the trash, and led Cassie through the conference room and into the lounge area. Gueyr and Knoal dozed peacefully on two of the couches, leaving one available. John opened the door to his quarters.

"You can stay in here tonight," he said. "I'm guessing you won't have anything to gain by messing with my stuff. I'll crash on this couch."

Cassie glanced inside the room. "Not a bad idea, strategically placing yourself outside the room. I imagine you've ordered Christie to keep tabs on my movements as well."

"Assuming she decided to come out of dormancy at some point."

Cassie entered the room and John followed her.

"Cozy," she said. "I was told you designed this ship. Why didn't you give yourself larger quarters?"

"I'm nobody special. There's the bed, and the bathroom is through there. If you want to take a shower, close the door. The whole thing doubles as a shower stall. Just make sure you put the toilet paper in the cabinet first."

John smoothed the sheets on his bed and randomly rearranged the pillows.

"I see," said Cassie, looking inside. "Pity there isn't room enough for both of us."

John twisted a pillow in half, almost tearing it. "You'll just have to seduce me some other time."

"Come back in ten minutes."

"Goodnight, Cassiopeia," said John.

John stepped out, closed the door, and took a deep breath.

"You should go for it," said Gueyr.

"You shouldn't eavesdrop on other people's conversations."

Gueyr rolled over and pulled his blanket over his head. "You left the door open, genius."

"We're both drunk. It's not the best idea."

"Are you kidding?" mumbled Gueyr. "Drunk is the best excuse for it."

John shook his head, and descended the stairs to the galley. Richter was passed out on the couch. He paced up and down for nine minutes, then got himself a drink of water. He slammed the glass down on the counter and looked at his reflection in the starboard H2O tank.

"I must be out of my mind," he said, and went back upstairs. A female figure stood at the top of the flight, her face in shadow.

"John," she whispered.

"You're right, babe. You're lonely, I'm lonely, we might as well be together at least once."

"That's awfully forward, John, even for you," said Arianna Ferro.

"Ari? Excuse me, I..." John climbed two more stairs. "Did you make up your mind already?"

"Who did you think I was?" asked Ari, smirking.

"Never mind that. What happened with Calico?"

"He did the right thing, apparently."

The cabin was at the end of a dirt road, two miles from Route 25A in Orford, New Hampshire. January had followed a bitterly cold December, a condition only made tolerable by the lack of any significant snowfall. Persistent sunlight had reduced snow from the previous year to small patches, revealing brown, fallow ground. That night was a relatively balmy 25 Fahrenheit, and for the lone occupant of the cabin, it was an opportunity to get bundled up and do some stargazing.

In his earlier years, the temperature wouldn't have been an impediment to the beautiful view the northern skies offered. As he passed his fifty-fifth birthday, however, he had to accept the fact that he couldn't tolerate the cold like he used to. The Air Force N3B parka that he'd been given as a gift several years ago had become invaluable for stargazing on nights like this, and allowed him to easily conceal his well-worn H&K USP .45-caliber pistol. He also donned a black watch cap and a pair of medium-weight gloves.

It was a perfect night for him to try out his new pair of binoculars. He had a telescope for more detailed observations, but binoculars offered a more convenient method of viewing in cold weather. He stepped outside and closed the front door, then walked up the small hill next to the cabin. He'd just found the Orion Nebula in his field of view when he heard a car coming up the road. He hung the binoculars from around his neck, drew his pistol, and put it in the front pocket of his parka.

A '21 Ford Expedition came down the road, dimming the headlights as it approached the cabin. The man confirmed that his flashlight was in his other pocket, and walked to the end of his short driveway. The driver turned off the engine and got out. The occupant of the cabin lit him up with the flashlight, and gasped in shock.

"Richter?"

"Hello, Kyrie."

Kyrie Devonai dropped his flashlight, which went out as he let go of the pressure switch.

"Is it really you?"

"You bet your ass, Devonai."

"Come inside!"

The two men entered the cabin. Devonai stripped off his gloves and shook Richter's hand. He stepped back and looked at his guest in wonder.

"My God, it really is you. But you haven't aged a day!"

"I wish I could say the same for you, but you look good for an old man."

"How...?"

"It's the effect of time dilation. Only a few months have passed from my perspective."

"Incredible! Please, sit down, I'll get us a drink."

Richter looked around the cabin as Devonai got a bottle of bourbon out of a cabinet. The main room was virtually unchanged from the last time he was there, although Devonai had added electric lights and an internet connection. Richter sat down at the kitchen table and accepted a tumbler from Devonai.

"Did you really go out into space?" Devonai asked, his eyes still wide.

"Oh yeah. I can't wait to tell you all about it. But you have more ground to cover, I'm sure. Tell me what happened to you after we left."

"Well, my career in the CIA was over, as you might imagine. I avoided criminal charges because of the clandestine nature of the case, and I was allowed to resign. I tried to rebuild my life, and Mara and I got married. We had two kids." Devonai took a sip from his glass. "It didn't last, though. There were no other jobs that held my interest, and I couldn't live the life of a stay at home dad. I had to get back into the action somehow. It was the only way to keep from going insane after what happened to us. I ended up kicking around with a private security company around the Horn of Africa for several years, but it was a decision that ended our marriage."

"I'm sorry to hear it. Mara was a good woman."

"She still is, and we've patched things up enough to remain friends. Anyway, ten years ago I got a call from the CIA. A new task force was being formed, and they wanted me as a member. Unexplained disappearances were on the rise around the world, and there was growing evidence that alien forces might be involved."

"The Kira'To?" asked Richter.

"Do you know about them?" asked Devonai excitedly.

"Only a little. We haven't encountered them directly. I'll fill you in. Go on."

"Well, I ended up pretty much like Mulder from the X-Files, traveling around the world with Evangeline Adeler, investigating abductions. There was a growing group of people we called the Left-Behinds, friends or relatives of abductees who had varying degrees of contact with the Kira'To. We also once ran into a group of Kira'To cultists, but at the time I wrote them off as a bunch of crazy nutbags. After that, most of people we met weren't too helpful, but occasionally we'd get a snippet of new information. I've been doing that for ten years. I'm actually on vacation right now."

"I'm glad to hear Evangeline is doing scut work, she always seemed to have the aptitude for it."

"Yeah, I, uh… I'll tell you more about that later. Anway, how did you find me?"

"We can find anyone if we know what to look for. In your case, we simply searched for the RFID chip in your Common Access Card. We found the names and locations of every case officer in the agency everywhere in the world."

"The director would go apoplectic to hear that. Oh, and you can probably guess who it is now."

"Lauren Hill?"

"You got it. So, we have an interesting collection of stories from Left-Behinds, but no definitive proof of alien contact. We wouldn't be able to justify our existence at all if not for the Portland Incident. We also had to share that incident report with the UK in order to gain access to their L-Bs. In fact, one of the most compelling disappearances was over there not too long ago."

"Miriam Colchester and her family?"

"Are you screwing with me, Richter?"

"I wouldn't do that, Devonai."

"Then I think it's time for you to tell your side of the story."

Richter leaned back, and smiled. "I think we should switch from bourbon to coffee. This is going to take awhile. But first, let me introduce you to my friend in the truck. Her name is Cassie, and she's from another planet."

Snow was falling on the bare hill in one of the many isolated knolls of Yorkshire County. Four freshly dug graves had already disappeared beneath the snow, and the audience gathered there shivered in the cold. No headstones could be placed, as the graves would have to remain a secret, but not one of the mourners would forget the location. They stood in silence as the wind picked up, the sky an even gray. After a few minutes, John stepped forward and turned around. He looked in turn at Ari, Ray, Dana, Aldebaran, and a tearful Miriam. Tycho was also there, sitting with stoic silence and looking back at John in a rather un-canine manner.

"I guess I should say something," John began, and cleared his throat. "We are here to say goodbye to Gabriel Ferro Colchester, Amelia Colchester, and Fugit Talvan, and to honor the passing of Christie Tolliver from flesh and blood to a being of pure energy. For those that have gone to a plane of existence that we cannot perceive, we celebrate their lives even as we mourn their deaths. They died before their time, in a manner that justice can never repair. For Christie, she lost her physical body but she remains alive in spirit. It is regretful that we lack the technology to preserve her body, but there may be some way in this universe for her to once again have physical form. For that, and for peace for the dead, we will stay hopeful."

Miriam buried her head in Aldebaran's jacket, and sobbed. He hugged her, a tear escaping from his own eye. Ray and Dana were sad, but reserved. Ari was stoic, as usual.

"Well said, John," said Ray.

"Christie," John said to Tycho. "Was that okay with you?"

Tycho nodded his head up and down. John smiled.

"Let's get back to the ship," said Ray.

The group turned and headed down the hill. As they reached the bottom, the cargo ramp revealed the otherwise hidden Faith. Once they crossed the threshold, Tycho ran up the stairs to the bridge. Miriam turned to get one last view of the hillside before the ramp closed.

"How did the connection go?" John asked the ceiling.

"Pretty good," said Christie's voice. Tycho's nose takes some getting used to."

"You mean in your field of vision?"

"That, too, but I mean his sense of smell. I was almost overwhelmed. John, thank you for what you said."

"It was the least I could do."

"Come on," said Aldebaran, leading Miriam up the stairs, "let's have some breakfast."

The others thought this was a good idea, and followed them.

"How long did you want to give Richter and Cassie?" asked Dana.

"A couple of hours should be enough," replied John. "If Devonai won't help us then we'll just have to be that much more careful."

"I hope we haven't made a mistake approaching him," said Ray.

The group entered the galley. Friday was sitting on the table and reminded John of her empty food bowl. John opened a bag of dry food and filled it.

"Good timing, Friday," he said, "this is the last bag."

Friday meowed. Ray filled the coffee decanter and set to work brewing a fresh batch. John and Ari sat down at the table with Aldebaran and Miriam while Dana set to work preparing the Freedmen equivalent of bacon and baked beans.

"Have you decided what you want to do?" John asked Miriam.

"I want to stay with you," she replied, wiping her eyes. "As much as it hurts me to keep my aunt and uncle in the dark, simply reappearing after a month will raise too many questions."

"Do they know your handwriting?" asked Dana, dropping a dollop of lox into a frying pan.

"Yes."

"Why not write them a letter? You don't have to be specific, just tell them that you're okay and not to worry."

"But what about mum and dad?"

"I... I don't know."

"Tell your aunt and uncle that they're gone," said Aldebaran, "and they're not coming back. Better to give them some closure, even if the truth is omitted."

"I suppose," said Miriam.

John stood up. "I'll get you some stationary, and we'll drop the letter off at the post office before we leave."

Miriam sniffled. "Okay."

Ari took Miriam's hand. "You may have lost your parents, Miriam, but we've both gained a sister. At least we can take comfort in that."

Miriam hugged Ari, and broke out crying. John headed up the stairs for deck one, and motioned for Ray to follow him. When they'd reached the corridor, he turned around.

"The flood gates are finally opening up," Ray said.

"It's just as well," replied John. "She needs to start the healing process."

"Indeed."

"Have you and Christie decided what you want to do?" he asked.

"We're going to hold off for now, John," replied Ray. "Our plan here on Earth is ambitious. If we're going to succeed, we're going to need to devote all of our attention to the mission."

"That doesn't mean we can't squeeze in a quick ceremony before we really kick things off."

"I know. Maybe, we'll see. In my mind Christie and I are already married, anyway."

"Are you sure she feels the same way?"

"I hope so."

"Well congratulations, then," said John, slapping Ray on the shoulder. "She's a real beauty."

"That doesn't mean I'm ready to start joking about the situation."

"Oops, sorry."

"Don't worry about it. What about you and Ari? Any progress there?"

"She still hasn't said anything to me about why she changed her mind at the last minute, although it seems obvious that Calico rejected her romantically."

"Perhaps she finally realized that the Reckless Faith is her true home."

"It's true whether she realizes it or not. Come on then, let's get some grub. I also wanted to show you my new design. Of course, we're going to have to come up with a better name than the Reckless Faith Mark Two."

GLOSSARY

AU: Astronomical Unit, the distance from Earth to Sol, approximately 93 million miles.

Dermaplasts: Biological gel-packs, used for rapid regeneration of damaged tissue.

FTL: Faster than light, usually in reference to a stardrive.

Genmod: A genetically-modified life form.

GFWG: Galactic Free Warrior's Guild, a reputable mercenary group.

HUD: Heads-Up Display, a holographic projection of information onto a surface, usually a transparent panel.

LMC: Large Magellanic Cloud, a diffuse sub-galaxy of the Milky Way galaxy, at a distance of 167,000 light years.

Nursery of the Gods: A local title for the Reticulum Globular Cluster, a star-forming region of the LMC.

Plank: Pejorative slang term for Planet Cop, a police officer assigned primarily to a single planet.

Res-ZorCon: Residerian-Z'Sorth Conglomerate, a heavy industries concern based out of the Tarantula Nebula.

Shuffler: Slang term for a bounty hunter.

SPF: Solar Police Force, the main law enforcement organization within the SUF.

SRC: Superluminal Relativistic Compensator, a device that allows ships traveling faster than light to accurately scan the surrounding area, as well as communicate with other ships at any speed.

SUF: Solar United Faction, a governmental body controlling the Residerian star system and outlying areas.

Superlume: Slang term for FTL travel.

UAS: Umber Astronomical Survey, a numerical catalog of stars compiled by Umberian astronomers. The standard reference for most of the Large Magellanic Cloud.

UMG: Universal Mercenary Guild, a loose confederation of mercenary groups with wide areas of operation.

Ultralume: Slang term for unusually long periods of FTL travel.

THE RECKLESS FAITH TECHNICAL MANUAL

Compiled by Christie Tolliver and Dana Andrews

INTRODUCTION
PRIMARY SYSTEMS AND COMPONENTS
WEAPONS SYSTEMS
FACILITIES
SECONDARY SYSTEMS AND COMPONENTS
APPENDIX A: TALVANIUM

Introduction:

Welcome to the Reckless Faith! Whether you have allied yourself to our cause or you are just hitching a ride, this manual will aid you in becoming familiar with this ship. Your clearance level is: ALL ACCESS.

History:

The Reckless Faith was constructed on Earth using a combination of Earth-based and Umberian technology. The design and layout were accomplished for the most part by John Scherer, currently serving as commander of this vessel. While some of our Earth-based technology was eventually supplanted by Umberian technology, the initial design and architecture remain.

Overview:

The Reckless Faith is classified as a Light Cruiser, although it is smaller than most craft fitting that definition. It carries the classification of Light Cruiser due to its maximum speed and offensive capabilities. Nominally carrying a crew of seven, the Reckless Faith can easily accommodate a larger number of passengers for a short duration. A full fuel load will sustain the ship during normal operations for 1,000 Earth years.

With a top speed of 1.56 million times the speed of light (c), the Reckless Faith is the fastest known vessel in the galaxy. However, due to the effects of time dilation, operating at velocities in excess of 900 c is only practical in emergencies. 900 c is also the most efficient operating velocity, as power requirements increase exponentially after that point.

The Reckless Faith is protected by a combination of Earth-based and Umberian weapons systems, as well as an Umberian designed Kinetic Energy Management System that absorbs damage from enemy weapons. A combination of firepower from both projectile weapons and directed energy weapons has proved to be effective against types of protection as ablative armor and energy-augmented structural integrity systems.

RECKLESS FAITH PRIMARY SYSTEMS AND COMPONENTS

Stardrive:

The Reckless Faith is powered by a cold fusion reactor, and driven by two superluminal (faster-than-light capable) engines. The reactor draws power from the fusion of Hydrogen into Helium, accomplished by gamma ray spalling of deuterium while contained in a cryogenically stabilized magnetic field. The engines function by the manipulation of gravitational fields of nearby celestial objects, which reduces the relative mass of the ship to almost zero while shortening the relative distance to the destination. Exactly how this is accomplished is not fully understood, but the mathematical transformations that determine time dilation effects have not proved to be any different from conventional relativity. In other words, the Reckless Faith is subject to the same time dilation effects as a ship operating at sublight velocities.

The reactor and the stabilized magnetic field also serve several other functions, which will be described later.

Quasi-Actualized Intraspace Quantum Grid (Orb):

Umberian in origin, this device is capable of containing an Artificial Intelligence Entity and an extensive database in a self-contained, self-sustaining quantum matrix. It acts as the central computer in tandem with Earth technology.

The original orb was the primary component of a deep space probe sent to Earth during the last days before the Zendreen invasion of Umber. The long transit time resulted in damage to the orb which limited the amount of technology available during the construction of the ship. The orb contained the Ego of Seth Aldebaran, which acted as the AIE until Aldebaran the pirate reconstituted himself with his Ego some time later. This process resulted in the destruction of the orb. Fortunately most of the orb's critical functions could be duplicated by our Earth-based computers, and some time later a new orb was replicated. The current orb contains the Ego, Superego and Id of Christie Tolliver, whose body was lost during combat operations.

Neutrino Doppler Scanning System:

A system that takes advantage of the property of quantum entanglement to scan and identify distant objects and substances. A neutrino is obtained from the storage coil and split into two identical particles. One particle is emitted toward the object to be identified, and the other is returned to the outer orbit of the storage coil. When the emitted particle passes through the object or substance, its path is slightly altered by the gravitational force of the object. The captured twin instantaneously demonstrates the same shift, and this change can be recorded locally. This device is limited to identifying objects and substances already in the database, although unknown anomalies may be partially identified by extrapolation.

The efficiency of the scanner depends on the distance of the ship from the target object or substance. The maximum range of the scanner is one light year, but information obtained at this extreme distance is unreliable. As the distance to the target object decreases, the quality of information steadily improves, with a sharp increase in reliability occurring at 10,000 light-seconds (approximately 1250 AU).

Matter Replication System:

This component utilizes matter-energy conversions, with an atomic redundancy compensator, to transport or fabricate inorganic matter. This system is more efficient if it is tied into the Neutron Wave Diffraction Scanner, but capable of longer range when used with the NDSS (3 kilometers maximum).

Superluminal Relativistic Compensator:

A device that allows ships traveling faster than light to accurately scan the surrounding area, as well as communicate with other ships at any speed. This is accomplished by a combination of measurements including Doppler shift (red/blue shift) of stellar references, active scanning with the NDSS, and communication with other public SRC devices operating within one light year. Accuracy depends on the level of processing power devoted to the task; a high degree of accuracy requires almost all of the processing time of our Earth computers or approximately 30% of the orb's processing time.

Talvanium:

A critical component in many of the Faith's systems, Talvanium has been the subject of intense study. It was exploited by Professor Fugit Talvan of Umber, who unfortunately refused to reveal all but a few details about this substance. See Appendix A for more information.

WEAPONS SYSTEMS

GAU 8/A:

A seven-barreled 30mm cannon originally manufactured by General Electric and used on the United States Air Force A-10 Thunderbolt II. It fires depleted uranium shells and is fed by a 1200-round helical magazine. The drive system is hydraulic; a pressurized hydraulic system had to be installed expressly for this weapon. The GAU 8/A has proved to be particularly effective in space combat as a mass driver weapon, especially in combination with the plasma cannon. The Reckless Faith originally mounted two of these cannons, but the rear-facing cannon was removed in order to supply material for the Umberian weapons systems.

Due to the fully integrated design of the magazine and feed system, the GAU 8/A can be reloaded almost instantly using the Matter Replication System. Empty shells are returned by the feed system to the magazine, where they can be reloaded in place. This convenient system can keep the cannon in action for an extended period of time, all other limitations notwithstanding.

The magnesium tracer component of the ammunition works in the vacuum of space due to a latent charge picked up while passing through the energy shield protecting the mount. This allows the tracer to burn for much longer than would be expected.

GAU 19/A Turrets:

Dorsal and ventral fully articulated turrets, mounting the GAU 19/A three-barreled .50 caliber cannon. These weapons can be controlled locally or remotely, but reloading is not automatic. With a conventional system of feeding and ejection, reloading must be done manually. The turrets were modified from existing B-29 turrets appropriated for this project. Similarly to the 30mm, these weapons are protected from the vacuum of space by an energy shield that protrudes slightly from the hull.

The turrets can be tied in to the Laser Banks to fire concurrently, if such an opportunity exists; however, they have different fields of fire.

Plasma Cannon:

A weapon that fires magnetically-stabilized superheated copper-alloy plasma, ignited by positrons. The plasma cannon is extremely powerful, but accuracy is detrimentally effected by intervening gravitational forces, magnetic fields, and space debris. This disadvantage makes it best for close range engagements.

Laser Banks:

Port and Starboard directed energy weapons firing high energy photons. While considerably less powerful than the plasma cannon, these banks act as turrets and can be individually aimed. As noted above, they can be fired concurrently with the dorsal and ventral turrets.

These weapons have excellent range and are useful for knocking out or disrupting enemy sensors, targeting equipment, or weapon emitters. They create very little explosive or vaporization damage, but are somewhat more effective when used in conjunction with the GAU 19/A.

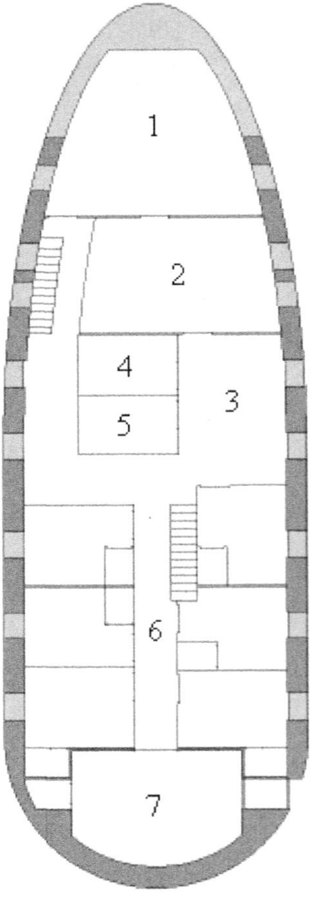

FACILITIES: DECK ONE

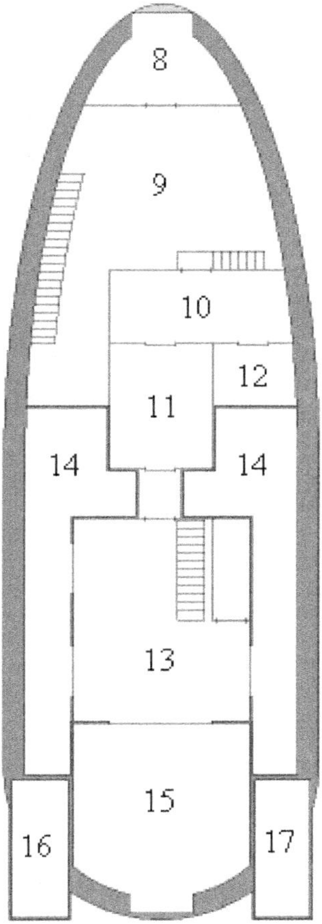

FACILITIES: DECK TWO

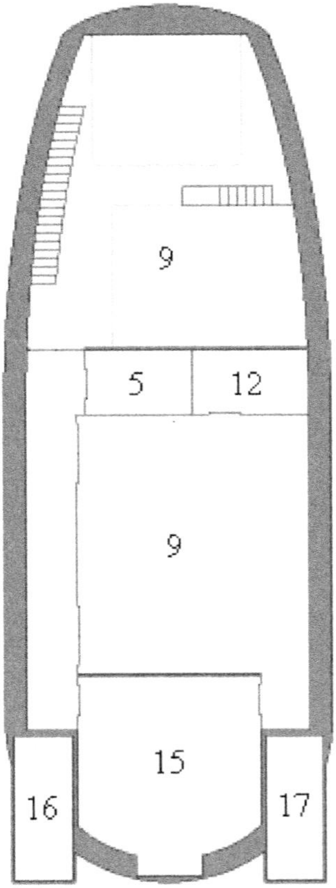

FACILITIES: DECK THREE

1. Bridge: The nerve center of the ship, the bridge consists of five computer consoles, one of which is also a dedicated piloting station. Each station can be used for any purpose, but they are usually configured, counter-clockwise from right to left: navigation, communications, pilot's station, remote weapons operation, and systems monitoring. The forward-facing window is also capable of projecting a wide-angle Heads-Up Display (HUD).

2. Conference Room: A room with eight chairs around an oval table, with a large wall-mounted monitor for demonstrations.

3. Lounge Area: An open area with several couches.

4. Secondary Server Room: This room contains two of the twelve computer servers, and is also used for spare storage.

5. Dorsal and Ventral Gun Rooms: These rooms provide gunner stations for and access to the dorsal and ventral GAU 19/A turrets. A limited amount of spare ammunition can also be stored here.

6. Living Quarters: Six nearly identical quarters, each with a private lavatory. The lavatory can also be used as a shower stall.

7. Zero-G Room/Airlock: A variable gravity area, this room can be used for Extra-Vehicular Activities (EVA) and for docking with other

vessels while in space. It is also used for spare storage and occasionally for recreational purposes.

8. Forward Gun Room: This area houses the GAU 8/A weapon system and magazine.

9. Cargo Bay and Cargo Hold: These areas are used for storage. The cargo hold has also occasionally served as a brig or spare quarters. The cargo bay has a ramp (outlined in gray) for accessing the exterior of the ship and loading large pieces of cargo. The cargo bay is double height, with the armory overhanging the rear portion of the bay.

10. Armory: All small arms used by the crew are stored here, along with ammunition, spare parts, and cleaning supplies.

11. Orb Room/Primary Computer Server Room: The Quasi-Actualized Intraspace Quantum Grid is stored here, along with ten of the twelve computer servers.

12: Storage Room

13: Galley: The galley contains a full kitchen, dining area, and a cold storage room.

14: H2O Storage Tanks: These tanks store 1000 gallons each of water for fuel, drinking, and sanitary purposes.

15. Engine Room: This area is home to the fusion drive and most of the secondary components. It also originally housed a rear-facing GAU 8/A, but that weapon was removed. Located on decks two and three (double height).

16 & 17. Port & Starboard Engines

RECKLESS FAITH SECONDARY SYSTEMS AND COMPONENTS

EO: Earth Origin
UO: Umberian Origin

Airlock/Ramp Control: This subsystem controls airlock and ramp operations, including manual override. UO

Air Exchangers: These devices regulate air pressure and temperature in each compartment, drawing oxygen from the H2O tanks and nitrogen from the Nitrogen Generator as needed. EO

Power Conversion Unit: This device converts power generated by the fusion drive into 120 volt electricity for use by other systems, and regulates power from the batteries when needed. EO

Batteries: Industrial grade dry-cell batteries, recharged by the PCU when not in use. EO

Computer Core: Twelve networked computers divided into primary and backup modules. EO

Electrical System: Standard power lines and jacks providing 120 volt power from the PCU. EO

Energy Shields: Low-power magnetic energy shielding that protects the ship's weapons from the vacuum of space. They may also be employed as emergency shields in the event of a hull breach. They do not provide any protection against weapons impact. UO

Fire Suppression System: This subsystem utilizes the Air Exchangers to rapidly deploy Nitrogen to suffocate fires. EO

Gravity Manipulation System: This system creates a zero-signature magnetic field to provide artificial gravity as needed. UO

Kinetic Energy Management System: This component uses nano-dynamos to convert kinetic energy into electrical energy, as well as heat sinks to convert heat energy into electrical energy. Used to shunt external forces into the engines or energy weapons. UO

Life Support System: This module backs up the Air Exchangers and ensures that they are functioning properly, and monitors the internal environment. EO

Liquid Oxygen Module: This module provides compression and storage of oxygen derived from the H2O storage tanks. UO

Maneuvering Thrusters: Twelve liquid-oxygen fueled thrusters. UO

Particle Storage Coil: A magnetically-stabilized infinite loop for capturing and storing useful subatomic particles generated by the fusion reactor. UO

Neutron Wave Diffraction Scanner: A system that uses neutrons of a small wavelength (one angstrom) to determine the structure of materials. As opposed to the NDSS long range device described above, the range of the Neutron Wave Diffraction Scanner is only fifty meters from the ship. However, the NWDS can be used to identify previously unknown substances, and is far more reliable for scanning radioemitters than the NDSS. UO

Nitrogen Generator: A component of the fusion reactor that produces 15O (an unstable isotope of oxygen) from engine exhaust products and captures and stores nitrogen (produced by $\beta+$ decay) in a liquid state. This process also generates a neutrino and a positron which are captured and stored in the magnetic coil. Energy generated by this process is also stored. UO

Radio Frequency/Very Low Frequency Transceiver: A device that provides short-range communication via a central receiver and hand-held devices, as well as the intercom system on board. EO

Waste Reclamation System: A device that uses ion filters to recycle water when possible. UO

APPENDIX A: TALVANIUM

History:

Named after Umberian research scientist emeritus Professor Fugit Talvan, this substance has been used on Umber for at least two hundred years, and has been known to the galactic community for at least one hundred years. However, its most remarkable properties were identified only 15 years ago, by a research team led by Professor Talvan. It is found only on Umber, Residere Alpha, and Earth.

Properties:

A complete analysis of this material is impossible due to the limitations of the scanning technology, but the following is known: Talvanium is a radionuclide of the element known on Earth as Neptunium, atomic number 93, with a neutron count of 238. This neutron count would normally decay into Plutonium 238, but measurements of alpha decay of Talvanium indicate a half-life of 150,000 years, a discrepancy that has not yet been explained.

Talvanium's usefulness stems from the drastic production of specific internal energy when the substance is exposed to a calibrated magnetic field of approximately 1500 amperes. This results in a net output of Joules/kg far in excess of what any known isotope of Neptunium would normally generate, although not all isotopes have been tested in this manner as of the writing of this entry.

Applications:

A few grams of Talvanium are utilized in our directed energy weapons, while 60kg is used to produce the required level of gamma rays to initiate the nuclear fusion process of the stardrive. It is probably not a coincidence that 60kg of Neptunium is also fissionable, but the relevance of this fact has not yet come to light.

Cryopathology:

Talvanium exhibits superconductivity at 50k, which is a relatively high temperature compared to other superconductive materials. This confirms the functionality of the Cryogenic Chamber component of the stardrive, which operates around the same temperature.

Talvanium also demonstrates superfluidity at extremely low temperatures, which is far more remarkable. The molecular lattice structure of Talvanium should preclude a liquid state at anything but extremely high temperatures (Neptunium is liquid at 910k), but for reasons yet unknown, the material will resolve into a superfluid state at 50k. This may be due to a variance governed by Cooper Pairing which allows the molecular lattice to expand into a liquid while maintaining a low temperature.

Zero-Point Energy:

These properties hint very strongly at the possibility that the true energy source derived from Talvanium is in fact Zero-Point Energy. Normally ZPE is a closed system, precluding any energy retrieval, but Talvanium consistently demonstrates properties that strongly imply such a relationship exists.

Conclusion:

We were originally led to believe that Talvanium is a naturally occurring element, but all of our research so far seems to indicate that it is, in fact, a synthetic material. Since Professor Talvan never took credit for inventing it, we strongly suspect that it was created elsewhere. It is unlikely that a naturally occurring element would have been found on only three planets in the entire known galaxy, leading us to believe that it was either abandoned at those locations or left there for reasons yet unknown. Based on the mining operation we encountered on Residere Alpha, Talvanium has been present in the strata there for at least a thousand years. It is also not known precisely how we obtained the Talvanium that was used in the construction of the Reckless Faith, even though we were all present during the initial synthesis of the structure and stardrive. Data logs of the event seem to indicate that it was absorbed from points scattered across the entire globe, but the Matter Replication System is not capable of that range. If it was obtained locally, that raises the problem that 60kg of a radioemitter as dangerous as Talvanium couldn't have been lying around the city of Chelsea for more than a few hours without making the nearest residents deathly ill.

The scientific method does not allow for coincidence, conspiracy theories, or deus ex machina. There has been considerable speculation among the crew that includes these distractions, and indeed Tolliver and myself have been guilty of indulging in them. However, they do not advance the study of Talvanium itself, and will not be included here. As of the writing of this entry we have exhausted our research, and without better scanning technology or outside assistance, these questions will remain unanswered.

ACKNOWLEDGMENTS

The Zendreen, Kau'Rii, Kira'To, Z'Sorth, Rakhar, and certain elements of galactic history are the intellectual property of John Wheaton and are used with permission.

Cover art by Alejandro "Alex Knight" Quiñones

Instagram: alexknightarts

Twitter: alexknight_

Thank you for reading Bitter Arrow, I hope you enjoyed it. Feedback is always appreciated, please take a minute or two and submit an honest review on Amazon. I always hope to improve my writing. Also, please visit my blog for updates and new fiction.

https://devonai.wordpress.com

Also available on Amazon:

Reckless Faith (The Reckless Faith Series Book One)

The Tarantula Nebula (The Reckless Faith Series Book Two)

The Fox and the Eagle (The Reckless Faith Series Book Four)

Dun Ringill (a stand-alone novel, sci-fi adventure)

Printed in Great Britain
by Amazon

57523199R00284